Excerpts from BELL, BO**K AND DYKE**

Clouds moved in to cov... ...rkness
total and complete. It was ... winds
seemed to be stifled, for no ... ...rtains.
The padding of kitty feet bro... ...here whisper of noise.
In the gloom, cat eyes glowed.

Lily felt the hands on her body. They were warm and soft. She
stretched into their caress, arching her back and willing them to
touch every inch of her.

—**SEA WITCH**, Barbara Johnson

Nothing was adding up to anything that meant anything at all
and dear sweet Hecate I could only hope that it hadn't all fallen
into the dark, evil realm of calculus, with all its imaginary numbers
and equations that proved two-plus-two did *not* equal four.

—**BY THE BOOK**, Therese Szymanski

My world was pulsing to the movement of her hand. The light
went and there was a hammering in my ears that let in only her
gasps and my sharp cries. I was a wound coil, ever tightened by her
body on mine. I tried for short, easy words like *coming* and *more*,
but they were caught behind my bared teeth.

—**UNBELIEVER**, Karin Kallmaker

Chameleon changed into her pink poodle pajama bottoms and
her Glinda of Oz T-shirt that read, "Are you a good witch or a bad
witch?" Taking the question on her T-shirt personally, she thought
of the choice she had made to go into the woods with Iris:
"Tonight I was a bad witch. But I'll try to do better."

—**SKYCLAD**, Julia Watts

BELL BOOK and DYKE

New Exploits of Magical Lesbians

Barbara Johnson
Karin Kallmaker
Therese Szymanski
Julia Watts

Bella
BOOKS
2005

Bella Books, Inc.
P.O. Box 10543
Tallahassee, FL 32302

Printed in the United States of America on acid-free paper
First Edition

Editors: Karin Kallmaker and Julia Watts
Cover designer: Sandy Knowles

ISBN 1-59493-023-6

Contents

FOREWORD

If we were in the mood to do so, we could expound at length on the long history of women, healers, midwives and workers of goddess magic. We could document the equally long history of oppression, violence and outright murder of so many of the women who dared to live outside their expected, constrained lives.

But that's not the mood we're in.

Regardless of history, being a lesbian in the twenty-first century already means living outside expected, constrained lives. Finding love, pleasure, community—such simple things—is for so many of us an every day wonder. Snatching happiness in the often violent world around us can render something as simple as holding hands an act of spiritual magic. That is what we mean by *lesbian magic* and it's what we've tried to capture in this *New Exploits* volume.

Along the way we've added a few black cats, some spell making, magic books, spooky twist and turns and a fair amount of just plain creepiness.

We're willing to admit, too, that when we contemplate a power that can leave us feeling as if a goddess has briefly visited our bodies, we're thinking about sex. Sex is the very magic that makes us lesbians. We have sex with other women, we enjoy it and we intend to share that joy through our stories.

That's the mood we're in.

Julia Watts & Karin Kallmaker
June 2005

SEA WITCH

BARBARA JOHNSON

Chapter 1

"Oh, yes . . . Yes . . . Don't stop . . ."

Lily writhed on the bed, her orgasm building to an electric climax. Her body tensed, and she grasped Jany's hair, urging her tongue and fingers to go faster and deeper. A sudden flash of lightning right outside the open bedroom window and the simultaneous crash of thunder made Lily shriek.

"Fuck!" Jany yelled as Lily jerked. She tasted blood.

"Damn bloody hell," Lily said. "Tara must be pissed off again." Still breathing heavily, she squirmed away from Jany, all thoughts of orgasms long gone. Another crash of lightning sent her scrambling off the bed to close the window and blinds.

Jany sat on the edge of the bed, ruefully nursing her injured lip. "I bit myself."

Lily sat next to her. "I'm so sorry. Let me see." She ran her finger lightly over the swelling lip before dabbing up the blood with a tissue and then kissing her.

"What about you? Did I bite you?"

Lily glanced down between her legs. Her thighs glistened, but not with blood. "Don't think so. But damn, talk about killing the mood."

Jany stroked Lily's bare breasts. "I'm sure I can get you back in the mood."

"Sorry, not while the storm's going." She winced at yet another rumble of thunder. "I am going to kill Tara."

"Why do you think it was Tara who did it?"

"Oh come on, the day was beautiful. No hint of storms on the weather report. You know she likes to show off. She probably conjured up some spell after a fight with her latest."

Jany settled back into the pillows. "You give her too much credit. She's not all that powerful."

"She's been practicing. A nice roiling storm is a piece of cake for her these days. And then she'll go collecting on the beach for all the crap that washes up." Lily frowned. "I don't approve of her using living things for her spells."

"Oh, what's a starfish or seahorse here and there. And you have to admit, she does make some gorgeous jewelry from shells."

"She ruins everyone's vacations."

Jany laughed. "You hate when the summer tourists come. I would think you'd ask Tara daily to 'roil up a storm' as you put it."

"Rain doesn't keep the tourists away, just off the beaches."

"And into your store."

"Okay, rain can be a good thing," Lily conceded. She got out of bed and reached for her clothes.

Jany enjoyed watching her wriggle into tight jeans and a skimpy tube top. "Those clothes make me want you even more. You know I love a woman with bare shoulders."

Lily danced away from Jany's reach. "I'm going to talk to Mandy. If she can't keep her coven in line . . . Well, maybe it's time for a new leader."

Jany laughed again as she lunged and grabbed Lily, pulling her down into her lap. "Better be careful. You never know what Mandy might do." She ran her finger along the top edge of Lily's tube top.

"Silly girl. You watch too many *Buffy* reruns."

"Can't help it. *Bewitched* isn't on anymore."

Lily kissed her again. "I'll be back soon."

"But it's still storming out. You hate storms."

Lily smiled and lifted up the blinds. As if on cue, the clouds disappeared as quickly as they'd appeared and the sun shone brightly. A few droplets of water on the window pane were the only evidence of the squall.

"Tara's temper tantrums only last about half an hour."

She scurried down the stairs, accompanied by four cats which had been hiding under the bed. All but one were solid black. Visitors always marveled that she could tell Lucifer, Merlin, and Morgan le Fay apart. In the kitchen she leaned down to pet Casper. "You been playing in the fireplace again? You're gonna be gray instead of white, silly kitty."

She dialed the phone. "Mandy? Yeah, how about that storm? I'm sure you know who caused it. What do you mean you don't? It was Tara, of course." She tapped a finger on the counter. "She's not even in town? Well, then who?"

Jany walked into the kitchen dressed only in black boxers and a white T-shirt. She got a beer from the fridge and raised a questioning eyebrow. Lily nodded yes, then took a deep gulp of the St. Paulie Girl Jany placed in front of her.

"I think one storm-happy Wicca is enough in this town. Someone new? God, we already have thirteen of you. Wouldn't a fourteenth throw off your auras or something?"

"Don't listen to her," Jany said on the extension. "She's just cranky because a bolt of lightning ruined her orgasm." She ducked as Lily threw an orange at her. "Hey, can you cast a spell to put Lily back in a horny mood?"

Jany hung up the extension and walked out to the back porch. She almost tripped as all four cats raced ahead of her. Cursing aloud, she vowed not to let Lily get another cat, like she'd been talking about just yesterday. One of Mandy's coven had a cat that had had yet another litter. Really, she knew these magical types liked cats, but didn't they get the concept of pet population control? Would she have to get a PETA person to come talk to them?

"No more cats!" she yelled as she stumbled over Casper and fell into a wicker chair, still managing not to spill her can of beer. He was the only cat she could definitely identify. Grumbling under her breath, she put her beer down and then snapped open the newspaper. The crackling seemed to act as a lure. "Go away," she said to four eager faces looking at her.

Lily came outside laughing. "I hear you, darling. Jacquelyn will have to find someone else to take her kittens."

"If she insists on letting her cat have so many kittens, she should have to keep them all."

Lily knelt beside the chair and kissed her. "She's promised this is the last time. Now, how about we go into town to the Frog Pond for lunch and gossip?" She took the paper from Jany and tossed it. Immediately, four felines pounced.

Jany couldn't help but chuckle, but then she grabbed Lily and forcefully kissed her. She ran her hands over Lily's curvy body, reveling in the softness of it. As she rose to her feet, she grabbed Lily's ass and pulled her close so their bodies molded together. She bit Lily's neck none too gently and whispered, "I have a better idea. Let's go back upstairs and finish what we started."

Lily moaned as she wrapped her hands around Jany's head. "Bite me," she said.

In response, Jany picked her up and carried her up the stairs to their bedroom. She dropped Lily on the bed and fell on top of her, kissing and biting her throat and naked shoulders. She swiftly removed Lily's clothes before getting up to close the window and blinds. "No sense taking any chances," she said as she fell down beside Lily again.

She ran her hands over Lily's body and down between her legs. She took an exploratory dip and smiled. "Mmmm, still wet," she said as she slipped her fingers inside. Lily arched in response, moaning deeply. Jany nibbled her way down Lily's body, all the while teasing with her fingers. In and out. In and out. It drove Lily wild. She groaned loudly while urging Jany's head downward. Jany knew exactly what Lily wanted, but she resisted, choosing to linger at her nipples, then her stomach, then her hip bone. Her fingers teased and played. She let her thumb caress Lily's clit.

"Jany, please. I want your mouth!"

"Mmmm, patience, my love. I want you to be nice and wet for me."

"I am. Dear God, I am. Don't tease me anymore!"

"You want me to bring out our little friend?"

Lily was squirming beneath her. "No," she gasped. "Just your mouth and hands. Please!"

Jany smiled and complied. Lily tasted like heaven. She left her fingers inside, searching as always for Lily's elusive G spot, while she sucked and licked Lily's engorged clit. She let her teeth graze lightly over the swollen bud and then felt Lily clench around her fingers as her body responded to her orgasm. Lily moaned long and loud. The sound always drove Jany into a frenzy. Moaning in response, she licked and sucked harder and faster as Lily thrashed beneath her. Her fingers pumped in and out. Lily tensed again.

"Jany!" she cried out.

She squeezed Jany's shoulders between her legs. Jany could feel them trembling, and then Lily let out one long sigh. She gently pushed on Jany's shoulders. "Enough, my love," she said. Jany crawled up and took Lily into her arms.

"You sure you had enough?" she asked as she played with Lily's soft hair. "You're usually good for more than two."

Lily snuggled deeper into her arms. "Oh yes. You have quite a mouth, my dear."

Jany suddenly felt like she was burning up. "I need to open the window again. I am so hot."

Lily laughed. "That you are." She sat up. "Okay, open the window, then take off those clothes and come back to bed."

Jany could feel herself blush. She quickly opened the window, standing in front of it for a moment to let the salty draft cool her. She took a deep breath. "I love the smell of the ocean."

"You're stalling."

Jany turned to face her lover. Despite their years together, she could never quite get over her own shyness, especially in daylight. She was a butch after all. But she did have to admit she liked it when Lily made love to her.

Lily smiled as she patted the bed. "I want you."

Hesitating only briefly, Jany walked over. "Let me help you with that," Lily said, pulling Jany's T-shirt off and letting it fall to the floor. Her warm mouth sucked in one taut nipple. Moaning, Jany knelt on the bed, giving Lily easier access. Lily's fingers played with the other nipple, rolling it between her fingers. Her other hand reached between Jany's legs.

"Mmmm, you are so ready for me."

"You know that making love to you makes me wet."

"I like that."

She yanked Jany's boxers down while simultaneously pushing her onto the bed. Instantly, she was between Jany's legs, nuzzling with her nose and mouth as her fingers continued to play with both nipples, squeezing them tight and making Jany moan loud and long. Normally much less vocal than Lily, Jany couldn't help herself when Lily was a bit more rough than usual.

Lily's tongue and fingers worked their magic. The breeze from the open window caressed Jany's body like a second lover. Jany could feel an orgasm begin to crest, and when Lily thrust deep with her fingers, Jany cried out as the waves rolled up and down her body like a high tide. The tangy salt air mixed with the heady scent of woman sex.

Jany opened her eyes just in time to see Merlin—or was it Morgan le Fay or Lucifer—seemingly wink at her before he walked from the room, tail twitching.

"No, really Mandy," Lily shouted above the music at the Frog Pond, "that storm this afternoon had the smell of witchcraft to it."

"You know, Mother Nature is perfectly capable of conjuring up a sudden tempest all her own," Mandy said, then grinned. "I know you and Jany were in bed together. Really, the way you two go at it, you'd think you were newlyweds or something."

"You're just jealous because we haven't been cursed with lesbian bed death."

Mandy took a sip of her gin and tonic, then pushed her long, gray-streaked brown hair over her shoulder. Lily hoped, not for the first time, that she looked as vibrant as Mandy did when she was fifty.

"If I didn't know better," Mandy said, "I'd think you were a witch yourself and had cast a spell on Jany." She glanced over at the handsome, auburn-haired butch who was the envy of many. "Before she met you, she was quite the player."

Lily rolled her eyes. "I've heard that old story so many times. You're just trying to change the subject. If Tara didn't create the storm, who did?"

Letting out an exasperated sigh, Mandy picked up her drink. "Get off it will you, or I'll turn you into a toad."

Surprised, Lily looked at Mandy. That seemed like a rather harsh statement from someone she considered a mother figure.

Turn her into a toad? Like that was even possible outside the realm of fantasy TV shows. Not that she didn't believe in witchcraft. Lily knew full well the Rehoboth coven had special powers, but transmogrification wasn't one of them. A love spell or a weather change was one thing, but changing a human into an animal was another.

"Darling, I'm just teasing you," Mandy said. She took a last gulp of her drink. "I've got some work at home to do, so I'll see you later." She leaned over and kissed Lily on the cheek.

As she watched Mandy walk away, Lily slouched down in her chair. She couldn't figure out why she was so peeved. It's not like Tara hadn't made it storm before. Tara, who always joked that she was the inspiration for the lesbian witch's lover on that Buffy TV show. And Mandy claimed Tara wasn't even in town. Well then, where was she?

Jany slid into the booth beside her. "You're frowning. What did Mandy say to you?"

"Nothing really. Just that Tara's not in town and I should get over myself."

"Really?"

"Well, no, not in those words," she admitted. "I don't know what's wrong with me. I'm so touchy."

"I know it's never easy for you when the tourists come to town. You like the money they spend in your shop, but not the people themselves."

Lily leaned over and kissed her. "You're so sweet to have put up with me these five summers." She started tearing the label off her beer bottle. "Jany?"

"Yes, sweetie?"

"You're satisfied with me, aren't you? I please you?"

"Of course I am. Why would you ask that?"

Lily couldn't look at her. "I . . . I know that before me . . . Well, you—"

"God, have you been listening to gossip again? Okay, yes, before I met you I liked the women. I dated a lot, and slept with a good many of them. But when I met you, it was different. I wanted to settle down. You can't let your insecurities come out just because someone mentions my past."

"I'm sorry. Like I said, I don't know what's wrong with me lately. I've been uneasy. Like something's gonna happen. Something bad."

Jany kissed her long and hard. "Whatever it is, it has nothing to do with us. I love you."

CHAPTER II

The haunting melodies of Loreena McKennett played softly in the background as thirteen women, all barefoot and dressed in diaphanous gowns of white or yellow, lolled about on oversized pillows. A number of candles sent the fragrances of sandalwood and clove mingling with the salty ocean air that wafted in through several open windows. Ruby red liquid glimmered in long-stemmed glasses. Seven cats of various sizes and colors also lolled about on the pillows.

Petting a large ginger cat, Mandy took a sip of her drink. "Mmmm, you outdid yourself this time on the drink, Lucy. Who'd have thought pomegranates would make such a good cocktail."

"I just got tired of the same old strawberry or banana. It wasn't easy finding pomegranates at this time of year, though. I ordered them off the Internet."

"I always thought Lucy held the best house parties," Clarissa said. "I vote we just have all our gatherings here."

"That really wouldn't be fair to Lucy, would it?" Mandy said.

"We'd all chip in for the food." Sarah glanced around the room. "It's such a nice space too. So open. You have to admit, when you come to my house it's a pretty tight squeeze."

Lucy laughed. "You know I wouldn't mind having everyone to

my house all the time. I do have the biggest place. And it's a lot more private too."

Jacquelyn rolled over onto her stomach. "Yeah, the rest of us live smack in the middle of town. All those freaky tourists trying to sneak a peek. You'd think they'd never seen a bunch of women having a gathering before."

"It's not just the tourists," Kathy added. "The townspeople have gotten curious too."

Tara groaned. "It's because of that damn article in *Letters from Camp Rehoboth*. You'd think people had never heard of Wicca before."

"Is that why you've been so cranky?" Judith asked.

"Yeah," Mandy said, "Lily accused you yesterday of causing a sudden storm in the afternoon. Even when I told her you were out of town, she still believed you did it."

"I don't know why Lily dislikes me so."

"That's not true, and you know it," Mandy chided.

"Well," Clarissa said, "it could be she's a bit insecure because you and Jany used to be involved."

"That was so seven years ago, before the two of them had even met. We were kids."

Kathy stroked Tara's arm. "I can see why Lily would feel threatened. You *are* the most beautiful woman in town."

Tara jerked away as if burned. "Insincere flattery will get you nowhere."

Kathy scowled. Two of the windows slammed shut, causing all seven cats to scamper. Then a strong breeze blew out most of the candles. There were small shrieks around the room as a glass shattered, spilling red liquid onto one of the silk-covered pillows.

"Okay you two," Mandy said, "I want no further hostility in our sacred space. Kathy, control yourself. You know I won't tolerate any kind of harassment."

"Yeah, control your temper," Lucy said. "Dammit, look what you've done to the pillow. I'll never get the stain out."

Kathy rolled her eyes. "Sorry. I'll buy you a new one."

An awkward hush filled the room. The music had even stopped

playing, leaving only the faint sound of ocean waves to fill the silence.

Abruptly, Tara laughed. "We're all too serious. Look at us, all somber faced. We're lying around on harem pillows and getting drunk on pomegranate juice laced with vodka. We should be relaxed and happy."

"Yeah, most people would think we should be having a drunken orgy while we dance naked around a campfire in the middle of the forest," said Sarah.

"I certainly wouldn't mind the orgy part," Kathy said with a leer.

Mandy shook her head. The woman just refused to get the message. She wondered if she'd have to take a vote on whether Kathy could remain in the coven. If truth were told, Mandy often thought most of the recent unwanted publicity came from Kathy. Mandy was sure she had some kind of agenda. She just wasn't sure what. The article in *Letters* had to have come from someone, and Kathy was as good a suspect as any.

She rose to ring a small bell. "I think it's time to call this meeting to order."

"I'll close the windows," Clarissa said.

"And I'll relight the candles," Jacquelyn said as she stood and stretched.

The other women pushed the pillows aside to reveal burnt into the wooden floor a five-pointed star surrounded by a circle—a pentacle, the symbol of the Wiccan faith. Mandy placed a large white candle in the center and lit it. She then anointed each woman in turn with juniper oil for purification and protection before they formed a circle and linked hands. In unison they raised their arms to the ceiling. "In the name of Hecate and all that's powerful, we call upon our protector," they chanted.

Hidden in the bush outside the smallest window, Lily couldn't help but gasp as she beheld the sight before her. Although the windows were closed, the women's sheer gowns fluttered around and clung to their bodies. The candlelight played tricks, turning the material transparent so they appeared naked. Their eyes were closed and Lily could see their lips move. She'd give anything to hear what they said.

Her coming here tonight had started out innocently enough. She wanted to apologize to Mandy for her behavior yesterday. Sometimes she felt like some teenager arguing with her mom. She had overheard Mandy tell a customer she'd be going to Lucy's tonight, and since Jany was out bowling with her buddies, Lily had thought she wouldn't mind spending an evening at Lucy's. After all, Lucy had a pool *and* a hot tub. She'd fully intended to invite herself to whatever they had planned, but after she'd parked the car, she saw several women arrive at once. As they entered the house, she counted. Eleven, plus Lucy and Mandy who were already inside. It was a meeting of the coven.

Lily could barely contain her excitement. She'd read the article in *Letters* like everyone else. True, she had known about the coven long before the article had come out. She and Jany were good friends with Mandy and Sarah, who'd both let slip they were practicing witches. Or Wicca, as they preferred to be called. But they'd also been secretive about who was in their coven, and now here tonight, Lily had seen them all. She knew about Tara and, of course, Lucy, as well as Jacquelyn who was forever supplying people with cats. The resident lesbian community in Rehoboth was not all that large. Everyone pretty much knew everyone. And tonight she recognized Clarissa, Judith, Gwendolyn, Cara, Sage, Ruth, Blossom, and, most surprisingly of all, the brooding Kathy. Lily watched as the opening ritual ended, and then they all sat in a circle. She shrank back into the bushes when Mandy glanced out the window and appeared to frown. Didn't witches have some kind of sixth sense? Could Mandy or one of the others feel that she was outside? And what would they do if they found her? A mild twinge of anxiety ran through her, but she could not leave. She felt drawn to what was happening, almost as if she belonged. The pull was so strong, she began to wonder if some dim memory was coming to light.

The discussion around the circle was lively. A lot of them talked with their hands. No one seemed angry, unlike earlier with Kathy and Tara. Lily had only heard snatches of the conversation, but she'd not mistaken the look on Kathy's face or the resulting physical manifestations. It was a regular *Carrie* moment. Lily shuddered just thinking about it. She'd have to remind Jany not to piss Kathy off. The two had a not-so-friendly competition—two attractive butches vying for attention from the femmes, though Jany's was, of course, only in fun. But there were times when Lily felt Kathy's rivalry wasn't only in fun. She'd seen the way Kathy would sometimes look at Jany, and it always made her nervous. Now she knew her instincts hadn't lied.

After a few more minutes, she backed out of the bushes, careful not to make any noise. She walked to her car, thinking about all she'd seen. She was more curious than ever about the thirteen, especially now that she knew who they were. Come to think of it now, she should have guessed about Sage and Blossom. Both born to flower-child mothers, they co-owned a mystical shop that sold salves and herbal remedies alongside crystals, candles, and books on the occult. But they were so obvious it made them not obvious.

What would it be like to be a witch? To be able to change things on a whim? Like, would she be able to change the lottery? Do some kind of spell to make sure her numbers came up? She paused getting into her car. Was there a spell to make sure your lover never strayed? She shook her head. Why would she even think she needed to do something like that? Jany loved her, of that she was certain. So why then did she feel so insecure and uneasy these days? Jany had done nothing to make Lily think she was losing interest in their relationship. In fact, she was more attentive than usual.

Lily started the car. That was it. She'd read too many of those articles in the women's magazines about how to know if your man was cheating, and unusual attentiveness was one of the indicators. Was Jany really bowling tonight? She shook her head again. "Stop it," she said out loud as she guided the car away from the direction of the bowling alley and to Sage and Blossom's shop instead.

Chimes sounded as she opened the door. The high school student behind the counter looked up as Lily walked in. "Hi, Miss Anderson. Haven't seen you in a while."

"Hey, Heather. Yeah, I've not run out of candles in a while."

"We just got a big shipment in. Lots of new scents." She came from around the counter and led Lily to an oversized wall unit stocked with candles of different sizes and colors. She picked up an orange one and sniffed it. "This one is pumpkin and nectarine."

"Um, I'm really more interested in some books tonight."

"What topic?"

"Witchcraft."

"What's that? I didn't hear you." Heather leaned closer.

"Witchcraft."

Heather laughed. "You and about fifty others. Since that article came out in *Letters*, we've not been able to keep them in stock."

"Really. What kind of people are buying them?"

"High school kids mostly. I think the teachers are gonna see lots of term papers on witchcraft this semester. Some have already come in wanting to interview Sage and Blossom."

Lily toyed with a set of votives. "They don't think they're witches, do they?"

"You talking about the students or Sage and Blossom?"

"The students. Do they think Sage and Blossom are witches?"

Heather laughed. "Well, yeah. Wouldn't you?"

Lily put the votives back. "Me? Of course not. I don't believe in all that."

"Oh come on, Miss Anderson, how can you not? And if you don't, why do you want a book?"

"I'm just curious, that's all. How does one go about becoming a witch anyway?"

Heather shrugged and walked back to the counter. "I don't

think you can become a witch. I think you either are one or you're not."

"But how do you know if you are? I mean, if I tried to do a spell and something happened, that would mean I had the power, right?"

"I really don't know. Look, Miss Anderson, I just work here selling their stuff. You need to talk to Sage or Blossom. They've been real nice to the curiosity seekers, so I'm sure they won't mind a friend asking."

Lily walked over to the books and scanned the myriad of titles: *The Magical Lore of Herbs*, *Druid Magic: The Practice of Celtic Wisdom*, *Celtic Lore and Druid Ritual*, *Healing with Gemstones and Crystals*, *Drawing Faeries: A Believer's Guide*. And sure enough, two shelves were entirely empty. She ran her fingers along the edges of the shelves, wondering what titles she might find there in the coming days. "When's your next book shipment due?"

"Don't really know. You might try the library. Perhaps interest has died down enough for the kids to return the books they checked out."

"Thanks for your help. I'll check back in a couple of days."

"You want me to tell Sage and Blossom you came by?"

"No need. I'll call them soon."

Feeling frustrated, Lily strolled to the coffee shop just a couple of doors down. After she ordered her latte, she picked up the local paper and took her coffee to a table. On page two, a headline caught her eye: *Navy to Perform Sonar Testing Off the Delaware Coast*. She skimmed the article in growing horror, then angrily crumpled the paper into a ball and threw it into the trashcan. "Damn them," she muttered under her breath as she stomped back to her car.

CHAPTER III

"Y ou were up awfully early this morning," Jany commented as she finally came downstairs. She poured a cup of coffee and put a bagel in the toaster.

"I had work to do."

Jany looked up at Lily's terse tone. "Something up with the shop? You getting ready to fire someone?"

"Nothing like that." She scrolled down the Web page on her laptop. "God, I hate these people!"

Jany sat at the table. It was rare to see Lily in such a mood. "Want to tell me about it?"

"Didn't you see the paper yesterday?"

"Yeah—"

"They are so evil!"

Exasperated now, Jany took Lily's hand to stop her from typing. "Will you just tell me what's wrong?"

Lily looked at her as if she should know. "You said you read the paper. Didn't you see the article on page two?"

Her bagel popped up, but Jany ignored it. "I'm sure I did, but I don't know which article you're talking about."

"The Navy!"

"Look, darling, I want you to take a deep breath and calmly tell me what's got you so irked this morning."

Lily closed her eyes and did as Jany had told her. When she opened her eyes again, Jany thought she looked calmer. "I have been up since five. I've written letters to the editors of the local paper as well as the surrounding communities. I have also e-mailed Greenpeace, the Natural Resources Defense Council, and the International Fund for Animal Welfare. I plan to e-mail the Navy's customer relations, if they have such a thing."

"But what is this about?"

"They're going to do sonar testing off the coast over the course of four weeks."

"And—"

"It is *so* damaging to marine mammals like whales and dolphins. It interferes with their own sonar. Some people even theorize that could be the cause of some mass whale strandings. On top of that, a couple of years ago, whales that had beached themselves in the Bahamas had massive ear hemorrhages that some marine biologists think were caused by nearby military sonar tests. You can find any number of articles on the Web to support this theory. And not just from so-called 'tree huggers.'"

Jany sighed. She should have known it was something like this. Nothing else would get her this worked up. "I'm sorry Lily, I had no idea this was such an important issue to you."

Lily got up and automatically slathered Jany's bagel with cream cheese. "I want to organize a protest." She placed the bagel in front of Jany. "And a letter-writing campaign. The first thing to do is publicize why this is not a good thing."

Jany bit into her bagel. It was barely warm. "I suppose you could always appeal to the town council, point out that having big Navy destroyers off the coast will mar the tourists' view. Maybe even interfere with pleasure boaters and fishermen."

"I don't care about the tourists!"

"But money is what the council understands. If they think it will hurt tourism, they might try to stop them. Think of how many whale-watching cruises leave from Lewes every day."

"Hmmm, you have a point there, counselor. I never thought of that angle. Who's gonna want to go on such a cruise if the animals are freaked or don't show up at all? Or vacation on a beach with rotting whale carcasses?"

When Lily got up from the table, Jany pulled her into her lap. "Hey sweetheart, how about we go back upstairs and I take your mind off the Navy for a bit?" She kissed Lily's soft neck, then moved her mouth down the vee of Lily's shirt.

"That feels so good, baby, but I need to get to the shop. We're having that big sale today, and I promised Marcia I'd not leave her alone with just the kids." She leaned down to kiss Jany full on the mouth. "But I'll take a raincheck." She stood up. "And besides, I don't think Mr. Hendrickson would appreciate you taking a day off when you're preparing for such a big case."

"You're right. It's not every day we try someone for murder."

Lily headed for the stairs, glancing back at Jany before she completely left the kitchen. "I still don't like tourists, but this time they could help me."

Jany laughed as Lily disappeared up the stairs. Ah, tourists. They were both the bane of Lily's existence as well as her livelihood. Lily designed much of her shop's unusual jewelry herself, but she also featured local artists like Tara, who made beautiful, one-of-a-kind pieces from natural items like shells and feathers and seeds. The shop was very popular with the lesbian community, both locals and visitors alike.

She got herself another cup of coffee. It seemed these days she couldn't drink enough of it. Lily was right. She did have a big case ahead of her. The picturesque seaside resort rarely saw violent crimes, and this particular murder had doubly shocked the community for its brutality.

She finished her breakfast and headed up the stairs. She heard the shower running and briefly considered joining Lily. With both of them naked and slippery, she was certain she could convince Lily to play. With a sigh, Jany went to the spare bathroom instead. Lily was right; Hendrickson would have her head if she played hooky this close to the trial. She had a feeling she'd be working some late nights in the next couple of weeks. She just hoped Lily wouldn't get into too much trouble with this anti-Navy campaign she was about to embark on.

"Hi, Mandy," Lily said when Mandy opened the door of her bungalow. "I need your help."

"Come on in." Mandy stepped back and let Lily walk in before her. "Care for some chai tea?"

"Do you have any plain old black tea? I can't figure out why everyone likes chai so much."

Mandy rummaged in a kitchen cabinet and found a beat-up tin. "Got some Lipton in here, but who knows how old it is."

"I don't mind if it's kinda stale." Lily slid onto a stool at the kitchen counter. "Did you see the article in yesterday's paper about the Navy testing? I've spent the whole morning writing letters, and I want to get other people to write as well."

"Write about what?"

"We have to stop it."

"Hey, I don't like the military in our backyard anymore than you do, but what can we do? What kind of tests anyway? Not missile firings, I hope."

"Sonar testing. And no, before you say anything, those tests won't hurt humans but they could prove dangerous for our marine mammals."

"I tell you what, you write the letter and I'll sign it." She poured hot water over Lily's tea bag. "Is that the only reason you came by this morning? To ask me to write a letter? You could have done that by phone."

Lily played with her tea bag. "I have a confession to make, but I don't want you to get mad at me."

"You saw us last night, didn't you?"

Lily looked up. "How . . . how did you know? I was so careful."

Mandy smiled mysteriously. "I sensed your presence. I am a high priestess after all."

"Oh come on, Mandy. You must have seen me or my car."

"Nope."

"Honestly?"

"Honestly."

"Look, I didn't mean anything by it. I overheard you telling someone you were going to Lucy's and I thought since Jany was bowling, I'd crash. I had no idea it was a meeting of your coven." She sipped her tea. "I wanted to apologize to you for my brat behavior."

Mandy took Lily's chin and made Lily look at her. "I know you are curious. I think you might even feel the power yourself."

Lily snorted. "Me, a witch? I don't think so."

"C'mon, Lily, you've never wished for something, only to have it come true? Something that had to be more than a coincidence?"

"I don't know."

"And how about that storm you accused Tara of causing the other day? I know you and Jany were making love. You're a very passionate woman. You don't think your passion could affect the weather?" Mandy grinned. "A storm inside and a storm outside?"

Lily felt her cheeks grow warm, especially because Mandy was old enough to be her mother. "People seem awfully curious about my sex life."

Mandy patted her hand. "It's just 'cause we're jealous. So, what did you think?"

"I was surprised at some of the women I saw there. I mean, I'm not surprised at Sage and Blossom. They've always had that Earth mother vibe going." She grinned. "But seeing the town's strutting butch in a see-through gown. Now that was something."

Mandy laughed. "Yeah, most people see Kathy as strictly a jeans-and-boots sort of gal."

"There seemed to be a bit of tension between her and Tara. What was that all about?"

"I probably shouldn't say anything, but Kathy's got a thing for Tara. And true to her nature, she's not too subtle about it. There's a right way and a wrong way to approach a woman, you know what I mean? Kathy could take some lessons from your Jany."

"Jany and Tara were involved several years ago. Was Tara a practicing witch back then? Did Jany know?"

"Tara's known since she was five that she had some special abilities. Fortunately, she chose to use those abilities wisely. Some people aren't so wise. They become dangerous. It's those individuals you have to keep watch over."

"Is Kathy one of those people?"

Mandy got up to put the kettle on. It seemed to Lily that she took longer than necessary to do so. Finally, Mandy turned to look at her. "I think it would be easy for Kathy to go the wrong way. She can be very volatile. I only tell you this because I also believe she is very jealous of Jany. She still resents that all those years ago Tara chose Jany over her."

"I've always wondered why Jany and Tara broke up. Everyone seemed to think they were the perfect couple."

"I don't know the whys or wherefores, but they were very young. I do know that Jany now loves you. And she and Tara had been apart a couple of years when you two met. I hope you have no insecurities about that."

"I used to, but I'm okay now." She thought back to her conversation with Jany. "At least, I hope I am."

Mandy poured them both another cup of tea and put out some homemade chocolate chip cookies on a plate. "Let's get back to the reason you came to see me. You want my help with this Navy testing stuff. I was a pretty good organizer back in my feminist protest days. Let me do a little research and we'll get the word out. I'll get us a rally permit, and we can have a nice little protest march."

Lily rose to hug her. "You're a darling. I knew I could count on you."

"I would also like to use some ritual magick to help you, but I need your permission to use it."

"I don't know how all that works, but if it will help, please do."

✦✦✦

After Lily left, Mandy called Tara. "I want you to call the others and meet here at seven tonight. One of our own needs our help."

"You're talking about Lily, aren't you?"

"Yes."

"Don't you think it's time you told her the truth? That she is indeed one of us?"

"She needs to discover it on her own, but I think this project she wants help with will enable her to do just that. She never knew her mother. And I feel bad that I didn't fill Rebekah's role and teach Lily about her legacy. I guess I just figured she would have discovered it long ago and that she would come to me."

"Well, it didn't help that her father took her away from here. You tried to follow, but he was determined to forget about Rehoboth and everything and everyone that reminded him of it. He was devastated when Rebekah died. I'm just glad Lily found her way home. We might have lost her completely."

"We will all need to work together to help her, not only with her cause, but also to truly find her way home."

CHAPTER IV

I know you are all surprised to be gathering again so soon," Mandy said as she looked around the circle at the other twelve women. They were a bit more cramped at her place than they had been at Lucy's. This time there were no comfortable pillows, just a wooden floor laid bare of its Oriental carpet to reveal Mandy's pentacle. "Lily has asked for my help, and I decided it was something we could all do together. After all, the power of thirteen is much stronger than the power of just one."

"Ah, time for a spell or two," Gwendolyn stated. "Not a love spell, I gather?"

Everyone around the circle tittered. Mandy was beginning to wonder if Lily was right in thinking people were obsessed with her love life. For Hecate's sake, Lily and Jany weren't the only lesbians in town having sex. She frowned, bringing the group back to order.

"No, this is not some trivial matter. It seems the U.S. Navy has decided to perform some military training exercises off our coast-line starting next week and going on for four weeks. These exercises involve mid-frequency sonar; studies have shown these types of tests can be lethal to whales and dolphins, possibly causing the animals to beach themselves." She paused, knowing they'd remember when such an event had occurred in nearby Dewey Beach.

"What does Lily think we can do? We can't stop the Navy," Sarah said.

"Maybe not, but we sure can give them some bad publicity. If we get the town to unite behind Lily, it will call attention to what's happening. And maybe a nasty storm or two will prevent the military from being able to conduct the tests."

Sage spoke. "You don't think we could stop the Navy entirely if we used all our power together?"

"This is more than just holding hands and chanting 'go home, go home' several times over. We will need a powerful protection spell."

"I think we can do it," Kathy said. Her eyes blazed brightly for just a few seconds, but it was enough to make windows slam shut and furniture rattle. Two of Mandy's three cats hissed and took off running.

Mandy shivered. Kathy's rage might very well help them get rid of the Navy vessels, but did she really want to harness it? Once released, could such power ever be contained again? If the truth were told, she was afraid of Kathy, but she'd never said anything to anyone. Her main reason for having Kathy in the coven was to watch her. What was that old phrase? Keep your friends close and your enemies closer? Kathy was not an enemy. At least, not yet. But she could be.

"Let's concentrate right now on bringing the townspeople on board with this."

They all stood and held hands, raising their arms to the sky. "By the power of Hecate, we call on thee . . ."

Within two weeks, posters were plastered all over town, advertising the upcoming rally to protest the Navy's sonar tests. The high school students who worked for Lily, as well as those who worked for Sage and Blossom, had shown great enthusiasm in helping. They had recruited fellow students, and now there was a mini environmental movement afoot. The school newspaper had run a series of articles, as had the local paper. Letters to the Editor were running four to one against the testing. Lily had convinced the radio and TV stations to interview her. The little town of Rehoboth Beach was attracting the attention of the surrounding counties as well.

"I am so surprised and pleased at how the kids have taken to this," Lily was saying to Jany one lazy Saturday morning as they lingered in bed.

It was looking to be another hazy, hot, and humid day. Despite her dislike of storms, even Lily had to agree a good thunderstorm helped break the triple H cycle, and in the last couple of weeks, they'd had one, sometimes two, almost daily. None of them lasted too long—an hour at most—but it was kind of uncanny. And what was even more uncanny was how Lily felt after each one—as if she herself was partly responsible for it. One day she'd even sat surrounded by her four cats while she concentrated on conjuring up a storm. Willing mind over matter, she'd focused so long and hard that she'd lost total track of time. Her next awareness was Jany coming through the door. By Lily's own account, she'd been unconscious of everything going on around her for nearly three hours.

Jany snuggled closer. "Me too. I guess we'd both written off their generation as a bunch of lazy slobs who care only about themselves."

Lily laughed. "Oh, I don't think we're off the mark too much with that, but it's good to see they have potential." She giggled as Jany licked her neck.

"You taste salty."

"It's so fucking hot. I'm sweating like a pig."

"Pigs don't sweat." She lightly bit Lily's shoulder. "I can make you sweat even more." Twisting around, she placed one arm on each side of Lily's body. "I can't seem to get enough of you."

In response, Lily pulled Jany down as she lifted her mouth for a kiss. Jany's tongue in her mouth elicited a moan. She could already feel the wetness begin between her legs. Sometimes just a look from Jany could make her wet, but physical contact almost always caused an instantaneous reaction.

"You feel so good against me," she murmured into Jany's ear. "I like being naked with you."

"Ditto," Jany replied. "That's the one thing I do like about this weather. You sleep naked."

"I suppose we could always turn on the air conditioning," Lily continued as she arched against Jany's touch.

"What? And have you sleeping in a T-shirt again? No way!"

She trailed her fingers across Lily's sensitive breasts, smiling as the nipples immediately hardened. She took one in her mouth, making Lily moan long and deep. Lily pressed against her and grabbed her hair. It made Jany suck harder. Her fingers traced their way down Lily's torso, lingering on her belly and then dipping between her legs to find Lily swollen and wet and ready. Lily arched against her fingers. "Please," she whispered, and then moaned again as Jany complied and thrust her fingers deep. Jany kissed her, going from mouth to throat to collarbone to breast. Her free hand continued to play with Lily's nipples—first one, then the other. She nibbled her way down Lily's smooth body, across her stomach to her thighs. Jany moaned herself when she tasted Lily's sweet woman nectar.

Jany sucked and licked Lily's swollen lips, teasing her before moving on to her clit. Lily squirmed beneath her, grabbing Jany's hair as she moaned. Jany used both hands to grasp Lily's hips, keeping her from thrashing too wildly on the bed.

"Jany—" Lily groaned. "Oh god, yes. Don't stop. Right there. Yesssss!"

Lily's hips bucked, but Jany held fast, steadily sucking Lily's clit until she felt Lily's trembling release. Lily sighed and released her hold on Jany's hair. Jany's tongue flicked across her clit. Lily pushed gently against Jany's shoulders. "Enough," she said, laughing softly. "Come up here."

"Just one more?"

"Not this time, my love."

Jany moved from between Lily's legs. Both their bodies

gleamed with sweat. She lightly stroked Lily's flushed skin. Lily stretched, raising up in response. "Mmmm, that feels so good," she said. She liked the tickling sensation. Even on such a hot day, she responded with goose bumps.

"I love you," Jany said.

"I love you too."

"This may sound incredibly corny, but I feel so lucky to have found you." She paused, looking deep into Lily's blue eyes. "It's no secret what I was like before I met you. If I didn't know better, I'd think you'd used some kind of love spell on me, making me blind to all other women."

Lily smoothed back Jany's damp hair and traced Jany's sensitive earlobe, making her shiver. One shoulder raised involuntarily as Jany turned her head away and smiled. "You know I'm a lot more ticklish than you."

Lily laughed. "It is such fun to tease you." She became serious. "Yes, I know what your reputation was, but when Clarissa first introduced us, I knew right then you were the woman I wanted to be with for the rest of my life. And yes, I know we sound like a sappy Hallmark card, but I look around and see our friends and know that no one is as lucky as we are."

Jany laid back against the pillows, willing a breeze to come through the open window to cool them. The curtains stayed bone still. "Yeah. You'd think though that all our Wiccan friends would be happy. I mean, they do have the power to cast spells. I saw how Judith manipulated that bowling tournament."

"Oh darling, there are just some things you don't want to manipulate artificially. I think falling in love is much better done naturally, don't you? I mean, if I had done a spell to make you fall in love with me, I would always know it was a false love. I don't know about the others, but after a while, it would no longer please me."

"If you were a witch, what would you use your powers for?"

Lily leaned over and lightly licked Jany's neck. "Wouldn't you rather I take care of you?"

"Mmmm, not this time. I feel very content right now."

"Well then, let's get up and have some breakfast. I'm famished." She pointed toward the bottom of the bed. "And the wake-up committee wants feeding too."

Jany looked. Merlin, Casper, Morgan le Fay, and Lucifer sat in a row on the footboard, their green and gold eyes unblinking. Then, one by one, they leapt off the bed and walked out of the room, tails twitching. Jany scrambled out of bed. "Sometimes those cats are too damn creepy," she said as she pulled on a T-shirt and her boxers. "I think they're familiars sent to spy on us."

Lily laughed. "You've got quite the imagination," she said, but she didn't entirely dismiss Jany's statement. After all, the four cats had come from Jacquelyn and Sage, two of the women she now knew were in Mandy's coven. She shook her head. Don't be silly, she thought to herself. Cats as familiars was a myth left over from the Middle Ages.

"Miss Anderson," Harold Jeeves was saying, "I find it admirable that you are so passionate about this cause, but the bad publicity from your campaign cannot be good for the town."

The head of the town council had contacted Lily via e-mail asking for a face-to-face meeting, and now she sat uncomfortably on a straight-backed chair in his office. "I don't know how it can be anything but good," she responded. "We've got reporters in town, plus the extra tourists. They're all generating extra income for the local businesses, and after all, isn't that what you care about? Revenue for the city?"

"After nine-eleven, it is not such a good thing to come to the attention of the U.S. military."

"Oh come on, Mr. Jeeves, you don't honestly believe they think Rehoboth Beach is a hotbed of terrorists? And think about it, would you rather have the bad publicity of an environmental disaster?"

"A couple of beached whales is not an environmental disaster."

"Maybe not to you." She took a deep breath. "Besides, protest is an American right protected by the First Amendment."

"I can revoke your permit."

"And I can take you to court!"

The coffee cup on his desk shattered, sending hot liquid spreading across his papers. "Damnation!" he yelped as he leapt out of his chair. Lily grabbed a fistful of tissues and began blotting up the spill. "Thank you, thank you. I'll take care of that," Harold said as he took the tissues from her.

"That mug must have had a crack in it," she said as she sat back down.

"Yeah, but what an odd thing—to shatter like that."

"Yeah, odd."

Lily waited patiently while he finished cleaning up the mess. She was very aware of her body. It was almost as if she'd had a minor electrical shock—the tingling in her extremities, the hairs on her neck standing up. Could she have made Mr. Jeeves' mug explode like that? Was she developing some kind of telekinetic abilities? No, that would be absurd. She wasn't even sure such a thing existed beyond the imagination of prolific horror writers. But suddenly she remembered something. Something from when she was a child. It was her fifth birthday. An obnoxious boy had been teasing her unmercifully, flinging her skirt up again and again to expose her ruffled underwear. She could recall his taunting voice, feel the bright flush that warmed her cheeks, hear the laughter of the other children.

"Stop it!" she'd said as she slapped at his hand for what seemed like the tenth time, a long time to a five-year-old mind. The flash of anger was a physical sensation as it coursed through her body. And then, the boy had been flung against a tree. The other children had gasped, their laughter stifled.

"Did you see what Lily did?"

"I'm gonna tell my mom."

"I don't like this party."

"How did you do that, Lily?"

"I didn't do anything. I didn't even touch him!"

By this time, the boy was crying. Lily stood in the middle of the yard while the other children whispered to each other. Lily's father came out, accompanied by two of the other kids' mothers.

"What's going on here?" her father asked.

"Timmy fell."

"Did not. You pushed him!"

"Did not! I didn't even touch him." She looked up at her father. *"He was teasing me. Pulling up my skirt."*

Her father's face turned white. *"I think you've all had a bit too much ice cream and cake."* The two mothers nodded, no doubt thinking all the kids were on some sort of sugar high. *"Lily thanks you all for coming to her birthday party, but I think it's time for everyone to go on home."* He patted the boy's shoulder. *"Timmy, you probably just tripped in all the excitement. Running around the way you were, you just fell with a bit more force than usual. You okay now?"*

Timmy nodded, the tears still streaming from his eyes. He hiccupped twice, then meekly followed the others into the house.

"You stay here," Lily's father said. *"You can call everyone later and thank them for coming. I want you to tell me what happened."*

"Nothing, Daddy. Honest."

He knelt beside her. *"Baby, I know sometimes we all get mad. And that's okay, as long we don't hurt anyone with our anger."*

"You mean, like hitting people?"

"Yes, like hitting people." He looked at her. *"Or even thinking bad thoughts about them."*

"I don't know what you mean, Daddy."

He took her hand. *"Did you think about making Timmy hit that tree? It's okay to tell me."*

She lowered her head, unable to look him in the eyes. *"Yes, Daddy."* Lily was crying now. She knew she was a bad girl.

He pulled her close and held her tight. *"It's okay, Lily. I will help you so you don't do that ever again. I love you, and I'm not mad at you."*

Lily sobbed into his shoulder. *"I love you too, Daddy."*

"Miss Anderson, are you okay?"

Lily looked up and saw Harold Jeeves staring at her with concern. "What? Oh yes, I'm fine. My mind just wandered a bit."

"Shall we get back to what we were discussing?"

Lily pushed back her chair. "I'm sorry, Mr. Jeeves. I really have to go. I'm sorry."

She hurried out of his office and headed toward Mandy's house. Something wasn't right, and she was certain Mandy would be able to help her figure out what it was. She was remembering things she wasn't sure made sense, and it was as if an inner voice was whispering to her, "Mandy knows the answers."

CHAPTER V

Mandy was in her garden when Lily arrived. Lily stood for a moment beside the white picket fence, watching as Mandy dug deep into the earth. Beside her stood several pots of miniature roses. Just as Lily was wondering how to get her attention without startling her, Mandy spoke.

"Hello, Lily." She set down her trowel before rising to face Lily. "You want to ask me about your mother."

"How did you know—"

Mandy smiled as she approached Lily. Wiping her dirty hands on an old towel, she opened the gate for Lily to walk through. "I know many things, my child. I knew this day would someday come. I'd just hoped it would be sooner."

Lily followed her up the path to the house. "Knew what day would come? I don't understand."

"Your father took you away from here in hopes you would never discover that you too are a witch, just like your dear mother. And without her nurturing to guide you, your powers never developed. At least, not so that you knew what they were."

"This is absurd. I'm not a witch." She heard the words come out of her mouth, but deep in her heart, she knew the real truth. It was just so hard to come to terms with it all. She felt quite lost.

Mandy indicated a chair. "Sit down while I make us some tea." She smiled. "Yes, I know. You want black tea." She bustled about the kitchen, putting on the kettle, getting teacups out of the cupboard, cutting up lemons. "Your mother, Rebekah, was a powerful Wicca. A healer. We belonged to the same coven, as did the mothers of all the women you saw here the other night."

"They're all daughters of witches?"

"In a word, yes." She set a steaming cup of tea before Lily and pushed the plate of lemons toward her. "And if things had worked out the way they should have, you would be part of that coven now."

Lily took a sip of tea. She didn't even notice that it scalded her tongue. "This is unbelievable. I've never even remotely thought of myself that way."

"It's because your true self has always been suppressed. Like any talent, it needs to be nurtured and encouraged. Yours never was, but obviously things have happened recently. Things you don't understand?"

"Just little things. I didn't even notice when they happened, but now looking back . . . I think I can conjure up storms." She looked at Mandy, chagrined that she had been right. "Tell me I'm crazy."

Mandy sat beside her. She pushed a strand of hair behind Lily's ear and stroked along the edges of her cheek and chin. "You look so much like Rebekah. Seeing you is like seeing her come back to life."

"My father would never tell me about her. I thought it was because the memory was too painful."

"It probably was. He loved her very much, but he blamed what she was for her death. That is why he took you away from us, spiriting you out of town in the dead of night. One day you were here, and the next you weren't." She sighed. "You must have been all of eight months old, but already your powers were evident."

Lily remembered finding her birth certificate among her dad's papers after he died. He'd always told her she was born in Hampton, just an hour from where they'd lived in Gloucester,

Virginia. She was surprised to learn at nineteen that she'd in fact been born in Rehoboth Beach, Delaware. And now, here she was ten years later learning yet again something she had no idea about.

"How do you mean? What could I do?"

"Oh, small things like having a stuffed animal float off the dresser into your crib, making the lullaby mobile turn on."

"But I don't understand how just taking me away from here would stop that. And why would it frighten my dad so, especially if he knew about my mother?"

Mandy waved her hand as if showing off a new appliance. "The atmosphere here is a conduit to the One, which is composed of everything it has ever created. The mighty Hecate, patron of witches and queen of the spirit world, guides us and nurtures us and protects us. It's not that we'd lose our powers by moving away. Once they've been strengthened, we never lose them."

Unable to stay still, Lily hopped to her feet. "You need to tell me everything."

"Let's move into the living room. The chairs are much more comfortable there." She took Lily's arm and led her out of the kitchen, placing her tea on the end table. As they settled into over-stuffed chairs, a large black and white tabby immediately jumped into Mandy's lap and settled there. She absently stroked his fur.

"Your mother and I were both born and raised here. We learned from our own mothers about our Wiccan destiny. We come from a long line of healers dating back to the Middle Ages. It has only been relatively recent that anyone other than those in the coven knew who and what they were."

"What do you mean by recent? Like in the last twenty years?"

"No, it's been longer than that. Mostly it was husbands knowing, maybe a couple of close friends. And of course, the daughters."

"So everyone in your coven is the daughter of a witch?"

"Yes, and our daughters in turn will take our places."

"But you have no children."

"Yes, as a lesbian I had none of my own. Of course, these days being a lesbian does not preclude you from having children. It's still a secret, but Judith is pregnant."

"Oh my god, Judith? She's the biggest separatist I know."

"Well, she used an anonymous sperm donor and, of course, manipulated things to ensure she'd have a girl." Mandy laughed heartily. "If people only knew the real reason why women out-number men."

Lily laughed too. She took another sip of tea. "I find it strange though that you're the only one left of my mother's generation."

Mandy was silent. For an instant, Lily could swear she saw genuine fear in Mandy's eyes. When Mandy next spoke, her voice trembled. "Starting with your mother, Rebekah, one by one all the others died until I was the only one left. The coven no longer existed, but each dead woman left behind a daughter. You were the youngest daughter left behind. Sage was the oldest; she was sixteen. The others varied in age, and those of us left helped to continue nurturing their powers. Until it was only me."

Lily shuddered. "This is too weird. Are you implying that someone killed them? And if so, why not you too?"

"I've asked myself that same question over and over. There's only one difference between me and the others—I am a lesbian."

"But everyone in the coven now is a lesbian, and if what you say is true, only Judith will have a daughter to take her place. How do you recruit new members? And if I was to take my mother's place, who took hers when she died?"

Mandy pushed the cat gently off her lap as she stood up. She paced the room. She nervously ran her fingers through her hair over and over. "First of all, we don't 'recruit' members. This is not like some country club."

"I didn't mean any disrespect."

"I know, child. I know." She smiled reassuringly at Lily. "I can't really explain how it happens. We are drawn to each other. We find each other. That is how Kathy's mother, Adrienne, came to be part of the coven. After Rebekah died, Adrienne came to me about two months later. She and Kathy had moved here from Salem the year before."

Lily raised an eyebrow. "Salem? As in famous-witch-trials Salem?"

"The one and only. And to this day I am convinced it was not coincidence, but I never had any proof no matter how much I called upon Hecate to guide my knowledge." She lowered her voice and looked nervously around the room. "I believe Adrienne or—and I hate to admit this—maybe even Kathy killed off the others one by one, for what purpose, I know not."

Lily could feel the hairs on her neck prickle. She got that fluttering sensation in her stomach as her heart began to beat faster. She too looked nervously around the room, feeling almost like they were being watched. She eyed the black and white tabby suspiciously. He seemed unaffected by the tension in the room as he continued to groom his whiskers.

"I still don't understand why you survived. It can't be just because you're a lesbian."

"I think she wanted to ensure the others had no more children. Daughters to be exact. I have no doubt the daughters would have been her next victims."

"God, that is just too spooky. I'm almost afraid to ask. What happened to Adrienne?"

Mandy looked grave. "She was attacked by a shark."

"What?" Lily gaped at Mandy in disbelief. She felt a shiver run through her body.

"It was strangest thing. It was late in the season, after Labor Day, so the crowd was sparse. Witnesses said there were other people in the water as well, but the creature seemed to go right for Adrienne. Pulled her under the water just like some reenactment of *Jaws*."

"That's awful. How old was Kathy when it happened?"

Mandy shuddered. "She was thirteen and on the beach that day. People said she stood staring at the ocean for the longest time.

When her mom was pulled under, Kathy didn't even react. After a few minutes, she just turned from the water, packed up her things, and went home."

Lily gasped. "You don't think—"

"That's exactly what I think."

Lily leaped out of her chair. She was more scared than she could ever remember. "Then why is she in your coven? Why do you have anything to do with her at all? And how can you let the others near her?"

"She frightens me, Lily. It's the only way I can keep watch on her. If she is as powerful as I think she is, or at least has the potential to be, then I am no match for her. The death of her mother probably stunted her ability. But even now I wonder how much she thinks I know."

"God, I'll never be able to act normal around her again."

Mandy grabbed Lily's arms and stared hard into her eyes. "You can never let on that you know any of this. She may lust after Tara now—or at least, pretend she does—but it's you she covets. I've been able to deflect her interest, but if she truly wants you, I don't know what she might be capable of."

She wrenched away from Mandy's grip. "This is insane."

Mandy grabbed Lily again and ran her fingers lightly across Lily's forehead. Immediately, Lily felt a calm descend upon her. Mandy laid her hand upon Lily's left breast; it was if she reached inside to stroke her beating heart. "I will protect you," Mandy said.

"I know."

"I want you to go home now, to Jany. Continue what you started this morning." She kissed Lily's cheek. "I loved Rebekah, but she loved your father. And I will protect her daughter with my very life. Fate brought you back into my life nine years ago, and I won't lose you again."

Lily gave Mandy a hug and a kiss. Still anxious but confident in Mandy's ability to protect her, she left the house. Not one to wear a watch, she could tell by the sun's position that the day was growing late. She'd been at Mandy's longer than she'd intended. A side movement caught her eye. Sitting near the garden tools where Mandy had been working earlier, the black and white tabby stared intently at her, his deep golden eyes catching the sunlight. She heard some leaves crackle, and without warning the cat jumped. He came out from the bushes and walked to where Lily stood. Tail twitching, he opened his mouth and dropped a dead bird at her feet. She could see a drop of blood ooze from its slack beak. Covering her mouth with her hand, she ran the rest of the way to her car, feeling as if some evil thing pursued her.

"It was creepy the way the cat dropped that dead bird right in front of me," she said later as Jany prepared salmon steaks for grilling. Determined to show she didn't dislike her, Lily had invited Tara and her new girlfriend over for dinner.

"I don't see anything creepy about it," Jany said. "Cats do that. They like to give presents to their masters."

"We're not their 'masters.' And besides, it was Mandy's cat, not mine."

"Something happen today at Mandy's to make you so jumpy?"

Turning away so Jany couldn't see her face, Lily said, "No, of course not. We just had a nice conversation. She told me about my mother."

"Stuff you didn't already know?"

"Yeah. Did you know Mandy was in love with my mom? And that my mom was also a witch? They were in the same coven."

"Really? Wow, maybe that's where you get it."

Startled, Lily looked up. Jany was not watching her, but was concentrating on peppering the salmon. "Where I get what?"

"I've noticed little things, like how the lights always change to green when you approach, how your flowers bloom longer and brighter than anyone else's, how nothing in our house ever breaks down."

"You think I do all that?"

"Yup."

"Since when?"

Jany put the salmon on a tray to carry outside to the grill. "Since we started dating."

Lily followed her. "You never mentioned it before."

"It wasn't a big deal. Look, I grew up here. I know all about the witches and the covens. I heard the talk in school just like everyone else. No one knew who exactly was a practicing witch, but I was always fascinated by it all."

"But I didn't grow up here."

Jany kissed her. "No, but your mom did."

"We've been together five years now and you're just now telling me this?"

"Lily, my love, it's no big deal to me. And besides, I know you're not a practicing witch—not that I would mind if you were. I just think you have some untapped talents you probably inherited from Rebekah."

Lily felt like she was in a world she knew nothing about. In the course of one day, her whole life had changed. And it had all started with a little temper tantrum in Harold Jeeves' office. There was no telling what she had done in her life. Had she really been a grade A student, or had she somehow manipulated her scores? When she was competing for a slot on the cheerleading squad, had Jennifer Moore really slipped on an unseen wet spot on the gym floor? When her dad told her she'd not get her allowance until the yard was cleaned up, had Bobby Tyler really just happened along with that leaf blower? When her store's landlord was talking about raising the rent again, did he really just have a run of luck in Atlantic City? And most disturbing of all, had Jany really fallen in love with her all on her own?

"Hey guys!"

Pulled from her thoughts, Lily turned to see Tara and another woman coming around the corner of the house. Lily could only stare in astonishment at the long-legged, redheaded stunner that walked beside Tara. Though she usually tried not to let society's notion of beauty influence her, Lily had to admit the woman could rival any Hollywood starlet. She would kill for a body like that.

"I knocked on the front door, but no one answered."

"Hey Tara," Jany said. "We're just back here putting the salmon on to grill." She wiped her hands on a towel before offering her right one. "Hi, I'm Jany and this is Lily."

Tara's glamorous companion took Jany's hand. "Rhiannon. Tara's told me a lot about you."

Finding her voice at a last, Lily said, "You look very familiar," as she, in turn, shook Rhiannon's hand.

Tara grinned. "You're looking at this year's Miss Delaware. You might have seen her on the Miss America pageant."

"Get outta here," Jany said. "Really? Did you win? I can't say that we watched the pageant."

Rhiannon blushed. "No, I came in second. You almost had a gay Miss America. I think I flubbed my interview question. I should have answered 'world peace.'"

"Isn't that from—"

"*Miss Congeniality*," Tara and Jany answered together.

Laughing, the four women went into the house to get drinks. Merlin stopped chasing butterflies and left the yard. He took a roundabout way through town and finally met up with Mandy's black and white tabby.

"Good kitties," Kathy said as she bent to pet them.

Chapter VI

The Saturday of the protest dawned clear and mild. Out in the garden, Lily heard the weather report and was pleased. A nice day without the usual humidity would likely bring out more people. Of course, she'd always known they'd be competing with the lure of the ocean. A knock on the gate distracted her from her notes. She looked up to see Kathy. Squelching a sudden rush of unease, she smiled and waved her in.

"Hope you don't mind me coming by so early," Kathy said as she stepped around Lucifer and Morgan le Fay.

"Not at all. Would you like some coffee? It's fresh-brewed Kona."

"Thank you, yes."

Lily went into the kitchen for another mug and the coffee pot. She filled both their mugs and indicated for Kathy to sit. "So, what brings you by?"

"I wanted to offer my help with the Navy thing."

"I know that you and the others have done a lot to get the townspeople behind the rally. Yes, I know about you and the coven." Lily paused, wondering if she should confess to having seen them that night. Kathy sat calmly, but the muscled arms revealed by her tank top rippled ever so slightly. Her intense, dark eyes unnerved Lily. "I have to confess that I came by Lucy's one night—purely innocently—and I saw all of you."

"Really?"

"Well, I of course knew Mandy practiced witchcraft, as well as a couple of the others. I just didn't know who all were involved." She took a sip of coffee. "I have to admit though that I was bit surprised to see you there."

Kathy laughed. "Not my style?"

"On the surface, no."

"Well, since you know the whole scoop, then what I have to say won't come as a total surprise. Yes, we've been using our powers to influence the way people are thinking, though I know it is a very worthy cause and you probably wouldn't have had trouble anyway. A nice storm or two while the ships are here might help hamper their efforts."

"I don't think we'll stop the tests, but I want to at least make people aware of the issue."

"What if I told you that we *could* stop the tests?"

"How?"

Kathy's dark eyes seemed to blaze with light. "Mandy does not know how to truly harness our collective powers. I believe I can get the others to work with me to not just create a storm, but to destroy the ships."

Lily felt a prickle of fear. "We don't want to hurt anyone."

Kathy grabbed Lily's hand so hard it hurt. "To get what you want, sometimes you have to take drastic measures."

Lily pulled away, but she felt out of control. "Not that drastic."

Kathy sneered. "That's the problem with you and the others. No one wants to do what needs to be done. You all take the easy way out. Passive protest."

"Killing or harming people does not create change."

"Sometimes it's the only way to create change."

Wishing Jany would come down, Lily tried a different approach. "Look Kathy, I appreciate your help, but I don't want any violence."

"Can I have more coffee?" Kathy got up and poured another cup at Lily's nod. "All right, Lily. I'll do as you ask. Just know if you change your mind, I'm ready."

"Thanks."

"On another note, how are you and Jany getting along?"

Startled at the change in subject, Lily said, "That's an awfully personal question. And none of your business."

The intensity of Kathy's dark gaze was almost too much for Lily to bear. "I've always liked you, Lily. From the day you arrived in town. I could have made you fall in love with me, you know."

"Kathy, please. I don't like the way this conversation is going. I don't mean to be rude, but I think you need to leave."

Kathy looked her up and down, making her feel as if stripped naked. "I'll go, but just remember that if you want me for any-thing . . . anything at all . . ."

Lily gathered her papers as she rose. "I'll see you at the march," she said and walked into the house. She was trembling. She wanted to look out the window to see if Kathy still sat in the garden, but she was afraid. Instead, she concentrated on grinding more coffee beans and willing Jany to come down.

"Good morning, gorgeous," Jany said.

Lily shrieked.

"Sorry to startle you." Sidling up behind her, Jany kissed Lily's neck. "You nervous about the rally today?"

"I guess." Twisting around, Lily kissed Jany on the mouth. "Thank you for supporting me in all this."

"Hey, my membership in PETA is up to date too. But really, I've sensed something bothering you these last few days. Is it all the stuff you learned from Mandy?"

"It's been a lot to think about. You know, I always felt drawn to the sea, though my father never took me to any beach. When I came to Rehoboth after his death, I felt like I was finally where I belonged. And now I know why."

Jany hugged her. "I'm certainly glad you found your way here. And if it turns out I have my very own Samantha Stevens—what a bonus."

"You always did have a thing for blondes. Too bad I'm not one of them."

"Ah, there's always the exception to the rule, and I happen to like my dark-haired, blue-eyed beauty." She turned to the refrigerator. "What would you like for breakfast?"

"I think just some raisin toast." She sat at the table while Jany made the toast, as well as eggs for herself. "Do you remember when Kathy's mom was killed?"

"Yeah, it was the talk of the town for weeks. Killed by a shark! That had never happened here before and never since."

"How did Kathy take it? I mean, she was all of thirteen. She must have been devastated."

Jany slid the eggs out of the frying pan onto a plate and sat down with Lily at the table. "Now that you mention it, she didn't really seem all that upset about it. I remember we all thought it quite odd. She didn't have a lot of friends in school. She mostly hung with Clarissa and Gwendolyn."

"Who'd she live with afterward? What about her father?"

Jany looked up from her plate. "Why all the sudden interest in Kathy? You don't really like her, do you?"

"No, I don't like her. She just scares me a bit. She's like a caged cat, ready to spring. She could be trouble."

"Trouble for whom? She's not said or done anything to you, has she? I'll take care of it if she has."

"No! Stay away from her!"

Jany pushed her chair back and stood up. "Lily, what's gotten into you?"

"Please, just do as I ask. Kathy is trouble."

"I'm not afraid of her, even if she is a witch."

Lily grabbed Jany's arm. "Please, just promise me?"

"If it will make you happy, I will steer clear of Kathy." She took Lily's hand. "Let's go get ready for the rally, okay?"

Rehoboth was not really big enough to have a full-fledged protest march, but it seemed as if thousands of people were gathered on the beach and spilling over onto the main thoroughfare. Looking out over the sparkling sand, Lily didn't see that many sunbathers. It appeared like everyone was there to support the cause. Many of them carried handmade signs. All her hard work to publicize this most passionate of causes was paying off. Across the shimmering water, Navy vessels anchored far into the distance. Could the sailors onboard even see them?

At the small stage located at the end of Rehoboth Avenue and near the beach, the guest speakers had already started. In addition to lesser known figures, Lily had managed to recruit a prominent university marine biology professor, as well as a Greenpeace expert on sonar's detrimental effects on marine life. Even a Navy representative was scheduled to speak. Shy by nature, Lily had declined to speak herself.

All along Rehoboth Avenue, various organizations had set up booths covering everything from the evils of vivisection to encouraging the spaying and neutering of pets. Loudspeakers erected along the avenue and at the beach allowed people not in the immediate vicinity of the stage to hear what was going on. Lily was thrilled to hear the reactions of the crowd to what the speakers had to say. At one point, a counter-protester managed to get up on stage and take away the microphone.

"You bleeding hearts will be sorry when we're attacked by extremists," he shouted. "You can't stop our military from protecting us by whatever means necessary! You care more about dumb animals than you do people!"

A police officer dragged him off the stage as the crowd surged forward. Lily was almost afraid her peaceful protest rally would turn into a brawl, but people calmed down after he was gone. It was inevitable that individuals with dissenting opinions would attend. Lily herself had been to Washington many times over the years to show her displeasure with various right-wing causes as their supporters marched down Pennsylvania Avenue.

She saw Tara and Rhiannon coming toward her. She smiled, thinking how they made such a cute couple. She couldn't remember seeing Tara so happy. Several people turned to look at them as they walked by. Some pointed and whispered. At one point a little girl ran up to Rhiannon and asked for an autograph.

"This is fabulous," Tara said.

"I am so happy. I only hope it helps make a difference."

"How can it not?" Rhiannon said. "Several reporters have already approached me for my opinion."

Lily hugged her. "That's wonderful. Quotes from a celebrity are always good."

Rhiannon blushed. "Well, I don't know if I qualify as a celebrity."

"Of course you do, my sweet," Tara said, then kissed her full on the lips.

Several cameras clicked at once. Lily frowned, worried that Miss Delaware might now receive some bad publicity.

"Don't you worry, Lily," Rhiannon said. "If I lose my crown, I'll be in good company with Vanessa Williams."

Lily grinned, remembering the scandal that had surrounded the former Miss America. "You two go on. Enjoy the day."

The sun shone brightly overhead. There was nary a cloud in sight. As the day wore on, many people put down their signs in favor of beach umbrellas, but Lily felt the day was a success. If even just fifty people would write to their Congressional representative, it could help make a difference. And people were spending money like crazy. Lily had even seen Harold Jeeves beaming.

Kathy disdainfully surveyed the throngs of people. Despite her words of support, she really thought Lily was making too much of the Navy tests. Who really cared if whales and dolphins had ear problems? She had relished the idea though of harnessing her powers, as well as those of the coven, to create some true havoc. Thunderstorms were so lame. What a triumph it would be to sink a ship!

Out of the corner of her eye, she noticed Jany walking in the street. Her nemesis. Sure, they supposedly had a playful competition, but Kathy resented Jany's popularity. And it still rankled her that not only had Jany stolen Tara away from her, but Lily as well. She could feel the anger welling up inside her. It would be so easy to hurt her.

As Jany walked under a streetlamp, Kathy spoke some words

under her breath. She smiled as she heard the sharp crackle of the glass globe. Then suddenly, the sound ceased and she literally saw the cracks disappear. She looked around and saw Mandy staring at her long and hard, her disapproval palpable.

Scowling with frustration, Kathy turned on her heel and left. Mandy was really beginning to get on her nerves, high priestess or no. And if the truth were told, it was a position Kathy felt was rightfully hers. Why should some relic from the old world run things?

"Are you okay?" Sarah asked Mandy as they headed home.

Thinking of what she had seen Kathy attempt, Mandy did not answer right away. Could she have been mistaken?

"Mandy?"

"I'm sorry? What?"

"You've been awfully distracted this last hour or so. Is everything all right?"

No, it's not, Mandy thought, but she answered, "Of course. I think I might just be a bit tired." *What am I going to do? I have to tell the coven.*

"It was a long day."

"But I think it was quite successful," Mandy said. "I can't believe the Navy even sent someone to speak to us."

Sarah snorted. "Yeah, like anything he said was true."

"It shows that they take us seriously. And it sort of lends us legitimacy, don't you think? In a weird sort of way." *Maybe I could try another binding spell.*

"I think Lily was very happy with the turnout. And all the local news stations were there. The Navy may have brought their ships to our shore, but they know we'll be watching them."

When Mandy didn't answer, Sarah touched her arm. Mandy jumped. Sarah was looking at her with wide eyes, her concern evident.

"Something is wrong. Tell me."

I can't. Not yet. Mandy kissed Sarah's cheek. "I'm fine. I'll see you tomorrow night at Lucy's. Nice of her to let us have our gathering there again." She stepped off the curb and waved her protest sign. "Be careful going home."

"Mandy! Look out!"

Mandy looked up in time to see a car swerve to avoid a ginger cat and head right for her. She stood frozen, unable to move. *Run!* her mind shouted, but her legs stayed still.

Sarah screamed as the car struck. Seconds later, the driver got out, visibly shaken. "Dear Lord, what have I done? I swear I didn't see her. Only the cat. Oh God . . ."

Sarah knelt beside Mandy's inert body. Blood gushed from a head wound. She felt for and found a faint pulse. "Someone call nine-one-one," she commanded.

Later that night, at a hastily called meeting, Sarah told the other members of the coven what had happened. "The driver swerved to avoid hitting a cat. Mandy had just started to cross the street."

"Is she going to be okay?" Sage asked, wringing her hands.

"She's got a broken shoulder and a severe concussion, plus lots of bruises and contusions. She needed stitches for a gash on her left temple." Sarah took a deep breath. "She was thrown kinda far. She's in a coma right now, but the doctors say it's nothing to worry about."

"How could this have happened?" Blossom asked, her face white. "I know she uses a protection spell daily."

"Maybe she got careless," said Ruth. "She's been preoccupied lately, and I don't think it's just about Lily's project."

Sarah started to cry. "I feel so responsible. Why didn't I do something?"

Judith took Sarah into her arms. "You couldn't have done anything, my dear. Don't blame yourself."

In the flickering candlelight, the women all looked at each other, apprehension and worry in their faces. All, that is, except

Kathy. The silence deepened, each woman lost in her own thoughts. Somewhere in the house, a clock ticked.

"What are we going to do?" Clarissa finally asked.

"We have to be strong for Mandy," Judith said. "We'll use our magick to make her well."

"But we're stronger with thirteen," Lucy said.

"I have the answer to that," Kathy said. "We know that Lily belongs to us—that she's one of us. Isn't it her right to take Mandy's place? After all, our mothers came first, followed by the daughters. Mandy has no daughters."

"If you want to get technical," Judith said, "she should take your place. After all, your mother took the place of her mother." She looked around the room. The others shifted uncomfortably, averting their eyes.

Kathy's eyes blazed dangerously. "Without me, you are nothing! Do you honestly think your little feel-good energies are enough to accomplish what needs to be done?"

"Just what is it you think needs to be done?" Judith asked. "What exactly are we talking about here?"

Kathy leapt to her feet. "Destroy those ships!"

There was a collective gasp.

"How can you think about that now? Our concern has to be for Mandy," Cara said, visibly shaken.

"Besides, you know the Wiccan Rede is to 'do no harm'," Judith said firmly. "If your agenda is so much different from ours, then maybe you should leave this coven."

Kathy clenched her hands, her stance rigid. "You can't push me out."

"Yes, we can."

"You'll be sorry if you do."

Uncomfortable with the direction of the conversation, Tara spoke up. "I cannot believe, Kathy, that you would threaten us so. We have embraced you into our circle. We have been sisters. What has happened to change you thus?"

Kathy seemed suddenly contrite. "I do want to help Mandy, but I also feel Lily's passion about what the Navy is doing. Desecrating the sea that way. I don't wish anyone harm." She looked around the circle. "Especially you."

"You all know our priority tonight needs to be Mandy. Nothing, and no one, else," Judith said, her tone disallowing any argument.

The woman all nodded.

Judith rose. "Let us call upon Hecate, goddess of magick and the moon, to watch over our priestess and make her well."

As they all stood, she made a mental note to later perform a protection spell for her fellow Wicca. Despite Kathy's seeming remorse, Judith didn't trust her, and she began to wonder if she ever had. She had always believed in that old adage about the eyes being the windows to the soul, and from what she'd seen in Kathy's eyes tonight, she wasn't sure Kathy even had a soul.

After their opening ritual, they sat together in their circle with three lengths of blue cord Blossom had provided from her shop. Swirling ribbons of smoke from incense curled around their heads. The open windows allowed in the sounds of wind in the leaves and ocean waves caressing sand. The tangy salt air was heavy with humidity.

They braided the cords together, chanting, "Infuse these cords, send healing power, have it grow with every hour." They repeated the chant until the cords were braided, then ended with, "This is our will, so may it be."

Into the cords, Judith added a topaz for healing and an onyx for protection against someone else's magick. "I will bring this neck-lace to Mandy tomorrow," she said.

Smiling, Kathy walked back to her car. Once she was sure the others had all left, she drew an imaginary pentagram in the air and raised her hands to the bright light of the moon. "From me to you, this spell I break, for it was not yours to make. Its path I will abruptly end, help to Mandy I do not send."

CHAPTER VII

Clouds moved in to cover the night sky, making the darkness total and complete. It was still and hot. Even the ocean winds seemed to be stifled, for no breeze fluttered the bedroom curtains. The padding of kitty feet broke the quiet, a mere whisper of noise. In the gloom, cat eyes glowed.

Lily felt the hands on her body. They were warm and soft. She stretched into their caress, arching her back and willing them to touch every inch of her. She felt her nipples harden as lips brushed against them before a hot mouth sucked them in. She groaned with desire, feeling the wetness begin to flow between her legs. Without warning, her hands were thrust above her head and her wrists were tied together to the headboard. She gasped, struggling against the binds, but feeling her desire grow tenfold. And then her legs were spread wide and the ankles in turn restrained. She was breathing more heavily now, her heart beating fast in her chest. She was completely vulnerable, yet it excited her even more. She had never been so tied up before, and she liked it.

She opened her eyes to see the dark form of a woman above her. Without the light from the full moon, she did not see the familiar features of her lover, but she was not afraid. Hands stroked her, almost feather light. She wanted more. "Harder," she whispered, and screamed when fingers clamped onto her nipples and twisted. And then the lover kissed her neck and shoulders and collarbone, sending pleasurable shivers up her spine. Teeth grazed her bare throat before biting her sensitive nipples. She whimpered, the shot of brief pain sending a jolt of want to her core. She could feel the wetness flowing from her now. Fingers played with her nipples, alternately squeezing and twisting and caressing. Her lover's tongue moved across her body, lower and lower until she lapped at her wetness, licking her clit, and thrusting inside her.

Then fingers replaced tongue, and Lily moaned and cried out as the fingers thrust deeper and deeper, harder and harder. She screamed as a fist rammed into her again and again. She fought against her restraints, wanting it to stop and yet not. She lost herself in the sensation of mouth and tongue and hand, fucking her over and over, felt the ropes cut into her tender flesh as she pulled against them. Her orgasm built until it released in an earth-shattering crescendo.

"Please," she whispered. "Please."

Laughter. Lips soft against hers. The sudden release of her wrists and ankles. She could feel the wetness on her thighs and on her cheeks. Desire mixed with tears. She held out her arms. The moon came out from behind a cloud, sending a pale glow into the room and across the face of the woman above her. No, not Jany, someone else. Kathy!

Lily screamed and screamed.

"Lily! Wake up! Lily!"

She slapped at the hands that held her. "Get off of me!"

"Lily, it's me, Jany. You've had a bad dream."

Sobbing now, Lily squirmed away until she sat at the bottom edge of the bed. Jany turned on the light before coming around the bed to sit beside her. She tentatively touched Lily's face before putting an arm around Lily's shoulders and pulling her in close. She stroked Lily's hair, softly as she would a child's. She kissed the top of her head.

"It's okay now. I'm here."

Lily clung to Jany now, tears still streaming down her face. "I don't understand. It was so real."

"Tell me. What was real?"

"I can't. I can't."

"Can you not remember?"

Lily hesitated. How could she tell a lie? Yet how could she tell the truth? She couldn't look at Jany. "No, I guess I don't remember. I'm sorry to wake you in such a way."

"Are you sure you're all right?"

"Yes. I just need to go the bathroom." She touched Jany's hand, still unable to look at her. She felt violated and betrayed. And guilty for the imagined pleasure. "Can you get me some juice?"

"I'll be right back."

When Jany left, Lily hurried to the bathroom and was violently sick. Afterward, she washed her face and brushed her teeth vigorously before taking the time to examine her own body. There were no marks, no flushed skin to indicate she'd had sex. She was barely moist, no swollen lips. She sat on the toilet, too shamed to go back into the bedroom. How could she have had such a dream? Such a hallucination? She'd never even liked Kathy. Increasingly detested her, in fact. What could it all mean?

A knock on the door. "Lily? Are you okay? I've got your juice."

"I'll be right out." She rummaged around in the medicine chest and found an old bottle of Xanax. They'd expired two months ago, so she took two of them. Tomorrow she'd go see Mandy in the hospital. If she was out of her coma, she'd know what the dream meant. And if Mandy was still unconscious, Lily would find another way. She had to.

The next morning, Lily left the house before Jany even woke up. She still could not face her. Though it had all been a dream— no, a nightmare—she felt as if she'd betrayed Jany in the worst way she could betray a lover, especially because at first she'd liked it. Feeling sick just thinking about it, she scribbled a vague note about

inventory at the store and left after feeding the cats. She knew
Jany's murder trial was coming up in just a couple of days, and so
she would probably not even give last night a second thought. She
stopped for coffee and a croissant before heading to the hospital.

"Hi, Judith," Lily said as she approached Mandy's room. "I'm
surprised to see you here this early."

"I could say the same to you." Judith held up a braided cord.
"This is for Mandy. It is a healing necklace."

"Is she conscious yet?"

"I'm afraid not," said a nurse behind them. "And visiting hours
aren't until nine."

"May I just leave this in her room? I promise not to stay."

The nurse eyed the rope suspiciously, then seemed to think it
okay. "You can go in for a minute, but not both of you."

"I'll wait here," Lily said as Judith went into the room.

Judith returned just seconds later. She smiled at the nurse.
"Thanks." She turned to Lily. "Are you okay? You seem wiped out."

"Is it that obvious? Judith, can we go somewhere to talk? I
needed to see Mandy, but I think you can help me too."

"Let's go to my house."

They walked silently to Judith's car. "I'll drive you back into
town later."

Once at her place, Judith made coffee and set out some muffins.
Taking their cups to the garden, they sat in lawn chairs under a
large oak. Lily leaned back in her chair with a long sigh. Judith
waited, giving Lily her space.

"How are you feeling these days? Any morning sickness?" Lily
asked.

"Nothing that a spell or two couldn't take care of. Thanks for
asking." Judith smiled. "But I don't think my pregnancy is what
you want to talk about."

"You're right." Lily didn't know quite how to begin. How do
you tell someone you were raped in a dream? Even someone who
believed in mystical powers? Not ready yet, Lily said instead, "You
have a lovely garden. I like your use of color. It is so peaceful here."

"That was my intention. That, and to make a haven for birds and butterflies." Judith laughed. "I'm the only one in the coven without a cat. Jacquelyn thinks it's sacrilegious."

"She just wants to guilt-trip you into taking one of her kittens. I swear, if she doesn't have her cat spayed, I'm going to take the poor thing in myself."

Judith touched Lily's arm. "Tell me what's bothering you. You're frightened about something."

"What can you tell me about Kathy?"

If Judith was surprised, she didn't show it. "What do you want to know? She joined our coven about five years ago." She hesitated but a moment. "I personally don't trust her. She brings negative energy to our midst. Destructive energy. But it wasn't always so."

"I don't understand much about your craft, but I know my mother was a witch and it seems I too have some powers. Untapped powers, as Mandy would say, but powers nevertheless."

"Yes, she has spoken of it. Is that what you need to talk to her about?"

Lily played nervously with a napkin. "This is difficult for me. I can't even talk to Jany about it."

"Anything you tell me will remain between us. You have my solemn oath on that. Does it have to do with Kathy?"

Lily started crying, the tears trickling down her cheeks. "She frightens me, and I think she has cast a spell on me. I had a dream last night, a vivid dream. It was so real, and yet when I woke, there was nothing to indicate it had happened."

"What was the dream about?" Judith asked as she handed Lily a tissue. She touched Lily's hand ever so lightly.

"I thought . . . I thought Jany was making love to me." She looked at Judith, pleading for understanding. "It was dark, the moon was covered. And when it was all over, after I climaxed, the moon came out and I saw her. It was Kathy, and she had made love to me. No, she had sex with me. Violent sex."

The blood drained from Judith's face. "Oh Goddess, you must have been terrified."

"It was horrible. I've never had feelings for Kathy in any way. Could she have made me dream of her? Is there such a thing?" She got up from her chair to pace. "Am I somehow responsible?"

"Of course not. No one is responsible for their dreams." She frowned. "And yes, there is such a spell but it's heavily frowned upon. Most practicing Wiccans would never use their powers in such a way. If Kathy did indeed do this, the coven will need to address the matter, but Mandy, as high priestess, normally would be the one to call such a meeting."

"Mandy warned me about Kathy." She whirled around to face Judith again. "Oh my god, do you think Kathy could have had something to do with Mandy's accident?"

"I don't like to think so, but I cannot be sure. I'm so sorry for all of this." Her eyes shone with unshed tears.

"I just hate to think my dream was some kind of unconscious desire on my part." Lily sat back down.

Judith took both of Lily's hands in hers. She looked deep into Lily's eyes. "I tell you again, you are not responsible."

Lily smiled, beginning to feel reassured that she had not betrayed Jany in any way. On impulse, she said, "This may sound crazy, but do you think you could teach me your craft? My craft? I'd like to be part of your coven. Is that possible?"

"You would be welcome. As a dedicant, you would need to study the craft for a year and a day. Because of her relationship with your mother, Mandy should be your teacher, but I will gladly take her place until she can teach you herself."

Lily hugged Judith tight. "Thank you so much. I will be a dedicated pupil."

"Rebekah, your mother, would be pleased. Let's have our first lesson be a simple protection spell. But I must tell you that while such a spell might make you feel more secure, it does not make you invincible." She rose, taking Lily's hand to lead her into the house. "Let's gather our ingredients, shall we?"

Walking to her car after Judith dropped her back at the hospital, Lily couldn't help but feel the spot on her forehead where she'd anointed herself with oil. She did indeed feel more secure, but she couldn't help wonder if much of the feeling was psychological. She wanted to believe in the power of witchcraft, but it was still so new to her. And she shuddered again to think of what Kathy was capable of doing with her witchcraft.

She put the key in the lock and suddenly felt the hairs on her head prickle. Glancing behind her, she saw Kathy approaching. A sudden panic overcame her, but then she remembered the chant. "I stand here in your guardian light. Empower this oil with your might. Protection from harm is what I ask; please accept this as your task," she said quietly as she touched her forehead, tracing a pentagram into the oil. She felt a calm descend upon her as she turned to face Kathy.

"Hello, Lily. Have you been to see Mandy?"

"Yes, but she is still in a coma."

"Terrible thing. She's usually so careful." Kathy looked at her closely. "And how about you, Lily? How are you doing?"

Was it Lily's imagination or was Kathy's smile a bit predatory? "I'm just fine. Slept like a baby last night. That always makes for a good day, don't you think?"

The smile left Kathy's face. "Glad to hear that. I thought you looked a little tired. Guess I was wrong."

More outwardly calm than she felt, Lily got into her car. "Guess so. You have a good day, Kathy."

That night, Lily was almost afraid to go to sleep. Very quietly, trying not to attract Jany's attention, she traced the protective symbol on her forehead and joined her lover in bed. The sound of Jany's breathing was relaxing, and she felt the pull of something safe and warm as she dozed off.

"Lily, my child."

Lily looked up to see the image of a woman she only knew from photographs. "Mother?" She felt the gentle caress of fingers along her cheek.

"I am here with you, like I've always been."

"Always? Even when daddy took me away?"

Rebekah smiled. "Even then. It was me who guided you. Let you experience what could be."

"I should have known."

"You did, for you are my daughter, born of my womb and descended down through a long line of Wiccans. We have suffered, and we have rejoiced. It is time now, Lily, that you take your rightful place."

Rebekah's form seemed to glow with light—an aura of colors in gold and purple and the blue of the ocean. The radiance enveloped Lily, drawing her into its warmth and protection, before fading away.

As Rebekah vanished slowly into the night, Lily murmured, "I love you, Mother."

"What did you say, sweetheart?"

Lily snuggled into Jany's strong arms. "I said, I love you."

And then she felt something cool and hard in her hand. Gently pulling out of Jany's grasp, she held the object up to the illumination of the moon. It was a pentacle on a silver chain. She slipped it over her neck and immediately felt a warm presence surround her.

"Thank you, mother," she whispered.

CHAPTER VIII

I need to tell you something," Lily said to Jany a few days later as they prepared for an afternoon at the beach. She stuffed beach towels and suntan lotion into a large straw tote.

"You're having an affair."

Lily's eyes got big as she stared at Jany. "What?"

"Only kidding, my love. Don't look so shocked."

"You've . . . You've never said anything like that to me before. Do you think I'm having an affair?"

"Of course not. Now, tell me what you wanted to say."

Lily hesitated, still a little shaken by Jany's joke. "I've asked to join Mandy's coven, and they have accepted me. I will be learning the craft from Judith."

"Your mother would be pleased."

"You don't mind?"

Jany took Lily into her arms and kissed her long and deep. "Why would I mind?" she asked when she finally ended the kiss. She touched the tip of Lily's nose. "Will you learn the Samantha twitch?"

Lily laughed. "Silly girl. No, my dear, it takes more than a wiggly nose to make things happen in real life. But I have to admit I finally feel like I know who I am." She pulled out of Jany's arms and sat on the edge of the bed, pushing Lucifer out of the way as she did so. "I didn't realize that I didn't feel complete, whole. And I'm not talking about my relationship with you."

"I know that. Can you tell me something though? What's going on between you and Kathy?"

Lily felt her heart leap into her throat. "Nothing. Why?"

"I just get a funny feeling. Every place we've gone recently it seems like she's there, and I don't like the way she looks at you. And you seem very uncomfortable in her presence."

"Mandy thinks Kathy has a thing for me. It does make me uncomfortable."

"I thought she had a thing for Tara."

Lily laughed, trying to lighten the mood. "Perhaps, but Tara is happily with Rhiannon now. I think Kathy's just jealous that you have me and she doesn't." She put her arms around Jany's neck and kissed her. "And I'm awfully glad of that."

Jany kissed her back, then pulled away, a pensive look on her face. "Kathy's always been a bit on the edge. All through school she never had many friends. Kept mostly to herself. Some people were afraid of her. We knew she had abilities." She stood up to lean against the dresser and seemed lost in thought. "I remember one time," she continued, "we were in biology class together. The teacher reprimanded her in front of the class—I can't even remember what for—but the wind came up suddenly and all our papers blew off the desks. It was almost comical the way they scattered, like someone had switched on a huge fan. And then the thirty-gallon fish tank just shattered, sending water and fish and little divers all over."

"You think Kathy did it?"

"I know she did. Her eyes had turned all black, and the look on her face . . . Well, it was one I'd seen before, and many times after I might add. She has telekinetic powers, on that I'd bet a month's salary."

Lily gathered up the tote and her sunglasses. "I don't want to talk about her anymore."

Jany took her arm to prevent her from leaving the room. "She's not done anything to hurt you?"

Lily felt a momentary flash of anger as she remembered what had been done to her. "No." If Kathy *had* been responsible for the dream, then Judith or Mandy would find out. Regardless, a dream was just a dream.

Jany ran her hands down over Lily's body, across the swell of her breasts and hips. Her mouth was warm against Lily's neck. Lily could feel herself responding. "Let's go back to bed," Jany whispered into her ear.

"Yes," Lily breathed, wanting to banish the memory of the dream once and for all.

Almost frantically, she stripped off her clothes and then Jany's. They fell naked to the bed, their kisses frenzied as if they hadn't seen each other in weeks. Their hands roamed over each other's body, feeling swells and curves and soft skin. Lily pushed Jany against the mattress, kissing her mouth and neck and breasts, down across her stomach to her thighs, pushing her legs apart as she explored with her fingers and then her tongue. Jany moaned, resisting little the role reversal. She was already wet and eager; they both were. Lily slid between Jany's legs, opening them wider with her shoulders as she trailed her fingers across Jany's breasts, tweaking hardened nipples, before continuing down her sides to her hips. She alternately licked and sucked Jany's swollen clit and lips, dipping her fingers deep inside her, feeling the grip of Jany's muscles as she tensed.

"Lily," Jany said, almost in a whisper. "Yes."

Lily moaned deep in her throat, savoring Jany's womanhood and inhaling the scent of her. She couldn't get enough as she felt Jany's vaginal walls clench around her fingers, once, twice, again. Jany arched against her, breathing out a long sigh. "Lily," she said again as she tried to wiggle away.

Pleased with herself, Lily acquiesced to Jany's wishes and withdrew her fingers. She licked Jany's skin, enjoying the hint of salt. She slid upward, liking the way their slick bodies squished together. "I love the way you taste," she said, and smiled as Jany blushed.

"And I love to make you moan," Jany said as she flipped Lily onto her back and without warning pushed her fingers deep inside her.

Lily did indeed moan, thrusting her hips upward so Jany's fingers went deeper. When Jany took one nipple into her mouth and then the other, Lily pushed her downward, not wanting to wait. Jany laughed as she obliged. She added her mouth and tongue to her fingers, driving Lily crazy with desire. Their bodies rocked together, pushing and thrusting, both of them moaning now. Lily grabbed hold of the headboard as her body readied for climax. She cried out Jany's name again and again as one orgasm and then another coursed through her body, a rhythmic tide that swelled along with the sound of the ocean waves crashing against the sand.

Beneath their open window, Kathy stood, rigid with jealousy and anger, fingers clenching and unclenching. The wind died down like air sucked out of a room, and an eerie calm descended. In the room upstairs, the moans didn't stop. "Jany," a voice called out. "Oh dear god—" Day became night as the sun was obliterated by ever-darkening clouds. With a roar the wind came back as the clouds unleashed a torrent of rain. Lightning stabbed the earth with crackling fury, the boom of thunder rattling windows and sending flocks of blackbirds soaring into the roiling sky.

And from the open window, the cries of passion didn't stop. Kathy watched the window before raising her arms, stepping away only as a bolt of lightning struck a tree and set it ablaze, seemingly immune to the rain. The flames leapt from branch to branch until they licked the sides of the house. Only then did the sound of passion change to fear.

Smiling, Kathy walked away, ignoring the hiss of water fighting fire. It didn't matter now.

Sitting on the sidewalk as if waiting for her was Mandy's black and white cat. She leaned down and whispered into its ear, then scratched its head. Tail twitching, the animal walked in the direction of town.

"Was that the scariest damn storm we've ever had, or what?" Blossom said to Lily as Lily browsed the bookshelf at the store.

Lily shivered at the memory of it, and the near miss they'd had as the tree burned outside their bedroom window. It was no ordinary storm, of that she was certain. And unlike previous sudden squalls, this one had lasted the rest of the day and into the night. She pulled out one of the new arrivals—*The Heart of Wicca: Wise Words from a Crone on the Path*—and flipped through the pages. "Yeah, it was pretty bad," she said.

"If I didn't know better, I'd say it was the remnants of some hurricane. Even the weather forecasters can't explain it."

"Oh, come on, Blossom, you know the reason why they can't explain it."

Blossom looked at her innocently. "What do you think is the reason?"

"Witchcraft, of course."

The door slammed open. Startled, Lily dropped her book as Sage rushed into the room. "Did you see the headlines today?"

"Not yet. What is it?"

Sage pumped her fist and whooped. "The Navy's pulling out!"

Lily and Blossom ran over and snatched the paper away. "A Navy spokesman today confirmed that the ships conducting tests off the Delaware coast will be leaving the area within the week," Lily read out loud.

"That's excellent," Blossom said, while Sage nodded in unison. "You should be so proud. Wait till Jany hears."

Lily scanned the rest of the article. "Listen to this—The Navy further went on to say that the recent protest rally in Rehoboth Beach played no part in their decision to abort the mission."

Sage laughed. "Of course they're gonna say that. You can be confident your rally *did* play a part."

Lily hugged them both. "With a little help from my magickal friends."

"Okay, I'll admit we in the coven have been conjuring up those daily rainstorms, but something as big and dangerous as the one the other day? Nope, not us."

Lily thought briefly of Kathy. "How can you be sure? Maybe your collective energies got out of hand? Or maybe one of you has an axe to grind?"

Blossom picked up the book Lily had dropped, glancing warily over her shoulder before she turned to face her. "I have felt a certain negativity lately, an antagonistic energy. It's hard to believe it would come from one of us." She lowered her voice. "I suspect it's related to Mandy's accident."

Sage shivered. "I've felt it too."

"Who in your coven would harbor such hostility?" Lily asked, knowing full well what Blossom's answer would be.

Again, Blossom glanced around the store. "Kathy."

"Do the others feel the same way?"

Blossom walked over to the jewelry counter and idly rearranged earrings and necklaces and bracelets. It was almost as if she needed to be doing something, anything. "Most of the ones I've talked to. I haven't spoken with Gwendolyn or Lucy yet, but I suspect they will agree. Only Cara voiced reservations, but I think that's mostly because she doesn't like to think ill of anyone. Plus, she and Kathy had a brief fling last summer."

"Something needs to be done, don't you think?" Lily asked.

Sage nodded, then spoke. "Other than Kathy, Mandy is the most powerful witch in our coven. She's still in that mysterious coma, despite all our healing spells and magick cords. She could handle Kathy on her own."

Lily didn't agree with Sage's statement. She remembered her conversation with Mandy, and how she too had said she thought Kathy was getting too powerful. But she decided not to say anything. At least, not yet.

The bell over the door chimed. Blossom looked startled, then scared, relaxing only when she saw Ruth. Mandy's black and white tabby followed her in. Lily felt a shiver of unease when she saw the animal, remembering that day in Mandy's garden. Normally, she loved all animals, but this particular cat gave her the creeps. She couldn't exactly say when that had happened. She watched as it settled on a rug in the middle of the room and began grooming itself.

"No change," Ruth said. "The doctors are at a loss."

"We were discussing it." Blossom looked over at Lily and Sage. "I think we all believe Kathy is somehow involved. Either she caused the accident, the coma, or both."

A slight movement caught Lily's eye. Did the cat appear to be listening to their conversation? It had stopped grooming and was staring at them intently, its ears and tail twitching. She shook her head. She was letting her imagination run wild. Still, she knew about witches and their familiars. It was not impossible.

"I think we need to take matters into our own hands," Sage was saying. "If Kathy's magick is becoming dangerous, she has to be stopped."

Lily realized if she shared her conviction that Kathy had been responsible for the horrible dream, Sage would be even more convinced it was time to act. She started to speak, but the cat abruptly moved toward her. Lily stepped toward the cat, intending to shoo him out of the store. He stood on all fours, the fur raised on his back, and hissed a warning. Lily glanced behind her, thinking the cat might be seeing something or someone threatening. No one was there. She moved closer, wary now. Intent on their conversation, the other three women paid her no heed. The cat seemed to grow three times his size. His ears flattened as he crouched into a predatory stance, his tail slashing back and forth.

With a snarl he leapt at Lily, his claws and teeth digging deep into her leg. She shrieked and instinctively hit the creature with all her might. He fell off of her, momentarily stunned, then readied for another attack.

With a shout, Sage smacked him with a straw broom. Hissing and growling, he ran for the door Blossom had opened. She slammed the door shut.

"Oh my god, what happened?" Sage exclaimed as she brought gauze and first-aid cream. "I've never seen him act that way. Did you scare him?"

Wincing in pain, Lily shook her head. "I only wanted to get him out of the store. I don't like or trust that cat."

Sage knelt down and cleaned the blood from Lily's leg with

iodine. Lily groaned at the sting of it. "I think you need to go to the emergency room. Cat bites can be highly infectious. When was your last tetanus shot?"

"Never mind that now," Lily said, feeling the tears in her eyes. Sage slathered on salve and wrapped the leg in gauze. "This may sound crazy, but I think that cat is Kathy's spy."

Sage and Blossom and Ruth all looked at each other. "It was Kathy's cat at one time," Ruth said. "She said she had her hands full with five of them, so Mandy said she would take him."

"When?"

"I'd say no longer than six months."

"I know I sound like some ignorant curiosity seeker, but can't witches inhabit the bodies of their familiars?"

"Well, yes, they're inhabited by spirit. The familiar helps the witch with her magick."

Lily shook her head. "This is going to take time to sink in. But right now our priority has to be Mandy and to, if need be, expel Kathy from the coven." Lily saw their looks of surprise. "I guess Judith hasn't told you yet."

"Told us what?" Sage asked.

"That she has accepted me as a dedicant. I will be part of your coven."

The others crowded around her, taking turns to hug her. "Oh, that's wonderful. We are pleased to welcome you," Ruth said.

Blossom sighed. "But that still leaves unfinished business. I will call a meeting together. We'll meet at Lucy's tomorrow night at nine-thirty. At ten, Mars will be in planetary rulership, and it is then we will conduct our ritual. You will need to be there as well, Lily."

Lily clenched her jaw, seething anew at what she knew was Kathy's second attack on her. Maybe even the third if she was responsible for the fire. "Oh, you can bet I'll be there," she said, knowing the time had come for her own reckoning with Kathy.

CHAPTER IX

I have to be at Lucy's tonight at nine-thirty," Lily told Jany as they cleaned up after dinner.

"Why didn't you say something this morning?"

"No real reason."

Jany scooped decaf coffee into the coffeemaker. "Is that why you've been on edge all day?"

"Yes, I'm sorry," Lily said as she threw down the dish towel. "I have a feeling it's not going to be pleasant. We're kicking Kathy out of the coven."

"Is that a serious thing?"

"Yes, but it's necessary. We suspect she is behind Mandy's accident and continuing coma. She brings an unhealthy negativity to the coven, to the town." She didn't add that Kathy had attacked her twice—another time she would tell Jany about it. The last thing she wanted was Jany deciding to do something macho. It was a crime of magick, and the coven had to deal with it.

Jany looked at Lily, her surprise obvious. "Are you planning on exiling her from Rehoboth? This is sounding more and more like some medieval ritual." She did a backward wave with her hand. "Banishment and all that."

"I know it all seems so melodramatic, but Kathy's witchcraft is dangerous."

Jany smiled, then quickly sobered when she saw the frown on Lily's face. "I'm sorry, I know this is serious to you. As a lawyer I just can't help but think the 'innocent until proven guilty' thing."

Lily snorted. "Oh come on, you're a prosecutor. You never believe anyone is innocent."

"All right, you've got me there." She poured them both a mug of coffee. "Do you want me to come with you? I know I can't join the gathering, but I could wait outside in the car." She took a sip of coffee. "Just in case things get ugly."

Lily kissed her. "Thank you, but I think everything will be fine."

"Okay, but if you're not home by three a.m., I'm calling in the cavalry. I think I'll head back to the office then and do some preparation for my closing arguments."

She was nearly out the door when she hurried back, all in a rush, and kissed Lily soundly. "Congratulations on beating the Navy. You were wonderful."

Lily watched her go out the door. She couldn't help but grin at the sight of Jany's backside in the tight black jeans she liked to wear, even in the heat of summer. The sight of Jany's body, clothed or unclothed, still gave her a thrill. And it seemed Jany still felt the same way about Lily. She giggled out loud as she remembered Jany's most recent gift—a trio of thong underwear from Victoria's Secret. She'd had fun modeling them, and the last pair had not stayed on but a few seconds. Nothing Kathy could do would change how they felt about each other.

With a sigh, Lily put the last of the dishes away and went upstairs to prepare for the gathering tonight. She hadn't had much time to work with Judith, which made her feel more anxious than she'd like. She knew tonight she'd be only an observer because she wasn't yet a member of the coven. She picked up the photo of her mother that she kept on the dresser. It was yet another item she'd found only after the death of her father. Though she had loved him dearly, she couldn't help but resent him at times for having kept so much of her life hidden.

"Watch over me tonight, Rebekah," Lily said, remembering the vivid dream she'd had of her mother. She retrieved the silver necklace from her jewelry box and placed it around her neck. The pentacle charm glinted in the mirror. Lily touched it reverently, feeling safe yet again as a warm presence encircled her.

Right at nine o'clock, Lily left her house with much trepidation. She had no idea what to expect tonight. Would Kathy already know what they were planning? What would she do? Or more importantly, what *could* she do? Was her power stronger than all of theirs combined? Mandy had seemed to think so.

When she got to Lucy's, the others had already arrived. Only Kathy was missing. Come to think of it, Lily wasn't certain Kathy had even been told of the meeting. The eleven women had already gathered round the pentacle burnt into the floor. In its center stood a lighted black candle.

Judith looked up as Lily entered. "We don't have much time," she said.

Surprised, Lily quickly donned her white robe and accepted the stick of burning incense Judith handed to her. She hadn't expected to be a participant. The incense, she knew, represented the elements of air and fire. The others already had theirs. It took Lily a minute to identify the smell—frankincense.

They walked clockwise in a circle, reciting the words Judith had taught Lily. "I walk the circle once around to cleanse and consecrate this ground."

Next, they each picked up a small bowl of water, which represented the element of water. Again, in a clockwise circle they chanted, "I walk the circle once again. Between the worlds all time can bend."

Lastly they picked up shakers of salt, which represented the element of earth. Sprinkling the salt as they circled clockwise yet again, they said, "I walk this circle thrice this time, for the protection of Hecate is mine."

With their sacred space now cleansed, it was time to define and protect their circle. Judith took a gnarled wooden staff and traced the edge of the circle as they walked clockwise around it. Lily, as taught, envisioned herself pulling up a circle. In her mind's eye, it was a circle of lavender light with a burst of golden energy. Once the circle was complete, Lily watched as Judith took vials of almond, black pepper, petitgrain, and clove oils. As she mixed them together, they chanted, "I stand here in your guardian light. Empower this oil with your might. Protection from harm is what I ask, please accept this as your task," to charge the oil with energy. Each woman then dipped a finger into the oil and drew a penta-gram on her forehead.

Afterward, they sat together in their circle, all obviously still nervous despite their protection spell. "I think we all know why we're here," Judith said. They all nodded. "I know some of you are uneasy with what we are about to do. With what we *need* to do." She looked pointedly at Cara and Gwendolyn. "But I think we all know that Kathy can no longer be part of this coven."

"Wouldn't it be easier to just put a binding spell on Kathy to stop her negative behavior?" Cara asked.

Sage looked a bit sheepish. "I already tried. It was soon after her outburst about destroying those Navy ships."

"But maybe if we do it collectively—" Cara argued.

"No!"

They all looked at Judith, surprised at her harsh tone.

"We want her gone from the coven, and gone from Rehoboth." Gwendolyn answered back. "You say *we* when you really mean *I*."

"Do you deny she caused Mandy's accident and that she keeps Mandy in a coma? You know that her mother came first to the coven, watching as one by one all of our mothers died. And now Kathy has taken her place. She defies the very Wiccan Rede we live by—to 'do no harm'."

"There was never any real proof that Adrienne had anything to do with our mothers' deaths," Jacquelyn said, her voice troubled. "And it's not like we have or will have daughters for Kathy to do away with." She looked at Judith. "Well, except for you of course."

Judith looked solemn, yet confident. "You're right about

Adrienne, but what I really believe now is that Kathy killed our mothers and then her own."

A collective gasp filled the room.

Lily spoke then, unsure whether it was allowed. "She's not the only one who feels that way. Mandy spoke to me about the very same thing."

"I had no idea," Clarissa said, shaking her head.

Lucy nervously played with the sash of her robe. "Why didn't she say anything to us?" She looked at Judith. "Or you too, for that matter."

Judith spoke softly, her eyes filled with remembrance. "We were all so young then. Motherless, one by one. Why would any of us have thought a young girl could do such a thing? It is not what our mothers taught us."

A hush fell over the room. One could almost hear the candle flames flickering. Lily felt a shiver go up her spine. To think such evil existed! But she knew from her own experiences just what Kathy was willing to do.

"I too have felt much negativity from Kathy," Tara said, breaking the silence, "but I'm still uncomfortable with this. She frightens me."

Lily knew it was time for her to tell them. She took a deep breath. "I need to tell you about something that happened to me. I think it will help you understand just what Kathy is capable of."

They all looked at her expectantly. She felt her throat tighten. Grasping Rebekah's silver pentacle, she took another deep breath. "A few weeks ago, I was violated in my sleep. The dream was so vivid, I thought it had actually happened." She felt tears in her eyes as she continued. "In the dream, a woman had sex with me." She shook her head. "No, she raped me!"

In the shocked silence, Lily looked round the circle. Judith looked grim, knowing full well what Lily would say next. She couldn't yet tell what the others were thinking. Would they dismiss it as just a bad nightmare?

"Who was it?" Tara asked.

"It was Kathy."

Once again, a collective gasp filled the air. Their voices rose and fell, then blended together. Disbelief. Shock. Anger. Horror. Lily trembled with her own anger. She told them about the second attack, wanting—no, needing—to make them believe.

"Oh, my god," Ruth said. "I remember that attack. It was Mandy's black and white one."

"Which used to belong to Kathy," Judith reminded them.

"Her familiar," Blossom said with conviction.

Judith looked around the room, her expression hard. "You know what we need to do. For Lily. For Mandy. For us."

The electricity went out as a chill wind blew through the room, blowing out the candles. Plunged into sudden darkness, the women shrieked as icy tentacles seemed to curl around their bodies, making them immobile. Lucy's normally placid cats could be heard hissing as they scrambled out of the room.

"Your puny powers can't defeat me!"

Kathy's cold voice sent licks of fear up Lily's spine. She strained her eyes, looking for the source of the voice. It seemed to be all around her. She tried to move, but she felt locked in place. She couldn't even wiggle her fingers.

"Did you really think your pathetic little protection spell could stop me?"

Tara spoke, her voice trembling with fear. "Kathy, why would you do this? We mean you no harm."

"Which is more than you can say," Judith said.

Kathy's voice slithered around them. "And why would you think I mean to harm any of you?"

Lily struggled against her invisible binds. She wondered if the others felt as trapped. She mentally ran through the spells Judith had taught her, but could not remember one to undo Kathy's binding spell. Kathy's voice was still disembodied, making it impossible to tell where in the room she stood. Lily's eyes adjusted to the darkness, but she could barely make out the shapes of her fellow Wiccan. They seemed to be sitting upright, as she was.

Judith spoke again. "Do you deny the part you played in Mandy's accident?"

Laughter. Cold and harsh. "She was using magick to try and force me out. I could feel her becoming more powerful. I had to stop her." She laughed again. "And she'd thwarted me for the last time."

Their heavy breathing filled the room. Gwendolyn spoke, her voice filled with betrayal. "I believed in you, Kathy. I defended you. How could you do this?"

"We can settle all this if you will but make me your high priestess. We can be the most powerful coven on the east coast. Others will fear and respect us."

"It's not our desire or right to intimidate others."

Lily gasped as she felt a hand caress her right shoulder. One by one, she heard each of the others react the same way, as if that same hand touched each of them in turn. The whole time, Kathy continued to talk. Her voice seemed to come from all corners of the room. Lily could feel her anger building. Did none of the others feel the same way? Kathy had betrayed them. Had violated their trust.

"Can we help it if people bow to our power? To our collective might? You saw how we made those Navy ships abandon their mission." Again, Lily felt a hand caress her. "And I know that made Lily happy."

"You'll not get any of our support by holding us prisoner in this way. And I know you can't keep it up indefinitely," Tara said.

"I wonder what you would do to save Mandy?"

It was as if time stopped. There was no sound, then only quiet sobbing. Lily had no idea who was crying, or how many. She could sense intense anger, but again knew not from whom it came. Her own fear struggled with her anger. Rebekah, she called silently, as she fought against her invisible binds.

"Oh my sisters, I would not kill Mandy. I'm disappointed you would think that. But I can keep her in that coma or I can set her free. In any case, she should be removed as high priestess." She paused, then sneered, "Her ideas are old, leftover from earlier times. She's rooted in the ancient past."

"You talk about Mandy as if she's hundreds of years old," Jacquelyn said, her voice high with panic.

"Her spirit comes from the ancient ones. They have no place here."

"That's not for you to decide."

"Ah Judith, you are so much the protector. You think you can take Mandy's place, but you are not strong enough." Laughter again. "The only thing you can contribute is that unborn child. She will make a good witch."

If the room could get any colder, it did. Lily felt the goose bumps rise on her flesh. The air seemed to crackle with charged electricity.

"You will not get your hands on my child!"

There was a surge of warm air, and the invisible binds loosened for a few moments. In a brief flash of light from the lamps, Lily saw the others stand as she did, their expressions pale and grim. Dressed in a flowing robe of black and red, Kathy stood in the north corner. Rage darkened her features. Lily caught a glimpse of Judith, whose rage was equally strong, before the room plunged once more into darkness and the binding tentacles again tightened around her.

"I need none of you!" Kathy snarled.

Lily cried out as the binds tightened further, and heard the others cry out as well. She struggled for breath. The pain in her lungs was excruciating. "Powerful Hecate, protector of those who serve, hear my plea," she whispered over and over again. As she began to lose consciousness, she could only say one word. "Rebekah."

Then, just as suddenly as the pain had started, it ended. And she was free! The room blazed with light from every lamp and every candle. Dazed, Lily looked wildly around her. Some women were on their feet; others had fallen to their knees. And then all looked stunned as they beheld the scene before them.

Judith stood tall, arms raised up, her expression severe and determined. Surrounded in a glowing light, she spoke a language Lily could not understand. Kathy seemed locked in place, her hands outstretched as she too spoke harsh, unintelligible words. Lily fully expected to see lightning bolts flash from both their fingertips. A tempest wind howled in the room, yet nothing was blown about. The light grew brighter. Lily shielded her eyes, straining to hear what the others were saying.

"Oh dear Goddess!"

"What is it?"

"Look! Look!"

"It can't be!"

"Mandy! It's Mandy!"

"Oh god . . . oh god—"

"It's my mother! How can that be?"

"And mine!"

And they were surrounded by thirteen images, twelve of them of those long dead.

"Rebekah," Lily whispered as she reached out, wishing she could touch her. Her mother's protection surrounded her.

The battle of wills seemed to go on forever. Lily called upon her own powers, her fury giving them strength. She could feel the collective energy of the covens, both spiritual and real, as they fought Kathy's astounding strength. And then Kathy fell back, shrieking as she hit the floor, the energy around her breaking into shards.

The room descended into darkness once more. The air felt cool, like a misty rain. Lily heard whisperings all around her and knew somehow it was the voices of those who had come before. She felt a touch, feather-soft.

"Lily."

Rebekah!

The whoosh of a gentle wind, then silence as the lights came up. Lily looked eagerly for her mother, but she and the other spirits were gone. Tired beyond belief, Lily grabbed Blossom's hand. She, like Lily, had tears in her eyes.

Shattering glass drew their attention as Kathy clawed her way back to her feet, knocking over a crystal vase. The rage and hatred in her eyes made those closest to her back away. "You'll pay for this," she hissed. "I will destroy all of you. Mark my words." Whirling away with the speed of a lioness, Kathy fled.

Judith started after her. Clarissa put out a hand to stop her. "Let her go. She can't hurt us anymore."

"She doesn't deserve to live!"

"That is not our way, Judith. She will leave Rehoboth. There is nothing here for her now. Don't let her poison your mind."

"I agree with Judith. She is dangerous. We have to stop her," Lily said.

Clarissa shook her head. "I promise you, she is no danger to us or anyone." She smiled. "Those who came before us have given us their protection."

"Our mothers," Sage said.

"And Mandy. How was she here?" Gwendolyn asked.

Sarah leapt to her feet, visibly shaken. "Oh no, does this mean Mandy is dead? Was that her spirit?"

"No my dears, I am very much alive."

"Mandy!"

Lily wasn't the only one with tears in her eyes as they one by one embraced their high priestess and mentor. In all the excitement, no one noticed a black and white tabby slip out the door.

"I guess all was quiet last night," Jany said as she and Lily snuggled in bed. "I didn't even hear you come in."

"No, everything went well," Lily said.

"Kathy just accepted being asked to leave the coven? No argument?"

"Well, she wasn't too happy, but she got the message that it was the best thing." Lily kissed Jany's cheek. "Someday, I'll tell you the whole story."

Jany traced her finger along Lily's jaw. "I'm glad. You seem so much more at peace now."

Lily smiled. "I think you're right."

Jany noticed the silver chain around Lily's neck. "Where'd you get that? I don't think I've ever seen it before."

Lily pulled the necklace out so the pentacle dangled in plain view. "It was gift from Rebekah," she said. "She gave it to me one night."

"But you were a baby when she died."

Lily ran her hands through Jany's hair, then kissed her. "She came to me in a dream. But I don't want to talk about that now. I want you to make love to me."

Jany pulled her down eagerly. "Gladly," she said as she untied the laces of Lily's nightgown.

Later that night, Lily felt the same warm sensation that had heralded the first dream of her mother. She stirred, feeling the heat of Jany's body against her.

"Lily."

"You came back."

Rebekah caressed Lily's cheek. "I never truly left."

"Will you help me? I want to make you proud. I want to be a good Wicca."

"You will be."

Lily sat up and looked into her mother's brilliant blue eyes. "But I allowed my anger to fuel a thirst for vengeance."

"It is something all humans have to deal with at times. But this time, your anger was justified." Rebekah frowned. "It is not right for a witch to abuse her powers and harm others."

Lily shivered. She grabbed her mother's hand for comfort, then raised it to her cheek, feeling the softness of Rebekah's skin. "I am still afraid. What if Kathy comes back?"

Rebekah took Lily into her arms and stroked her hair. "You needn't worry about her. No, her offenses have been added up, and the payment taken by the spirits who pursued her."

Lily enjoyed the comfort of her mother's arms. It was something she'd not had growing up. She let her thoughts slip away to what her mother had said. Lily didn't like to think about what might have happened to Kathy. Was she in some sort of hell? Did those same spirits exact some retribution of their own? Despite what Lily had endured, once her anger was spent, she could not wish ill on anyone.

As if reading her mind, Rebekah said, "You are a good person, Lily. You will make a fine witch." She looked over at Jany's sleeping form. "And you have someone who loves you with all her soul—a powerful force indeed." She gently pushed Lily away. "But now I must go. Hecate, our protector, calls for me."

"No, please . . ."

Lily felt her mother's light touch, then she was gone.

Awakening briefly from her dream, Lily reached out to touch Jany, then rolled over to go back into sleep. As she turned, a glimmer of white at the foot of the bed caught her attention. Blinking sleepily, she noticed a black and white cat sitting on the footboard, watching her. *I must still be dreaming*, she thought drowsily as she drifted off into sleep.

BY THE BOOK

THERESE SZYMANSKI

Prologue

Screaming, he charged me with his sword raised. I back-flipped off the wall and landed neatly behind him.

He yanked his sword out of the wall, from the spot where my neck had been only moments before.

I ran to the far wall and yanked a sword out of the display just in time to whip about and counter his thrust. Metal clanged as we danced through the well-choreographed moves of our duel. Our swords flashed under the hot lights.

I kicked a lamp into his path, but he was unrelenting in his pursuit. I leapt over the coffee table, flipping around to keep facing him. I didn't dare let him at my back. I let my body act and react, keeping my motions fluid and fresh.

He laughed and grabbed the table in his beefy hand and tossed it aside. It was all theatrics on the part of the big, bad man, but it bought me time to readjust my weight and grip.

I dodged to the right, hurdling the shards of the coffee table, but he swung his arm around, striking me across the back and sending me tumbling forward.

Fucker. He hit me and it hurt! But I had no time to dwell on such things. I rolled off my shoulder to land on my feet. I had to focus and concentrate, or I could get hurt. I flipped over the futon, still holding onto my sword, and ended up on my knees on the far side. I blocked his blade just before it met the soft flesh of my neck.

I looked up at him. I grabbed the tip of my sword and used the full length of the blade to throw him back, leaving me room to somersault forward on my shoulder and swing my weapon just across the backs of his knees. After all, I wasn't in a position to deliver a killing blow.

But just before my sword struck, I hit instant migraine, with a terrible pain drilling my skull. I lost control of my body and dropped my sword, fell forward onto my face, and . . .

. . . *I knew my parents were dead.*

"Cut!" the director yelled. "Ty, are you okay?"

CHAPTER THE FIRST

I stood at the edge of my parents' grave and dropped a blood red rose into it, watching as it fell to earth, just as my parents had fallen out of the sky and down to the ground when their stunt went oh-so-wrong.

My best friend Christie squeezed my hand and wrapped an arm around me, offering me a warm shoulder to lean against.

I watched the rose fall, unbuffeted by breeze or wind, and thought of it as happening in slow motion. Maybe it was my show-biz mind thinking it would be slo-mo on film that made it seem so, or maybe time really does slow at those crucial moments in one's life.

"It's fine to hold the steering wheel like that in regular life, Ty," Mom said from the passenger's seat as I made a right-hand turn. *"In fact, I believe in driver's ed the dictated hand-over-hand method requires such measures, but remember if you're doing a car crash scene, never hook your thumbs over the wheel like that—keep your hands entirely on the outside, or else you might break your thumbs."*

One of the coolest things about having a stuntperson Mom was that she was supervising my driver education quite calmly—not grabbing for the "oh-shit" handle of the car or jamming the invisible passenger-side brakes. Plus, well, she was always imparting knowledge about what would likely end up my career.

"I've never broken my thumbs, thank goodness, because a lot of things

become more difficult when you've broken your thumbs—and I've seen people struggling with such." She leaned into the turn as I followed a curvy road. "After all, opposable thumbs are one of the things that set us apart from other animals. And Ty, dear, remember speed limits are not mere suggestions, but actual laws."

"Uh, Ma? We're practically in the middle of nowhere, and I need to work on my fast driving as well."

"You don't want to waste all your karmic bonus points on not getting tickets. So you can drive up to nine miles over the limit—when you're older. The cops aren't as lenient with younger drivers, so until you're no longer a teenager, just drive the speed limit. Unless you're at work."

"C'mon, how bad can the Canadian cops be?" Dad and Mom were working in Vancouver during my summer break.

"You don't have your U.S. driver's license yet. I probably shouldn't even be letting you drive here, so don't go getting us into any more trouble."

"Okay. Fine. So where are we going anyway?"

"Hank's working, so I thought we'd just go to this cool place I found years ago—before I had you. It's very calm and peaceful and it has a gorgeous view. I thought you might enjoy it."

"Cool."

"So. Tyler. After this job—"

"Mom, can't I ever just go through an entire school year at one school, without interruption?"

"Tyler. Keep your eyes on the road. And you have attended a single school for an entire year."

"Yeah, when you stick me with strangers while you two go running all over."

"Tyler Black, I do not appreciate that tone, and unless you can keep your eyes on the road and hold your temper, we will have to pull over and I will not be pleased. How can I trust you to drive in L.A. and crash cars if you can't keep your focus?"

"I'm focused here. I'm all with the focus on both the driving and what you're saying and I'm holding my temper."

"Yeah, right. You might be the best actor of us, though. Pull over here."

I parked and got out of the car. She was right. The view was incredible.

She put her arm around me. "Ty, what I was saying was that after this job, your father and I would like us to take a little trip to the Michigan house—turn right here, and just keep to the right—there's no tenants at the moment, and we want to check the place out. Plus, we can stay there since there's no tenants."

At least they always kept me abreast of plans, contracts and obligations. But it wasn't like I had any say in anything. "Okay. It's near Detroit, right?"

"Yes. And, by the way, Ty? Your Dad and I are planning on you staying with us for your last three years of high school—and that you'll be at the same school for all three years."

I turned to her and wrapped my arms around her. "I love you, Mom."

Ever since I'd discovered my folks died I'd been having nightmares that left my sheets soaked and my heart hammering. Sometimes they weren't terribly horrifying, but they were vivid. And they always told me I had to move back to Mom's old house.

They died on my thirtieth birthday. If my life was a movie, the music would swell and fade as I thought that, because it had to mean something. Anything. They couldn't just die on my birthday and it mean nothing.

It was my choice they shared a grave. They always seemed so meant for each other—like they belonged together forever plus a few years. Or millennia. A few forevers plus a few more. They'd love that they went together. They'd also love that their final stunt made it to film. (Obviously, only the DVD would have the *entire* stunt on film. For the actual movie it was cut early, so people in theatres wouldn't see my parents plunge to their deaths.)

The rose hit Mom's coffin and bounced, somersaulting into the air.

I knew everyone at the funeral by face, name, and association with my folks and myself. But my folks had each other while I was alone.

They were gone and would never be back.

They were all I'd ever had.

I looked into their grave, at their caskets, and wondered if any of the many people gathered around me were truly friends to me or my folks—or were they just *associates*? People who were here, with me, at their funeral, just because we were in the biz and any chance to be seen was considered a good P.R. move?

Even Christie, who held my hand, rubbing her thumb lightly over its back, sending tingles throughout my body, had gotten every acting job she'd ever had through me, because of me. She'd been by my side ever since I'd found out they were dead—helping me get the bodies through customs, pick out the coffins, arrange for the service and all the other details of death. She was there, by my side, with me, for them.

And she was here with me now, holding my hand and scanning the crowd, as if assessing who was present and what they could mean to her or do for her. Among the many other thoughts rampaging through my brain was the growing one that I had been in this town too long.

Christie was lovely—beautiful even—and nice, and my best friend. It would be so easy to love her. But she was straight, and she wasn't The One. But she was here with me now, and I was grateful for her support. But did she look out for me just because of what I could do for her?

I was born and raised in sunny SoCal. I belonged here and couldn't imagine living anywhere else. I was following in my folks' footsteps and that was as it was meant to be. Or at least I had thought so, until they died jumping out of an airplane.

I suddenly realized there wasn't much keeping me here now. The folks had left me with a wealth of stocks and insurance payoffs so I was now rich and never had to work again. I could just up and leave and move to the house in Michigan Mom'd left me—just like I'd been dreaming I ought to. But I'd *always* done what I'd wanted. And what was I without my work? Who was I?

I loved getting beaten up on a regular basis. I loved pushing my body to its limits. I dug running with scissors, taking candy from strangers, jumping out of perfectly fine planes and off totally respectable cliffs. We—my parents and I—did stupid shit and got banged and bruised and hurt and kicked when we were down. It was what we did.

But now they were dead.

My world was built on topsy-turvy and crazy. I'd always known I could die at any time, but I didn't really believe it. The rules had changed suddenly, however. Now I *knew* that I, too, could die at any time.

I'd been taking gymnastics, fencing, and martial arts all my life. I honestly couldn't remember learning how to ski (water, downhill or cross country), because I'd been skiing, skydiving and jumping off cliffs for as long as memory.

And, like my folks, I'd never missed a day of work, no matter what I broke, sprained, dislocated or concussed. I'd been raised to be a stuntperson, just like my folks. I was resilient by nature and didn't get hurt nearly as often as I ought to due to sheer dumb luck. Or else I had a wicked-cool, with-it guardian angel or something.

The rose had come to rest between their caskets and I stared at it for a moment. The minister eulogized about how my folks had worked toward ensuring safer standards for stuntpeople—even going so far as to stage a walk-out. There were many times they could have gotten more money, but instead they focused on safety and security for those like them and those yet to come.

Like me.

I stood in my black suit, looking like maybe I was ready to go to the Oscars or something, and knew I could dive down into that grave and land without injury. I knew my body and myself and my folks, but I didn't know anybody else. Not really.

With the folks gone, there was no reason for me to stay here.

They weren't supposed to go. Not yet. They still had so much to teach me. So much to tell me. I always knew there were things they were hiding from me, and those things, especially Mom's things, became more apparent as time went on. I only wanted to be worthy, to get worthy/become worthy enough, some day, for her to tell me.

One day, when I was in high school, Dad was in Tonga filming, and I was supposed to go over to Christie's to study and we were working on Marsha Norman's *'Night Mother* and I realized I hadn't told Mom I loved her for way too long. To my surprise, when I got home, she was surrounded by incense and candles, humming, as she sat cross-legged on the living room floor. I stared at her for several minutes before she realized I was there. As soon as she became aware of my presence all the candles snuffed, she stopped humming and became the mom I knew again.

I guess that was the moment I knew the folks, or at least my mother, were/was hiding something from me. And I wanted to know what it was.

"Some day I'll be able to tell you, Ty," she had said when I asked what was up. "We'll both know when the time is right. I can't explain more now, though, because there are those who would take advantage of you if they could."

Christie wrapped an arm around my waist, pulling me back from the grave. She stood next to me while people came and went, shaking my hand and offering condolences. Or I guess that's what was going on. I wasn't paying attention.

These were all fake people, Hollywood people. Not real. Not like my parents. Why was I even still here in L.A.? Besides for their funeral?

Christie squeezed me. "It's a real shock. I've been with her ever since she found out. It's just awful. I know."

I looked up at the person Christie was explaining to. Michele.

"Ty," Michele said as she took my hand. "I know everyone's telling you this, but if you need *anything*—"

"I'm here for her," Christie said.

I was surprised by Christie's possessiveness, because usually she'd be fawning all over Michele, trying to get work. But I couldn't complain because Christie had been with me ever since they died.

"Have dinner with me Friday," Michele said, holding my hand in both of hers.

"Give me a call," I said. Her hands were warm.

"Why don't I just pick you up at seven?" she asked. I wanted to collapse into her arms. I wanted to curl up and cry on her lap.

I had to run. I had to get away from her. Michele wasn't good for me—she was rich, famous and important and I was just me— plain, simple, nobody me—and I loved her way too much.

"She'll meet you at Piccolo's at seven on Friday, how's that?" Christie said, nodding toward the rest of the mourners who wanted to pay their respects to me. She tightened her arm around me and got Michele to move along and I wished, yet again, that Christie was The One, even if she was just using me. I understood the rules in Hollywood, at least I thought I did. But as each day passed without my parents, I felt those rules were no longer work- ing for me. I needed to get out of town, and I knew just where to go.

CHAPTER THE SECOND

H ow are you doing?" Michele asked, reaching across the table to place her hand on mine. Her hand was soft. It felt nice. Comforting. "Really?"

"Uh, okay." I twisted my neck a bit, cracking it. "I don't think I'll even have any bruises tomorrow. Or not many, at least." I tried to withdraw my hand, but she wouldn't let me. We'd just finished shooting the season finale that day. I hadn't taken any time off the show since the folks died. I knew they would've liked that.

"Ty, you've been doubling for me for more than six seasons now. I know you. Somewhat. And there's something troubling you lately."

"My folks just kicked, how am I *supposed* to be acting?" I poked my salad with my fork and didn't look at her.

"I know my own father was basically a sperm donor, nothing more. But I can't imagine losing my mom, too."

"All things considered, I'm fine. Okay? I'm getting over it all." I tried to yank my hand from hers. It wouldn't be good for her rep to be caught holding hands with another woman in a restaurant.

She kept her grip on my hand with both of hers. It was becoming a territory war. "Tyler, I just want you to know I'm here for you. If you need a friend. Someone to talk to. Anything like that— anything at all."

"Fourteen years and how many meals have we shared, Michele?"

"Hundreds. Thousands even, maybe."

"But how many with just the two of us?"

"Don't shut me out now, Ty. You need me now more than ever."

"Is that a threat?" I stood, looking down at her. We were about the same height, but she had long, dark hair, was stacked and was hot. Wicked hot. "If you're threatening to cut off my work, to kick me off the show . . ."

"No, Ty, I'm not. I'm just—"

"I don't need you, or the show, any more anyway." The words were coming out of my mouth and I was hating myself for them. How bloody stupid could I be? She could blacklist me and make sure I didn't ever get another job again. Unless, of course, I wanted to work at Mickey D's or Wal-Mart.

She seized my hand again and wrote some numbers on my palm. "This is my home number, and my cell. I don't know what you're going through, and I can't imagine what it must be like. But if you need somebody to talk to, call me. And I'm not just saying that, I actually mean it."

She looked at me earnestly and I believed her in that moment. But then I remembered she was a TV star, a multi-millionaire, and so much else I wasn't. I had just realized I couldn't trust my best friends, since they weren't my friends at all, but were simply using me to get work in a town so networked knowing anyone was a huge step up. "Why should I listen to you? Believe you?" The words were out of my mouth before I could think. I *so* needed to fire my internal censor.

"I can't give you a single reason," she said. "I just know I can't let you run away from me like this."

I looked at her and remembered how I used to cherish every single touch from her. It wasn't just the blacklist I was afraid of, it was that I wouldn't be able to leave her. "I've got enough cash to retire now. I'm not sure if I'm going to or not, but I *am* taking a break. See, Mom left me a house out in the Midwest. I've been dreaming of it every night since they passed, in fact. I feel like I have to go there. Move there. And I don't know why I'm telling you all this."

"I just have to tell you, I'm a huge fan of yours!" the waiter gushed, placing the bill by Michele's elbow. I realized a number of folks were staring at us now and finally I succeeded in freeing myself from her grasp.

I grabbed the check, glanced at it, and threw some bills into the folio. "You ready then?"

"We don't have to work tomorrow," she said, autographing something for the waiter. "The season's over, after all." She could never be mine—she belonged to everyone else.

"I'm not quite comfortable here." I led her outside.

"Tyler, you have to deal with this."

"I'm fine, I'm cool, I'm copacetic even." I took her keys and opened her car door for her.

"And I'm following you home. We're not done."

"Micky, I'm not gonna risk your career by hanging too close to you."

"It's not your choice. You do what you have to, and I'll do what I must."

I looked at her. Apparently she wouldn't get into her car until I agreed.

"Ty, I'm going to follow you to your home, and we'll finish talking there," Michele said. "I'm surprised I got you away from Christie for this long, and now you're telling me you're planning on moving away. I don't want to lose this chance. It might be our last, okay?"

Christie *had* wanted to join me tonight. It was when she'd commented that Michele could help her as well that I realized it was time to redefine our friendship with a firm *no*.

I looked at Michele. She didn't know where I lived, and I knew I could lose her quite easily if I wanted to. But of all the Hollywood people I knew, she was the one who had nothing to gain by being a real friend.

"I'm hoping you'll give me a ride on that bike of yours some-day," Michele said in my apartment parking lot.

I was embarrassed as I led her into my meager dwelling, but she didn't seem at all disturbed by it.

"Dear lord, you own a lot of books," she said as she draped her jacket on the sofa.

I shrugged. "I like to read. I like to know things. And I've always hated having to wait to find things. To get info." I didn't mention all the stories I'd written. All the stuff I'd written. All the book clubs I belonged to. So I simply rolled my eyes and shrugged.

"And I'd always thought By-the-Book Black meant you fol-lowed the rules," she said, "not that you were such a voracious reader."

"Being a stuntperson you have to be careful and pay attention to all the details, because there's just way too many ways to get hurt doing this job. As my folks so amply proved. So I read." She was just so incredible, I wanted her to see me for more than just . . . as more than just . . . well . . . some stalker-loser guy. She got those every day of the week since the start of the second season, when her popularity took off.

She could be The One, but everyone thought that about her. She didn't need me acting like that, too.

"Can I get you something to drink?" I asked.

"Sure, a diet soda would be great."

When I returned with a soda for her and a beer for me, she'd taken off her shoes, curling up against an arm of the couch with her feet curled beneath her.

I handed her the soda and went to the stereo to put on some music.

"Most people in this business live it up," Michele said. "I'm sur-prised you live here. Like this."

"I don't need much. My space, my books and my computer. I'd rather save up for the hard times." I sat at the other end of the sofa, far away from her.

"So you're just selling your parents' house here, packing everything up, and moving to Michigan?"

"Ayeah, that's about the size of it."

"Have you ever been to Michigan before?"

"We visited the place a few times while I was growing up."

"And you're doing this because . . . ?"

"Micky, my world has gone all David Lynch since my folks passed. But see, I remembered that house right after I found out they'd died, and then, just after the funeral, Christie and I were going through a drive-thru, and all the quarters we got back were from Michigan."

"Why did your Mom have a house in Michigan?"

"The house—and property—has been in her family forever. She grew up in it."

"So it's just been sitting there empty?"

I shrugged. "It is now. I'll need to figure out what's been up with it. I know they rented it sometimes."

"So you're giving up everything—and everyone—you know, selling or packing everything, and moving to a place where you don't know a soul?"

"Ayeah. That's about the size of it."

"But what if it doesn't work out for you out there? What if you don't like it?"

I shrugged. "I'll move back here. Buy a new place. I wouldn't want to live in the folks' place, since it'd remind me too much of them, and I shouldn't keep throwing money away on rent when I can just buy a place, y'know?"

"And all this doesn't seem the least bit strange to you? Why now?"

"I've always known what I'd do—it was laid out for me. I idolized my folks, and simply followed in their footsteps. I did what they did. But it's like with them gone now, I've realized that I can die, and will die someday. And then I look around me, at everything we've always done, and realized it's all an illusion. Fake."

"Ty, you work in TV and movies. Of course it is."

"I know. And it can be nice. I can pick up DVDs and videos and say I worked on this or that—but do I affect people? Does my work make a difference? I feel like I need to stop and look at everything. I don't need to keep hustling for a living, so I should take this chance to figure things out and decide what to do next. And where better than the Midwest? Where people are real?"

"I guess I'm not real enough for you, huh?" Michele averted her face.

I put my hand on her arm. I didn't like her turning from me, especially not since we were connecting like we never had before. I was starting to think maybe something could happen between us—maybe not an affair, but maybe a friendship.

"Yeah, what?" she said.

"Sorry. Thank you for your help. Thank you for trying. It means a lot, even though I've been an ass. I just need to do what I need to do, okay?"

She leaned closer to me and cupped my cheek. "Just remember I'm here for you, okay?"

I wanted to kiss her so badly. But she was way out of my league.

"Tell me," she said. I could feel her warm breath on my cheek. "I hear about you and all your *conquests*. Is it all true?"

"No. Nothing here is real, remember?" I picked up my beer and finished it off. I didn't like her believing all those bizarre rumors about me—I hadn't been with that many women. She was too close, and it wasn't safe. I'd had a drink with dinner and one since. "Michele, I'm thinking about having another drink. You maybe might wanna leave."

"Do you have any wine?" She looked up at me through her lashes. She *so* had to know what she was doing.

I picked an appropriate bottle, poured her a glass, and snagged another beer for me. I sat back next to her on the couch and handed her the wine. I felt an intense jolt when our fingers brushed. This situation was unreal and I closed my eyes for a moment.

She had turned off the lights, lit the candles, and unbuttoned another button on her blouse, but I looked at her face, into her eyes. I wanted her too badly to give in to her for just one night, if doing so meant that was all we'd ever have.

I'd seen her in just a bra and panties before. This was far hotter than that because that'd merely been thespians changing costumes. This was her getting comfortable around me, and starting to undress for me. Acting as if she was going to seduce me.

I focused on her eyes.

"Your mom told me you'd listen to me," she said.

"You talked about me with my mom? That's kinda weird, babe."

"Yeah, but she was right, wasn't she?"

"I didn't even know you knew my mom." She was so close I couldn't resist touching her. I brushed my fingers softly through her hair.

"She knew I liked you in a more-than-friends way, and so she trusted me. She told me things. She wanted me to help you. She knew we had more powerful things in common and that I could be here for you when she couldn't. She didn't want to tell you, because she knew how powerful you could be—and how someone else might try to take that power for themselves. She didn't want you to know, for fear that it'd only make you stronger and draw even more attention to you."

"I don't want to be talking about my mom right now." I feathered my lips up her neck and to her delicate earlobe. "Besides, she's dead."

Michele lay back, bringing me down on top of her. "God, Ty, I've been thinking about this since I first saw you."

"Me you too." I looked at her full, lush, pouty lips and needed to taste them. I leaned down, brushing my lips over hers, and she raised up so she could feel my lips with hers. I slipped my arm under her head and lay by her side. "You are so unbelievably beautiful."

She took my hand and placed it on her breast.

I kissed her again, and she opened her lips, allowing me to enter her. I caressed her breast. "I can't believe this is happening," I said.

"Maybe it isn't, not really," she said.

I unbuttoned her blouse as we looked deep into each other's eyes. Her nipples hardened and I caressed them with my tongue and fingers.

"God, yes, please."

"Don't call me god. Not yet." I slipped off the sofa to pick her up and carry her to the bedroom. I laid her on the bed and she sat up so I could remove her blouse and bra. It was like she could read my mind—as if she knew what I wanted.

She lay back, naked from the waist up. She was looking up at the ceiling as I pulled her skirt, stockings and undies off. "I love your biceps. It turns me on when you carry me."

I lay on top of her.

"Please, Ty, I need to feel you," she said, tugging at my T-shirt. I sat up and pulled it and my sports bra off.

I lay back upon her and groaned at the feeling of her breasts against mine. We kissed long and deep and I kissed down her body and wrapped her legs around my shoulders and slowly tasted her.

"Ty, yes, please."

I ran my tongue up and down her. "Open yourself for me."

She reached down and opened herself, even as she arched up into my mouth, tempting me to further ministrations.

It got even hotter seeing her touch herself.

I buried my tongue in her, then replaced it with my fingers. I ran my tongue up and down her.

I fucked her with my fingers, and added another and another. I was knuckles deep in her and eating her up like the tasty treat she was.

"Yes, please, Ty, now! God yes!"

Her legs tightened around my shoulders as I buried my face in her. I loved having her. I loved being in her and touching her like this.

I loved her.

I felt her tighten and convulse and she almost dislocated my shoulder.

I kissed her thighs and then, in the dim light . . . well, that wasn't right.

Michele was a brunette, with thick, rich, gorgeous wavy dark locks. This woman was blonde.

I lifted myself to my elbows and saw . . .

. . . not Michele.

But she was familiar.

"Stop brooding," Michele said, shaking me lightly.

"Michele . . . Micky . . ." She was now so thoroughly distracting me that I felt like a high-schooler and then I realized how much younger than me she was, and she was straight and that vivid fantasy I'd just had was an enormously bad idea.

"What?"

There was no way this meant what I thought. Plus, if something happened here, now, I couldn't leave. And I knew I had to leave. Later tonight, I'd wake up again soaking wet from head to toe, fighting off demons in my sleep. The only safe place was mom's house. I had to get out of here before I completely lost my mind.

And even when Michele left, I tried not to feel disappointed and really, I hoped she wasn't as disappointed as I was.

Or maybe I was hoping she was every bit as disappointed as I was.

CHAPTER THE THIRD

Everything happened so quickly it was almost like magic. The folks died. Christie helped me pack up their place and sell it. Movers moved, I drove and next thing I knew I was sitting on my Harley in my driveway, staring up at my new home. I took off my helmet and looked up at the huge, old house looming at the top of a tree-lined drive in a quiet Royal Oak cul-de-sac.

It was dusk and the sun was setting just behind the building, which looked the same as it had when I was a kid. It didn't feel the same, though. Maybe it was my trepidation at starting a new life, or maybe it was my road-weary ass, but something wasn't feeling right here.

As I glanced around, I saw my new neighbor pulling into her garage. A few seconds later a petite blonde wearing a short skirt appeared. When she bent to pick up the paper her hair fell down to catch the last remaining rays of sunlight. She had wonderful legs and a great figure. The slight breeze wrapped her dress around her like a second skin.

My tongue dropped out of my mouth and I was left panting like a dog running across Death Valley in the summer. During the hottest, longest day of the year. Without water. Or food.

I gotta say, it was all like some perfectly scripted TV moment: She, nonchalantly walking out to gather her paper, me noticing her (in slo-mo, of course). She, glancing toward me whilst picking up the paper.

The only thing missing was front lighting while swelling clouds of mist and fog came up from behind her.

That and her actually noticing me.

She walked inside without even glancing toward me. I studied her house for a bit longer, then turned my attention toward my own again. Everything suddenly seemed very right. Things were starting to make sense, because I realized I'd been pulled more than halfway across the country for Her.

The One.

My new neighbor.

I investigated the house and started unpacking all the boxes the movers had left all willy nilly throughout it. The stereo was a priority—music always made everything better and easier. For instance, I could unpack faster to some good 70's tunes like ABBA.

But there was already a little skip to my step, even without the music. I'd finally found The One. She hadn't noticed me, not yet, but she would. I just knew we were meant to be together. I couldn't believe that just a few weeks before I'd been thinking Michele might be The One. In retrospect, it was almost like Michele'd laid a spell on me or something—seducing me with her fame and fortune and all the trappings thereof. She'd tried to trap me in her trappings.

I felt a cool breeze. But the back door was closed. I stepped outside to look around. It felt as if someone was watching me. I wondered if paranoia was one of the five or six stages of grief?

Oh, for fuck's sake, I was an idiot. My neighbor was a hottie and I was overreacting to it. I didn't know her, and Love at First Sight didn't exist. I'd only just seen her.

I double-locked the door behind me and finished putting the

last of my kitchenware away, then faced the wall of boxes I had just emptied. I picked up the dagger I was using for such things, and quickly broke them all down.

Some crazy collectors would probably pay quite a lot for some of the props I was using as regular household implements (this dagger had come from the set of *The Good Die Young*), but me and my folks had always walked away with some remembrances from all our movies.

But I couldn't remember ever just seeing a woman and having the reaction I'd had with my neighbor. Just seeing her had done something to me.

I went downstairs and started unpacking my swords. If I still lived in an apartment I couldn't be drilling and mounting things for display this late at night. But, also, the walls of my old apartment didn't seem to hum when I touched them. When I was twelve, I read *Pet Semetary* by Stephen King. It was late at night and I was all alone and wicked freaked. And I got more and more freaked with every page I read, yet I read on—pulling my feet from the floor so no nasties could grab them, running as fast as I could when I had to go from one room to another, and then leaping onto my bed from the doorway without turning off the light first.

I was feeling just like that—that I was surrounded with something out to get me.

It was spooky.

But hell, I was able to get to sleep that night, and I'd do it again now. Fear was something to be overcome. Plus I was exhausted. Unfortunately none of the beds were made up, so it looked like it was the couch for me.

I was accustomed to catching some Zzzzs whenever I could, whether it be in a trailer or in a chair, so with the exhaustion of my long ride, it didn't take me long to fall asleep.

"Tyler Black, what is this?" Mom said.

I was eight. "Umm, my backpack and bag lunch? Ooo, do I get Ho Hos today?"

"No, I mean this?" She held out a videotape.

"Oh, that." I reached for it. She held it up over her head.

I ran up to her, bounced off the wall behind her to yank the tape out of her hand.

"Wow! Ty! That was amazing!" Dad said, coming up behind Mom.

"Hank! That is the wrong message to be giving Ty—though it was perfectly performed—because she'll have to wash the wall after school."

"Which she'll do, right?" he glared at me.

"Yes," I said, sticking the video down my pants.

"And this isn't about that anyway," Mom said. "It's about the video. Ty was about to explain just what it was and why she needed to take it to school with her."

"Tyler?" Dad said.

I gave it to Mom. "I just wanted to show everybody at school that you guys do work in the movies."

"Tyler, some people look up at movie people, so you saying that your parents are movie folk is bragging, and bragging isn't nice. Your Dad and I are just regular people. We just have certain talents and use them to our best advantage—it doesn't mean we're any better than anyone else. Do you understand?"

"Yes, Mom," I said, toeing the ground in front of me.

"Tyler," Dad said, "You need to learn how to use and respect power and talents. Not everyone is equal, but that's no reason to flaunt what you have and others don't."

"I understand."

I knew I was asleep, and was dreaming, again. But I couldn't pull out of it.

The boy stood across the common staring at me. He'd been older last time. I'd been younger.

This much I knew. And this time I had the power to ensure next time I'd remember. Just as each time I built my power and played with the strings of fate to increase my chances as each life progressed, I was also stacking the deck to ensure my ultimate success.

He'd been young. I'd been old. And we'd been Navajo. All three of us. He'd gotten her that time—but I'd used the time to develop my power . . .

The dreams had stopped while I'd been road tripping and staying in motels while I drove cross-country on my Harley. But now they were back. I wanted them to stop, but my mind was drenched with sleep and I fell back in.

The first time I was ever on a set, Mom warned me to be very quiet. But when that man attacked Mom, I knew she could take him, and I kept my mouth shut, but so much of me inside was screaming as I jumped up and down (silently), waving my arms, knowing she could so kick his butt from here clean to the next room.

And she did. Really.

Much embarrassment abounded that day, 'cause she so didn't know how she'd kicked this guy like twice her weight across one room and into another—clear through a wall.

I tried to wake up, but couldn't. I slept on.

I was digging a hole. A deep hole . . . with my hands. I'd already bespelled the book I was putting into the earth, chanting as I did so.

I touched my abdomen and found my hand was covered with blood. I had been stabbed in the gut. I was dying. I was burying this book as my last act. Burying it beyond the secret room even I might never find again.

He might be able to find me, track me down here.

But he'd never find the book.

And I'd come back and someday, someday I'd win.

I put my blood-covered hand on the upturned dirt, sealing the promise.

He was behind me again, I felt him coming and I forced myself to run. It was more of a drunken stumble, but I tried my best to escape.

I sat up gasping for breath, and peeled my sweat-soaked T-shirt from my body.

I glanced out the front window at the quiet night and saw a figure standing at my curb, staring at my house. I jumped to my feet and pulled on my jeans.

When I opened the front door to confront the person, he or she was gone.

I don't know how I fell asleep again, but I do know the rest of my night was no more restful than the beginning, and when I awoke it was already noon, and I had a lot of work to do.

After all, the movers might have unloaded everything, but I had boxes to unpack and things to arrange and a home to make. After food and a shower, I dove into my unpacking, starting with the basement, since you always got to start with the weapons.

I hefted the swords Dad had used on *Samurai Midnight*, the dagger Mom mistakenly got stabbed with on *Whirling Dervish* (no big—it was just a flesh wound), the scripts, crossbows, armor, books, battle axes, boxes of weird and unidentifiable smelly herbs that reminded me of the day I walked in on mom humming, surrounded with a bunch of candles. I wished now more than ever that we'd come to the moment when we'd both known it was time for me to hear her secrets.

She was dead now, and I could never be good enough. The scales had been balanced and I was found lacking. It was the only explanation—I hadn't been good enough.

I never liked seeing my parents get their butts kicked. Especially since I had inside knowledge—they could kick the butt of any of their so-called foes.

They rocked, after all.

I hadn't been working too long when I first crossed paths with Patrick Peterson, the infamous director of *Sometimes It's Tuesday* and untold other classics. After a particularly difficult day's work, Patrice (as those of us in the know refer to him) looked at me and said, "Oh, honey-child, nobody's ever gonna have to DNA your cute ass—nobody but Frank and Hank Black could be your parents." (Mom's name was Francine, so everybody always called her Frank. When I was growing up it made me feel hip, like I had two daddies or something.) "What you all do for me is pure magic. Nobody but y'all could pull off the things you folks do and not only live to tell about it, but escape with nary a scratch!"

I was eighteen when I did that film and even then I knew things weren't . . . quite right. I should have died from my stupidity during filming, but I lived to tell the tale. Less than a year later I heard someone calling me By-the-Book Black behind my back. He was making fun of me, but I took it as a compliment. I had learned to follow procedure and protocol, to practice and do my job well. I followed the rules and so got injured a lot less than many others.

I now picked up the last sword Mom had ever used, needing to burn off some energy. I flipped it around and hurried outside to the backyard I'd envisioned using for just this sort of practice.

All the while I was driving across country I'd been thinking about the great many stunts I'd been doing my entire life, from the first one to the most recent (perhaps last?). It was like I couldn't stop myself—it was a tape playing on and on in my head.

I swung the sword around me, acclimating to its weight, and then danced across the yard, thrusting, parrying, flipping and high kicking. Then I got into it, using my entire body as a weapon, leveling any and all opponents in my way, throwing one foot against the railing and tossing my body into a neat backflip. I landed on my feet, then dropped to one knee to deliver the killing blow to my invisible opponent. "Yah!" I yelled, in a bold, brave voice, followed quickly with, "Aieee!" when I saw *Her* in front of me.

"Gah!" she yelled as she stumbled backward.

"Uh, who are you and what are you doing here?" I said, scrambling to steady her. Her hand was as warm and soft as Michele's.

"I . . . I'm your neighbor and I saw you out here when I was coming home from work and decided to come over and say hello. I never knew real people could move like that."

"Oh, god, I'm so sorry." She had the greenest eyes I'd ever seen, and she was standing so close I could feel her breath on my lips.

"I'm Sydney Pierce. I live next door."

"Ty. Tyler Black." She had fantabulously soft hands. I cupped them, just wanting to prolong the tingling.

"All of us neighbors here have been talking about you, you know," she said. "I mean, the place has been vacant ever since the last tenant, who moved out a few years ago. Or so I heard. I just bought the place next door about six months ago myself." Her beige skirt was cut just above her shapely knees. Her silky long-sleeved brown blouse showed a bit of cleavage, with a gold cross nestled between her breasts. Her boots had three-inch heels and were not sensible at all. They were, however, sexy as hell, and I wanted her to use them to walk all over me.

No woman had ever done this to me. I was Hollywood bred

and knew how to hold my own. I was By-the-Book Black and never got distracted. Never. "Wow," I said, "so you're still moving in yourself, huh?"

"Oh, I'm situated now. Took a while though." She looked down and glanced upward through her lashes. "But I understand how it is, especially when you're trying to do it by yourself. That's the real reason I came over, to tell the truth. I wanted to help you unpack."

Nobody ever seriously offered to help someone else unpack unless they were dating. But she hadn't said, "if you need anything" or "call if you want help." She put it all in the active and I knew better than to question such help.

Especially since it was the perfect opportunity to get to know her. Her hand had felt perfect in mine, as if it always had been there and always would be. Great, I thought. Leave Hollywood but start thinking like some stupid romantic movie.

"I might not be the spiciest taco at the picnic," I said, "but I'm still not about to let such an offer go. I could use the help—so come on in!"

"Have you had a chance to meet the rest of our neighbors yet?" Sydney's boots made a light tap on the hardwood floor as I led her inside.

"No, not really."

"Well, we seem to be the lone singles in the valley of the families. If you *are* single, that is"—she paused, looking into my eyes.

"Very much so." She was going to be mine. I knew how to go after things with a single-minded enthusiasm, and that's exactly what I'd be doing with Sydney.

In the basement she admired my weapons and I told her I was a stuntperson. Ex-stuntperson. In the living room she marveled at how well I'd set up the stereo. She liked my two-man Henckel knives. She caressed the spines of books. She went from room to room as we chatted, giving herself the tour and discussing where things would go as we walked. She even knew enough to ask if I'd like my CDs alphabetized, and how I was planning on setting up my books.

"This is a nice space," she said. "Basement, kitchen, living room, family room, dining room—and four bedrooms with two-and-a-half baths?"

"Uh, yeah. Have you been here before?"

"Oh, uh, no."

I stopped. I tapped my booted foot on the floor and crossed my arms.

"Okay, fine. I was curious. I had to check it out when I heard Hollywood folks owned it. It was just kinda exciting, you know?"

"Oh, good grief. It's not like we—they—were famous or anything."

"Ty, this is the Midwest. Anything to do with Hollyweird is exciting. Oh, sorry."

"It's okay. We've referred to it as such."

"I snuck in when that guy you paid to take care of it left a door open by mistake. I made sure to lock up behind myself, though! It's just, I was bored and curious and dear god, could I sound any more retarded and loserish?"

I smiled at her and took her hand. "We're nobody. I'm nobody. They were nobody."

"No—you and they were somebody. Somebodies. You still are." She led me to the bedroom and I was filled with trepidation, since it was the bedroom. My bedroom, and of course it was a shambles. "Your bed isn't made," she said, noting the bare mattress on box springs. "You don't strike me as the type to sleep on a bare mattress."

"Uh, no, I'm not."

"Then where'd you sleep last night?"

"On the sofa."

She was still looking at me when she opened the closet and walked into a black hole.

I hadn't realized the house came with one of those.

I launched after her, grabbing her as she screamed.

We tumbled into cold unending blackness (it *was* a black hole—it's not like I had this much closet space), and I broke into a sweat and held onto her as tightly as I could and . . ."Ooof!" We hit a hard surface and it was dark, but at least I could breathe and she landed on top of me keeping us together, and I'd been able to cushion her landing, so it was all good—except maybe that we could perhaps be on some other planet, or, even worse, we could be someplace frightening, like inside the brain of some truly terrifying right-wing politician.

"Oh god, oh god," Sydney said, squirming in my arms. "Where are we? What happened?"

"Calm down. Are you hurt?" It was nice to be able to focus on her. I already knew I was all right, but this situation definitely wasn't.

"Uh, no . . . no . . . I don't think so. I think I'm okay."

"Then just take a deep breath and calm down." Only when I felt her relax did I loosen my hold. "I can't see anything, so we shouldn't let go of each other since we might get separated."

"I'm not going to argue that," she said in a shaky voice.

"Good." I helped her stand, keeping an arm around her.

"Um, Ty?"

"Yeah?"

"Where are we?"

I was afraid she was going to ask me that. "I don't know. I can't see anything. We were in my bedroom. You weren't looking where you were going and you walked into my closet and disappeared. I jumped after you."

"How very gallant of you—saving the damsel in distress and all."

"Yeah, that's me. Always willing to do the stupid."

"So saving me was stupid?"

"No—I just mean, me not thinking. Looking before leaping and all that. Anyway, we're apparently all right, though quite lost." Actually, not looking before leaping was not like me at all. I was By-the-Book Black and I did things methodically and with precision. But this was an emergency situation, so I guessed what I had done was all right. I had to save the girl, after all.

"It sure is dark here," she said.

I kept an arm around her while tentatively reaching out with my hand to see if I could feel anything. I couldn't. I slid a foot forward, hesitantly searching for a clue.

"Do you have your lighter?"

"Oh, yeah, of course." I pulled it out of my pocket. During an adolescent rebellion I'd smoked. Once. The cigarette had felt as if it belonged in my hand, and about ten minutes later I was craving another one.

The experience made me realize how easily addicted I was. It was good to learn that lesson then. Ever after I was careful around drugs—down to the painkillers I was put on for various breaks, sprains, dislocations, concussions and such. But I'd always carried a Zippo. It felt like I ought to. Plus, when some lovely lady needed a light, I could be her prince in black leather.

"How'd you know I carried one?" I asked.

"Aren't you a smoker?"

"No."

"Oh, I just thought you were, I guess."

"Do I smell funny or something?"

"No, silly—you smell great. It's just with the bike, leather jacket and, well, you've got this entire dark, handsome thing going on. It's like you *should* smoke."

"I don't bow to peer pressure."

"I get that now!"

In the light of my flickering Zippo, I could see we were standing at the end of a long, narrow hallway that seemed to stretch on forever. The walls were so close it was amazing we hadn't scraped them. The dirt floor made me think we were in an underground tunnel.

"Um, Ty?" Sydney asked. "Where did we come from?"

I looked up and saw a solid ceiling of dirt. "There's something not right here."

"I'm with you."

She was afraid, so I had to appear confident in order to keep her as calm as possible. I nodded forward. "Only one way to go."

We walked and I kept my eyes open for anything I could use to create a torch or lantern, since I didn't think my Zippo would last very long. The tunnel went on and on. It was as if we were rats in a maze, looking for cheese.

And then we came to the boarded-up dead end.

Sydney stepped forward and ran her fingers over the boards. "This isn't good. What do we do now?"

"Hold this," I handed her my lighter and kicked the boards. They were tightly together, blocking any view of what they covered, but when I kicked them I could feel a give, so I figured they weren't mounted on a wall. In other words, they were blocking the passage.

I'd been doing karate and kicking things down for most of my life, so it only took a few kicks for the boards to fragment and split, allowing us access to the rest of the tunnel.

"This is not right," Syd said, again grasping my arm like it was her life preserver. The passage gaping in front of us seemed to go for an eternity and beyond. "This is like something out of Harry Potter, all magical . . . mystical. There's no way all this could fit in your house."

"Yeah, to all of that," I said. I was having serious flashbacks to Tomb Raiders or Buffy or that *Raiders of the Lost Ark* rip-off I'd worked on. One key difference: this was real. I pulled away from her momentarily so I could take off my shirt. I had a sports bra on beneath it. I cut the sleeves off with my keys, then put it back on. I wrapped one sleeve around a chunk of the wooden boards. I took the lighter back from Syd and set the material aflame.

The Zippo was hot when I put it back in my pocket. I picked up several more large pieces of wood and shoved them, with the other shirt sleeve, down the back of my jeans.

"Let's go," I said.

Chapter the Fourth

A little farther down the corridor we came to another obstacle: a huge chasm. I looked at this gaping hole and thought of a huge maw, waiting to eat us up whole.

But there was a rope hanging down just over its middle.

"This isn't good," Sydney said once more, but she didn't move, she just stood staring across to the far side.

"We can do this." It was my first stunt ever. I had been so young, I was flat-chested enough to double for the adolescent male lead of the film.

The stakes then hadn't been high in some ways, since there was a cushion just a few feet down, and we did it all in sections which even further decreased the danger. With the safety precautions, it required agility and stamina, but there was no risk.

For me, the real stake was Mom watching. She was there, assessing my work as we did the scene over and over again, moving the cameras around to get different angles at different moments.

I was glad she never looked nervous. In fact, she looked as if she had no question that I'd be able to do the job as many times as it took. I still remembered the purple amethyst she wore that day. I had the random thought that I hadn't found the necklace among her things yet.

That was the first time I ever worked with Michele. She was the girl. They had wanted someone to stand in for her during those scenes, but she'd insisted she could do it. She always was rather spunky. I'd been especially careful with her.

"When I say, jump into my arms," I now told Sydney. "I'll catch you."

"Wait a second," she said, holding up the torch. "Do you think you can throw this to the other side? We don't want to lose it."

"Good thinking." I took it and carefully threw it across. I knew that if it extinguished I could create another with the spare materials I had, but I didn't want to waste anything.

Once it was safely on the far side, giving us even greater perspective on the crossing, I smiled at Sydney and squeezed her hand. "We'll be fine. Trust me."

I ran a few steps and leapt out over the pit, easily grabbing the rope and swinging on it. When I was sixteen I could do a standing long jump of six-and-a-half feet. This was a joke to me now, even though it was a good ten feet out to it.

I did my Tarzan and yelled, "Jump!" just as I was approaching the apex near Sydney.

She was perfect, leaping right into my arms. Of course she was perfect, I thought. She was The One.

"Hard part's done," I said, as we swung back and forth, gaining momentum. "Now I just have to toss you to the other side. On the count of three."

"Ty!"

I held on. "On the count of three. One . . . two . . . three . . ." She seemed ready, so I tossed. She landed and fell to her hands and knees.

I followed on the next upswing, just before the rotten boards holding the rope split.

They crashed right behind me. If I had still been swinging, I would have plunged to my death. Seemed a bit cliché.

"Oh my god, Ty, that was incredible!"

All I could think was that I did that when I was sixteen. It wasn't a challenge. At all. But Sydney hugging me didn't suck.

"Do you have any idea what's going on?" Sydney asked, holding onto my arm as we walked further down the hall.

"This could just be a dream." I was hoping it was, since it was all impossible, but I was sure it wasn't. Bottom line, I was clueless and didn't like it one bit.

"No, it can't. We're both here, together. Plus, we hit the floor pretty hard back there. Something like that would've woken us up for sure."

"Unless we just dreamt we hit the ground and that the other is here. But anyway, what do *you* propose is going on?"

"I'm not sure but this doesn't look good."

I stared up at the bare wall of dirt. "This is like stunts one-oh-one. When I was driving out here, I was remembering every single stunt I ever did, and it seems like maybe somebody or something was listening, 'cause the Powers that Be certainly ain't trying very hard here. I could do this drunk with a broken leg and a dislocated shoulder." I stepped back and ran up the wall as far as I could, using my own momentum to propel me up it until I could grab the ledge overhead and haul myself up. I glanced around, but didn't see anything to aid me with pulling Syd up, so I pulled my shirt off, lay on the ledge, and stretched down. "Grab hold."

"Let's do the torch first," Syd said, tying the end of the sleeve around the torch so I could lift it up. I liked how practical she was in such a bizarre situation. When I dropped the shirt back down, Sydney stared at it for a moment before looking up at me. "I . . . I don't know if you can lift me so easily. I weigh quite a bit more than a torch you know."

"Take the shirt already, Syd."

"You are strong," she said when I'd pulled her up.

"I'm . . . I *was* a stuntperson," I said, leading us ever onward. "A lot of the job requires knowing how to fake—fake punches and fake getting hit . . . fake kicks and smunches and all that." At each turn, I peered ahead, ensuring we wouldn't step into anything worse by accident. "But for the work the Blacks do . . . *did* . . . I needed to stay in shape. And keep learning more and more—sword play, martial arts, gymnastics, acrobatics. Bottom line, I can squat you, bench you, hell, I can probably even curl you without break-ing a sweat."

"Brag much?"

I had to laugh. "Just a bit. I'm from Hollywood, after all. And I actually worked there, which means I had to learn how to sell myself."

She stopped dead in her tracks. I ran into her back. "Ty? Please tell me you have a clue?" Syd laid a hand on my arm, sending warm tingles through me. When I didn't answer immediately, she con-tinued, obviously finally freaking out about our situation, "God, I don't know how we got here in the first place and now you're off in La-La Land and I can't—"

I grabbed her by her arms. "Syd, I'll go through it, get to the other side, and figure out how to turn it off. 'Else I'll come back through and get you, 'kay?"

"Nobody can get through that!"

"Maybe nobody else, but me . . . no problema. Just watch." Whoever had been looking through my mind for my worst night-mares had misread this one. This one I had down.

If you've seen many movies in the past decade, you've seen the whirly-blade obstacle—the one where the hero(es) have to leap and twist and time their moves to avoid becoming thin-sliced sandwich fillings because huge circular-saw blades are busy slicing down from the ceiling and cross wise. A seemingly impenetrable barrier. But they never hit each other, so there was a pattern. One merely had to watch to figure it out.

I slowly stretched my body, reaching forward as far as I could with my fingers spread. I rotated my head, feeling the cracking of my spine. I brought each leg up in turn, grasping it and pulling it tight against my chest.

And all the while I watched the blades, learning their pattern, memorizing the timing and making it a part of me.

If you were fighting someone you had to react. In stuntwork, you had to react, but know exactly how to do so, when to pull back, and have wicked good reaction time. And you also had to know your blocking and timing—when to jump, when to kick, when to thrust.

This was just like learning my blocking.

Except with fatal consequences if I failed.

Good thing I never failed. At least, almost never.

I took one, quick deep breath and ran into the melee of blades, flipping into the air and twisting to the side to pass above the first cross-wise cutter. I hit the ground and dropped to my back, bending my knees fully so I could lie on the floor while the blade passed just above me.

"Bend, hop, jump, down, run, over, wait," I spoke my actions aloud, repeating my blocking to myself. One fuck up would be my death. "Go!"

I twisted, turned, danced and flipped through it all.

Well, almost all of it. I was flipping over a horizontal blade so I was horizontal with the floor when I noticed a big switch a dozen feet up and back. Quick change in blocking.

"Up, over, jump," I muttered. "Right, right, up, flip and grab!" I grabbed the pole that ran wall-to-wall, and used a basic hand-to-hand to flip the switch and turn off all the blades.

All told, it was fun. Difficult and challenging, but fun nonetheless. Which wasn't surprising, since I enjoyed puzzles and . . . trials. It was almost as if someone had been systematically testing me, like they wanted to know what I was capable of—or else remind me what I could do.

Now, it was pretty silly that there was an on/off switch, but that was just the nature of predetermined trials. I stood on a blade and looked around the shiny room and suddenly realized there was something I needed to learn—needed to do—and this wasn't the way to it. But I had to get Sydney out of here, wherever here was, safely first.

Syd made me hold her hand while we walked through the maze of stilled blades, just in case they reanimated.

At the far side there was a door.

I almost hated to see what was on the other side of it. But I couldn't let Sydney see me filled with trepidation and fear, so I boldly opened the door, stepped through and conked my head against my shoe rack, knocking my combat boots to the floor as Sydney fell onto me.

. . . Sydney was moaning and thrusting upward against . . . Him.

He came inside of her, even as she screamed, "Tom!" and looked at her wristwatch.

He collapsed on her and I knew this was the current Sydney and her current boyfriend and it was just last night.

"Ty, Ty—what's the matter?"

"Huh?" I shook my head, pulling myself out of the vision thing and back into reality.

Sydney reached a hesitant hand out to touch me.

Here she was, worried about me, touching me, after she spent last night with *Tom*. I wanted to call her on it, point out how she was acting—flirting with me after she had sex with Tom just last night and now she was sitting here, caressing my cheek.

What was she? *Some sort of common whore?*

Where the hell'd that come from? This was a woman *I'd loved for centuries*, what the hell was I thinking?

I released her hand and lowered my face so she couldn't see my expression. "I'm fine. Now. I just phased out briefly. Conked out." Somehow I knew the dreams I'd been having were real, and so were these visions. It was all the truth and it made no sense.

"Ty, why do I feel like you're not exactly telling me every-thing?" She was now petting my hair, running her fingers through the strands.

God, that felt good. Calming. "Uh, we just fell out of a black hole in my closet. And now you're questioning my veracity?" I entwined my fingers with hers, pulling our hands down to her thigh and effectively changing the subject. Or so I figured.

"So what are you gonna do next?" she asked.

"Dunno. I'm thinking shower, eat—"

She pulled her hand away to smack my thigh. "I meant about all the mysteries of this house."

"*All* the mysteries? We've found one. As in singular."

"Well what are you gonna do about it?"

"You seem stable and understanding about all of this. This is just freaky shit. And it's my house." I scrambled to my feet to gain the relative safety of my bedroom.

"And so it's your freaky shit, again—what are you gonna do about it?" She followed me out of the closet and flitted restlessly around the room.

She had a really nice ass. And why the hell was I noticing such a thing? "I'm gonna eat and shower. Then maybe search the house for any other freaky shit, secret passages, black holes et cetera."

"But what are you going to do about your closet?" She closed my closet door and then opened it. It was still just my closet.

"Move my clothes? In case that happens again? Or else maybe build a brick wall to effectively close it off and could that get any more metaphorical?" I put a hand on her waist. It was like I couldn't help but touch her.

"Glad to see the prioritization. You don't want to lose your shoes, after all." She stepped so close to me I could feel her breath on my cheek.

"Hey, there's some jeans hanging in there that I've *finally* got broken in right."

"I've been dreaming about this house." Her eyes grew intense. "I didn't want to tell you that because it's freaky shit, as you say. But after what we just went through, I think I should at least be honest."

"So, what did you dream?" My own murky nightmares were starting to solidify in my brain. Secret rooms and endless terrifying tests were a big part of them.

"It was mostly about a secret room, hidden behind a stone wall, and there was something important about that room. But I was terrified to go near it, and knew everything bad that could happen would happen if I did," she finished, pretty much whispering as we grew closer and closer.

A hidden room? This was beyond freaky shit, this was freak-out time. "You maybe might wanna go home now." I was thinking that if I remembered enough of my dreams, I would know how to find the secret room, and now I believed it existed. This house had secrets. Maybe mom's secrets. The room was down there, somewhere. I just couldn't find it with an audience, in case I failed.

"You want me to leave just when it's getting interesting?" Her chest was heaving and I could tell she wanted me to notice. And notice I did—as well as that an extra button or two had come undone on her blouse during our adventure. I remembered how good her nubile body felt in my arms as we swung over the pit of peril.

"It's my freaky shit, so no worry to you," I said. Adrenaline was coursing through my veins, pumping me up, exciting me, turning me on. "And . . . fuck, you'd better leave. Now." It was more than just adrenaline, though. It was like during everything that'd happened I'd started tapping into something within me, something powerful and primal—and now all that energy and power was juicing me, and I *liked* it.

"Why?" She put her hands on my arms and stepped even closer to me, looking right into my eyes. She licked her lips, slowly and sensuously.

"If you don't leave now, I'm gonna pin you against that wall— the one right behind you—and make you scream."

"Please." She was practically panting as she stood with her shoulders and hands flat against the wall.

"Please no or please yes?"

"I don't know."

I felt like a predator as I advanced on her. Her nipples were standing up, hard and rigid, under the covering of her blouse. I took her hands in mine and lifted them above her head, holding them against the wall. Pinning her to the wall. "You spent the night with *him*. You were with *him* last night, at least your body was. But you"—I suddenly knew that when she had looked at her watch the night before she was wondering if I was asleep yet— "you were thinking of *me* when *he* was inside of you." I shoved my thigh up into her crotch so she moaned and opened her legs more.

"I don't know what's going on," she said. "Please, Ty, don't do this."

I realized I could easily overpower her and take what I wanted. "What is *this*?"

"Ty, do you really want to . . . do this?" She was gasping for air. Our bodies were grinding together.

"You're mine," I said, grasping both her hands in my left. I touched her hair . . . her cheek . . . her breast . . . Down to her hip, tracing over to her inner thigh. Her crotch. My sense of reason tried to scream for my attention, but it was as if I had lost control of myself.

My phone started ringing. Which was strange, since almost no one knew my number. I hadn't even given it to Christie yet.

Sydney was frozen, pressed up against me. "Are you going to get that?"

I suddenly realized how we were standing, where my thigh was, where my fingers were. "Oh, god! I'm so sorry!"

My answering machine, set up on the floor on the other side of the room, kicked on. " 'All the world's a stage, all the men and women merely players.' This is Ty. Leave a message and I'll get back to you if I feel like it."

Syd was staring at me with a somber expression.

I couldn't believe I'd almost . . . It was almost rape. Except it wasn't, since she was going along with it. Quite a bit along with it, in fact. But still, she'd asked me to stop and I hadn't. I'd been enjoying it. What was going on with me? This wasn't like me. Who was I becoming?

"Ty," a voice said over my machine. I wanted to grab the phone before the caller said another word, but it was too far. "I got your new number from your agent. I . . . I just wanted to see how you were doing. I wanted to make sure you were okay. Give me a call, please?" She rattled off a series of numbers, then said softly, "Oh, and this is . . . Michele. Micky. In case you didn't know."

Syd was leaning against the wall, staring at the machine. "That wasn't who I thought it was, was it?"

I shrugged, looking down at the floor. "Who'd you think it was?"

"I dunno."

"You wouldn't have said anything if you didn't."

"It's stupid."

"What already?"

"Michele. She said her name was Michele. That *wasn't* Michele Anne Browning, was it?"

"Uh, yeah. It was." It was time to let go of Sydney. I had to pry myself away. Once there was some distance between us a drink seemed a good idea. I headed down to the kitchen and grabbed a Miller Lite.

Her boots sounded on the stairs as she followed me. "Ty. She just left her home *and* cell numbers on your machine!"

"Did you eat dinner?" I opened the fridge and stared inside, scoping out the options, which were none and none. "Or should I find enough for two?"

"No, I haven't eaten yet. I was just climbing out of my car when I saw you in the backyard. But that doesn't matter. That's not the topic."

"Okay, so what I'm seeing in the quick-dinner options here are—somewhere that delivers."

She came to my side and wrapped an arm around my waist. Like we were together. A couple. "What can I do to help?"

"Tell me the name of your fave pizza delivery joint and what you like on your pie."

"Order from Cottage Inn. They're in the book. I can't actually stay for dinner, though. But I still want to know why Michele Anne Browning calls you."

"I was her stunt double. We got to be friends. Kind of." I turned to face her. "Why can't you stay for grub?"

She started edging toward the front door. "Well, um, my boyfriend—his name is Tom—is coming over to . . ."

I walked toward her. She wouldn't be so worried after being so comfortable unless she was attracted to me.

"Uh . . . spend the night . . . We're having dinner first, though and he's due over at any moment." Her back was against the front door.

I was all but dry humping her again. It was like I couldn't control myself. "Your perfume is driving me insane," I said, the heady aroma filling my senses and overwhelming me.

"Ty, Ty . . ." she moaned, then, as she tried to pull away, as if she was trying to change the subject, "Tell me . . . so tell me . . ."

"What?" I asked, gently sucking at her pulse point.

"Is it true Browning stands on boxes during filming since she's so short?"

I pushed away. "What is with your fixation on her?"

"I don't have a fixation on her—it just seemed odd her calling you at home and all that."

I was uptight. On edge. Not myself. I wasn't sure who I was, but it definitely wasn't me. I tried for sarcastic humor. "You would so not believe how much money goes into boxes each year. And it's such a pain, how big the boxes are for each person—the bigger the star, the bigger the box. I mean, Tom Cruise's box in his next movie is taller than I am. It's ridiculous."

She stared at me like a squirrel standing in the middle of the road eating a nut and waiting to get run over.

"I'm sorry," I said, pushing away from her. "I'm not quite myself today. I'm By-the-Book Black. Even keel and all that. Not like this."

"It's all right," Sydney said, pulling me into her arms. "You've been through a lot lately. It's okay." She was soothing me and then I heard a car door slam outside. She pushed away from me. "That's Tom."

It looked almost as if she was afraid. "You'd better go then, huh?"

"Yeah."

As soon as she'd gone I went downstairs and grabbed a sword, strutting through the house yelling about ghosts, comeuppance, come and get it. "Oh, for fuck's sake, don't play all hard to get." I was still way off-keel, and going ever further off-kilter with my failure to be my usual calm, cool and collected self.

I went through the house, searching it from top to bottom, for any other secrets, passages, or additional mystical crap.

It was clean from what I could see. Even my closet was normal now.

From my bedroom window I saw an Expedition parked in Syd's drive. It obviously belonged to a man with a very small penis.

I wandered outside, pretending to check on the front lamp, but wanting to get a better look at Syd's place. I saw the lights go out in her living room and go on upstairs, in what I assumed was her bedroom.

And then those lights went out as well.

And no one left.

I went back inside, stomping my way to my bedroom, to my closet. To anything to keep me from getting any more stalker-like.

I was going to try it again and again until it worked and got me back there. I wanted . . . no. I *needed* to find the room I knew had to be there. Sydney had dreamt of it, and so had I. It was hiding something. I just knew it.

I slunk toward my closet. "Oh, closet o' mine, the cause of such torment, such pain, such trouble, and now such wardrobe-suckage!"

Just because I was just a stuntperson didn't mean I couldn't drama queen with the best of them. I slapped the back of my hand against my forehead and then, just to catch it off-guard, slammed the door open.

Chapter the Fifth

I looked into my closet and saw my suits and trousers.

I closed the door. Opened it again, and saw my shirts, ties, and sweaters.

Closed it again. Opened it again. Still just as neatly organized as the last time I saw it before it all became a black hole.

I closed it, went down to the kitchen, cracked another Miller Lite, slipped my pocket Maglite into my, well, pocket. Then I returned and reached for the closet door.

I paused, thinking about what Sydney had been doing when she'd fallen in. Maybe I needed to be equally distracted in order for it to happen again. After all, things happened when you were looking the other way all the time.

So I looked the other way, opened the closet and stepped in . . . to some other place. Wherever that was.

I fell, hit the ground, rolled and jumped to my feet, ready to rumble. Just in case. But then I realized I wasn't where I'd been before—I was someplace else. This wasn't a dirt passage, it was a dark, paneled hallway leading toward a light in the distance. I carefully made my way toward it, wondering why Sydney had taken me somewhere else than I ended up by myself?

It was annoying that my focus kept drifting to Sydney. Sydney was straight. Or at least she thought so and I wasn't in the habit of recruiting. I'd never figured out why so many liked straight girls so much. And, well, I already had a toaster oven. Plus she had some beefsteak of a boyfriend, who *so* had nothing on me.

It was when I got to the end of the hall and saw the room in front of me that I understood a big difference between the place Sydney had taken us and this place I had brought myself: that place had been filled with the greatest challenges of my career, whereas I was now looking directly at my greatest fear. This was something only I would know, but even I would never admit it, until now.

The last challenge in that other realm had been whirly blades that were easy to do in movies, but dangerous as hell in real life.

But now I was looking at a room that was the set from my most difficult work—the day I'd almost died. I should have died, but I hadn't. I still couldn't figure out why I hadn't died. But now I knew . . . I realized . . .

There's something worse than death.

Life. Life with death, actually.

Or, more precisely, life *after* death.

I realized that this wasn't the first time I'd lived. I'd been alive before, and found The One, but I kept losing her and had to go on without her. So many times before.

I knew that to understand what my dreams meant, to figure out who I was in the greater scheme of things, to know what I needed to do, I simply had to overcome this challenge that I'd obviously set up for myself.

I got it now. In some other life, I'd set all this up to guard my secrets from anyone other than me. This was the secret place I'd been searching for.

But was I going to have to relive that stunt? Feel the certain pain of death again? I realized I was sweating and for the first time in my life, I couldn't make my body obey my thoughts. I wanted to go inside and face whatever it was that waited. My body obviously didn't agree.

I don't know how long I was frozen, warring with myself. Finally, I managed a small step, then another. I could feel a wave of cold as I passed from the dark passageway to the brightly lit set, and the strain of making myself move had my heart pounding hard in my ears.

One more step, and I was through.

I did a flying backward somersault through the window, out onto the balcony. It was all happening exactly as it had that day, horribly the same. He was coming after me and hitting me before I could find my footing. My foot glanced off a piece of the window frame and I was tumbling toward the railing, hitting it and flying backward off the end of it.

The pads were set up on the ground off the side of it. There was only a car where I was about to hit. Like that day, I hoped they caught it on film, since it was going to hurt. Seemingly in slo-mo, like the most awful times in life, I flipped in the air, trying to work out how to best land while breaking as little of my body as possible when I noticed something wrong—Michele was standing next to the director, next to a camera. Watching me.

But she wasn't part of this movie. I realized that wasn't right and so I could control this. I landed on the car hood on my feet and then jumped to the ground. The crew began rushing around, but I ignored everyone except Micky.

"Nice job," she said. "But—"

"Don't even try it," I said, waving a hand so all the window-dressing disappeared. None of that belonged here, so it went away now. All it took was a single focused thought. "You have something to show me. You're hiding something, and I need to know what is." I looked deep into her eyes, and I knew I was dreaming or imagining or something, since I thought, looking into her now, that she had feelings for me. But Sydney was The One.

I didn't think, right then. I didn't have time to figure it all out. I couldn't afford to be confused, but I was.

Fuck it. This wasn't real.

But yet I still couldn't even try to kiss Michele, who was looking at me like that was just what she wanted, since this was the place I'd nearly died. Should have died. Was I even alive, now?

"This isn't about that." Michele pointed at the door of the building in front of us. "It's about that."

The door flew open and it was as if I was looking down a long corridor toward a dark room where a figure crouched. I stepped toward it and the room churned into a black hole that swallowed . . . everything. I was alone in the universe except for the crouched figure.

I realized the figure crouching was me, and I looked like a Native American. Then the other me disappeared and I was alone in this hole in the ground, a dark, dank room in the ground and there was no one there at all.

On one wall was a bloody dagger with an elaborately engraved hilt. There were some strange markings on the blade. The blood was dried on it, and I guessed it'd been on there for a long, long, longer, longest time.

I didn't touch it.

Mounted on another wall was a beautiful sword that I wanted to play with. It was incredibly balanced, delightfully designed, and fit my hand and the strength of my arm as if it had been made for me. It whistled as it sliced air.

Mama liked. I'd be taking this with me. It felt as if it was mine—belonged with me, was a part of me.

Next to where this fabulous sword had been hanging was a wicked cool battleaxe, and crossbow, shield, long bow and quarter staff.

This was just like Toys "R" Us for psychotic adults! Cool! But then I had to wonder if I could take this stuff with me when I left. That is, if I could figure out how to leave.

One step at a time. I'd gone through a lot to get here, so I wanted to figure out where I was and what it contained. This was what I had been meant to find, and I still didn't understand why.

In the middle of the third wall was a stand with a box on it. I picked it up and realized it wasn't a box at all—it didn't have any sort of a latch or opening or seam where the wood came together. It was a solid block of wood without any way of opening. *This box was mine, and only I could open it.*

I held it in my hands, pressing my palms against it, trying to figure it out. *Just holding it made me want to strut. It made me feel powerful and in control.* My palm suddenly sank into the wood as if it was making a mold of my hand. It felt like the stuff makeup artists used to create casts and molds and impressions. But just a moment before it had been solid wood. Oak, I think. *But the only thing that mattered was that I had it now.*

And then the wood was entirely solid again and the block opened, revealing an ancient book with leather binding. The pages were brittle, and it looked as if the text had been hand-inked. By several—many—different people. I sat on the floor and began reading . . . reading writing that looked to be from more than a dozen different pens, but was all probably illegible to most people in the galaxy today. I could read it because it bore a strong resemblance to my own writing.

I wrote this. And my energy had unlocked this book—a karmic fingerprinting had just occurred.

I flipped through the pages, reading passages here and there, and taking note of the strange-looking recipes peppered throughout. They all had crazy-ass ingredients, like eye of newt, twice-blessed sage, the legs from six dung beetles that drowned in single-malt scotch, and the finely ground lungs from an anemic cow. Ingredients that were to be added in a specific order while reciting certain phrases and words.

Well, duh. I wasn't always the spiciest taco at the picnic. Sharpest needle in the haystack. Best-aged single-malt in the cellar. These were spells. My spells, collected over many lifetimes, over a lot of long, searching years. I had hidden them myself and somehow my mother's house had been the conduit to this place. The black hole, the freaky shit, it was all my shit, and all about leading me to this moment in my life.

I was a witch, and I had power.

I started seeing all the ways I'd avoided injury at work, and realized it wasn't just dumb luck. It was magick. I saw how I'd influenced the laws of physics, right down to not dying when I should have.

Dear sweet God, I was stupid. I'd been doing shit and looking the other way for years. Mom and Dad had done it too—beat the odds so many times that a less skeptical world would have called them magicians. Just call me Cleopatra. What a selective memory I had!

Patrice had said as much. I wondered how much he knew.

I wondered how much anyone knew.

But if Mom and Dad both, or either one of them, had power, how had they died?

And I also wondered what, exactly, were the specifications and ramifications of the spells I'd cast in previous lives. And just how powerful was I?

Did I kill my parents? Did I cause them to die? Was that part of me remembering? Was it the triggering event to make me remember and bring me to Michigan and this house and Sydney and . . . Where the hell'd that thought come from?

This was the book from my dream. The book I'd buried and put a spell on, so it would always bring me back here. So I could keep building from one life to another, gaining greater power with each life.

I sat on the floor and read. And read. And read some more.

I read about the power and how to use it. I read about my past and those in it. And I read about me and Sydney—our multifarious lives and names. There was always just the one love: each other.

And as I read I felt the power welling up within me, gathering for greater things to come.

Chapter the Sixth

I took the sword with me when I used my new-found telekine-sis to propel myself back into my home. As I'd read, I'd worked on some of the things the book was teaching me—tapping into the powers I had. I knew I had a ways to go to master them all, but I was beginning to know what I could do and how to do it.

But for now, I could try to learn more from the book, or else I could see what I could teach myself.

The bar was crowded. Noisy.

The bass pumped through me. My feet started moving all on their own, even as my palms started to itch.

I looked around the dimly lit joint, assessing the space and sitch. There were a lot of women here, including a bunch of butches and andro-dykes. Fortunately, there were also some major femme hotties.

I took a deep breath, centering myself and my energies. I'd always had a problem cruising and trying to pick up women—or even just a woman—as in singular. You'd think I could simply slip on another persona and become someone else, like I did when I auditioned. But even though I was in the biz, I was rather shy.

want to rumble with her. *Or maybe I did. I could win, after all. I'd always win.*

"Um, balloons?" I said, pointing to the b-day balloons. "And since all of you," I waved my hand, indicating the couples, "are paired off, well, it made sense it'd be Zoë."

This conversation was pointless, I abruptly realized. I'd come here to work my power and increase my knowledge, but I'd chickened out. Now I was flirting with a stranger, even though I knew Syd was the one for me.

It suddenly occurred to me that I had no reason for being here.

I leaned over and laid a light one on Zoë's lips. "I need to go." I feigned a yawn. "Moving and all has been taxing."

I was walking out when a fight broke out over the pool table. A bunch of drunken straight boys started arguing and one threw the cue ball at the wide-screen TV, fracturing it. Now that sucked moldy moose meat.

All of the worst badass butches were charging toward the boys who were now armed with pool cues. I raised my hand and laid out a sweet peace spell, calming everyone.

Wow. I wondered if I could do that to the world? That'd be wicked cool—world peace through magick. I wondered if there was a de-testosteroning spell in my repertoire as well?

As everyone stopped in mid-roar, looking lost as they wondered why they had been upset in the first place, I walked up to the boys and looked right at them.

"So you're all leaving now, right?" I said. "And you're never coming back again since you had such a suck time."

"Yeah, man, this place is the pits," one guy said, leading the rest of the pack outside, and forgetting whatever it was that had caused issues in the first place.

That left the broken screen, and after a long stare from me, it wasn't broken anymore. I felt wicked cool. Oh, dude, I was *so* the stud tonight. I was handsome and charming and smart and could have any girl in this bar. I was in better shape than most butches here, and sure-as-shit dressed better than they were.

And for fuck's sake, this was the Midwest, and I was a gen-u-wine Hollyweird stuntperson. My stories could so rock their worlds.

"I thought you were leaving." Zoë slipped her warm hand up my arm, and it broke me out of my reverie.

I looked at her. I was in tune with so much now, it was as if all my nerve endings were standing on end like little radio towers picking up every single feeling in the room.

Many eyes were upon me. I touched Zoë's elbow, ran my hand down her arm till I grasped her hand, which I brought to my lips and kissed gently, looking up to wink at her. "Yeah, I was. I'm going, now."

I looked around the bar, meeting many eyes. And then I left. After all, you always gotta leave them wanting more.

I felt Zoë still reaching for me when I was long gone. I was now in tune with so much; my power grew with each moment.

I was on the highway, my Harley purring in the night as I merged to the right when a Hummer shot up from behind me, almost running me over. I swerved to the left, but someone was already there. I was about to be sandwiched when the Hummer yielded me enough room to bolt ahead.

I looked over and noticed it was a boy driving the beast. *Of course.*

People who drive big vehicles can't seem to behave like normal people, so less than half-a-mile down, that same damn Hummer decided it needed to exit and damn anyone in his way. *I needed that de-testosteroning spell again.*

He cut me and two other cars off, then rammed his brakes so I almost rear-ended him. He needed to wreck himself before he took others out with him.

The light turned green. He veered to the right and I passed him, hoping that was the last I'd see of him. I happened to glance in my rearview mirror and the Hummer was spinning down the embankment, rolling over and over.

He deserved it.

✿

I pulled into my garage, listening to my neighborhood—the sounds as well as thoughts. I knew I could hear more, but it was only this cul-de-sac I was interested in. I wasn't interested in all the dirty, nasty thoughts the neighbor boys were having. None of them were original in the least. And, well, the girls' thoughts were equally gross to me. Ick!

Sydney was having sex with Tom. But she was thinking about me.

I made my way to my bedroom without moving a muscle, and only when I got there did I realize my feet weren't on the floor. I was hovering.

This was a dream. This couldn't be happening. No one should have this much power. Strength.

I raised my hands and looked at them. When I touched my fingertips sparks fell off them.

I was strong. *Too strong.* I could make things happen. I could do things purely by the power of my will.

No one should have this much power. *But I did.*

For a reason, I thought, even though right then I didn't know what the reason might be.

I went to bed. I fell asleep without undressing or even brushing my teeth.

I ran along the edge of the forest, leaping logs and other debris. I loved the sure and graceful feel of this body. I looked up and saw them talking at the edge of a cliff. Fog shrouded their figures, but I would always know her, as I would always know him.

She seemed so small and frail next to his large and ungainly form. I watched from afar, ensuring her safety as he took her into his arms and kissed her.

She let him kiss her. *I stepped out of the forest, revealing myself to* them. He grinned wolfishly at me, reaching for the crossbow on his hip, but she kissed him and sent him on his way.

I felt arms entwine around my neck, pulling me down. I reared from the unexpected grasp, bucking away from her, surprised at the strength in this lithe form.

"Ice, oh Ice," she said, practically swooning about me. "We are to be wed! He proposed marriage to me and I accepted!" She was kissing all over my furry face. I caught a glance at my appearance in a puddle and realized I was hidden in the guise of a doe.

I felt my body . . . melt and change and twist and . . . morph, until I was in human form again, holding her lithe body in my very human arms.

She was on top of me, still kissing me. "Isolde, I am sorry, truly. I sometimes forget myself when you take such shapes!"

Chapter the Seventh

The next morning I awoke feeling gratified and powerful and . . . guilty. And then I felt a particular sense ting, letting me know where Syd was. *She was my soul mate. What I kept searching for.*

Lifting the drape, I peeked at my neighbor's drive. Syd was just parking her Honda. She was nearly to her front door when she turned sharply to look at where I stood.

I dropped the drape. I didn't want to appear the stalker. I stood with my back against the curtain, panting. She'd seen me. *I'd been made. She'd caught me.*

"I'll always love you," I called out with what was left of my voice as the flames engulfed me. It took more than an hour for me to die. The lucky ones died from the smoke early on. The not-so-lucky ones were slow-cooked.

I'd never been lucky.

It was excruciating as the fire peeled the skin from my body.

I could no longer speak. I couldn't use what was left of my hands or arms, since they'd been chained behind me to the stake, but I focused everything I was, had been, would ever be, to ensure we'd be together—some day, some time.

I was crying, screaming from the pain, but still I wove the complex web of spells necessary—knowing that years and lifetimes of spells would some day come to fruition.

In my dreams, she came back to me—again and again. She wore different bodies—blonde, brunette, tall, short, slender, full-figured. I wore different bodies, too. But it always came down to us two, meeting life after life.

I followed her, knowing some day I'd win. We'd be together. Some day I would have the power to make it happen.

Someday it'd happen. Some time, it'd be forever. Like it was meant to be.

I showered, thinking about how those pissed-off guys at the bar would've ended up hurting others, and instead I'd calmed them (and everyone else) down.

I hadn't actually meant to hurt the dude in the Hummer, but now I wasn't so sure I hadn't simply taken him out just before he killed someone else.

I was good. Not bad. Not evil. I did right. By stopping him I had saved countless others.

I slicked back my still-wet hair, dressed in all black, and finished my unpacking (telekinesis is wicked cool), while eating breakfast.

I wanted to know what was going on with Sydney and Tom, so I reached out to her mind with mine but barely brushed into it before I pulled back.

It just felt wrong. I couldn't do that. Not to Syd.

But I didn't trust myself to listen through him without controlling him and making him do things. After the Hummer, I didn't know what I could set in motion. But as I pulled back, I realized I could still see what was happening in the room, even if I wasn't in either of their heads. I could see places I wasn't at.

Yet another new power. Cool beans.

"Tom," Sydney said, *putting a plate of food in front of him, "we need to talk."*

"Uh-oh. That sounds serious. Where's the syrup?" he replied, digging in.

"I'll get it for you." She left her food to serve him. "Where's this relationship going?"

He was such a selfish bastard he just started chowing down, mumbling between mouthfuls. "I was thinking maybe marriage—sometime.

Children. A family. I mean, that is what you want, right?" I was sur-prised he was already awake.

"Tom, I'm just not feeling it. I'm not sure if I've ever felt it."

"Sydney, what are you saying?"

"I'm not in love with you."

"Sydney, are you breaking up with me? Was last night just a . . . what's it called? Sympathy fuck? I thought you were there with me. I thought you were feeling everything too. Sydney, I love you!"

"I thought I loved you, too." She was crying now.

He left his food to pull her into his arms. "I know all of this stuff can get scary. But see, I love you, so I'm not gonna give up so easily."

She pulled away, staring up at him as she backed up. "Tom, I . . . I hate that I've hurt you and, but—it might be best if you left. Now." She was afraid. I didn't have to read her mind to know that.

I stood. If she was afraid, I was worried. I hadn't even needed to look inside her to see her fear, but now I tried to read Tom and realized I couldn't. I could see inside Syd, but not Tom. I used my mind to pull a book from my upstairs' shelves and I intercepted it at the door. If things started going downhill, I could run over to her place pretending to either loan or return the book to her.

"Sydney . . ." he said. "I love you and I don't want to lose you."

"There's someone else. You do need to leave. Now."

"I can't . . . I can't believe you're doing this to me."

"It's not about you. I just don't feel it."

Part of me wanted to lean into his brain and make him be an asshole, but I knew that would be wrong. And since I couldn't read him, I wasn't sure I could do it. So I just listened to make sure he didn't hurt her, poised with the book should I need a plausible excuse to ring Syd's doorbell.

I should just destroy him, my inner demons whispered. I could practi-cally see the burning mass of his vehicle—how they wouldn't be able to get him out of it, how he'd be stuck . . .

My doorbell startled me. I let Sydney in.

"I broke up with Tom," she said.

"Omigod, really?" She slipped past me into the house and I could feel her confusion and depression.

She sat on my sofa, holding her head in her hands. "I don't love him. And I don't want him touching me."

I knelt in front of her. "Sydney, what are you telling me?"

"I always thought I was straight, but then I met you . . . and I can't help the way I feel when you touch me."

"So you like it when I touch you?"

"Yes."

In a single motion, I picked her up, tossed her over my shoulder and carried her upstairs.

"Ty, what are you doing?" she squealed, kicking slightly.

I tossed her onto my bed. "Isn't this what you wanted? Get me out of your system?" I raised an eyebrow.

The phone rang. I ignored it.

"Ty," Syd squealed, squirming up the bed against the headboard.

"What?" I said, jumping on top of her. I had the thrill of watching her light up because being with me made her feel better. I grabbed the remote and rolled over and said, "I thought we could snuggle and watch some TV."

"You are so evil," she said, beating me.

I held her hands and pulled her into my arms.

"Aren't you going to answer the telephone?"

"It's just Michele again," I said, burying my face in her hair and breathing deeply of her scent. With a flick of my brain, I turned down the answering machine so we couldn't hear what was said.

We lay on the bed, spooning, all innocent-like, and she entwined our fingers and laid our hands under her shirt on her tummy. I felt her shudder at the intimate touch. It worked for me, too.

The television was forgotten as we fell into a quiet, warm space where touching seemed like the best thing in the world. It was sweet, tender but always edged in ripples of earthy desire. I caressed her naked flesh, feeling more and more of her as I unbuttoned her top. I buried my face in her hair, kissing her neck. I cupped her breast over her bra, insinuating my leg between hers, then pulling her upper leg over mine, opening her up.

I still wasn't reading her mind, but I did reach out some feelers to see if she was liking this, and she was. Very much.

I ran my tongue the length of her neck. She moaned and rolled onto her back.

Leaning on one elbow, I brushed her hair off her face. "I'm going to go get us some drinks. Why don't you get undressed and slide under the covers?"

"What?" I could feel her heart speed up as a surge of adrenaline hit her system.

"I was thinking you could use a full body massage. I give good ones."

"Oh." Our gazes tangled and she knew what I meant, and I knew she knew.

When I returned I could sense she was anxious and untrusting, but nude nonetheless. In my bed. Under my blankies. I put our drinks where we could both reach them. I lit a candle with my mind, and flew my massage oil into my hand.

She wasn't watching me. I poured the oil into my hands, warming it before touching her skin. I used lots of oil as I started with her shoulders, working the tense muscles there. I ran my hands down her back, then focused on the tight areas.

I worked and kneaded her back, her arms, her shoulders . . . her hands and fingers . . . I moved the sheets so they only covered her butt, and I massaged her feet, her shins and thighs, caressing her flesh and letting her know by my touch how much I loved her.

I knew she was getting wet, turned on, as I worked her thighs. But she was too embarrassed to stop me. So I stopped myself.

I pulled the sheet up to cover her completely again, and said, "Roll over."

We snuggled, not saying much. I had never been much of a snuggler, but the feeling of her in my arms was heaven after so many years of searching.

We eventually fell asleep.

When I woke the next morning she was wrapped around me, her head resting on my shoulder, her leg tossed across mine in a possessive manner. God, her hair smelled wonderful. *She* smelled wonderful. Simply intoxicating.

I didn't want to leave her, but I was sure she'd freak if she woke to find me caressing her so-soft, warm, naked flesh. Also, I was reckoning she might enjoy a nice breakfast—maybe enough to remain in my bed for a while. Naked.

When I brought in breakfast (pancakes, eggs, sausage patties, toast and Kona coffee), Sydney was awake. The sheet was draped almost artistically across her nude form. I put the tray in front of her, and she tucked in. I sat next to her, devouring my own plate of chow.

The way she ate was a wicked turn on. She feasted, she ravaged, she devoured.

"Glad you enjoyed," I said, moving the tray to the side when we were done.

I had a sudden flash of me touching her, and it took me a moment to realize it wasn't my thought—Sydney was projecting her thoughts so completely that without even trying I was reading her mind—and she wanted me to touch her.

I laid a hand on her cheek, leaned forward and kissed her. As my tongue entered her mouth, my hand dropped to her shoulder, caressing her naked flesh. I slowly pushed the blanket down so I could cup her full breast.

She gasped and arched into my hand, her nipple hardening. She squirmed and I crawled on top of her, moving the blankets so they covered only the apex between her legs.

I caught a brief image of her fantasizing about sitting in front of me, naked, with her legs spread wide. She wanted to masturbate for me, and just thinking about it turned her on.

Dear god, that was . . . this was . . . she was . . .

A dream come true.

Our tongues tangoed as I learned her again, caressing her breasts, squeezing her nipples, making her groan and squirm. I nibbled her earlobe and then tasted her down to her breasts until I bit her nipples, taking them each in turn as she pushed up into me, struggling under me.

I insinuated myself between her legs, forcing them open farther, until I finally yanked the covers away so she was naked beneath me. At that moment her mind, her fantasies, became naked to me, too.

She'd read things in books, things that scared her but also excited her. Especially when she thought about them in conjunction with me. She wanted to feel me inside her. She was projecting her thoughts so loudly I couldn't help but hear them.

I rolled to the side, letting her curl her body around me and then climb on top. We kissed, intensely, as I enjoyed the warmth of her body on top of mine, feeling her everywhere. She took my hand and placed it between her legs, so I felt how wet she was.

She gasped.

I looked into her eyes as I wrapped my arms around her. "I love having you naked in my arms."

She buried her face in my neck. "Ty, just touch me. Please. I've been wet since you got me naked last night." She sat back in my lap so we could look at each other.

My hands were everywhere. I let my tongue and lips wander—down her neck, over her shoulders and collarbone, between her breasts. I settled her on her back and I worked down . . . Worshiping her breasts, sucking her nipples, cupping the warm weight of them . . . pulling her hips up into me, against me, while I pushed down against her . . .

I loved that there was plenty of light here, in the day, so I could study every inch of her body. She was a natural blonde.

I reached down and touched her there. Felt her wetness. Enjoyed the way my fingers glided through her slickness until they slid up into her. Inside of her.

She bucked against me when that happened. Squirmed and jerked and forced my fingers into her more deeply.

Once they were there, I left them there.

She opened her legs wider.

I caressed inside her while I tasted her mouth, neck and breasts. "I love you. I've always loved you."

She pushed against me, riding my fingers, her eyes closed.

"Look at me, look at me!" I insisted, wanting to feel that deep connection.

She opened her eyes and came while we stared into each other.

Then I reached over, lubed my hand, and continued my magic as I did what she had been thinking about since yesterday. Gently, carefully, I slipped my whole hand into her.

"Oh yes!" she screamed.

She was naked in my bed, giving herself to me. She didn't realize I'd been stalking her for eons, for more years than either of us could conceive.

She was mine.

Chapter the Eighth

I was holding Sydney's sweat-dampened body, lightly caressing her while she trembled with the aftermath of the many orgasms she'd just experienced. The doorbell rang and I ignored it. I had no need for Jehovah's Witnesses or the cross-eyed Midwest version of such. Nobody knew I lived here, so those were the only options as to whom could be calling.

But when it rang again, and then again, I let my brain wander down to identify the pest. As soon as I did, I jumped from Syd, threw on jeans and a shirt, and charged downstairs.

After all, this woman wouldn't go away. Not yet. Not soon. Not now. Not after she'd obviously come so far to see me.

I'd actually studied acting somewhat—done workshops and classes and gone to university and everything, so why I didn't do better answering Michele's knock is anyone's guess. "What are you doing here?" I said. I didn't even attempt subterfuge. Or even contemplate disguising that I knew who it was before I opened the door.

"I was worried about you. You weren't returning—or even taking—my calls, and I kept having horrible dreams of bad things happening to you." She took my hands in hers as she stepped into my home. "I was worried."

Syd came down wearing only my bathrobe. "Uh, Ty? What's going on?"

I saw her look from me to Michele and saw that moment of recognition when she realized who Michele was.

I stepped from Michele and said, "Syd, this is Micky—Micky, this is Syd, my neighbor."

"Pleasure to meet you," Michele said, tilting her head and smiling just so.

"Oh my goodness," Syd said. " 'Micky?' Michele Anne Browning? Ty . . ."

I took Syd's hand in mine and looked back at Micky. "Syd's my neighbor. And maybe more."

"And you've always said your life wasn't interesting," Michele said.

Syd turned bright red and pulled the robe more tightly about her lithe body. "Ty, you could've warned me!" She ran up the stairs.

The silence that fell could not have been more awkward. I struggled for anything to say. "You have a bag with you. I don't suppose you were bringing that with you to my door wondering about the nearest hotel?"

"This trip was so last minute, I didn't have time to make reservations or anything, so I was hoping I could crash with you the few nights I was in town."

"And you got here from the airport . . . on your magic carpet?"

"I grabbed a taxi."

"And what were you gonna do if I wasn't here?"

"That wasn't in the game plan. Do you think I ever plan for failure? I'm an actress, and forward optimism is the thing."

"Micky, I know you have to have fucked a lot of auditions, and lost a bunch of jobs before you got this one, so you can't feed me that crap."

"Yes, yes, and I guess I would've done what I did before—suck it up and keep moving. Now, here, I guess that would've been to either camp out on your property till you returned, or else grab a cab to a hotel. Since there's no cabs here, I would have either been screwed, or worked my improv."

I knew she was telling me the truth, and I was only being hostile because I was embarrassed. "Let me take your bag up to the guest room and get you settled, then you can explain exactly what you're doing here."

"Nice place you have here," Michele said, following me up the stairs. "Why don't you give me the tour?"

"Y'know me too well. I always forget the little hostessy details like that." I led her to the guest room. "Fortunately, I'm pretty much moved in so I'm not too embarrassed by the joint."

"Uh, Ty," Sydney said, coming into the room, fully attired now. "I'm just gonna go home now, seeing as you're all busy with your friend . . ."

"Oh, Syd," I slipped an arm around her waist. "Why don't we make this official? Sydney Pierce, meet Michele Anne Browning. Michele."

"Ty said that was you on the phone the other day, but I thought maybe she was just trying to impress me," Sydney said.

"You two seem to have gotten to know each other quite well in a short time," Michele said.

"I think I'm just going to rush on home now," Sydney said. "And lock myself in a room to dwell in my own embarrassment and let you two catch up."

"I'm sorry," Michele said with a smile as she touched Syd's arm lightly. "I'm just harassing you. Ty here's a real catch, so I'm not surprised you jumped on the chance, though there's gonna be a lot of girls back home who'll be awfully disappointed."

Sydney blanched. "Ty, give me a call later, okay?"

"Hey," I said, "why don't you come on over later for dinner? I'll grill something up for the three of us. Say, about six?"

"I'm just going to take a moment to unpack," Michele said.

"Why don't I walk you out?" I said to Sydney, leading her downstairs while Michele remained in her room.

"I . . . I've enjoyed spending time with you," Sydney said.

"Me too. I just can't understand why Michele suddenly decided she had to come visit. We're friends, but not bestest or nothing like that."

"Well, it looks like maybe she's got something in particular on her mind."

I frowned, unsure of what she meant.

"I think she likes you, Ty."

"Naw, she's not like that."

"Neither was I." She wrapped her arms loosely around my waist. "Now, I know you've made jokes about all the Hollywood gossip and stuff, but seriously, you've got to wonder just what someone like her has to gain by coming all this way to see you. She's got to want something from you."

"I think she's just concerned. I mean, she was worried about me even before I moved out here." I had thought I would spend the next few days figuring out how Syd and I fit, and reflecting on everything I had found in this house. I wanted life to get simple again, for a while at least, before I went on to the next step. As it was, it was getting kinda scary.

Syd ran her hand over my cheek and leaned in to kiss me. "Just watch out, okay? I have a bad feeling about this."

"No worries," I said, kissing her. "I'll see you at six, baby."

"So you two have known each other for how long?" Sydney asked Michele.

"Ever since the pilot," Michele said. "How long have you been living here, anyway?"

"Just about six months now. You ever meet Ty's parents?"

"Just in passing. You always live in Michigan?"

"Born and raised. You a native Californian?"

"Grew up in San Diego. So what do you do out here?"

"Funny, I never thought of here as 'out here' before."

It was like listening to a ping-pong match, with everything moving so quickly I barely had time to think about what was going on. I concentrated on my grill, the chicken, steak and my glass of wine.

"Well, both Ty and I come from the West Coast," Michele said.

"But still, we're all here now," Sydney said.

"Fine. So what is it you do here?"

"Is that a nice way of asking how I pay the bills?"

"Yes."

"I'm in advertising. So how'd you pull all this time off work?"

"We just finished filming the season finale, and I have a bit of time before I start on my break project."

"And you came here why, exactly? I'm still not quite clear on that. I mean, it doesn't seem as if you two were best friends before Ty moved here."

"I'm hoping to talk Ty into coming out to help me on my break project. I've yet to find a double as talented as she. Plus, she's fun to work with and gets everything done perfectly. She's By-the-Book Black for a reason."

"So how long are you in town for?"

"We don't start filming till a week Monday."

"And you want to spend all your time off here, in Michigan?"

I missed Michele's response because this was getting wicked intense. I was waiting for smoke to start pouring out of their ears, and could only wonder what sort of challenge had erupted between them during the few minutes they were downstairs selecting a few bottles of wine to go with dinner.

Part of me wanted to ask Michele to leave, since she had come here uninvited and Sydney seemed to be my girlfriend now. But then again, I'd known Michele longer, and I did like her, and she could either help or hinder me with getting further work—if I wanted more work. Of course, I was still wondering why Michele had come visiting, and if she had been trying to seduce me back in California, and maybe Sydney was jealous and why the hell Michele lied about how well she'd known my parents? And when we first worked together?

I just wanted to scream because nothing was making any

sense—nothing was adding up to anything that meant anything at all, and dear sweet Hecate, I could only hope that it hadn't all fallen into the dark, evil realm of calculus, with all its imaginary numbers and equations that proved two-plus-two did *not* equal four.

"I'm not hiding anything—they *did* work on the show, I *did* meet them, but it's not like I was a regular visitor to their house or anything. We all knew each other in passing. It's Ty that I worked with regularly," Michele was saying.

I could not figure out why they were back to that or why Michele was so adamantly denying things she had said to me before I left California.

"Then why did several publications quote you talking about how they were good people and that you'll miss them?"

"What?" Michele whispered. I'm guessing she was kinda stunned, 'cause that's exactly what I was.

"I Googled you when you two were off grocery shopping." Sydney shrugged. "I was a bit jealous, and worried. I wanted to find out more about the relationship you had. And I've got to say, it didn't seem as if you two were all that close—'specially not so much that you'd come all the way out here on the spur of the moment just because she didn't return a couple of phone calls. I have to say, it makes me wonder what it is you're doing out here."

I reached out with my mind to gently caress each of theirs—not to calm or affect them in any way, but instead to figure out what was going on. Then I thought about what I was doing and who these women were, and paused.

"We may not have been going-out-to-the-bar-to-get-drunk-once-a-week buddies, or 'Gee, we just met, but let's go screw like bunnies' types, but we've known each other more than a few days," Michele said.

I wasn't going to totally violate their minds, or make them do anything they didn't want to—I was just gonna figure out what the hell was going on. And I needed to do this because of how everything was heating up.

"We didn't *just* meet," Sydney said to Michele. She was concerned for and worried about me, and worried Michele had some nefarious reason for being here. The only idea she could formulate about it was that Michele wanted to use me. I could understand her reasoning—Michele didn't seem the type to risk everything, including her career, especially when she was starting to maybe make it big, for a lesbian relationship.

"—and that means something to me," Michele said. "I was concerned about her, and I had the time and means to come visit, so I did. But as far as I'm concerned, I still don't quite understand why you decided to research me so thoroughly." I'm guessing Michele suddenly realized she had my close regard, because she turned to me with a questioning look, as if wondering why I was staring at her. See, the thing was, I couldn't read her mind—not at all.

"Dinner's almost ready," I said, glancing at the food and pulling off the finished steaks. The corn still needed a bit, but no way was I waiting for it, so I sent a spark of energy flying toward each ear to finish it off so we could eat and—please, god!—finish off whatever the flip was going on that was so evil between these two women.

Them catfighting over me might be wicked hot—especially if some sort of oil was involved—but whatever the hell it was that was going on right now was simply wrong.

And I was wicked worried that I couldn't tell what Michele was thinking. It made me wonder what the hell she was up to.

I topped off each wineglass and sat next to Sydney, across from Michele. Sydney worried I was upset because she Googled Michele.

I put my hand on Sydney's. "Sydney, honey, I understand you're worried about me, but you have to understand that some of the folks I know sometimes get itchy if you start looking too stalkery—"

"Sorry if I seemed to have overreacted," Michele said to Syd, cutting me off. "It's just that Ty's right. I had a stalker earlier this year and I'm still worried about people who seem too interested in me."

Sydney wasn't believing her for a moment, but still she said, "I'm sorry. I'm just concerned for Tyler. I wanted to know a little bit more about your relationship." Sydney knew Michele and I were friends, and so she wanted Michele to like her, but I could tell she was afraid she'd ruined any possibility for that.

It's simply amazing how many different thoughts one person can have in just a few seconds time. In rapid succession I sensed that she wasn't sorry, because she didn't trust Michele, and that she also couldn't shake the feeling Michele was after something with me.

"Looks good," Michele said, unwrapping her corn and helping herself to salad.

"Yes it does, baby, thank you for inviting me over for dinner with you and your friend," Syd said, giving me a quick peck on the cheek.

I felt a quick flash of . . . was that jealousy? From Michele?

"This is really good," Syd said, tucking in.

"Ty, these are beautiful wineglasses," Michele said.

"Thanks on the food, and thanks about the glasses. Mom got them years ago in Scotland. She really loved them."

We ate dinner and the fur didn't fly for a while. I was wrong to relax.

Chapter the Ninth

I managed to avoid any further confrontations between the two women during the rest of the meal, but then I had to worry about how I could possibly clear the table, and/or get another bottle of wine, and/or ask Sydney to go home, *et cetera*, without further badness occurring.

I definitely had to separate these two, though. During dinner, Michele kept pulling me into remembrances of our times on set, working together, and both Sydney (in her mind), and myself (in my mind), wondered if she did it just to make Sydney jealous.

"Hey, Michele," I said, when we finished eating, "would you mind finding another bottle of wine while we clear the table? Just bring it into the kitchen, okay?" I piled everything to take into the house. "Syd, can you grab the wineglasses and salad dressings please?"

I led us int the kitchen where, as we put everything away, I said, "Sydney, baby, I don't know why Michele's here—why she came or anything, but I think she and I need some time alone, because I don't think she's going to talk to me while you're here."

"So you want me to go home now."

"No, I don't, but I think you need to. She came a long way to see me, and I need to find out why. I don't think I'm going to while you're here."

"I just wish I knew what she wanted."

"That's what I'm going to find out."

"I'm worried about her. And you."

"Don't be," Michele said, coming up carrying a bottle each of white and ice wine. "Wasn't sure what you two would be in the mood for."

"Oh, let's just go for the dessert wine," Sydney said with a smile, taking it from Michele's hand. She pulled out my ahso and quickly opened the wine, pouring some into each of our glasses.

Michele put the other bottle on the counter and washed her hands. I picked up my glass from the table, and Syd handed Michele hers. Michele took it in her graceful fingers and as she raised it to her lips, it oh-so slowly slipped to crash to the kitchen floor.

Oh shit!

I heard the words as Michele's slender fingers rose to cover her mouth, her face a mask of disbelief. "Oh, god, oh god, Ty, I'm so sorry," she chanted.

"It's all right," I told her as I set about cleaning the mess on the floor.

"I'm so sorry, your mother . . ." Michele put her hand on my arm.

Sydney couldn't believe Michele had dropped the glass. Michele was hoping I'd forgive her.

"It's no big," I said.

Sydney wanted to spend the night. She hoped I wasn't too attached to the glasses. She hated even thinking about me losing any of the few remnants of my folks I still had. Especially not something that meant anything. She couldn't believe Michele had broken a glass I had just expressed fondness toward.

I was throwing the paper towels and glass shards into the trash when I heard them both clear their throats and make mumbling noises. There were not a lot of huggy feelings going on. I got clumsy with the glass.

"Dammit," I said, sucking on my now-bleeding finger. Both

women were suddenly at my sides. "Enough!" I said. I grabbed a paper towel and applied pressure to the wound. "Michele. Stay here. Grab another glass of wine—just, please, use a fruit glass or something. Sydney, let me walk you home."

"But Ty—" Sydney said.

"No. Michele—feel free to drink the entire bloody bottle. I may be gone a few minutes, 'kay? Good." I grabbed Sydney by the arm, then loosened my grip. I didn't want to hurt her or scare her off. "C'mon." I took her hand on the walk to her place. "Syd, I know you and Michele aren't getting along, and it's awkward trying to deal with both of you at once. I'm sorry about this, but—"

"And which one of us is your girlfriend?"

I smiled. "We're girlfriends now?"

"I thought . . . Well . . . Last night . . . This morning . . ."

I grabbed her and kissed her, hard. "I *want* to be your girlfriend. You saying that makes me very happy."

She smiled and hugged me tightly. "So you'll spend the night here? Or are we at your place again tonight?"

"Whoa, whoa, I've got to deal with Michele. My folks taught me to never burn bridges."

"But I thought you'd given all that up now?"

"I don't know what I'll be doing the rest of my life, so I don't want to piss her off or anything, okay?"

"God—was she the one who dumped her boyfriend of a couple of years for you, or, huh, was that me?"

I let go of her hand. "Oh, no. Don't do that. I thought you dumped him 'cause he was a co-dependent, overly jealous jerk. You dumping him for me after we've known each other this little bit of time is not a good sign for the future of this relationship."

"Ty. I'm sorry. It's just I've got to go back to work on Monday and I was planning on spending some time with you. I'm not good with spontaneity, and I don't like plan changes—especially not when I'm . . ." She wrapped her body around mine and whispered into my ear, "looking forward to something the way I was to spending tonight and tomorrow with you. You're an amazing lover, you know?"

The shiver that ran through her sent waves of pleasure shooting through me.

I wondered if I could get Michele to spend the night over here and take Syd to my bed again tonight. "I need to do this, okay? Let me have tonight and I'll do my best to get her to leave tomorrow, okay?"

"Are you sure about that?" she asked, staying wrapped around me and pulling us till her back was against the front door of her home. She lifted herself up so her legs were wrapped around my waist.

I practically melted into her as our mouths met in hot, wet need. She arched against me and I sucked her pouty lower lip as I caressed up and down her sides with my hands, cupping her breasts and running my thumbs roughly over hardened nipples.

"Oh, god, Ty," she said, bucking against me, grinding her heat into my bulky belt buckle. "You could probably make me come right here. Out in the open like this."

Dear sweet Hecate and Hecuba, that was one fucking hell of a thought that turned me on to no end. I reached down to put my hands on her feet, which were shod only in amazingly sexy strappy sandals, and slowly ran them roughly up her smooth legs, spreading my fingers to touch even more flesh as I got higher and higher up her legs.

We were both breathing heavily by the time I reached her sweet, soft thighs. Never breaking contact with her hot body, I moved my left arm to wrap around her waist and help support her, while I used my right to cup her through her underwear.

She gasped and writhed even more urgently against me as I began to rub her, and slowly explore her swollen folds through the silky material.

Oh, for fuck's sake, I was in love with the girl, but that didn't mean I couldn't just fuck her. I fingered her through her soaked panties, and then slipped my fingers under the material to feel her directly. I used my thumb to play with her clit while my fingers stroked up and down until I thrust first two fingers, then three and four into her.

I fucked her hard while my thumb flicked her swollen clit, teasing it back and forth.

"Oh god, oh god, oh Ty, yes . . . yes . . . please . . . yessssss . . ." she said, riding my fingers even as I fucked her. With each thrust, she shoved herself harder against me, her breath hot on my neck, her nipples hard under her dress, her wetness all but pouring out of her.

She kept biting, licking and kissing my neck as she rode the waves of pleasure, and suddenly I felt her tighten around my fingers.

"Ty!" she screamed briefly, before biting my neck, hard. I continued stroking inside of her even as she ground her hips against me and spasmed around my fingers and scissored me with her legs. I held her against me, using the wall to help hold her aloft as she rode out the waves of her orgasm, till she was panting and hanging from me, wrung out like a piece of fine silk.

"God, Ty, you're amazing," she whispered, still gasping for air. Her head rested on my shoulder, and she slowly lowered her feet to the ground.

I reached into her little bag, pulled out her keys and unlocked her front door, all the while supporting her with an arm around her waist, since her legs were obviously quite shaky.

Door open, I picked her up, and carried her swiftly and easily up to her bedroom. There was no way I was getting out of this without looking like a bloody asshole. Sure, yeah, I could spend the night here and totally blow off Michele, thus being an asshole to her. But even if she didn't blacklist me and burn my effigy at the stake for that—if she didn't leave town first thing in the morning—I'd eventually have to have it out with her.

Now, there was no reason to put off till later what could be done now, except that I'd be being an asshole to Sydney, because then I'd be screwing her and leaving, which wasn't nice. But of course, she had seduced me on her front porch.

Suddenly, the answer came to me: I laid a sweet sleep spell on Sydney as soon as I placed her on her bed. I took off her shoes and dress, leaving her only in her thong, and tucked her in. Then I snuck out of her house, being careful to lock the door behind me. I hoped she'd stay unconscious till morning.

It was when I was walking back home, thinking about Sydney, and feeling guilty not only for putting a spell on her, but also for just leaving her like that after we had just, well, it wasn't *making love*, certainly. After we'd just *fucked* on her front porch. That led me to thinking of guilt and I remembered Michele dropping the wineglass and how she'd thought *Oh, shit*, and then I realized I hadn't been able to hear Michele think all night, so that led me to wonder if she'd just thought that loud and hard enough to break through whatever barrier she'd had up, or if she'd let down her barrier for just the moment it took for that to get through.

Of course, that supposed it had been Michelle thinking it. Who else could it be, since we three were the only ones present? It made no sense for Sydney to think so loudly and vehemently *Oh, shit*. Unless, of course, she was reacting with empathy toward me.

Or if there'd been some other reason she didn't want Michele to drop the glass. Like if she'd put something in the wine.

I stopped in my tracks. Where the hell'd that thought come from? I hated that bad thoughts kept popping into my head. Why would I think such a thing of my lover?

When I walked into my home and didn't immediately see Michele, I sent out little mental sensors to try and locate her and yelled, "Michele?"

A pulse of her presence came from the basement. "Michele?" I called again, walking toward the stairs.

"I'm down here, Ty!" she called. It seemed like it was only then that the downstairs' lights came on, but maybe it was just that I was approaching the staircase at an angle.

"Whatcha doin'?" I asked, jumping the last few stairs.

"Studying for a math test." She was gracefully moving through some motions with both hands on the leather grip of one of my short swords.

"You been down here since I left?" I hoped I had been imagining the lights coming on only as I approached the basement. It'd be pretty embarrassing if she had seen Syd and I on Syd's porch and *holy-mother-of-God I hadn't washed my hands!*

"Pretty much so." She turned to face me and smiled. "I just couldn't resist—so many fun toys! I hope you don't mind."

Clasping my hands behind my back I said, "No, not at all. Why don't we go upstairs, have a glass of wine and talk?"

She put the sword back and followed me up to the kitchen.

"Why don't you pour us a couple of glasses and I'll be right back?" I didn't give her a chance to answer before I bolted up to my bedroom to check my pants and use the bathroom sink. I had no excuse to scrub my hands, except for having a lot of Syd still all over them, and I didn't want to share that with Michele.

Granted, it can sometimes be wicked nice to smell a woman on your hands—y'know, just catch a whiff when you put your Chapstick on or such—but right now, when I was about to have an intense convo with Michele? Not so much.

But as I was leaving the bathroom, I realized my *closet door was open*. No way no how had I left it like that. Ever since my last visit to Black Hole land, I'd been careful to ensure I kept it closed tight.

Its being open now meant one of two things. One, someone had gone from the house into my closet. Two, someone (or some thing) had come from my closet into my house.

When I had walked into the house, I did not immediately sense Michele in it. Then she was in the basement, as if from nowhere, and then the lights came on suddenly.

Huh. *Curiouser and curiouser.*

I sent out my sonar and found Michele in the living room. I still couldn't read her mind. I widened my sonar enough to ensure Sydney was still asleep in her bed.

I snuck down the hall to the guest room, and cursed when I realized I ought to have brought a flashlight with me. I could probably turn on the overhead light without Michele noticing, but I didn't want to risk it. It wouldn't be so easy to accuse her of malfeasance if I was caught searching her possessions.

But I was going to search, regardless. Without thinking about it, I lifted my hand, palm up, and said, "*Illuminate.*"

A ball of fire appeared in my hand, and I almost screamed and dropped it before I realized it didn't hurt at all.

I had just performed my first spell. Well, unless of course quickly whispered prayers before my more difficult and dangerous stunts were spells of safety or some such.

It felt good. It felt right. I felt powerful.

Michele was tidy. Her clothes hung in the closet, her intimate items were in the drawers of the bureau, and her toiletries were in the attached bathroom, as to be expected. But what happened to her suitcase? Well, she would've tucked it neatly under the bed or in her closet. I'd already looked in the closet and it wasn't there—but it *was* nicely hidden under the bed.

And lookie there, little Michele hadn't quite completely unpacked.

At first I thought it was a script she'd maybe read on the plane and disliked so much she left it in her suitcase. It was a script-sized and -shaped binding of papers. But when I opened the binding, I found it was actually newspaper clippings, computer print-outs of articles and other Internet materials, such as historical documents, spells, genealogies and a tasty looking recipe for a three-layer chocolate mousse torte. There were also a few drawings and pages torn from magazines included in it.

It was all about me and my family. Trade and industry papers reporting on things about us. Our history.

"I would have brought that downstairs, but I couldn't in case you weren't alone when you got back from Sydney's," Michele said from the doorway.

I just about jumped through the roof. The binder and all the papers went flying, and the ball of fire almost touched the ceiling. Given all choices, I rushed to catch the flying flames. I was normally a calm and collected sort of person, but this was all too much. "What the hell do you think you're doing, sneaking up on someone like that?"

"I didn't sneak up on you, and anyway, you were searching my stuff."

"Well, it might be your stuff, but it's in my house!"

"So that gives you the right to search it?"

"No, but that isn't the point. The point is that you snuck up on me and almost scared me witless. I could have burned down the whole damn house!"

"With that ball of fire you've got in your hand."

"Yes with this"—I flipped on the overhead light and closed my fist on the fire—"ball of flame which is a magic trick since I'm thinking about taking up magic during my retirement from Hollywood. And all of that is beside the point."

"And what is the point?" she asked with a little half-smile and a raised eyebrow.

"The point now is . . . well. Michele, this is all stalker-crazy shit." I indicated the binder and pages now all over the floor. "What the hell are you up to?"

"Doing what your mother asked me to and helping you."

"Helping me? How is getting all stalkery and searching my stuff helping me?"

"Searching *your* stuff? Excuse me, whose room are we in and whose stuff were you looking through?" She stepped up into my personal space.

"Hey, it's technically *my* room since it's in the house that belongs to *me*. And I only did it when I realized you'd been snooping around while I was walking Sydney home!"

"Hold on. What do you mean I was snooping around while you were gone? I was just playing with your swords."

"Then why was my closet door open?"

"Oh."

"Yeah, precisely." We were practically dancing, each of us pushing forward with our bodies when we took the offensive, and backing up on the defensive. But we kept getting closer and closer.

"Fine. You caught me. But now explain to me why you have an enormous power source in your closet?"

"Stop making this about me. It's all about you," I said. I noticed I was breathing heavy. *Huh, when did that happen?* The room was practically crackling with energy. "You're the one who came out here without warning. And you have yet to give me a good reason." I was backing her into a corner. Every time I'd thought about being with her, it was always sweet and gentle with waves and rose-petal-covered beds and lots of sunrises and sunsets and all that mushy stuff. "You've been lying to my girlfriend, clearly, and right in front of me. And you've been making cryptic comments about my mom." Right now I just wanted to shove her up against the wall and fuck her silly. Then I'd rip her clothes off, tear them from her body, bend her over a chair, counter, desk, whatever, and fuck her from behind.

I wanted to make her scream.

And this want—this need—scared me with its intensity.

And also, there was the whole thing of having a girlfriend and just recently screwing her on her front porch.

Michele was backed into a corner, staring at me with fear in her eyes. Fear and . . . *lust.* I could feel the power coursing through me. It was practically sparking at my fingertips.

"It's not about me," she whispered. "It's about you." She grasped my biceps in her hands and held me like that for a moment.

I scowled at her. I knew I could turn her arms to cinder without even trying. "No baby, it isn't." I didn't even need magick to flip her around so her face was against the wall and I held her arms pinned against her back. "Now," I whispered malevolently into her ear, "are you going to start talking, or do I have to make you?" I ran my tongue up her neck and nipped lightly at her earlobe.

She groaned and I knew she liked it. She seemed about ready to start humping the wall, in fact.

" 'Course, we might both prefer it if you make me make you talk," I said. I moved her wrists so I could hold them both in one hand and use my now-free hand to roughly caress her ass.

The unmistakable rumble of Tom's big penile-enhancing vehicle came through the bedroom window, distracting me from my mission. I reached out with my mind to see what was on his.

Who the fuck does she think she is, dumping me like that? Like she can do better than me. I wouldn't be surprised if that new dyke neighbor of hers is part of this, getting her all high-and-mighty and thinking her shit don't smell. I'll show her. And if she still don't see we belong together, she'll never be anybody else's neither.

I could practically smell the Jack Daniels on his breath.

I wondered if I should just let Sydney sleep while I dealt with him, but then realized that not only would her being awake be safer, in the almost-impossible case I failed to stop him, but also she could see what he was really like. She would never go back to him.

Even if he lived.

If he didn't, well, she wouldn't mourn him, either.

CHAPTER THE TENTH

N o, no, Ty, don't," Michele was saying, squirming against me even though it was obviously painful. She apparently heard his car, saw the look on my face, and did the math.

"Don't you hear that asshole out there? You know as well as I do some guys don't get it. They need to be taught a lesson."

"Just call the police, please. Let them take care of it."

"Yeah, right. As if they'd do much of anything. He'd keep coming back. You've had a stalker. You know how it is."

"You can't let it take control," Michele said. "That's what your mother wanted me to watch out for—that *you* stay in charge, and not let the power take over. You're in charge, Ty!"

"Yes. I am." I reached around to none-too-gently stroke the place where her hip and thigh joined, and up and down a few times till she squirmed some more. "You remember that now." Then I tapped her on the shoulder, said, "Sleep," and carried her to her bed.

Next I woke Syd, and with a single hand gesture, raised both the window and screen of my guest room, and jumped to sit on the sill, looking down toward Tom pounding on Syd's front door.

"Goddammit, Syd, let me in!" he bellowed. I saw the lights go on in her house.

Soundlessly I dropped down to my front lawn. I slithered through the darkness thinking I could kill him where he stood without him ever even knowing what was going on—but then he wouldn't learn anything to take with him to his next life, even though he deserved to return as nothing more than a slug, or better yet a fish fly or locust, since neither of those really lived more than a few days. He shouldn't ever come back, actually.

I wondered if even I could arrange such a thing. And I was proof that reincarnation was real, so there were no questions about *that*.

"Sydney, you bitch! Open this door *now*! Tell me face-to-face what a fucking whore you are!"

I could reach inside his chest with my mind and squeeze his heart till it popped like a really disgusting zit, but where was the fun in that? Instead I gave Sydney's mind the barest of caresses, so when she got to the door, she invited him in.

This way, there would be no witnesses. Just the few who would testify he came over drunk and started yelling and threatening her. I made my way stealthily over and glanced around to ensure no one saw me entering.

The door closed silently behind me. Sydney and Tom were standing just a few feet into the living room. I stood with my legs spread, my head tilted slightly down. I was looking up at them and smirking. I was *so* gonna make him pay. I had it *all* under control.

"It *is* that fucking dyke," he said, backhanding Sydney. Horrified, I watched as she smashed against the wall.

TV and movies show normal people getting hit like that and much worse but still being able to get up and walk away without a scratch. I knew it was all a lie—I had the bruises to prove it. Sydney was badly stunned, if not unconscious. "That was one of the last mistakes you'll ever make," I said. I'd been fighting him for centuries, but he didn't know that. This time, I would end it for good.

He swung at me. I caught his arm and threw him against a wall. He was fairly resilient. He leapt to his feet and charged me again. "Why you little—"

I raised an arm so it cut across his windpipe and he landed on his back. I kicked him in the ribs until I heard a couple crack.

"Don't feel so hot being on the receiving end, now does it, *Big Boy*?" He was stunned, thinking it was just little ol' me doing all of this. He didn't have a clue about my super-charged engine and how I could do all this with just my mind.

"Oh, god, Ty, please stop!" Sydney was behind me, trying to wrap her arms around me, trying to pull me from her downed ex.

"Why do people keep saying that to me?" I said, kicking him once more. "He hurt you. Don't you understand? He came here to hurt you and he was going to hurt you some more. He'll kill you if I let him."

"But don't you understand? If you kill him, you'll be no better than him."

"But I'll be right."

A look of fear passed over her face and she stepped back with her hand over her mouth. "Oh, god, Ty—"

And then everything went black.

I wasn't out for long, but when I came to, I wasn't just pissed off—I was wicked pissed off and had a helluva fucking headache as well.

"You Goddammed, fucking, bitch," Tom was yelling. He was holding Sydney by the shoulders and smashing her into a wall. Her barely moving feet couldn't even touch the floor and I could see blood on the wall. "She hurt me!" he yelled.

Even as I summoned the power to make him stop, he threw her against the fireplace. When she landed, her neck was at an odd angle to the rest of her body.

"*NO!*" I yelled, using my mind to pull him through the air to me. I shook him by his shoulders, so his feet didn't touch the ground. "*NO!*" Goddammit, he'd won *again*! I threw him to the ground so hard the floor shook, and then I kicked him so violently his body arched up and he flew halfway up the stairs. He tried to stand, to move, but his broken body wouldn't let him.

I stood, looking at him, my fists clenched, and I growled.

I slapped my hands together, hard, building my power, focusing it, and finally giving in fully to centuries of rage, anger and hatred. I felt it pulse through me, and I did not care that every light bulb in the house—in the neighborhood—popped from the explosion of energy that surged up within me.

I raised my arms and held my palms toward Tom, channeling it all at him—tearing his skin off, ripping it from his body, even as he screamed and I—

Holy fucking shit! I dropped to my knees, feeling as if someone had run me through with a sword. I looked down to see that someone *had* run me through with a bloody, rutting sword. I fell forward onto my hands, but then a strong arm twisted me around so I ended up on my back and the sword plunged farther into me.

I could feel the blood gurgling in my throat.

She straddled me, kneeling on my hands so I could not use them to defend myself magickally or physically. She ripped my shirt open and placed her hand upon my heart.

"Oh, god," Sydney moaned as her hand started to glow. "You are *so* juiced this time—you've got more power than ever before! It was all worth it, waiting in nowheresville for you to break down all those protective spells. Six months I'd been trying to get past the closet. I finally set up the first set of challenges to make sure you'd find your power, and go back into it as soon as possible."

"Sy . . ." I couldn't breathe. She was sucking my power from me.

"Oh, baby," she said, slapping my cheek lightly with her free hand, "you shouldn't bother wasting any life force trying to figure out how you can make this end up better for you next time. The power you're giving me will be mine forever—that's how much you've got for me this time! All I needed was to get you here, and that was easy once your parents went kerplop from a great height. For paranoid people with a zillion protection spells, you'd have thought they'd have seen me coming."

She blurred in my vision, then steadied again. The picture she made still wasn't pretty. I wanted to scream, to rage at her for taking my parents from me, but the world was getting fainter by the moment.

"I almost worried when Michele showed up—that she might

get you to see how well I was playing you. But she's still as insipid and powerless as ever. Did you really think *she* could block your little mental probings? Or, better yet, that *you* could actually read *my* mind? You only heard what I wanted you to—*oh, baby, let me play with myself for you.* Such a typical butch!"

I tried to fight her, but things were getting darker and the sounds were fading but I thought I heard a crashing . . . and then the weight, the pressure on my chest was gone. I rolled to my side, relieving the weight from the sword. The room got a little brighter, but still I was gasping for air and in terrible, terrible pain.

Sydney hit Michele and Michele went tumbling back against a wall, dropping her sword. I saw that the new light was coming from the tongues of flames dancing all around us. Fires had started when the light bulbs popped.

Sydney flung Michele across the room. I knew I had only moments. It had taken me a bit to learn to use my power, so Sydney ought to have a learning curve as well, but once she got up and running with my power, we were in trouble. I dropped face down onto the carpet so the sword was pushed back out of me. It hurt and I was dying, but the least I could do was try my damnedest to save Michele from my stupidity.

Michele leapt off the couch she had landed on, and started grabbing anything she could to hurl at Sydney.

"I don't care what magick Ty's mother taught you, *little girl*," Sydney said, pelting the items back at Michele almost as quickly as Michele launched them, "you have no chance of standing up against me. Why do you even try?"

"Like I didn't know you'd poisoned the wine, *amateur*." Michele looked at me, a fatal giveaway.

Sydney, with little more than a flick of the wrist, tossed me across the room. The sword clattered onto the ground. Now I didn't even have that to fight with or staunch the flow of blood. But I had landed right where Michele'd dropped the other one.

"Go!" I yelled at Michele as I picked up the sword in both my hands, using almost all of my remaining strength.

Sydney turned toward me, but I was already running full tilt at her. We collided and went flying into the flames right behind her.

I felt my skin sear as she screamed, but I stood as she tried to pull herself from the fire. I was on fire and it hurt like hell, but I was used to it. I could ignore it to get the job done. After all, I was By-the-Book Black, and I'd been burned at the stake before.

Using all the strength I had left I swung the sword, and watched Sydney's head hit the floor with a satisfying *thump*.

"Ty!" Michele screamed.

I lurched toward her. "Go," I said. Someone had to live to tell the tale.

She pushed me to the floor and dropped a blanket on me, smothering the flames. "We've got to get out of here, now!" she yelled, trying to get me to my feet.

"You."

"This is nothing, Black! Your mother'd roll over in her grave if she saw you giving up this easily!"

I pushed myself to my feet, wrapped my arms around her, and guided us up the sofa by the window, then through the window. I turned in the air to ensure I'd land on the bottom.

And then it all went finally and completely black.

Epilogue

A shes to ashes and dust to dust . . ."
I tuned it all out. I couldn't believe everything that had happened. I had to be here, had to see this, because it was all utterly impossible.

Syd's house was ashes now. When the wreckage was cleared and the body parts collected and identified, Tom's injuries appeared consistent with those caused by a fire and a fall from an upper floor, so it was easy to assume there was no foul play with regard to his untimely demise.

The discovery that Syd's head had been neatly severed from her body raised both alarm and questions. However, when the neighbors testified that Tom had shown up at Sydney's, belligerent and drunk, it was far easier to put it down to a domestic dispute gone horribly wrong than to try to implicate someone as famous as Michele Anne Browning.

After all, the firefighters responding to the call saw us both exiting the residence at the same time, and if I was involved, her high-profile celebrity ass was as well.

The police and D.A. decided it was just easiest all around to take the simplest solution.

I took Michele's hand in mine. "Okay," I said. I just needed to see Sydney put into the ground, to know she was really and truly dead and gone.

"Let's go," Michele said to the attendant who turned my wheelchair and pushed me out of the cemetery toward the waiting ambulance. The doctor hadn't been too happy with my insistence on attending the funeral, and Michele wasn't too happy with my insistence that she go ahead with her hiatus project—but it did make her feel a lot better that I was moving back home—to California—as soon as I could and was even coming back to the show.

Who knew where things would go from there? I knew where I wanted them heading, and I was pretty sure Michele had about the same idea.

Fortunately for me, Mom had helped Michele develop the very little power she did have—and that's how she was able to overcome my sleep spell. Mom was hoping that keeping me from my power would keep me from evil, and from Sydney, so she hadn't told me I had a multi-lifetime stalker after me. But just in case, she had appointed Michele my guardian angel.

Ironic, really. I kept her from harm at work, and she was supposed to keep me from harm in life. I wondered if we could trust each other with our hearts?

Before I headed back to California, I had to pack up what was left of my stuff. The fire had spread to my house as well, and at this point, with all its secrets looted, I was thinking about having it demolished.

What I knew for sure was that I'd destroy the book and everything in that room. It was all bad. I still wasn't sure what had happened, kept happening, or would happen, in the pasts and present, but I did know Syd had played me.

All the drama had been playing out over centuries. Lifetimes after lifetimes. Sydney wasn't the woman of my dreams; she had been the one screwing with my dreams, creating the fiction she wanted. I always lost, until this time around. I held Michele's hand on the journey back to the hospital. I had won this time because of her and I would happily spend the next fifty lifetimes repaying that debt.

꙰

"I hate leaving you like this," Michele said, sitting on the edge of my hospital bed. She brushed the hair off my face as I sunk into the pillows. "You really overdid it, going to the funeral."

"Don't worry, I'll be up and fighting again soon. You go do your movie and I'll be back on the show when break ends."

"Don't rush it. Don't strain yourself. And let me know if you need any help packing up here or anything, okay?"

I was feeling particularly brave, so I took her hand in mine and kissed it. "I'll be fine."

"Remember, if you need a place to stay in California, *mi casa, su casa*. In fact, I already put my key on your ring. In case you need a place before I get back."

"Thank you. For that, and for pulling me back from the brink."

"C'mon, I know you've had days when you've felt invincible. I'm sure your mom did, too. You keep me real, Ty. And I'll always be there to keep you real, too."

There's all these platitudes about absolute power corrupting absolutely, people not being islands unto themselves and that one cannot decide what's best for the masses. Well, yeah, it's all true. I'd had all that power and thought I knew best. I felt bad about the guy in the Hummer because I was nearly certain he'd rolled because I'd thought of it. There was nothing I could do about it now, though.

I'd thought about making everyone in the world all happy and peace-loving.

Which, I still thought, could be a mighty fine idea, but people want and need free will.

And magick could be addictive.

"I hate to say this," Michele said. "But I'm glad she tapped you out. I know it hurts now, but there's a reason you had to keep Sydney from that power."

"I'm cold turkey. No worries." I knew now how it could grow and swell and take me over. "But you have a plane to catch."

Michele looked over her shoulder, ensuring that the door was closed and we were alone. Then she leaned over, taking both my hands in hers, and her eyes were so green and serious and . . .

"Oh," she said, sitting up and blushing.

"What's the matter?"

She glanced down at her loose-fitting top. "Not exactly the sort of blouse to lean in."

Even though it hurt like hell, I sat up and touched her face. "You have the most beautiful eyes I've ever seen."

She leaned forward again and brushed her lips over mine. "I've been wanting to do that for the longest time," she said when she finally pulled away minutes, or lifetimes, later.

"So have I." I pulled her back to me, running my lips over hers, enjoying the softness of her lips, and how she tasted and how her tongue felt in my mouth.

"I've . . . god . . . I've got a plane to catch. Be on. To get home," she said, her eyes still closed. Her breath was warm on my lips.

"Yes, you do," I said, sinking back into the welcoming pillows. "You can't afford to cancel on a project like this right now in your career. Especially not to babysit an injured stuntwoman."

Michele smiled at me. "By-the-Book Black is back. But you still haven't figured it out, have you? Sydney didn't create those dreams. She just made it seem like she was the one you were dreaming about."

"What are you saying?"

"Come back to me and find out for yourself."

I watched her leave. Then I sat up to pour myself a glass of water. My hands were shaking. I knew I couldn't sleep. I *so* wished I'd asked her for the remote before she left.

I thought about hitting the call button to get a nurse to bring it to me, but I was apparently losing my mind, since it was already in my hand.

I turned on the TV and lay back, letting my mind wander.

World peace would be nice. Especially these days.

And, after all, I could make it happen. I had the power.

UNBELIEVER

KARIN KALLMAKER

Chapter 1

"I n conclusion, it is essential to understand that use of words such as *primitive* or *modern* are value judgments and unnecessarily juxtapose . . ."

My own droning voice was putting me to sleep—it was one of those afternoons that I understood why some students dozed off in my lectures. The overheated room was muggy from fifty jackets piled near the hissing radiators to steam off snow, and the packed-to-capacity lecture hall had taken on a quiet that spoke more of dazed insensibility than of rapt attention.

However, the echo had not died from my final remarks when an intrepid young woman with a serious expression raised her hand. "Professor Carnegie, I just want to be certain that this class fulfills the Values and Concepts Curriculum."

I held back my sigh. "If you'll note the opening disclaimer on the syllabi I handed out when you arrived, you'll see that it fulfills the VCC only if you elect to complete a twenty-five-page thesis in addition to the weekly essays and attendance."

A massive sandy-haired youth in the back was still not sure, apparently. "So if I do that, it counts?"

Words of one syllable work best sometimes. "Yes, if you do that it counts."

I presumed he, and those of similar build near him, were football players. Go Blue Hawks. Like the rest of my students, some of the athletes would be bright, some not, some looking to get through easily and the rare few inspired by the topic. "Twenty-five pages does not mean twenty-four and a half, nor will fifty meandering pages be better than twenty-five well-conceived ones. The largest font you may use is twelve-point Courier, double-spaced, one-inch margins. That information is on the syllabi as well."

Oh, the cleverness of me, I thought as I answered more questions. Clever to have figured out how my own academic interests could fulfill a core curriculum credit, thus guaranteeing a minimum enrollment every semester for *Persistent Theology: A Survey of Godmaking*. Certainly I had colleagues who considered my astute positioning to be pandering to administrative dictates and abandonment of academic ideals. Our students should learn for the sake of learning, not for the sake of employment—that was a sentiment I often heard, and from colleagues who had completed the last bitter detail of their Ph.D., just as I had, solely for the purpose of being able to teach at such august institutions as the University of Massachusetts at Danvers.

It wasn't in my nature to point out that their academic career objective could render, by their own definition, a Ph.D. a "vocational" degree. Truth, like falsehood, is a matter of perspective.

As for the legitimate goals of the required course I had created and taught for the last four years, I personally believed that a course that imparted a critical approach to learning, be it about peanut butter or piebald ponies, was badly needed by most college freshmen.

"As my very last comment in setting the tone for this course, I want to make it clear that use of the terms *Right* and *One True* in regard to mystical, spiritual or theological belief will not be tolerated in this course. You are not here to debate cultural holy books or determine which—if any—stairway to heaven is real. You are here to learn the history and social mores of twenty-four different cultures, how to compare their similarities and differences, and view the use of formalized religion as a social maintenance mechanism. To pass this course you must demonstrate that you can discuss the use of theological and spiritual ideas to create social governance, rules and order. Lectures will not be derailed into discussions of Right and True. Anyone who exhibits disrespectful behavior of any kind will be asked to leave."

The faces of two young women in the front row fell and I hoped that didn't mean they'd spend the course answering every fact I presented with, "But Dr. Carnegie, Jesus said that was wrong."

As the students gathered books and jackets and eddied out into the hall, I heard one of the young men say to a buddy, "Stairway to heaven—never heard it called that before."

"Me neither," his companion replied as they muscled their way out the door.

Feeling old, I slowly packed my satchel as the room emptied. The lecture hall ceiling was ablaze with rainbow prisms caused by the winter sun reflecting off the snow outside. The light was beautiful, but cold. I mused to myself that at least one lover in my past had said the same of me. My twin, Kylie, had received all the warmth, and once upon a time I'd groused about the random act of nature that had given her, it seemed, so much life, and me so little. The perspective of time had changed my outlook. Sighing, I gathered my things and braced myself for the rest of my afternoon.

The beginning of a new quarter provided a fresh start with fresh students, and a reconnecting time with the graduate students in my care. The holidays now behind us, the serious ones would buckle down to their research and questions with renewed enthusiasm. Snow and ice were just proof that being inside with books and a crackling fire was not just good sense, but essential to both physical and academic survival.

I was beginning a new year and would, in all probability, see its ending. At home, Kylie would be taking a long nap after a scant lunch. She would not see spring, let alone another new year. We both knew it. We were both scared. The winter had never seemed so bleak, so desolate. A department meeting was the last place I wished to invest energy.

Carl was in the power chair, coffee steaming on the table in front of him. We had to select a new department chair today. Carl wanted the job, of course, but he'd not approached me for support and his "Good afternoon, Hayley," was distant.

Mike, Trina, Jenny and Lotham, professors of history all, were in the "not even thinking about running this meeting" mid-table spots, leaving me the chair facing Carl. It was the chair of the tacit second-in-command. Susan's goals were higher than that, so she stayed at the window, pulling power to her by standing.

Annoyed with the predictability of it all, I took a folding chair, abandoning any pretense of participation in the meeting's outcome.

Carl started talking and I stopped listening. My success as a teacher was two-fold: my courses were well-attended, and I refused to get caught up in factions. The week three lecture in my course was all about the use of factions to enforce social order and divert social pressure for change. I liked to think I was smarter than that.

Smarter, usually. This year, with the frozen Massachusetts winter making it hard to breathe and even more difficult to stay warm, it was just smart to stay below Carl's and Susan's radar. I was cold, tired and wanted to teach my courses, read my books and spend time with Kylie.

To my immense relief, Susan, it seemed, had done her politicking before the meeting. She'd rightly figured I couldn't care less, and had spent her time on the swing voters, Jenny and Lotham. Carl had presumed his ego was the Ohio of electoral votes somehow, but Susan carried the popular vote, which is how we played the game. I cast my vote for her because she already had enough to win and I knew that people in folding chairs got to vote last. Presidential elections were sometimes decided with less care.

Free to head for home, I bent my head into the bitter wind and began the short walk.

After I gratefully shut the front door between me and the now swirling snow, I gave Bast her dry food and fresh water and received my daily dose of fur, purring and disdain. Kylie's lunch dishes still contained a half a boiled egg and half a slice of toast, both of which showed signs of nibbling by Bast. At this point, Bast ate more than Kylie did. We were quickly approaching the time when someone would have to check on her during the day when I could not.

I quietly slipped upstairs to her room to make sure she was asleep. She didn't have much strength, but as usual, she'd kicked off the blankets. I pulled them back over her and she didn't stir; she'd rest for at least another hour. Bast, now sated, cuddled on the comforter against Kylie's back. Kylie had wisely told Bast she hated that, when in fact she adored Bast's warmth. But, as anyone who has shared living space with a cat can advise you, it never pays to tell the creatures your true feelings.

My nose had barely begun to thaw over a steaming cup of peppermint tea when the doorbell rang, followed by the rumbling sound of a departing delivery truck. I scooped the package off the porch before the temperature in the house fell fifteen degrees. My brief look at the snow took in its change from light, fluffy and picturesque to heavy, wet and slushy. The temperature was dropping; in the morning there would be ice everywhere.

Bast, having no doubt thought I had left the house again, had roused herself and was, therefore, caught in the act of eating the Dreaded Dry Food. After a surprised glance at me, she retired quickly to a corner to heave up most of it. Our nightly rituals of one kind and another complete, I took the package and tea up to my study while she returned to the comfort of Kylie's warmth. A touch to the switch and flames blossomed in the fireplace under the wood that I'd left stacked ready for a night's work. When Kylie woke she'd join me, her toes close enough to the fire to get crispy.

Computer grinding to life, I tore the thick envelope from my parcel and tossed it on the fire. A layer of black paper—thick, slightly sticky—was tightly bound around what was obviously a large book. I had a few things on order, but what emerged from the wrapping was not anything I recognized. At least I didn't think so—the heavily tooled leather cover was crowded with designs but nothing that could be construed as a title.

I set it down for a moment to poke the now crackling fire and switch off the gas, then returned to examine the heavy book. It was oversized and at least four inches thick. Lounging into my large, comfortable desk chair, I studied the cover again, tracing the most prominent design with my eyes. And again. It almost seemed familiar. Celtic? Teutonic? My eyes followed the whorls a third and fourth time, but now the design didn't seem familiar at all.

Slightly dazzled, I jumped when the study door banged open. Kylie gave me a brilliant smile. I thought fancifully that, when we were kids, Kylie had been the brilliant flare of the sun and I the pale moon. Her smile today, for all its brightness, was like the last flare of a candle before the wick drops forever into the wax.

I was surprised to see that half the logs were well-consumed. They'd been fresh only moments ago. My computer screen was slowly changing hues, indicating it had been idle for some time. But I'd just turned it on. A glance at the clock on my desk reminded me the night was not so young—had cleaning up after Bast taken that long?

"I'll get dinner started," I told Kylie, after settling her in front of the fire.

"I was going to try," she paused to fill her lungs. "Try to make it myself. You were . . . so quiet."

"Here, let me put this on your lap and you take a look. I can't make anything of it." I glanced guiltily at the fire where I'd tossed the outer envelope. "I don't even know who sent it."

The book seemed to weigh more than Kylie did. Even as I looked at her, my mind replayed moments in the past, delighting in watching her surge with speed to intercept a pass and run rings around the other team's forward. College glory seemed so long ago.

Her thin fingers traced the cover design. "Beautiful work."

"Yes, but I can't place it."

Shaking my head free of the beginnings of a headache, I slipped on my reading glasses and immediately felt more clear-headed.

Eyestrain, I decided, and I popped a few tablets once I reached the kitchen.

Kylie's appetite was difficult to tempt. The key was to offer her variety in small quantities. A strawberry sliced into five delicate pieces would work, along with a plump Medjool date, pitted and sliced as well. Several mouthfuls of cottage cheese would provide badly needed calories. I found a tin of olives from New Year's Eve preparations and added several to her plate. When we were kids our mother had called such a meal "French" and we'd both felt quite worldly munching a bit of brie with crackers and sliced apples. Only now did I appreciate that our mother had been cleaning out the icebox with such meals. A couple of cashews finished her plate. I'd be pleased if she ate it all, but it was unlikely.

Using most of the same ingredients, I made myself a curried chicken salad and headed back to the study where it would be warmer.

Kylie looked as if she was waiting for a kind, easy breeze to take her someplace warm. When once I had envied the gene sequences that had made Kylie such a glorious star, I now felt a familiar stab of guilt. She would die before our thirty-eighth birthday. I would not.

She ate the olives slowly as I sorted through mail. Bills from specialists went into the tub where I put the details of Kylie's deterioration. I tossed my 2004 Queer-Quotes-for-the-Day into the recycle bag. My 2005 appointment book was empty except for departmental requirements, but mentally every day was marked "Save for Kylie." I would not allow myself to see the emptiness of spring, summer or the rest of my life.

"I could have done chemo," Kylie volunteered. "And I'd have eaten as much." She slowly hooked a soft lock of dark hair behind one ear. "I'm sorry. Not that hungry."

"It'll keep. I'll put it on the table next to you so you can snack if you want. So, what did you think of the book?"

"You were always the thinker." Kylie lifted the cover. "You know my best work. With rule books."

"You're the only person I know who can recite the balk rule in baseball, that's for sure." Kylie's passion had always been for sports. Not being able to play, after the disastrous collapse in college that had led to diagnosis of her heart condition, had been a crushing blow to her spirit. Even with a bad heart, however, one could officiate from the sidelines. Even with degenerative bones and joints one could keep score and run statistics. Even chronic fatigue allowed her to watch, for an hour or two.

Advanced uterine cancer, however, was the Bitch Goddess, the Destructor, She-Who-Must-Be-Obeyed.

"What will you do with this?" Kylie patted the cover.

I lifted the book from Kylie's lap, still trying to discern the title. "Read it—I'm sure I ordered it for research."

"It's blank."

I realized then that I'd been so taken with the cover that I'd not opened it to look for a title page. Quickly thumbing through the tome I saw that Kylie was right. Blank, every last page. The book felt old, but perhaps it was someone's idea of a gift? A journal or elaborate notebook?

When I'd tossed the envelope on the fire I hadn't realized there was no packing slip. I had no idea who had sent it. Frustrated, I pulled up my list of items I had on order for research and scanned it for anything I might not have understood was the book now propped up on my desk. But my quick perusal didn't turn up listings that noted my loan request was a "leather-bound edition" or even an "antique."

"Well, that's vexing," I said to Kylie. "I have no idea what this is." I flipped the pages once again as I considered how to go about identifying the book and, more importantly, to whom it should be returned. It was nice to look at but useless to me. My shelves were already far too full.

"I'm sure you'll figure it—oh, damn!" Abruptly, there was only firelight to illuminate us.

"Don't worry. I was thinking we'd lose power." My computer switched to battery and the monitor glare helped me find the long-nosed lighter in my desk. A few minutes later my office was softly illuminated by several oil lamps. The fire continued to warm the room and I'd slept on the small divan near it more than once when weather insisted we all remember our tenuous grasp on survival. Kylie, however, would quickly chill, so I brought several more blankets as I helped her to the sofa. I'd be able to warm up my own bed enough to sleep.

Kylie drifted to sleep after swallowing her meds. Reading by oil lamp light was a prescription for a headache, but I could sort and file papers with no trouble. And so I filled the rest of my evening with tidying up for the new quarter's onslaught of papers to grade and administrative memoranda.

From university paperwork I turned to the large pile of reports and letters from all the specialists who had seen or wanted to see Kylie. Most of them wanted to see me as well. We were a pair for the medical textbooks. Our DNA had been sampled and resampled, compared, clucked over and declared a puzzle. Our genes were identical but our physical health had diverged wildly. I'd been tested for everything Kylie suffered from and been judged soundly healthy, if a bit too wide in the hindquarters.

I had letters from geneticists wanting to clone us, scientists wanting tissue samples, researchers (sometimes with a shocking lack of humanity) asking to conduct Kylie's autopsy. Hospitals from Los Angeles to London asked for pieces of her as if she was a bit of furniture. They asked me, as if I knew, how two things that were the same could be so different.

A lot of it I chucked, but a few things I kept to discuss with Kylie at some other time. There would come a point when she needed to be in a hospital. She had choices with a dozen worldwide offering to provide care in return for her body, both before and after her death. She'd accepted there was something to learn in the process of her dying, but we'd agree to be in denial, for a little while longer. If she could get out of bed, use the toilet and make a meal, she wanted to be here.

As I swallowed back tears of bitterness and depression I would not allow Kylie to see, I came across our father's Christmas card to me, reminding me that I was obliged to send him some sort of response. Last year I'd put it off until nearly Easter, and then only written a letter so that his Easter missive didn't begin with a comment about not getting a reply to the Christmas card.

Figuring a handwritten note might look longer than a few sparse paragraphs from my word processor, I found writing paper and pen, took the brightest oil lamp to the chair next to the fire, and sat down to compose something suitable. At the last moment I grabbed the mysterious book to serve as a writing platform.

I supposed that Kylie had written him back, though it would have taken her some time to do so. When our parents had divorced they'd had the brilliant idea that they should each take one of us, and Kylie as a result could talk to our father in ways I could not.

Dear Father, I wrote dutifully. My pen stilled as inspiration faded. I glanced at his Christmas card, postmarked Montpelier, for help. *I am glad your rhododendrons will survive the frost again this year.*

The rare acquaintance who inquired about the rift with my father rightly concluded that it was due to the fact that he was a fundamentalist bigot and I was, though not put into practice recently, a lesbian. It did not help that I was also a "heretic" in his estimation. Kylie, who had embraced some of his religion during her teens, could stand him; I could not.

We exchanged greetings at all major religious holidays when piety is at its most false and obligatory. I knew that somehow or other I was supposed to be old enough to forgive his rejection of me, but given how little actual affection there had ever been between us, I saw no reason to change the status quo. I was old enough to decide what was and was not worth my time and attention. Changing my father was not.

My pen had not moved for several minutes and I set it and the paper aside with a heavy sigh. With just the book on my lap I could not help but turn it over to examine it one more time. Peering through my glasses I studied the cover again, but whatever pattern I had seen earlier refused to reemerge. I set my glasses aside to rub the bridge of my nose as I idly flipped pages one last time. Just as I was about to push the heavy thing onto the floor, a log split on the fire. In the abrupt flare of light, the page under my hand appeared now to have writing.

I closed my eyes for a moment, then cautiously looked again. A handwritten script spilled across the pages. The fire dimmed and so did the writing. Intrigued, I carried the book closer to the fire. The ink leapt into full color, deeply blue.

I turned to the very first sheet and discovered what might be a title page, but the letters were so crowded and stylized I could still make out nothing of use. I studied it for a moment, turned the page to the next, studied it, then on to the next.

After twenty pages or so I suddenly yawned. To my amazement the mantel clock reported that my next class began in less than five hours. Kylie had not stirred in all this time. Her meds knocked her out for the majority of the night and most of the day.

Bast agreed reluctantly to share my bed with me, as long as I shared the down comforter with her. The deal was struck. My head spinning with fatigue, I plunged into sleep.

I woke with a serious ache in my back. I supposed it was from hunching next to the fire for so long the previous evening. The power was back on, and it took only ten seconds to discern that I had twenty minutes to get to my first class of the morning. Students hated eight a.m. classes only slightly more than their instructors did.

I woke Kylie with a gentle hug after I set a steaming cup of Irish Breakfast tea, a cookie and her morning meds on the table next to the sofa. "I'm terribly late—will you be okay?"

"I will when I'm not dizzy." Kylie closed her eyes again. "You go on."

I swore my way through my shower, appeased Bast, then hurried out the front door, already late.

My boots hit the first patch of ice and I involuntarily skated the short length of my walk. My yelp of alarm warned off other pedestrians as I windmilled madly for balance. A man grabbed for me but missed and—certain I was about to beat Kylie to whatever happened after death—I spilled across the hood of a slow moving Jeep.

The amazing thing was that I landed on my feet. Though I was shaking like a leaf, I had injured my pride more than any part of my body. Oh, my shoulder would tell me all about it for a week, but that I was alive seemed miraculous to me.

The driver of the Jeep clambered out with expressions of alarm and I recognized my neighbor. She'd moved into the cottage next to mine at the beginning of winter break, but I'd seen little of her after the moving van had departed. Kylie sometimes reported on comings and goings and the return of the odd piece of misdelivered mail.

"Are you okay?" She put one arm around my shoulders, being about my height, and guided me toward the sidewalk. "That was some dance number."

"I forgot about the ice. I'm fine, really. It wasn't your fault." I thanked the man who'd tried to save me and assured everyone I really was okay. "I'm late for class . . . power outage . . . no alarm."

"Can I drive you? Though I don't know why I bother. It's such a short walk."

"Driving is actually not a good idea today."

She shrugged, her blue eyes alight with mirth. "I grew up in Phoenix and have been hoping to find someone who could tell me things like that. Oh—stay still."

She had the look of someone who had spotted a spider about to bite my jugular. I froze. She very carefully reached toward my left eyelid, however, and pulled her hand back to show me a fine fiber from my snow cap.

"It was headed right for your eye." There was no mirth in her gaze now, but an intent, evaluative look. "Why don't I put my car back and we can walk together. You can tell me how to assess this white stuff all over the ground and I'll convince myself I really didn't break four of your ribs with my car."

A few minutes later we hurried toward the university gates with our breath steaming the air in front of us. Credentials were quickly shared and absorbed in academic shorthand. Her summary was, "Lit. comp, no tenure in Phoenix. Perishing for lack of paper, but hope to put out next year."

I answered with, "Humanities, tenure barely. Unspectacularly published . . ." I hesitated, but decided that I had no energy for academic posturing. I am what I am. "See that building over there? Gray roof? That's the business and economics building. I've got the same last name as the robber baron who paid for it, so . . . I am left alone to research what is of interest to me and very few others."

"Which is?" She tramped without hesitation across the icy ground, her shiny new boots breaking the crust easily, though I guessed she weighed a good twenty pounds less than I did. The slender frame was discernible even under the winter wrappings. She looked perhaps in her early forties but I had yet to see her hair—it was tucked up inside her snow hat without a single tendril to give a clue.

"The intersection of religion and social code. The divergence of morality and scripture."

She avoided a snow-covered hummock. "You mean why is 'thou shalt not kill' a matter of morality and not religion?"

"It is a nearly universally held law, regardless of supporting scripture."

"If you don't count women and children." She had a tiny frown line between her light, finely sculpted brows.

"Exactly. Religion can be surprisingly amoral when it comes to treatment of what is considered property. One can kill property in most religions. The differences are often in the definition of what a person is or isn't, hence one can kill nonbelievers and infidels, too."

"The current climate in our country must frustrate you."

"Not particularly. I'm a historian. This is a phase." Our steps matched in rhythm as we neared the social sciences building.

"Ah. So, all of history is one passing phase after another?"

"For the most part, yes."

She smiled then, a perfectly readable I-know-something-you-don't-know smile. I hate that. "When does a phase take on permanence?"

"Depends on your timeframe. Humanity is a phase in the longevity of the planet."

"But the planet is not?"

"It is in the timeframe of the universe."

She held the door open for me. "Then it really does matter where one sets one's frame of reference, doesn't it?"

Ahead, I spied two of my grad students whisking into the classroom, no doubt immediately relieved to see I was not yet there. "A day trader sets it in seconds. A geologist in eons." I shrugged.

She waved in parting as I put my hand on the classroom door. "Our souls set the only timer that matters. Thanks for the walk."

Hoping her last comment didn't indicate some sort of cultish adherence to the latest God of the Week, I breezed into the classroom to apologize to my students and begin the working part of my day.

It was only later, feeling tenderness in my ribs and reflecting on a surprisingly intriguing conversation that I realized I did not know my neighbor's name. I would have to ask Kylie when I got home.

"Aurora Lowell." Kylie stretched her feet toward the fire as she picked at her dinner. "She's hot and she's gay."

Kylie's frank assessment startled me. "How would you know? Are you finally coming around to my way of thinking about sex?"

"We got her *On Our Backs*." Kylie's wan face lit with a teasing smile. "Good article about G-spot stimulation." She took a shaky breath as a laugh threatened. "You girls aren't shy."

"No," I agreed. "When it comes to pleasure and the female body, I think we dykes lead the way."

"Pity I never tried."

Oh, how I agreed. Our father's attempts to indoctrinate both of us into his Temple of Righteousness had failed utterly with me, but Kylie had been attracted to something in it. The ritual, the comfort of knowing your spiritual place in the order of things, whatever it might be for her, I didn't understand it. But I firmly believed that it had kept Kylie from exploring her sexuality fully. "Honestly, I can say there are a few high points to it, though I've not often experienced them."

"You should ask her out."

"Don't be ridiculous."

"Hayley."

I looked up from my monitor. "What?"

She gazed at me for a minute before saying, "I won't be here forever."

My eyes stung with sudden tears. "I know that. I want to spend all the time with you I can."

"I worry about you."

"Don't waste the energy, I'm fine."

"When was the last time you laughed?"

"Today, reading the latest government promises to build unity between the parties."

"Danced?"

I shrugged.

"Fucked?"

"And your point?"

"Life's short, even if you live to be a hundred." She set her barely touched dinner to one side. "I wish I'd tried a lot of things."

I surreptitiously dabbed at my eyes. "Such as?"

"Xstasy—wish I'd tried it."

"You're not serious!"

"Just once. And I wish . . . I'd danced naked around a bonfire."

"Sounds fun until the cops show up."

"There was a woman who loved me."

I blinked. "Really? I mean, I'm not surprised, but you never mentioned it."

"I wish I'd said yes. I think . . ." She turned her head to gaze into the fire. "Wasting love is a real sin."

"Didn't you love what's-his-name? In college. You wore his ring for a while."

"I think I did. I got sick and he left." She shrugged, or at least I thought the tiny movement of her shoulders was a shrug. Then I realized she was crying.

I held her gently against me, trying not to cry myself. One of us had to be strong, but with our bodies so close I could feel our hearts beating in the same rhythm. Her depression echoed in me.

"I'm so scared, Hayley."

"I know."

"What happens afterward? Where am I going?"

I cursed my academic mind that could so easily distance me from the emotion in her plea. It was the eternal question of all societies. But this was not some theoretical discussion—this was Kylie.

And there was no comfort I could give her, no superstition or faith that she would believe from me. Kylie hadn't been shocked when I said I'd been to bed with one of her teammates in high school, but she'd turned ashen when I'd announced I did not believe in God. There was no tale of Cloud Nine or Heaven Hereafter that I could convincingly offer. Our father would pour her full of his assurances that there was a Plan for us all, and when she surrendered to the Will she would be Healed or Taken, according to the Design.

That was why he did not know how sick Kylie was. If our mother had still been alive I'd have told her. But not him—he'd take Kylie away to pray for healing and forgiveness because only a sinner was struck down. In his world, the sicker Kylie got, the more it must be Kylie's fault.

I held her tight until she cried herself out, then helped her to bed, feeling utterly inadequate.

It was barely nine o'clock and there was certainly work I could do. The study always seemed quiet and dark after Kylie left, as if she still cast light wherever she went. Bast made a huge show of loving me, but I knew she was really after the warmth from the computer monitor. We settled which part of the desk I'd be able to work on and she curled up, watching me with her pleased yellow eyes.

The damn mystery book took up too much space. I didn't know how to send it back from whence it came, and I could hardly spend another long night poring over pages that only revealed themselves by firelight. The scribe had been very clever, to be sure, but it was useless to me.

I pushed it away, then decided I could at least get it off my desk. Next to the fire would be fine. I'd show Kylie the writing tomorrow night. As I set it down I saw the remnants of my ill-begun letter to my father and cast it wearily into the flames. I sank down in the chair with the book on my lap, warming my hands, and considered what to do next.

I jumped when Bast brushed past my ankles with her "I want out of this room" yowl. I had no recollection of opening the book, but it was on my lap and I was tilted awkwardly toward the firelight to make the writing visible. I shut it, annoyed with myself, and then gasped in pain as I tried to stand. My left leg was asleep and my back stiff.

Stamping to get the circulation going in my leg, I stared in amazement at the clock. It was past midnight. And yet I'd just sat down.

I let Bast out and she resentfully scrambled downstairs toward her litter box. I peered in on Kylie, but she appeared to be asleep. I felt stupid with fatigue and guessed I had simply fallen asleep after not enough rest last night.

CHAPTER 2

"Professor Carnegie?"

I paused on my way out of the classroom. "What can I do for you?"

Greg, one of my favorite grad students, looked uncommonly nervous. "Your last notes, I'm afraid I can't read part."

"Handwriting that bad?" I took the paper he proffered as I slipped my reading glasses onto my nose.

Consider Shaeffer and Pollard, I'd written, then . . . I blinked. The rest was unintelligible. It looked like . . . but couldn't be . . . the script from the book that I had been studying for a week now. What on earth had I been thinking? More importantly, why hadn't I noticed?

"Oh for heaven's sake," I said, letting my chagrin show. "I must have been really tired." Unbidden, I temporized, "It's shorthand. They're letter groups formed into single characters."

Greg seemed satisfied but I was stunned at what I'd just blithely said. Looking at what I'd written, I was flabbergasted to realize I could read it. "It says this is very good work." Which was, in fact, what I had written.

We talked a little bit more, but inside, I kept asking myself how all of a sudden the damn book was now understandable to me. I knew no such code. Osmosis had been thoroughly debunked by science, so I didn't believe that, either. Where had this knowledge come from?

My obsession with the book was inexplicable. I hadn't told Kylie about it because I couldn't explain it myself. I was missing hours and hours of my time and the more I told myself I was dozing off, the more I knew it wasn't the right answer. I've never been big on meditation but that was likely closer to what was going on. If I told Kylie she'd worry that I ought to be having an affair with a real live person, not a book.

"How are the ribs?"

I spun around to face my neighbor, and felt myself flush as I remembered Kylie's succinct assessment: hot and gay. "They're fine. I'm fine."

"Good. You know, the other morning I didn't realize at first that there are two of you."

I stuck my hand out for a proper introduction. "Hayley Carnegie. You met my sister, Kylie, I believe."

"Over my magazine and your water bill. Aurora Lowell. You're twins, aren't you?" She shook my hand and gave me another of her evaluative stares.

"Yes. Identical, though most people can easily tell us apart." I abruptly wanted to explain how Kylie's spirit had always flared brighter. I let the classroom door fall shut behind me, finally, and turned toward the main doors. Aurora matched pace with me.

"So you never pretended to be each other?"

"No. It wouldn't have worked. We never dressed the same, at least, not after our parents divorced."

"They didn't do that *Parent Trap* thing, did they? Split you up?"

"As a matter of fact, they did, for a couple of years." Neither of us had been the same and the bond between us had taken years to recover from the separation.

Aurora didn't voice the scorn over parental choices that showed in her eyes. Green eyes, green like a deep river. "But you live together now?"

"Yeah, it's convenient." I sucked in my breath as we went through the outer doors to the courtyard.

"Oh mother, I don't think I can get used to this," Aurora muttered. "I have never had to force myself to breathe."

"Hot drinks. Keeps the lungs open," I advised. "I'd say today the temperature is bracing. Tomorrow is predicted chilly." I zipped my vest halfway up.

"Show off." She cinched the neck of her fleece jacket tight and pulled her hat down more firmly. It once again completely covered her hair. "Hot liquids? Have a cup of coffee with me, then?"

I hesitated. Normally, I headed home to settle in and make dinner for Kylie, who wouldn't eat unless I did. "I actually don't drink coffee and the New Englander in me can't bring myself to spend two dollars for a single tea bag."

The light, clear bell of Aurora's laugh seemed to glide across the snow. I thought fancifully for a moment that I could feel it on my face and found myself blushing again. Kylie had put illicit thoughts into my head, that was all.

"How about some hot chestnuts, then? I know they're not liquid, but I'm famished and cold. Have some pity on me."

I grinned. "They're a weakness for me too. I'll take some home to Kylie."

Wax paper bags in hand, we lingered near the vending cart because it was out of the light wind. Aurora ate one of the nuts with a speculative expression. "Okay, that's rather good. I like that a lot."

"Never had them?"

"No, only heard about them in the song. Open fires and Jack Frost, et cetera. We have California almonds by the bushel in Arizona."

I stepped out of the way of a jostling backpack, then realized I knew the woman carrying it. She ignored me as she smiled at Aurora. "Hey, Rory."

"Hi." Aurora smiled congenially at one of my least favorite people on campus, but she had the blank expression of someone desperately trying to recall a name. Her eyes seemed to plead *help me*.

Forcing a polite smile to my lips, I asked, "How have you been, Lexi?" Aurora gave me a grateful look.

"Great." Lexi didn't take her avaricious gaze off Aurora's face. "The year is off to a good start."

"Hayley has introduced me to hot chestnuts." Aurora offered her bag. Of course Lexi had to have one. She needed no invitation to help herself to items belonging to others, so of course when actually invited, she said yes. "I don't think I'll get used to the cold."

"I was thinking about what we were talking about the other day." Lexi paused to lick her fingers. "It's such a short drive, even in the snow."

"Oh." Aurora gave me a controlled but panicky look. "I'm not ready to sightsee yet."

Not sure what was being implied, I silently chewed on another nut.

"It's really just a day trip. You can see all of Salem in an afternoon."

"I'll do that. When the weather's better." Aurora concentrated on the chestnuts.

"That won't be until April," Lexi complained. She wasn't oblivious to Aurora's signals, of that I was sure. She just had no intention of paying them any heed. "I'd have thought you'd be anxious to find those Lowell graves, you being descended from witches and all."

I shot Aurora a glance. She looked pained, so I said, "It's better to see the cemeteries without snow. Some of the markers are in the ground. At least one museum closes for January, too, and you can't see several of the gable houses until March." Lexi treated me to an evil glare.

"I think I'll wait." Aurora glanced at her watch. "I've got one more class today. I'd better go."

Lexi unexpectedly touched my arm with one of her claws. "Oh, Hayley, I'm sorry. I didn't mean to be insensitive earlier."

I gave her an enquiring look, and held myself still to avoid shaking off her hand.

"That my year is looking so good. Kylie and all . . ." She waved an airy goodbye, leaving her knife in my heart.

Aurora was obviously puzzled, but I had no voice to explain. "I need to get home," I murmured.

"Sure. Are you okay?"

"Yeah."

"Thanks. I hate being called Rory."

"I'll remember that."

She smiled then, a light, easy curve of her lips that eased the pain of Lexi's parting stab. "Good. You and she have a history?"

"No. She and an ex of mine have a history. Except the ex wasn't my ex at the time they began their history."

"She poached."

I shrugged. "I can't say the fish was unwilling. Somehow, that made me the bad guy." I had to smile a little bit then, picturing the faithless Maggie as a fish. It suited her. It had been hard work to make things a go with Maggie, and it had ended in failure. I'd not found the energy for even a date in the two years since.

"Well, thanks for the save. I didn't want to be rude to her."

"You might have to be. Lexi's approach to everything is binary. Loves you or hates you."

"What's wrong with Kylie? If you don't mind my asking."

I didn't mind, actually. Standing with her in the cold air, feeling a conflicting mix of alive and dead, I wanted to tell her. "Everything. Just about everything. She wants to be in her own bed for as long as she can make it."

Aurora touched my arm in the same place that Lexi had, and I felt cleansed of Lexi's spite. "I'm sorry. You were wanting to get home and I need to get to class. But, um, if you'd like to talk over a two-dollar bag of tea, you know where to find me. Heck, I've got tea at home now. I'd give you some for free." She winked and I felt good enough to smile back.

"Sounds good. I'll . . . let you know."

She walked away a few steps, then turned to walk away while facing me. "When the snow's gone I'd really like to see Salem. With a good guide."

I hoped that my expression didn't look as shy as hers now did. "I'll see if I can scare one up for you."

I watched her disappear into the swirl of coats and hats, then headed for home. My mind was overwhelmed with too many thoughts and feelings to name.

Bast and I went through our nightly greetings and I bolted upstairs as soon as possible. Kylie was sleeping but pain would wake her soon. I wanted to know why she'd told me to ask Aurora out. It was unsettling me too much, the idea that maybe, just maybe, Aurora was flirting with me. I didn't have time for that. Between classes and papers to grade, I had barely enough time for Kylie, who had no time at all.

In my office I scowled at the book. I was *not* going to spend another night hunched next to the fire. I didn't know how to read or write what was written in that book. I put a hand to my suddenly throbbing head.

No, I thought, I won't waste time on it again tonight. I need to do the work for which I am paid and I need to be with my sister in her every coherent moment.

I covered it with a pillow and my head cleared. I was happily working at my desk when Kylie shuffled in, complaining of the cold.

"I'll go get some more wood."

The brief trip outside cleared my head even more, and I panted up the steps to the study, cursing the architect who had thought a second-floor fireplace useful, but planned none downstairs save the kitchen.

Kylie had somehow gotten the book onto her lap and I struggled with myself not to snatch it back. It was mine.

"I could have sworn," she said slowly, "that this was blank."

Dumbfounded, I stared at the pages with her. The handwritten script was perfectly visible under the ordinary incandescent bulbs. "It does funny things in the light. I think the ink is old."

"What kind of writing is this?"

"I *think* it's someone's homemade code," I managed to say. What was with this book? I didn't need mysteries right now, and neither did Kylie. I ran my hand over the page that Kylie held open. "*Today is truth. Yesterday is memory. Tomorrow is hope. Tomorrow requires time. Yesterday is water.* Huh."

"Yesterday is water?" Kylie touched the page. "I guess in a way it is."

"I think this is someone's journal." My hand stilled and I decided I would read no more to Kylie.

"Tomorrow requires time—that's true, too."

"I'll get you some dinner," I said, lifting the book from her lap and carrying it to my desk. "Back in just a bit."

We didn't speak of the book again, and a few hours later I tucked her into her freshly made-up bed.

She gave me a grateful smile. "Clean sheets are better than sex. Sometimes."

"Less work, usually." I refused to let Aurora dance in my head. If she subscribed to *On Our Backs* she was likely an adventurous woman and I had no use for that information.

"Promise me something." Kylie slumped onto the pillow, clearly exhausted. She coughed slightly and I felt a brush of fear that she might have a cold.

"What?"

"You'll go out. On a date. Or go to that club, remember?"

"All the way in Boston? Not likely. Besides, I'm too old for that crowd now."

"You tried to shock me."

"I had no idea you'd dance all night."

"Wish I'd gone home with someone, the way you did."

The memory of that and several other college-aged trysts, no strings and nearly anything goes, washed over me. "It was foolish of me. And risky."

"You need . . . a life. Other than caring for me."

"Kylie," I pleaded. I didn't want to put it into words, but she waited. I finally whispered, "I'm going to have a life."

"Start now," she answered immediately, clearly having guessed what I had been going to say. She grinned. "Start now so I can enjoy it, too."

"Voyeur," I accused after clearing my throat.

"Most of my life. How I envied you knowing. Doing what you knew you wanted."

She'd envied *me*? Kylie had had friends by the bushel, trophies by the dozens. She'd traveled to tournaments and Olympics and *everyone* loved Kylie. "I never knew that."

"You weren't scared to live."

"Neither were you." I kissed her on the forehead. "You did things I never would have tried."

"When I had a cheering section. Nobody cheered you. You succeeded anyway."

I had to laugh, though tears swam in my eyes. "This is true. I'd have been quicker to ask Pam Steinbech to take her clothes off if there'd been a bunch of cheerleaders yelling 'go for it' in the background."

"As long as they're cheering the right thing for you." Kylie closed her eyes. "When it came to love, sex . . . My cheerleaders were all wrong. Promise me."

"I promise," I said, hoping she was so sleepy now she'd be comforted by the words, but not remember them in the morning.

I stood at the doorway to my study for a few minutes, staring at the book as it lay on my desk. I finally shook myself out of my foolishness, and carried it once more near the fire.

I don't believe in these things, and yet I'd given them power over me by not telling Kylie what else I had read in the book. If it was all nonsense and superstition, why had I not told her?

My finger tracing along as I read, I said aloud, "*Yesterday is water. A spell to conjure memory.*" Honestly, the idea of someone sending me, of all people, an unreadable spell book was ludicrous. "*The past comes to thy mind in thy time. Prepare ye well lest ye recall ill. Think as thou would to recall to thee good.*" Even the poetry was poor. After so much study and effort I had in my hand the ravings of some lonely adherent to a long-dead belief system.

Good memories or bad, I teased myself, what shall it be? I recalled Kylie's earlier mention of the club. Yes, the ease with which I'd allowed that woman to pick me up had been youthful folly. I'd been trying to shock Kylie into . . . acting. Doing *something*. I'd thought our father's hold on her had lasted far too long. I remembered his mournful gaze the day he'd dramatically declared that the Lord had sent him two daughters, but only one was Truly His.

I took a deep breath and struck a dramatic pose. The next words were meaningless, so I sounded them out according to basic English rules. "*Arc-nim-tah-pellum!*" Then I put the book under one of the cushions on the sofa and set about doing a much needed review of this week's essays.

I worked long into the night and no memories, good or bad, came near me. Bast did not hiss at shadows, and no spirits tapped on the windows. The fire burned clear and true.

Hocus pocus, my eye. Some time after midnight I brushed my teeth, scrambled into flannel pajamas and crawled into the cold bed.

The throb of disco music stunned me awake.

Kylie shouted, "Is it always like this?"

"I've only been here twice before!" I pulled her by the hand into the throng near the bar, but by the time we were in a position to order something, she'd been asked to dance. I watched my sister, younger by eleven minutes, swirl into the pulsating mass of bodies.

We were very similar in looks, but Kylie always danced and I always graced the wall. It could make a sister bitter. On the other hand, I was certain that even my limited experience of sex had been more satisfying than hers. It was, so far, a leveling of the scales. If the night went as I planned, though, I would lose my advantage. I was willing to pay that price to see Kylie truly happy.

If her tastes were anything like mine—and I really did believe they were—that inviting, smiling woman she was dancing with might be able to succeed where I knew others had failed. Two years of that stinking Bible school would perhaps finally get washed away tonight.

"You look like you're trying to get a drink."

Smoky was certainly the word for the fine pair of eyes gazing down at me. They belonged to a leather-jacketed brunette whose stance said she was looking to take someone home. It was a posturing I had long detested in men, but in women it sometimes stirred me, like it was stirring me right now.

Condensation beaded on the beer that she bought me and I committed every inch of her face, particularly her mouth, to memory. Her lips were moist and pale, in that alluring combination of soft and firm. "I'm Hayley."

"Jane."

"Not plain."

"Nor in the rain in Spain."

I smiled as I glanced toward the dance floor where Kylie was just visible, dancing hip to hip with her own smoky-eyed companion. If I were out of the way, I mused, she might feel free to act. Who wants to get seduced with their big sister watching? "Rain is mainly a pain."

"Oh, with the right woman it can be damned fun, rain."

Relieved I didn't have to think of more rhymes, I said, "I prefer showers to rain, but I'd give rain a try, in Tahiti."

"Sorry, I am fresh out of Tahitian rain this week."

"But you have a shower, right?" The little voice reminding me I had two exams in the morning was very faint. I liked Jane's eyes and wit. I wanted Kylie to see that it was okay to say yes.

"I do." Jane's hazel eyes were sparkling with mirth. "Would you like to dance?"

It wasn't precisely dancing, but Jane had smooth moves on the small square of parquet, somehow keeping our breasts in contact as our hands roamed. She feathered kisses over my face, a few at a time. I liked her slow approach after my boldness. It was as if even though I'd practically said I'd go home with her, she still wanted to seduce me properly.

It was working. The mixture of her eyes and her mouth, the kisses, the alluring cologne she wore, and the occasional laughing comment, was all making me want to experience her as well.

When I located Kylie again, she was dancing with all the grace and exuberance that she showed at soccer. Maybe soccer was her first love but there was no reason a woman couldn't be her second. That son-of-a-bitch, our father, had done his Lord's Work. Now I was doing Sister Work.

Jane leaned in to kiss me again and the room was filled with a silence so profound it hurt my ears. I became slowly aware of a distant, steady beeping in another place, another time. That heavy, damnable voice said, "I wish it were you."

I flinched from the returned onslaught of dance music and Jane said, "It is loud, isn't it? Would you like to leave?"

Kylie was hip to hip with her increasingly attentive partner, not far from us. I waved to get her attention, then turned the gesture into a mimed, "Bye, bye." Turning back into Jane's embrace, I kissed her full on the mouth. We moved together toward the door. I hoped with all my heart that Kylie got a clue.

I welcomed the humid, warm air. The night was heavy with the scent of cut grass and jasmine. A rose bush, laden with yellow blooms gone silver in the moonlight, drooped over the fence near Jane's car. The street lights flickered in the reflection of the dark hood, and bluesy jazz piano sparkled from the speakers as we drove. Jane's hand was on my thigh and I was warm where it rested. The warmth was spreading.

The wallpaper near her bed was white with small diamonds of purple and blue. The lamp Jane left burning cast a soft lavender light on her features.

"Make yourself comfortable," she said softly.

"Okay." I ran one hand under the waist of her jacket, inhaling the tang of the leather and the sweet spice of her perfume. "This is comfortable."

Her hands moved sinuously over my body, setting my nerves on fire as she undressed me. My skin chilled deliciously at the touch of the sheets against my bare back. Jane left the light on and the reflection of a skinny woman with dark hair, hunger plain on her face, glistened at me from the depths of her eyes.

"I think this is the best part," Jane whispered. Her thigh slipped between mine, warm and muscled.

I arched up to her, feeling the shock of all my nerves jangling at the warmth of her body. "What?"

"All my skin. All your skin." With the scent of the club fading, her cologne was more pronounced, mingling with shampoo, soap and woman smells that I so adored.

I responded to her touch with a sigh and shiver. "I'm not usually so—"

"Don't," she said quickly. "It's okay to be whatever it is you need and want."

I lost myself in kissing the freckles that spilled across her shoulders and chest. As a young teen, with singular abandon, I'd learned all the clinical words for where Jane was touching me. Some were sexy, like *vulva*. It rolled through my mouth, sounding and feeling like inviting velvet. I liked *mons*, with a moaning *M* to begin it. Her hand was cupping me there and slipping down the slope. She paused to smile as I gasped.

"I think that's the best part, too. It's *all* the best part."

"When you do that I am so glad to be female—" I arched my back as her fingers slid over my clit. *Clit* was sexy to me, *clitoris* was not. *Clit*, short and sharp, like the prickles that jolted through my body, puckering my nipples and tingling down my thighs.

"I take it you like that?"

"Can't you tell?"

"Yes, I can tell. Does my talking distract you?"

"No—I like that, too."

Her voice a low purr, she brushed her lips to mine as she said, "I want to fuck you."

Her words and the firm pressure on my clit made my body jerk. "Yes. Please." I thought of Kylie for the last time, hoping she had found her way to a moment like this. "Yes, please."

Her fingers explored my vulva, parting folds and finding wet heat. "Right now, or shall I wait a little while? This is very fun."

"Now," I whispered. Her fingers slipped through my folds again and my legs quivered in response.

"Are you sure? I can do this for a very long time." One finger almost slipped inside, but withdrew.

"Please, now." My hips rose in frantic response to another brush of her finger near my opening.

She laughed, low and sexy, and her mouth captured mine as a lone finger tipped inward. I pushed myself down, but she moved her hand, too, keeping me hanging in the frustrating, arousing space of almost.

"You do want this, don't you?"

"I won't beg." I gritted my teeth to hold back a hoarse, needy plea. "Don't tease me."

She kissed me again and moaned, and I felt her fingers fill me. Her thumb pressed down firmly on my clit and I arched into her next push. My world was pulsing to the movement of her hand. The light went and there was a hammering in my ears that let in only her gasps and my sharp cries. I was a wound coil, ever tightened by her body on mine. I tried for short, easy words like *coming* and *more*, but they were caught behind my bared teeth.

Her fingertips danced on the nerve cluster I could no longer coherently name, high inside me. My legs spasmed, my arms went to jelly and my nipples tightened to hard, red aches. There were no words in me that would pass my lips now. I always lost them even as my mind burned with their red afterimage. *Don't stop. Fuck me. Please don't stop.*

I felt as if I was screaming, loud, long, fierce. Neighbors would think I was dying. Some might know I was in the throes of life. My body shook as I screamed inside but I knew, as always, I did not make a sound.

It was a long journey back to my body, hand over hand climbing up from depths—or down from heights, I could never tell. I did not want to sleep, not yet. Sound came back to me slowly.

" . . . incredible. The way you moved."

I swallowed, not yet certain I could speak. I made a sound and I don't know what Jane thought I said, but she kissed me, hard and furious, then her hands gripped my arms as she turned me over.

"You can do that again. I can feel you still clenching down on my hand. I know you can." Her voice was heavy with passion as she pulled me to my hands and knees. She did not tease me, but pushed inside me before I could manage a yes or a no. I had always rested after that kind of orgasm and for a moment I almost struggled to escape her grasp. But the stunning truth that she was right—I could go that high, that hard again—spun me back into that space without words, beyond where light could reach me. The only sound I heard was her hand fucking me.

I broke into a sweat and felt it chill on my hot skin. That another woman could do this to me, another woman could know how to get me to this place—every time was more than the last. I was down on my elbows, my head on the sheets between my forearms. My breath came in great gasps. I wanted to beg her never to stop. I wanted to groan and scream. The harder she fucked me, the quieter I became. My body did all the talking.

Enough time passed to form the thought that I had never taken this long. I wanted to come so that the words trapped in my body could flow again. Frustration tightened my muscles around her fingers. Even though my eyes were open all I could see now was black streaked with yellow.

More yellow when I felt her other hand knotting into my hair. She pulled me up to my hands again and into my silence she hoarsely said, "This is how you want to fuck, we'll do it all night!"

More yellow, pushing away the black. When her hand let go of my hair to grasp one nipple just as fiercely, I ached to cry out. My nerves were dancing with fire like sunlight. Everything felt so good, but the last bit of the arc toward climax eluded me. I was too hot, too high.

And then I felt the cool whisper of her breath on my spine, and the hand at my nipple let go, instead smoothing over my chest and stomach. Gentle, sweet even. Her touch brought a flush of emotions and my head jerked up. She fucked me hard, but touched me soft. It was soft that brought my shivering release. She moaned as I came on her hand. Crumpling to the sheets, I found words at last, a jumble of them. "So good . . . just like that . . . how did you know . . . more . . . everything . . ."

"Oh, baby," she murmured as she collapsed next to me. "Baby, you are very, very fun to fuck."

My body was melting into the bed. I was glad she'd found it fun, but *fun* was not the first word I would have chosen to describe how I felt. But I could think of nothing better, so I nodded and echoed, "That was fun."

Her hand stroked my shoulder and arm. She pulled me half on top of her so I could rest in her arms. The sound of her heartbeat seemed to push away the last of the black. My senses stirred as my thigh eased between hers and was immediately smeared with wonderful, slippery excitement.

"You can rest a little more," she suggested softly.

I kissed my way from one nipple to the other. "I'm dying to go down on you."

I had the satisfaction of hearing her swallow, hard. "I've wanted that from the first time I kissed you."

A throaty laugh escaped me. "I was hoping you'd get that idea."

Words were no problem for me now. *Labia* seemed too clinical, as did *pubis*. In this mood, given what she'd just done to me and what I intended to do to her, only one word worked. I lightly coiled my fingertips in her pubic hair and gazed in hunger at the reddened, wet lips. "Your cunt is beautiful."

"Aren't they all?"

"Indeed," I agreed. "You know, a Valentine's heart shape is nothing like the human heart. Scholars believe that it was originally drawn to represent female genitals."

"Really? I suppose—" She sucked in her breath as I kissed her clit softly. "Oh, yes."

My kiss lingered as her legs spread more for me. "Next time you look at a Valentine's heart you'll see it. You'll smile, seeing vaginas all around you."

"That's all very interesting, but right now I want your mouth doing this." Her hand cupped the back of my head and pulled me in.

Sweet, soaked flesh, soft under my tongue, shuddering when I pulled it into my mouth. My tongue learned every inch of her, each fold, the way bone and skin formed the swooping curve of her cunt that invited me to push inside her. I tasted deeply. *Cunt* was a word used to wound, to diminish, to make a woman hate that part of her body. Jane was, at that moment, all cunt to me, and she was glorious. I drank and suckled, lapped and buried my face there. How could anyone not love this?

I thrust my tongue into her, then licked up to her clit. She cooed when two fingers went where my tongue had been and I could feel goose bumps rising on her thighs. Her knees rose and her hands left my head to cup her breasts as her chest heaved.

The sweet salty taste of her flooded my mouth, soaked my chin. Laughter bubbled throughout my body, so wonderful was her response and my joy at having brought her to such pleasure.

I rested my head on her thigh for a moment, petting her soaked hair with my hand. "You have a beautiful cunt."

"I'm glad you think so." She sighed deeply. "Come up here and bring the covers with you."

Cool white sheets settled on our bodies and I appreciated the beauty of the curve from her hips to her fingertips as she stretched to turn out the light.

Dark settled around us. Her breathing steadied and I closed my eyes, ignoring the distant beeping, regular and steady. There was a squeak of shoes on linoleum.

The hated voice said, "I wish it was you."

My sudden movement to sit bolt upright dislodged Bast, who clawed my leg through the bedclothes by way of protest.

Heart pounding, I turned on the light. I was in my own bed. My own room. Jane was from long ago. A fantastic night never repeated. Coffee, toast and goodbye in the morning. I'd forgotten the music in the car, at least I thought I had. My recollections of sex were not so precise. I had not realized that when I was close to climax I couldn't even speak.

Hands over my eyes, I didn't even want to begin analyzing why I heard my father's voice mingled into a dream of incredibly hot sex. It was just too damned icky.

I heard the muffled sound of the toilet and realized Kylie had to be awake. She was never up in the middle of the night. I hopped out of bed and discovered my legs were wobbly and my crotch soaked. For a dream, it had been incredibly real.

Kylie was standing next to her bed, looking as if the task of getting into it was more than she could manage.

"How come you're up?"

"A dream woke me." She reached for her flattened pillow.

"I'll do that. You turn around and sit down. Are you okay? Was it a nightmare?"

"No—not scary. Sad." She perched on the edge of the bed as she watched me fluff her pillow and straighten the sheets. "I didn't know," she mumbled.

Bast hopped up and immediately set about kneading herself a place in the covers. "Tell me about it in the morning. Bast is here to see you to sleep."

"Steal my covers, you mean." I helped Kylie lift her legs into the bed, pushing away the comparison of them to how she had been even a year ago. "That cat's a user."

"The cat's a cat. Are you going to be able to sleep or should I get you a pill?"

"A pill. My back."

She dutifully took the small glass of milk and pain pill I brought her a few minutes later. The pill went down and she chased it with several more swallows of milk.

"You'll drop right off," I reassured her. I switched out the light and crossed to her door.

"Hayley?" Her voice sounded pale in the dark.

"What, sweetie?"

"Dad—did he ever say . . ."

"What?"

"Never mind. In the morning."

"In the morning," I echoed as I quietly shut the door. Shivering with cold I returned to my bed, but sleep was elusive. My hands roamed over my body as I tried to relax, but I know the clock had passed four a.m. before I finally dropped into restless sleep.

CHAPTER 3

My eyes popped open when the alarm went off. For a moment my weariness was so profound I nearly cried.

The life of a professor has many freedoms, but being able to call in sick without causing a great many people a great deal of stress isn't one of them. My first class was at nine and I *could* cancel my midday office hours and come home to nap. It was just a matter of getting myself up and moving.

I was just sipping a strong cup of Irish Breakfast tea when there was a quiet knock on the kitchen door. My first reaction was of surprisingly strong pleasure to see Aurora on the step. My second thought was that I was moving around like someone twice my age and my hair looked like Bast had used it for a toy. "Hi. Come in, it's freezing out there."

Her pert nose was red from the frigid air. Bundled from head to toe, she looked frozen. "I've locked myself out of the house."

"Oh, what a pain. I wish I had a key."

"A phone will do it. I'd rather call a locksmith than break a window."

Phone book located, I carried up Kylie's milk and pills. She stirred as I set them down. "Whenever you're ready."

She said something incoherent and I wasn't at all sure she wouldn't go back to sleep. I paused for a moment in the bathroom to rake the brush through my hair, but it was hopeless.

As I walked back into the kitchen I caught Aurora warming her hands on the tea kettle. "How rude of me—please pour yourself a cup. Bagel? Butter or cream cheese?"

"Cream cheese. I've not met any of my other neighbors and didn't want to bang on doors unknown. I'm so glad you're an early riser," she observed as she joined me at the table.

"I could have used a few more hours this morning," I found myself admitting. "Kylie was up for a while."

She gave me a look of intermingled understanding and sympathy. "It must make your frame of reference very short." She warmed her hands over the steam from the cup.

I blinked, then recalled our first conversation. "It does. Temporarily. Kylie is the one with the . . . without much time."

"My father was very ill the last six months of his life," she said softly. "I know what it's like to care for someone. Raging against the dying of the light yet welcoming it when the pain is bad."

Tears welled in my eyes. If anyone else had presumed to talk to me about how I felt I'd have uttered the classic New Englander brush off, "We'll get by." Instead, I found myself saying, "It's getting hard to keep her comfortable."

"But she wants to be here as long as she can. I understand."

It was clear she did. We sipped companionably until Bast arrived to vet the newcomer. It was, apparently, love at first sight. Bast could not get enough of Aurora's legs, and wrapped herself around them in a display of adoration the likes of which I'd never seen.

"She seems to like you."

"Cats and I usually get along. My old kitty passed away last year and I haven't been adopted by a new one yet." Aurora reached down to scratch Bast with one lazy finger and Bast's purring became a palpable throb in the room. Lucky damn cat.

I heard Kylie's halting step in the hall. There had been a time when her compact, well-muscled body had creaked the flooring and stairs, but she was so slight now that I hadn't even heard her. One of my biggest worries was that she would fall. Moving her bed downstairs would likely happen in a couple of weeks. Given her prognosis, that seemed like a long way in the future.

"I thought I heard a voice." She struggled to the chair I pulled out for her, wrapped up tight in her fleece-lined robe. "Trouble?"

Aurora smiled over her cup of tea. "I locked myself out of my house. I was just going to go for a walk because the sun is shining. I made three trips back inside the house for extra layers, a cap, the really thick gloves, and so on. Last time in I must have set my keys down somewhere."

"Nanook of the North," Kylie said.

"It's pathetic, isn't it? I saw two women go jogging by in nothing but pants and lightweight shirts. I might not ever adapt to the cold."

I set down a mug of milk-doctored tea and a small plate of chopped dates with honey-glazed almonds, Kylie's favorite. "Can I get you some of these? They're delectable."

"I'm already scrounging plenty." Aurora hefted her bagel.

"Here," Kylie said. "Have a taste."

Aurora said something back and they both giggled, but I was too busy watching my sister to listen. She'd dropped one shoulder lower than the other, and one thin hand carefully tucked surprisingly well-brushed hair behind one ear. Her gaze was lowered for a moment, then raised to look sidelong at Aurora as she laughed.

I'd not seen Kylie do that in ages. For a wonderful minute, she glowed with life and sensuality. I mentally added twenty pounds to her, and the healthy sheen her hair had always had. Flirting with Aurora gave me my sister back for just that moment and I savored it all that I could.

"Actually," Kylie was saying, "I only woke up because I had a bad dream. Not that it was bad, except . . . it was a dream about things I've never done and wish I had." She glanced at me, then, a question in her eyes, but she didn't voice it.

"Is there still time?" Aurora's acceptance of Kylie's condition contained no false cheer or hope. It was, for me at least, refreshing.

"No. Not that." She opened her eyes meaningfully and I was reminded for some reason of my own explicit dream of last night. "It's too late for some things. Maybe I can still get in skydiving, though."

"No way," I said firmly. "I'd have to go with you and I'm not jumping out of a plane."

"I could find someone else, you know. Not everyone is a 'fraidy cat." Kylie popped another almond into her mouth and chewed with gusto.

"Oh, yeah?"

Aurora interrupted our bickering by saying, "The phone book is right here. We could look up lessons."

"Stop that!" I gave her a meaningful look and she allowed me to put the book out of Kylie's reach. "You'll give her bad ideas."

"Aw, Hayley." Her face alight with laughter Kylie was about to bait me, but a nut slipped out of her fingers. By the time she picked it up off the floor the spell had broken. The light faded and the smile, though still present, lost its glow. If Aurora was aware of the change it did not show in her face. At least not until Kylie had begun the arduous climb up the stairs to bed again and we were alone at the table.

"I imagine your sister never wanted for a date. That's some kind of magnetism she's got."

I shrugged. "She was very popular but didn't go out much. Heaps of friends, not many lovers."

Aurora asked, sounding as if it was almost against her will, "And you?"

Our gaze met and the light in the room seemed to flicker. Aurora's face sizzled in my brain and I realized I was covered in goose bumps. "Not many of either."

She tried to smile, but it didn't quite materialize. "Me, neither."

I wondered if my inner purring was as loud as Bast's. I flattened my hand on the table and it took all my strength not to slide it toward hers. I saw her fingers twitch reflexively. I extended mine, losing the fight with my composure—then a horn sounded outside.

"The locksmith," Aurora breathed.

"The locksmith." She rose to put her mug in the sink. It was completely out of character for me to imagine her nude, gracefully moving across my line of sight. Yet I did so, and realized again that I still had no idea what her hair looked like.

"Thank you for the tea and warmth. I'm sure I'm quite rosy." She glanced at me, one hand on the kitchen doorknob.

"Me, too. You're welcome, I mean." Cary Grant I was not. The ticking of the clock seemed very loud in the silence that fell between us, then I unwillingly looked at it. "Oh my lord, look at the time."

I lingered long enough to watch her step across the snow to talk to the locksmith. She spoke a few words to him, then stole a look over her shoulder. I waved awkwardly, then hurried upstairs.

I paused to make sure Kylie was tucked back in bed. She was draining the last of the water from the glass by the bed.

"I told you she was hot and gay. I was right, huh?"

"You were sure flirting with her."

"Yeah. I'd give you a run for your money if I had a chance of finishing the game." She rested back on her pillows, her eyes going a little glassy from the meds.

"I suppose it's a good thing we never competed for the same women, then. I'd hate to see you lose." I smiled at her as I pulled the covers up.

"Yeah, right." I went for more water and heard her say more loudly, "You promised me you'd go out. So ask her."

"Maybe," I hedged. It was not an onerous prospect, given the electricity we'd been generating in the kitchen. But there was time for that later.

"My dream was about sex," she admitted as I set the refilled glass of water on the bedside table.

"What's wrong with that?"

"It was—I mean, I've seen porn. And it wasn't like that. I didn't know women . . . looked like that. Could be so fierce about it."

I didn't know what to say. My own dream had been explicit and, yes, fierce. "I hope you have more dreams, but that they don't make you so sad."

"Me, too." She sighed softly and her eyes closed. She whispered something.

"What, sweetie?" I leaned close to her mouth.

Gasping, I hurried to my shower, certain I had heard wrong. I don't know what Kylie had said, but it could not have been "plain Jane, rain in Spain."

Classes, office hours—my mind was in a whirl throughout. I felt as if I was waiting for something to happen. I heard Kylie's whispered words from my dream, my father's condemning voice, Aurora's laughter. By the time I got home I was in a state of nervous excitement, but I couldn't have explained to anyone why.

I fairly burst into my study and then I knew what was pulling me there with this bizarre sense of anticipation. The book seemed to gleam in the dim room. After I turned on the lights it nearly glowed.

I opened the page to the spell for memory, reading again. I could hear a voice, very like my own, pointing out that I'd been warned. I hadn't been very careful about my choice of memories before I'd gone to sleep, hence the intermingling of the night with Jane and my interaction with my father the first time Kylie had been hospitalized.

Next time, I began to muse, then I snapped the book shut. Next time? There wasn't going to be a next time. This was absurd in the extreme. There was no such thing as spells and charms, any more than there were gods in the fireplace and fairies in the snowflakes.

Caught between anger, fear and arousal, I dumped the contents of a hutch drawer onto the floor, put the book in the drawer and closed it. I felt better once it was done, but even after I put a chair in front of the hutch I thought I could see light seeping past the edges of the drawer.

It was all absurd.

I measured time by the day, as Kylie's illness demanded. Within a week it was the half-day, as I began dashing home between classes or shaving time off my office hours to check up on her. On one of my two trips back and forth to campus, however, Aurora was usually on her way as well. She did not offer tea or chestnuts again, but half the time we'd arrive at campus or the foot of my walk and I'd realize I had no idea what we'd talked about, just that during those minutes I forgot my stress, forgot my grief for Kylie. Her quiet touch on my arm when we parted was *not* one of the highlights of the last year.

On a day when I'd seen nothing of her, I would chide myself for missing the sight of her heavily swaddled figure, pink-chilled nose and a smile that I would not let myself crave. Today was a good day, as we plodded toward home in the swirling snow.

"I'm telling you this is a warming trend." I batted a snowflake off my eyelash. Between the cold cover and the early sunset, it was unnaturally dark.

"That sounds suspiciously like a chamber of commerce lie. What's so warm about this?"

"Another degree and the snow would turn to rain."

"Freezing rain, you mean." She sidestepped a dog out for a walk. The dog was happy, the owner was not. "I'm not saying it isn't beautiful and that all this snow and cold is unnatural for this part of the world, it's just not natural for me. I thought I'd get used to it easier, somehow. A lot about the countryside seems familiar to me."

"Your people hail from these parts, don't they?"

"Two hundred years ago, maybe. I think—" She yanked her ubiquitous cap down harder on her head. "I think the blood has thinned."

I paused to look up my walk. No lights on, which meant Kylie was still asleep. "I think I'd likely melt in Arizona."

"Maybe not." Her voice was so soft I glanced at her curiously. The look on her face stopped my heart, it was so tender and inviting. "You might like it."

I would if you were there, I wanted to say. I was in no position to utter those words, I told myself. My life was not my own and wouldn't be for—a while. Though I knew Kylie would not see the spring, I would not make any plans. Did that mean I was hoping for some sort of error in the diagnoses to be found? Maybe. Or maybe I just didn't ever want to start a thought or sentence with "after Kylie is dead." I stared at my feet, and said only, "Maybe."

She touched my arm the way she always did when saying good-bye, but this time she added a squeeze. "I understand."

Her boots, which had lost a lot of their new-purchase luster, crunched over the sidewalk toward her own house. I wanted to ask her in for dinner. I wanted to ask her to stay the night. How would that make Kylie feel, watching me . . . happy?

I made a couple of typical French plates for dinner, and set them down on the table in my study, planning to get Kylie in a half an hour if she hadn't woken on her own. Forcing Aurora out of my mind, I made myself focus on papers to grade. It was several minutes before I realized that Kylie had been calling for me, her voice increasingly upset.

"What is it?" I found her sprawled on her bed, one leg over the side.

Through tears, she answered, "I can't get up. I can't . . . try."

No, I thought. No—she had at least five more weeks at home. At least, the doctor had said. But he'd also cautioned that her decline, when she took the last turn for the worse, would be rapid. Privately, he'd added that the rapidity with which the inevitable occurred would be a blessing.

I crawled onto the bed next to her so I could take her in my arms. I shushed and rocked her, not knowing what else I could do. "I'm sorry I took so long to hear you. Sorry, Kylie, so sorry."

Her tears calmed, slowly, and when I suggested we try to get her to a sitting position, she agreed.

"It's so frustrating. I tell my muscles to do something and they won't." She swatted weakly at her thigh. "And I have to pee so bad."

She'd once high jumped seven feet, flopping over the bar with a triumphant whoop. I couldn't let memories break me down right now. One of us had to be strong. "Next stop bathroom."

Something was clearly wrong with her legs. For several weeks I'd been imagining the downstairs parlor into a bedroom so she did not have to climb the stairs during the day. Now was the time, I thought. I'd get the home visitation nurse, too, and then wearily recalled that I needed the specialist's concurrence if I hoped for insurance to cover even a part of the cost.

Kylie finished on the toilet, but as I was getting her to her feet, her pallor intensified. Without warning she vomited on both of us, then melted into helpless tears.

"It's okay, it's okay. It's not like there was anything in your stomach. Fresh clothes and we'll be fine. And I think it's time for a trip to the emergency room."

Her hands gripped my arms. "You won't leave me there. You can't. Please, Hayley, don't take me there. I want to be here. I won't . . . I won't . . ."

I shushed her, holding her tight against me in spite of the mess. "I will do everything I can to bring you home again." *We're supposed to have more time. They promised!*

It was nearly an hour before we were both clean and I had Kylie in the car. The night air was cruelly cold and Kylie shivered all the way to the hospital. The intake nurse knew us, which always helps, and the resident oncologist arrived quickly. Kylie was given a concoction to both calm her and relieve the rising pain, and was quickly wheeled away toward the imaging center.

"I suspect it's not the cancer right now, and I've paged the neurologist." Dr. Gaines gave me a look that didn't even come close to hopeful. "I think she's at another stage of the bone degeneration. How has she been eating?"

"Poorly. Her electrolytes are probably a mess. I've had to coax her to drink anything."

His beeper went off and he glanced at it with irritation. "I have to see another patient, but I will check back. She'll need to stay here for the night."

"Can you sign the paperwork for the home visitation nurse?"

He nodded and wrote something on the chart tucked under his arm. "It's time. You can talk to her while she's in imaging but she's going to be pretty doped up by now."

I wearily made my way across the building and found Kylie extremely groggy. Still, I knew she'd understand some of what I was saying, so I told her everything I knew. Speaking slowly and clearly, I added, "You have to stay here tonight. Tomorrow I will come and get you. Do you understand, Kylie? I will come back and take you home."

She squeezed my hand and closed her eyes with the slightest of nods. After that all I could do was wait for the neurologist, who told me, about an hour later, that Kylie's results needed further review. In the morning he would know more.

By the time I pulled into the driveway I was so tired that only the rapid chill overtaking the car made me get out. I hauled myself up the steps, my body tired but my mind whirling. I told myself to do something useful, but standing in the parlor, trying to decide where to put Kylie's bed, was surreal. We could not be at this milepost already. We were promised . . . it wasn't fair.

I sank to my knees and indulged myself in a bitter, frustrated crying fit. None of this was fair. It wasn't fair that she was sick, and by the flip of the same coin, it wasn't fair that I was healthy. It wasn't fair that we were both so alone. I felt small and useless.

Eventually I made myself get up and mop my face in the bathroom sink. The red blotches and puffy eyes I regarded with some satisfaction. At least I looked as wretched as I felt.

I didn't care that I was exhausted and midnight was behind me. I wanted to get something useful done, something that would make a difference in Kylie's few tomorrows.

My decision to move her bed turned out to be ill-advised. With the mattress stripped and leaning against the doorway I realized, through sniveling tears, it was foolish to do it alone. Sleep for me would be more important. I'd get the local handyman and his helper to come over in the morning.

Bast coiled around my legs and I shooed her away. She resentfully stalked from the room, tail lashing Kylie's now upright mattress, which as far as Bast was concerned, was Bast's rightful nighttime sleeping place. I set her on my bed and turned on the electric blanket to appease her. She didn't exactly purr.

I found myself sitting at my desk, too numb to turn on the computer. Sleep, I reminded myself. It took a great effort to shut off the light and stand up. As I turned toward the door, a soft light caught my eye. Moving closer, I realized what it was: white light seeped from the drawer where I had put the mysterious book.

Mystics throughout the centuries write of crossroads. They tell of the conflict between their old teachings and the new ones clamoring at their minds to be taken in and believed. Hearts pounding, senses overloaded with portents and symbols, they reached into the unknown and pulled a belief formerly outside their world into their being. The transformation became the pivotal moment of their lives. In the most common version of the tale, the mystic would then spend the rest of their lives trying to coax others to their way of thinking.

I was no mystic converting from one faith to another. I did not believe in this book. I did not believe in fairy tales either. My father looked in his book for all the answers and I would not follow in his footsteps.

Because I was so tired, maybe, I heard a little voice of doubt for the first time in forever. What if, the voice murmured, he was right? But I'd never turn to *his* book—it had too often been pointed at women and gays like a gun.

What if, the voice persevered, *your* book is right. What if there is a cure for Kylie in its pages? What if it came to you precisely so you could save her?

What if . . .

Trembling, I pulled the book from the drawer. I had said a word from it yesterday and had a dream. A dream that Kylie had also had. But it had saddened her, I told myself. Hurt her, when she was hurting enough. Kylie did not need to know now what she had not chosen. Knowledge was sometimes cruel. But I was a researcher, an academic. Cruel, knowledge could be, but it was never without a point.

I couldn't *not* open the book. It would be a test, I told myself. The dream could be a fluke, a twin thing. I needed to do something of which I could be certain.

An index or table of contents had not occurred to the scribe. It began on the first page with a spell to "purify" water. There was a special word to say, but the spell itself was to bring the water to a rolling boil for ten minutes. Basic sanitation. *Presto open sesame* not required. It was foolish to read any more of them, I told myself, but read I did.

Page after page, I read. Magic words to soothe, rituals to sanctify, recipes for healing cakes and restorative syrups—page after page of silly, pointless information. I did not believe in this. Angrily, I decided I would prove it useless.

"*Thought is a river. Distance is a thought. What is desired shall come to thee, even if unwilling or spirit not free,*" I read aloud. Well, that sounded powerful and amazing enough. All I needed was to light a pure white candle, pick what I desired, and say the word.

What did I desire? A cure for Kylie, more than anything, but the spell seemed to be for tangible objects. An apple from downstairs? A blanket from in front of the fire? Aurora flickered across my mind and I shook my head to free it of her image. I wanted to hold and be held desperately at this moment, if I was being honest. An apple, that would do it. Or not. I was quite certain the apple on the counter downstairs would remain there.

One of the emergency candles from my bottom desk drawer was white. I let the flame steady before I struck the same dramatic pose as last night, clutched the book to my chest, and intoned the magic word. "*Ah-null-nath-rack!*"

Nothing happened. I peeked into the hallway and no apple was floating up the stairs. Quelling a sense of disappointment, I seriously considered putting the book in the fireplace and setting it alight. What a waste of my time and energy, getting me to hope for something that was—

The fireplace was turning into mist.

The andirons were quickly lost in a gray fog that rapidly expanded toward me. I couldn't move. I wanted to, but my brain didn't seem to have control of my legs. Gasping in the kind of fear that encompasses shock and surprise and outright terror of the unknown, I watched the mist coat the sofa, my desk, the piles of paperwork. It was coming for me.

I held my breath as it billowed to my face. I felt the cold of it on my arms, but it came no closer. Even though it was a freak of air, an assortment of molecules colder than the rest, I felt examined and considered. I wanted to look away but it was staring at me. Staring at the book, too. I wondered if I should offer it up. It wasn't really mine, even though I could read it.

I went on trying to hold my breath and nothing seemed to change until, in the measureless depths of the fog I saw a swirl of vibrant red. It seemed to be dancing, or spinning, or struggling, I wasn't sure.

It was getting bigger, though. I was frozen in place and my heart was hammering as if I had run up ten flights of stairs, screaming. Red . . . my apple? All this for my apple?

But this apple wasn't just red. There were creamy hues, now, and something that glittered. Rippling and twisting, it came closer and closer to me and it grew. Whatever it was, it refused to solidify. Red spinning, cream twisting, glitter twinkling.

As it grew past the size of a child, the mist began to recede. The chill that had not quite touched me was drawing back, blanketing the figure in its depths. But the gray was no match for the red, and abruptly the shape took on edges and depth. Long, swaying locks of waist-length red hair obscured the woman's body. It was a woman, easy to discern as she wore no clothes and her shapely attributes were quite noticeable.

Hair blew violently to one side as the mist retreated behind her. Around her neck was a strand of sparkling clear stones.

Standing in my study, where only minutes earlier I had been completely alone, stood an unknown woman with vibrant red hair on her head and between her legs, and a slender, yet curvaceous body that my own responded to in a purely Pavlovian way.

"What in mother's name do you think you're doing?"

I looked more closely at her face and realized she was very angry—and familiar. I mentally erased the hair and added a snow cap. The pert nose I tinted with pink.

We stared at each other as the last shimmer of the mist subsided. Then Aurora, her hair settling on her shoulders like a mantle of fire, her voice seething with outrage, shouted, "And what are you doing with *my* book?"

CHAPTER 4

"Mother spare me amateurs and the foolish!" Aurora, wearing Kylie's robe, continued to glare at me.

I couldn't say I blamed her. I said again, "I had no idea anything would happen. I don't believe in this kind of thing."

"I was busy, you know. You can't just grab a person—"

"I didn't think I was doing anything. I wished for an apple."

"Oh, please."

"I'll show you the page, and I thought of an apple. It was a test, because I don't believe in it."

"So you say, over and over, but here I am."

"You could go home."

"Not without my book."

"It must have been delivered here by mistake."

"If you don't believe in it, how come you can read Goddess Hand? I didn't think they taught that in college."

"Is that what this is?"

She blinked. The book lay on the kitchen table between us, and she had yet to touch it. "If you don't know Goddess Hand, how did you read it?"

"I don't know. At first I thought it was blank, then I realized I could see characters by firelight, and then I'd wake up hours later with a backache."

Her mouth opened for a moment, then she shut it again without saying anything. Her fingers drummed the tabletop, then that stilled, too.

"Are you sure you don't want some tea?" I was glad of the hot cup in my hands. I was feeling more drained by the minute.

"No, thank you. You've never been initiated? You've never danced the spiral? Called the moon?"

"I don't believe—"

"Stop that, of course you do. How did I get here?"

"You don't understand. Superstition is—"

"I am not a superstition or a hallucination."

"I'm so tired and scared and worried that maybe you are." There had to be a perfectly logical explanation for everything, I thought. There *had* to be.

"Give me my book back, and you won't have to worry about doing something truly foolish."

"It's yours. Take it." I swallowed back tears of exhaustion.

"No, you've read it and used it. You have to give it to me."

I pushed it toward her. "There."

She picked up a cotton tea towel, felt it between finger and thumb for a moment. "You don't have a square of silk, do you?" I just stared. "Okay, this will do. Wrap it in this and hand it to me."

"And if I don't?"

"It'll go on tempting you to try what you don't understand and can't control. I inherited that book and sent it to . . . a friend . . . to have the binding repaired. I've only used it twice in five years. Thank goodness you've only used it once."

I didn't want to tell her about the dream spell. I wrapped it in the tea towel, my hands shaking. "Here, then."

She wouldn't take it until I was facing her, and I looked her in the eye. With a hard swallow, for something in me did not want to give it up, I extended it toward her.

Her hands rested on top of mine for a moment and she gasped

as something that felt like static electricity seemed to dance on the surface of the book. I snatched my hands back and then she had it. From within the folds of Kylie's robe I saw her necklace shimmering with light.

"You used it more than once."

"Twice, but the first time I thought it was a joke."

"You shouldn't fool around with what you don't understand. You might as well play with electricity."

I'd had enough lectures. Tired, cold and feeling more tied in knots by the minute, I said, "Can we continue this discussion tomorrow?"

"As long as tomorrow you won't pretend it never happened."

"I'm sure there's an explanation. Something that makes sense."

"The most obvious explanation *does* make sense." Something flashed in her eyes that made my heart pound. "There was a time when a safely delivered, healthy baby was considered an act of magic. Then science explained it. The moon would blot out the sun—magic, until science explained it."

"What's your point?"

"Just because science *can* explain something doesn't mean it's still not magic. Everything around us is magic. Just because science *can't* explain it doesn't mean it doesn't exist, either. Atoms existed before the electron microscope. Science, reasoning and comprehension are gifts of nature. Understanding magic does not rob it of the goddess's power."

I couldn't help but roll my eyes. "Oh please. Don't tell me you hanker for the good ol' days of matriarchy. Matriarchy is a construct, just like patriarchy. It's what its believers created to give order and sense to their world."

"You say that like it's a bad thing," she snapped back. "I believe our world is magic. I visualize that magic and the order behind it as the female divine. I don't care how others view it. It works for me."

"But if I don't then I'm an idiot."

"Believe what you want." She clutched the book against her

chest and turned abruptly to the kitchen door. I had always thought Kylie's fuzzy blue slippers were amusing, but on Aurora's feet they were abruptly very, very sexy. "You don't have to believe in an apple for it to ripen."

"Then how did you get here?" The last thing I could handle right now was her talking like a fortune cookie. I didn't know why we were fighting but I didn't want it to be my fault. She was the one who thought that crazy book was . . . real. I couldn't believe it.

"How should I know? I haven't gone wading through this book like a kid on an egg hunt."

Stung, I shot back, "That's not what I was doing. It made me read it!"

"Oh, and how does a book do that? An ordinary book, isn't it? Isn't that what you think?" She abruptly lowered her voice. "I'm sorry, I forgot about Kylie."

"She's not here. I had to take her to the emergency room."

"Oh, no." Aurora left the door, skirting the table to reach for me with a gentle touch on my shoulder. I could feel the nearness of her and the book all over my skin. "Is it serious?"

"It's all serious." I tried to shrug lightly and failed. "I thought . . . I'm so tired. I don't know why I'm so tired."

"You did a major spell working, for starters. It takes energy."

"It's not like I had any left." There was a fatal quivering in my chin.

"Adrenaline, then. You must be so worried."

"Yes." I didn't want to cry in front of her, but a lone tear broke free of my eye. "I don't believe in that damn book, but I thought if it were real, I thought, what if . . . I'm such a fool to let that nonsense give me hope."

I cried for the second time that night, but this time with the warmth of Aurora's body holding mine. Kylie's robe did a lousy job of hiding every curve of her that I had glimpsed earlier. Her neck was lightly scented with rose and the heavy silk of her hair, too, blanketed me with warmth. I wanted to crawl inside her and get lost for a long time, but I couldn't do that. Kylie needed me.

After a tissue was found and used, she said gently, "You tried to find hope. That's not nonsense."

"So that book has no spells for curing cancer, bone decay or synaptic meltdown?"

"Not that I know of, no." She abruptly let go of me. "I should go."

"It's late. I'm sorry. I disrupted your night."

"I was in the middle of something, yes, but I can recapture it another time."

"Dancing?" I could not stop staring at her shoulders and tracing the swell of her breasts with my eyes.

"Some might call it that." She took a step backward. "I really should go."

Her insistence hurt a little, but I understood. It was now closing in on the real witching hour, three a.m. "Are you a witch?"

"Yes. Got a problem with that?"

"No. Not tonight. Tomorrow I'll be cranky and confused." Tonight I wanted to be back in her arms, held close and safe. Why a near stranger should make me feel that way I could not explain. Snuggling was not all I wanted, either.

"Tomorrow I'll be less argumentative. I'm sorry for being so prickly." She went to the door again, hand back on the knob.

"Will you be okay? It's very cold out there."

"I'll run. Thank you for giving the book back. That it let you read it means you could have kept it, so thank you." With a blast of cold air, which drew a painful gasp from her, she was gone.

The scent of her lingered, gentle rose and that mix of aromas that are so female. I inhaled all I could as I stood to set my mug in the sink. A bang at the kitchen door nearly caused me to drop it.

"I'm locked out!" Aurora slammed the door behind her, robe askew, slippers dotted with snow. "It's fr-freezing out there!"

I did the only thing that made sense, which was to put my arms around her to warm her up. "You didn't put a spare key outside somewhere after this morning?"

"Not yet." The book was pressed between us, giving off heat

that I couldn't help but enjoy. "There's an upstairs window slightly open."

"I've got a ladder."

She shivered. "Hayley . . ."

"Stay here tonight," I murmured and then, because she tipped her head back and her eyes were velvet with tenderness, I kissed her.

She breathed my name again, between our mouths. I wanted to stop because, yes, she was attractive, and yes part of me wanted her in a very basic, earthy way. But I was so tired and if we didn't stop we'd end up doing more than kissing and I was . . . disheveled, weepy, exhausted. If I went to bed with her I at least wanted to be clean and full of energy.

One of her hands was twined in my hair, and it slipped down to cup my neck. I couldn't help but open my mouth to hers. We kissed until the snow on her slippers had melted.

"We shouldn't do this," I finally whispered.

"Why do you think I was trying to go?" She opened her mouth to me again.

I was submerging into the heat of her, the femaleness of her scent, her eyes, her mouth, soft blended with strength, sweet mingled with fire. "You have to stay now."

"Hayley . . ." The robe was slowly coming undone.

I could feel the chill of the door on my arms as I pressed her against it. The book was gradually sliding toward the floor as she moved in small waves of response. "Stay, please."

"Hayley . . . I want to." She arched slightly into me, and my body answered with a brushing of my thigh between hers. "We can't . . . it's not . . . right."

"It feels right to me." My clothes felt as if they were tightening on my body. The next kiss worked over my mouth like a slow, sensual drug. "It feels incredibly right. I don't know why."

"I do," she murmured. "We have to stop."

"We will. Eventually." My hands slipped from her waist to her hips, and I pulled her more firmly against my thigh. The book was getting in the way now. It was warm, tingling even, but I wanted her fire and nothing else.

"Hayley . . ."

I loved my name on her lips. "I won't call you Rory."

"You've been in my head since I hit you with my car." She laughed a little, but gasped when I nibbled at her lower lip. "Hayley . . . Gaia help me, stop, please."

"Why?" I was swollen with wanting her, heavy and ripe.

"I put a spell on you."

She was sprawled in a tangle of blankets on the sofa in my study when I slipped in to get my assignment book for morning class. I didn't know if she had a class she was about to miss, and I didn't care. I'd barely slept and it wasn't just the events of the night that had kept me awake. Visions of her naked, dancing for me in ways that had nothing to do with music, had tormented me.

"How dare you?" I'd demanded.

Beet red, she'd fired back, "But you don't believe in it."

"You do!"

"It wasn't supposed to lead to this. It was just a fantasy."

"Some fantasy!"

"Yeah, and I'm here because you *weren't* thinking about me? Don't think I don't know how that summoning spell works. You were thinking about me, plenty."

"At least I didn't mean to do anything. But you did!"

She'd said, in that calm smug way of hers, "Only to myself. Being here with you was none of my doing."

I was not at all happy that somehow the situation was my fault. "Oh, so your little spell wore off on me, is that it? A fantasy and eye of newt? Bubble, bubble, toil and trouble?" She was right, I didn't believe in it, but it was the mere idea of it all that bothered me so.

She had pressed her lips together at that. "I'll sleep anywhere if you'll just give me some blankets."

With one last look at the creamy bare leg that emerged from

the pile of down and flannel, I tried to begin my day. Another call to the hospital yielded no new information. I'd leave my cell on, and make apologies to my classes should it ring.

I was two steps out the front door when I knew I had to go back. I hadn't slept well, and was up earlier than usual. I had just enough time to wake her and offer help with the ladder.

At my first touch her eyes flew open and I was bathed in that rich, river green. I kicked myself, hard, and made myself picture her bending over a cauldron, cackling Shakespearean rhymes. It might have worked had my vision of her included any form of clothing.

"I don't know if you're late for anything."

Seeming remarkably lucid, she glanced at the clock on my desk. "Nearly."

"Do you want that ladder and some clothes?"

She nodded. "Thank you."

Okay, we'd be coolly polite this morning.

She took the offer of a pair of my boots and a running hat, but claimed the robe was enough to cross the yard. I think she was sorry when the first knife of icy wind hit her, but she'd opted to be the stoic.

Once the ladder was unfolded and against her house, under the window she said she'd left barely ajar, I took pity on her. "Why don't you go back to my kitchen and I'll wave from your kitchen door and let you in."

She was going to refuse, but a chance stab of wind blew open the lower half of Kylie's robe. Her legs were gorgeous, I couldn't deny that, even if they were mottled with red from the cold. She clutched the robe closed and bolted for the house. "Thanks," she called over her shoulder.

Climbing the ladder was easy but I went carefully because my hands were stiff on the frozen metal. The window was indeed ajar, but I could barely work my fingers under it. Finally, it gave another inch, then all way. I slithered over the sill and closed the window firmly behind me.

I had thought I'd be in her bedroom, but the room was nearly empty. A large round area rug of deep red covered the hardwood floor. In the center of the rug was a candle, burned down to a hardened puddle of wax in a crystal bowl. I followed my nose to the other crystal bowl—it was filled with fragrant rose petals.

I stood again and then blushed hotly. On the far side of the rug was a red towel, and just protruding from under it was a vibrator. The only other object in the room was a CD player in the corner, plugged into the same outlet as the vibrator.

I couldn't help myself. After I pressed play the room filled with a quiet, rhythmic drumming, quickly joined by the tuneful humming of women's voices. Obviously, Aurora had been having a very private dance when I had interrupted. I was chagrined, embarrassed, even. This was crazy—she was crazy. I didn't have time for her or how I felt, but I was grinning ear to ear.

I don't know, I guess that her calling herself a witch was so foreign to me that it was nice to see she was wholly a woman, with needs and desires I understood. Needs she took seriously enough and tended to by devoting an entire room and considerable energy to a night of solo passion. That vibrator was the kind with *wow*, *oh wow*, and *splat on the ceiling* settings—and a match to the one I had at home.

She was alive, I mused as I hopped down the stairs, and I felt alive when I was with her. More alive than I'd felt since . . . since Kylie's cancer diagnosis.

I came to a stop at the foot of the stairs, all the humor draining out of me. Kylie was dying and I had no right to be wasting my time on sex rooms and Aurora's body. I should have called the handyman about Kylie's bed. I needed to call the hospital again, and again. Kylie counted on me.

Aurora was peering across the distance separating our kitchen doors. My wave was solemn. She was pink when she reached me, the book clutched to her stomach, and it wasn't all the wind. She knew what I had to have seen.

We stared at each other awkwardly. Finally, I said, "I've got a class."

"So do I."

I was washed over with a vision of pushing her up onto her kitchen counter so I could open her legs and run my hand through the luxurious red hair I'd glimpsed last night. I knew I would find her eager. She was breathing hard. So was I. A magic spell? I don't believe in it, I don't, I can't. But I do believe in lust and we were both under the influence. I viciously reminded myself that even if she felt it, Kylie couldn't act on it. So how could I?

"I'm sorry," she said quietly. "It's the kind of spell that's a wish more than anything else. It hasn't . . . run its course."

I closed my eyes for a moment, thinking of the many delicious ways we could complete each other. When I looked at her again there was a hint of tears in her eyes. "I have to go."

"I noticed you're moving furniture."

I paused, hand on the doorknob. "Kylie can't go up and down stairs anymore."

"I'm free at four if you need a hand."

I was grateful. "Thank you. That's a big help." I left before I would let myself think about how much I wanted to be in her company again.

Insane woman, crazy lady. Had she bewitched me somehow? The last twenty-four hours made no sense, I thought. Kylie was supposed to have more time. I'd conjured Aurora into my study. There was no explanation except the one that Aurora offered and I could not accept it. Superstition and hocus pocus played no part in my career, my life, and least of all my heart. I kept repeating that to myself all the way to my first class.

I started awake and looked up in time to see the lunch cart pass the open door of Kylie's room. The hospital seemed oppressively quiet and the moment I'd sat down I'd had trouble staying awake.

Kylie made a soft noise, like she was trying to surface out of her meds-induced haze.

"I'm here," I said quietly. "Do you want some water?"

She nodded, then sipped when I slipped the straw between her lips. A grimace of pain crossed her face as she swallowed, but she sipped again and the next wasn't so bad.

"I don't think they're going to let me take you home today. I haven't seen the neurologist yet, but they've got you really doped up, haven't they?"

Her attempt to answer was a croaked affirmative.

"Are you hurting?" Another croak. I gently touched her shoulder as I rang for the nurse.

She was too jovial for my mood, but she quickly checked Kylie's vitals and noted them on the chart. "I'll page the doctor. I need instructions before I can give you anything more," she told Kylie.

We waited an interminable fifteen minutes. I babbled on about my classes that morning and the weather. I wanted in the worst way to tell her about the book and Aurora. If she weren't under the influence of the meds, she'd happily speculate with me about what really happened. Our father's queer—in the good old-fashioned meaning of the word—sect of Christianity thrived on debunking the supposed relics of other branches of the faith. Bored children saw holy figures in clouds. Tourism-minded priests claimed bones were from martyrs. We'd laughed together over the account of a grilled cheese sandwich, half-eaten but appearing to have the visage of the Madonna, which had been auctioned for tens of thousands of dollars.

I clutched my stomach as I waited, not wanting to face the fact that the Kylie who would help me make sense of what I'd experienced might be gone forever.

The neurologist from the night before came in with the customary bustle of a man with too much to do. He addressed us both, though his gaze settled more on me. "I'm afraid the news is not good."

I wanted to shut off his voice, leave the building, but I forced myself to listen. I didn't want to translate his long, technical words into ones I could more easily take in, but I did it. He droned on for several minutes and I boiled it all down to the fact that Kylie's vertebrae were disintegrating more quickly than anticipated.

There was a little silence when he stopped talking, then Kylie's rasp made me jump.

"So we can tell the oncologist to kiss off?" She might have been smiling if I had had the courage to look at her face. "It's the bone thing that'll get me?"

"The pressure on your spinal cord can have unexpected results. But you've got the most common—partial paralysis."

"Next I get the whole deal? My brain's messages get blocked? Heart stops?"

She was asking all the questions I could not. Brave, fierce, determined to know the worst, while I cowered from truth.

"Possibly. I can't tell you how likely because your other conditions are probably accelerating the deterioration in ways we don't yet understand."

"Wish I was around for the autopsy." I could hear her hard swallow. "I'm kinda curious, myself."

I don't know how the doctor could smile. Bits of me were freezing.

He made a note on her chart. "Leave a forwarding address and I'll send you a copy."

They both laughed. *Laughed.*

I struggled to find my voice. "When can I take her home?"

"I'm not sure that's wise."

"I want to go home," Kylie said.

"You're going to be on an IV and loopy from the drugs. You may not be able to easily get out of a bed, which means a bedpan or catheter."

"There will be someone checking on her all the time," I assured him, vowing to make my statement true.

"I'm liking morphine so far." Kylie gave a thumbs up.

"Let's decide tomorrow," he finally agreed. "If your vitals are stable, then it might be possible the day after." I walked with him to the door of her room. In a lower tone, he added, "You'll need someone to check on her three times daily and nightly."

"How long?"

"I can't say. The cancer is more predictable."

"And that's two months at the most, right?"

"I'm not an oncologist, but I see a rapid acceleration of her deterioration."

"So not even that?"

"Not in my judgment, no."

"A month?"

"For the cancer, at the most. But perhaps sooner for the spinal collapse, unless we put her on a respirator."

I shook my head vehemently. "She's signed all those waivers. Absolutely not."

"I know. It's in her chart."

"Thank you for your honesty. And for not dealing in false hope."

He grimaced. "Some people prefer it, but your sister is a realist."

"She played soccer at the Olympic level."

He gave me a look that said he wished I hadn't told him that, and was obviously grateful for the chirp of his beeper. I understood there was a certain distance necessary to do his job, but I'd suddenly needed him to be able to describe Kylie by more than the sum of her disease, syndromes and symptoms.

At her bedside again, I gave her more water as I said, "I've got to dash to class and office hours. I will be back this evening, okay? Home tomorrow."

"Yes. Thank you. I want to go home."

"I want you there, too." I squeezed her hand. I had to be brave because it was the last thing Kylie would ever ask of me.

CHAPTER 5

When I walked in the door after my early afternoon office hours the answering machine was a welcome distraction. Seven messages awaited me, from home visit nurses who had picked up the authorization for their services from the hospital posting board. I had feared it might be hard to find someone, but it was a relief to know that was not the case. It took only two phone calls to arrange for a visiting schedule to commence when—if—Kylie could come home again.

I'd had my sabbatical last year. If I'd known . . . I could still take leave, though Kylie protested vociferously every time I mentioned it. I stood there, lost in thought, until a soft tap on the kitchen door startled me.

Aurora smiled shyly at me. "Is now a good time?"

Any time was a good time, I wanted to say. Her abundant red hair flowed freely around her shoulders today, and I had that overwhelming desire once again to crawl inside her and stay there. She looked warm and glowing in her thick Shetland sweater. "Sure. Thank you, I really appreciate this."

"It's no problem." She followed me up the stairs and surveyed the half-assed job I'd done in the middle of the night. "Have you thought about renting a hospital bed? She'd be more comfortable, and have grips to help sit up and move. Position changes to make her more comfortable."

"I have—she objected."

"I know it's really none of my business, but maybe you should insist."

I snorted. "Kylie is incredibly stubborn."

"What a surprise."

Her tone was so dry I gave her an evil look that she returned far too blandly. Turning away, I sighed. "You're right. Okay, can you help me get this back together? I'll make some calls, then."

We lifted the box spring back to the frame with a minimum of chatter, and the mattress was in place in moments. So much in life is easier with two, I thought. I wanted to look forward, but my mind was trapped in the past, seeing only Kylie and I catching lightning bugs. She'd handled the net and I'd managed the jar.

"Got clean sheets? You might as well make it up."

"I can do that."

"I'm sure you can," she said quietly. "Let me help. I know what it's like. I'll do this and you go make those calls."

It was unnerving to be moving around my study yet deeply aware of Aurora elsewhere in the house. Every creak of the floorboard and whisper of fabric on the bed distracted me.

I was just finishing the call with the hospital furniture rental people when she paused at the door to my study. As I swiveled my desk chair around to face her, I realized I was hearing the familiar rumble of the washing machine from the basement.

"You didn't have to do that."

"Truthfully," she said with a gentle smile, "I wasn't going to, but there were some clothes needing attention on the stairs."

I blushed upon realizing the sight and smell that must have greeted her. "Oh, I forgot. Kylie was sick."

"When is she coming home?"

"Tomorrow I hope. Maybe not for long." She stayed at the doorway, but the ten feet or so separating us felt like inches.

"Back to the hospital?"

I tried for the same macabre humor Kylie had shown with the doctor. "Or the funeral home."

One look at Aurora's face told me I'd failed. "I'm sorry," was all she said.

"My fault. I'm not handling this very well."

"It's not like you've ever done it before, so who's to say if you're handling it well or not?"

"You make me sound sensible and sane."

She shrugged. "In this situation, it seems to me you are."

"You don't know what I'm thinking," I said before I could stop myself.

"You could tell me." She hadn't moved from the doorway but she felt closer.

I could not blurt out that I could feel her hands on my thighs and her mouth blowing cool air on the parts of me that seemed burning hot. This sexual fixation on a woman wasn't like me. Therefore it had to be about something else, about Kylie because Kylie was the most important thing in my life right now. "She needs me and yet I keep thinking about escaping, for just a little while."

"Caregivers do that, they do escape. They have to."

She didn't know how I wanted to escape. That I was thinking about her red rug and drumming music, the towel and the accessories we could explore. That my fantasy of escape seemed to be her body. I drew in a sharp breath, realizing I had forgotten to breathe. "Kylie needs me."

"She needs you in one piece."

My mouth was dry but there were tears in my eyes I didn't want her to see. What could I tell her that made sense? Why did making sense to her seem to matter so much? "It's not fair," I finally said.

"That she's ill?"

"That I'm not."

She sighed, softly. "Yes, and worse because you're twins."

"I should be sick. I should have all the same problems. We're identical."

"Obviously," she said gently, "you aren't."

"So many tests . . ." I stared at my hands while my body tracked her quiet footsteps toward me.

"They did not measure the things that make you different."

Heat covered me. Had she cast another of her spells? I was swollen and heavy with wanting to bury my face in her hair. "That even wasn't what I meant, really. It's not fair that I get to . . . escape when she can't. Why should I have pleasure when she won't ever again?" My laugh was bitter. "Why should I have what she denied herself her whole life?"

"Hayley . . ."

Her whisper washed down my body like warm rain. I was steeped in her gentleness but seared by the fire I saw in her eyes. Against my will I said, "Only now, now that there's no time and she can't do anything about it, only now is she realizing she'd probably have liked to have gotten to know you or a woman like you. Only now is she letting her real self emerge, so how can I turn the knife in the wound by flaunting my health, my sex life and . . . you . . . in front of her?"

She knelt in front of me and the urge to kiss her made my hands clench. "Do you want me?"

"Yes." My answer was nearly a growl, and came from a place so primal that I did not recognize my own voice.

I heard her hard swallow. "It doesn't have to be complicated."

"What doesn't?"

"Sex. Desire. Escape."

"I don't use . . . sex that way."

"Whyever not?" She smiled, but her words sent a spark of anger through me.

"I'm not even sure what's real anymore." I turned my head. "How do I know you didn't put another spell on me?"

"Because I am telling you that I did not. And the way I feel when I'm near you is one of the most real things I've ever experienced." Her hand gently touched my face, turning me to look at her again. "It can be as easy as yes."

"I don't want to use you."

She trembled. "You can't use the willing. You're not the only one in need."

Her thumb brushed over my lips and my control broke. Burying my hands in her hair, I tipped her head back so I could capture her mouth with mine. She made a small noise, but it wasn't pain and my blood seemed to pound with a repeating *Yes* that flowed from her body to mine.

I gathered her body in my arms, pulling her up from the floor and onto my lap. She coiled eagerly into my embrace and we kept on kissing—long, wet, hot kisses that intensified the burning behind my eyes. My brain was on fire and her mouth, her body, seemed the only thing that could save me.

"Is this for real?" I feathered my lips across hers, sublimely aware of their softness.

"I hope so," she whispered into my mouth. "This is all us, just us."

"I don't want to hurt you." I stopped kissing her long enough to meet her gaze. "I'm not feeling gentle right now. I don't know why—"

She bit my lip almost hard enough to draw blood. "Maybe because I'm not either."

The next kisses bruised my lips and the sensation made me feel wonderfully alive. I matched her moan for moan, muscle for muscle, until our mutual writhing had deprived her of her sweater and left my shirt unbuttoned.

With a gasp she repositioned herself so she was straddling my lap and I could only groan a long, low, "yes," as I watched her pull her bra straps down her arms, exposing her erect nipples to the supercharged air between us.

She quickly took her nipples between her finger and thumb and tugged, hard and firm. "Like that."

I lifted her hands to my shoulders and pushed her bra down even farther. The confinement shaped the lush roundness of her breasts and I stroked them for a moment, savoring the smooth texture of the soft sides while exploring with my thumbs the roughness of the puckered skin around her nipples.

She was breathing hard as I gazed into her eyes. I was bathed in deep, old green and both our mouths went slack as I captured her nipples just as she had and slowly pulled as I squeezed. She shuddered. Her hips jerked on my lap and I envisioned us just a few minutes in the future, with my fingers deep in the heat I could feel against my crotch.

"Is this okay?" I knew the answer before she nodded, but the question was meant to focus her on not just what I was doing, but what I was going to do. I pulled harder, as roughly as she had bitten my lip, and was answered with a moaning gasp as she closed her eyes.

"You know it is." Then, inside my head like a confirming bell, I heard her say again, *You know it is.*

We kissed, her mouth panting against mine as I continued to enjoy the play of her nipples. They felt warm in the grasp of my fingers and I wanted to feel that heat in the rest of her body. I crushed her body to mine, pulling her hard down onto my lap. She strained against me and made another of those small, arousing noises that I knew, with certainty, meant she wanted more.

I could feel the temperature rising on her skin as my hands caressed her back, her ribs, then sensuously cupped the curve of her ass through her jeans. She shivered against me and broke our kiss with a half laugh. After the boldness of her showing me how she liked her nipples touched, I was smiling to see her looking shy.

"I really like that." She tightened the muscles under my hands and laughed again. "I really do like that."

I brought my hands to her waistband. "Then I think these pants are in the way."

"Definitely." She went up on her knees as I undid the buttons on her fly. I gently loosened the jeans from her hips, letting them fall around her thighs. The panties underneath were two small pieces of lace, a mere excuse of covering. Their only use was to delight my hands as I cupped her ass again through the sheer fabric.

"Oh, Hayley . . ." She arched against me as I touched my tongue to one reddened, plump nipple. I pulled back and she followed my mouth until her nipple met my tongue again. I bit down softly, pulled less gently and her moan was like an electric charge down my spine.

I was momentarily distracted by the ringing thought that I love women, and this was why. She was female, soft and strong, needing and able to cup the back of my head and say in a low, intense voice, "Please, Hayley, take me to bed."

"What's wrong with here?" I coiled my tongue around her nipple, licking the underside as it stiffened. I loved the way she responded to me, and I loved the way it made me feel. My hands slipped under the lace of her enticing, useless panties and I stroked her ass with my palms.

She moaned as she grappled for the back of the chair. "I want both."

Her hair fell in heavy silken waves around me and I felt enclosed in a world of her making. There was nothing for me to think about but her, nothing for me to do but love her body. The focus was liberating and I thought in amazement how simple it really could be. I was older and wiser than I had been that night with Jane, but that did not mean I couldn't say yes to something that felt as wonderful as her body in my arms.

"Hold on tight," I whispered.

"I will . . . sacred mother . . . *please*." She arched her breasts to my mouth and as I licked each sensuously in turn I felt the brush of her pubic hair against my stomach. "Please, Hayley, touch me."

Looking up into her face, I reached for her nipples again. Her shoulders were flushed with pink and I could see the fire rising in her eyes. A prolonged squeeze drew a hoarse, responsive whimper and I was dizzied by the wonder of her cunt dripping on my stomach. "Now. Like this."

She moaned loud in my ear as my fingertips brushed her open lips. That fevered slick welcome that made touching a woman so wonderful trickled over my fingers and down my hand. I lazily found her firm clit, moving more slowly the harder she panted. I don't know how I knew she would like that except that I could read every reaction of her skin to my touch. I stroked to either side of her clit with two fingers, almost still while she moved more and more frantically.

"*Please.* Oh, Hayley, please."

"Ask for what you want."

She lifted her head from my shoulder and the green of her eyes enveloped me. She was high on lust, but not insensible. Her gaze was full of intent and though it was her body open and needing me to be inside her, I needed to be inside her as much. In that moment we were both equally moth and flame, blazing with matching need.

Her hips slowed slightly as she said, firmly and clearly, "Fuck me until we both melt."

I surged into her with two fingers as she kissed me. We both moaned as the heat between us flared and I knew the time for slow and teasing was past.

"Oh, yes, like that."

"More, I'll give you more."

"Don't stop."

"Oh, I'm not going to stop. I love that sound. You're so wet."

The red of her hair and the green of her eyes seemed to mix inside me, a blazing sunrise on a rolling ocean. Her kisses tasted of violet and the feel of her cunt around my fingers was so sensuous that my own body clenched with hers. I watched her body rise and fall with a swoon of arousal that surpassed any I'd ever felt in my life.

Our gazes met and I found I could not look away. Her eyes were talking inside my mind. *Do you feel that? Those muscles, right there, squeezing your wonderful fingers? Female sinew and bone, tender flesh, press there . . . there . . . and feel that wonderful moisture explode.*

I gasped and pushed into her more firmly. "Like that?"

Yes, her eyes said. Her panting breath reverberated on the inside of my head.

We were kissing and her voice was in my head again, repeating that divine *yes* and wild *more*. Something other than carnal fire was rising between us, something natural and alive. Something I could not put a name to, not yet. The sensation of being inside her was sharp with pleasure. This new, building feeling was soft by comparison, but vast. It seemed to well up into any places between us that did not yet touch, filling in all our distance.

My world went away. I had no thought of anything but my body and hers, and the wonder of our union. She was making short, sharp sounds that echoed the message in her eyes. *It's supposed to feel this good.*

It had never felt this good before, but I didn't know why. This was something beyond my experience, to be so focused on her that I could tell when that electric jolt of near climax spiraled through her hips.

It should always feel this good.

She stiffened against me but where my fingers touched she was melting, pouring. Muscles tensed in violent spasm. My lap was wet and I couldn't breathe until her long, deep groan subsided.

All around me was the quiet of snowfall. Familiar things were shrouded in silver and gray. She was a swirl of crimson and, looking at my hands, I felt suffused with golden light.

Aurora was laughing and the clear bell of her pleasure found a response inside me in a place that wasn't physical. I was laughing, too, because it had felt *that* good.

We could have been in a gladed forest, so fresh and alive was the air. Light was soft on my skin, as soft as her touch as she pulled me to the sofa. I laughed as we tangled with my jeans, now wet, and we fell into a breathless embrace, me on top, my knees embracing her thighs.

"That was amazing. Did you do something special?"

She blinked. "Wasn't it all special?"

I kissed her to hide my blush. "Yes, of course. I was just wondering—"

"Oh, you mean did I sacrifice an eye of newt?"

There was no hiding my blush and she laughed at me, not one iota of mercy in her dancing eyes. "Something like that."

"That was all us, just us," she said softly. "You really let your energy go. Are you always like that?"

"I'm not sure what you mean." Something had been different, but I could not yet explain what. "It felt as if I was touching you everywhere . . ."

"You were. With every part of yourself. With everything you could expose." Her next kiss was slow, nibbling along my jaw as she gazed up at me. "You were inside me with more than your fingers."

"So is that . . . oh." Her hands swept over my hips, leaving a trail of heat in their wake.

"What?"

"Is it magic?"

"Don't you think it was?"

"I think your sophism is showing."

"No. I think you see dividing lines that I do not." One finger snaked between our thighs to open my swollen lips. "Sweet mother," she breathed out.

"Oh . . . Aurora." My mouth watered in response to her touch and we began kissing again, hot and wet and seemingly endless. My hips could not stay still and her curled fingers opened and explored me as I moved against her. That feeling of losing my shape and form rose again, and there was no space between us. I was in her arms, dancing for her the way I had envisioned her dancing for me. The way she had danced, in my arms, like some mystical creature of passion.

I tend not to believe in things I can't see or feel, and I didn't believe in magic. But the way she felt under me, the way I felt when her fingers slipped inside me, the way her voice and mine twined in matching ohs of pleasure—those things I had to believe in. Nothing in my life had ever felt more real.

She caught me again with her green gaze and her talking eyes. *It feels good, doesn't it? Weren't our bodies made for this? Aren't women fabulous?*

"Yes," I answered her, not trusting my eyes to speak for me.

It's all magic, everything. The air, your smile, the world, our lips. This passion. All magic. We are the goddess divine. We are women. We have no beginning, no end because we are bound to the magic of our existence.

A thousand lectures about social constructs played in my mind. Anything taken on faith is a superstition and yet I was sharing this . . . experience with Aurora. Experiencing something that was more than her touch. She did not ask me to believe what her eyes were saying, for nothing I felt required it. There was only the one word that worked and I whispered again, "Yes."

Her skin was as flushed as it had been when I had loved her, and the writhing of her body under mine while she fucked me was equally passionate. Her fingers plunged into me and I took all her energy and pushed back with my own. I clenched her hand, hard, and she moaned. She shoved into me again with a loud groan and my last reserves were broken by that sound. Crying out, I pushed down on her hand. "Yes!"

"Let it go," she crooned. "Come to me, my dearest. Let it go."

My body seemed to pour out light, beading down on her body like sunbeams. The light was pure white, then softened to gold. Patches of green dappled her body where she was not in my shadow and I reared up with a gasp, loving the feeling of her inside me.

She was smiling shyly, proudly. "Didst thou enjoy that?"

"Minx," I managed to say. "Thou knowest that I did."

"Again? Thou needest further treatment." Her eyes were stars of laughter and I loved her with a profound ache. "Does that soothe?"

Her fingers turned inside me, feeling so good that I moaned and spread my legs. Her other arm pulled me close. "Your touches are fire in my womb."

"'Tis good I have salve near to soothe thee." Her eyes were knowing as she fluttered her fingers against that place that made me melt.

The sensation was so pleasing I threw my head back and she quickly kissed my throat. Our gowns were strewn on the floor next to us and in their midst our cat had made a bed, even now thoroughly cleaning one paw.

Her touch made my eyes want to close but before I would succumb to that sweet temptation I glanced one last time toward the fire, where a half-dozen cookpots hung close and kettles contentedly spit steam. The abandoned churn would require more work when our attention could return to it. The items on the sturdy table where we'd begun our afternoon's pleasure were safe from the fire, though the cat had been known to tip the inkwell in the past. A vellum page in the thick, leather-bound tome my beloved had been slowly filling with her secrets lifted in the refreshing breeze. The moving air spoke of rain, a welcome break in the humidity that had both of us dripping.

I dripped for her in more ways than one. It was a beautiful, lazy afternoon we were having in our kitchen. The light was green from the thick trees that sheltered our cottage. Her earthy sigh brought me back to the rolling of green in her eyes.

"Come to me," she pleaded. "Let it go, my dearest."

The light shifted, lost its green luster of life and fresh beauty. The study was cold but her body incredibly warm under mine. I lost my voice, lost my words, could not speak. I could only push down, taking all I could of her hand. I tried to tell her with my body how much I needed her touch. Her eyes told me she understood, and she moaned the deep, needy sound that would not break free of my clenched teeth. Her touch, her desire, they broke me. They always did. My flood began, contractions swept down my body, then I crumpled over her. Silent tears began.

Her voice, as sweet as the past, as soft as the present, wrapped me in close warmth. "Let it all go. All of you is welcome and sacred. All is precious and nourishes, especially tears."

Tears washed away the dizzying vision of my study's fireplace crowded with cookpots and kettles. They washed away the burning confusion inside me. For that brief while, curled in her arms, everything made sense. No beginning, no end, the perfection of circle and flame was blissfully clear. No beginning, no end. There was only the magic of our existence and the air we shared as we kissed.

CHAPTER 6

Just take the apple," Aurora insisted. "Turn it in your hand and think about what it is." Just as she had this morning, she looked fabulous in Kylie's robe.

Still hiding the fact that my legs were shaking, I took a large bite out of the apple she insisted would explain her entire philosophy of life to me. After a half-hour's doze we'd moved to the bed to start all over. Growling stomachs had finally called a halt, and we'd struggled down the stairs, half laughing and holding each other up. "It's fruit, red and round and ripe." I blushed.

"What's that look for?" She took a similar chomp from her own apple, grinning at me.

The feeling inside me could only be called *mushy*. "I wanted to say, red and round and ripe, like you."

"Oh." Her smile faded, but in surprised pleasure. "Thank you."

"I've never felt . . . that before." I didn't even know how to bring up my puzzling vision of some circa-1750's kitchen and the two of us seemingly . . . involved.

"I've had some . . ." She chewed thoughtfully, cleared her throat and continued, "some very good sex. But nothing like that. It was intense."

"I've had intense. It was more than that."

Her lips parted as if she would say something, then closed again. She chewed thoughtfully. "How so?"

"You talked to me without words."

"Perhaps you're perceptive."

Feeling better with a bit of food in my stomach, I shrugged. "I'm not usually. Believe me, I could get witnesses on that count."

"Perhaps . . ." She again focused on her apple.

"What?"

Shaking her head, she said, "So about that apple. Red, round, ripe. What else?"

"Fructose, raw, crunchy."

"How is it different from the table?"

I blinked. "Well, the table isn't edible."

"But it's organic, just like the apple."

"It's dead."

"Technically, so is the apple."

I was getting annoyed because she was driving at something and I hated being made to guess. It was one of my father's old ploys to foster confusion and put himself in the position of wise lecturer. I didn't think Aurora was playing that kind of game with me, but it rankled. "They have a different molecular structure."

"Yes, and yet . . . where did those molecules come from? Where did all of our atoms and molecules begin?"

"Big bang or the hand of a god, take your pick."

"Does it matter?"

"To some people, yes. It matters a lot, and they're willing to fight and die over the difference. To construct elaborate belief systems and rule books to explain the difference."

She brushed her fingertips over the back of my hand. "I believe there is no difference why or how we began. What matters is that we are all made of the same stuff. The same building blocks. The dust of exploded stars or the breathing out of a supreme being, it is *all* a miracle. It created our planet, our brains, our ways of processing information." She paused for a moment, blinking hard. "I'm sorry, I get very passionate about it."

The glitter in her eyes reminded me of the glitter of the necklace she had worn only last night. "It's okay. I get worked up about things, too."

"So being a witch is about doing things that connect and honor the gift of my molecules. The apple in your hand—what's left of it—is exactly what you and I are. A gift. A miracle. Pure magic. I recognize that, and every day, throughout my day, I stop to notice."

So far it sounded rational. "So where do the spells come in?"

"I believe that a magic spell is science unexplained. If you have the energy to bring me across space, science *will* explain it, when scientists have the words and understanding to do so."

"Well, that's just it. How is it I have the energy for such a thing when I don't believe in it?"

"You have me there." She grinned, then rose gracefully to put her apple core in the kitchen trash. "Belief isn't necessary for nearly all common magic. As I said, you do not have to believe in the apple for it to ripen. Higher workings, well, belief usually plays a key part. It's part of the energy."

"Seriously, I did not believe anything would happen." I joined her at the trash can, tossing my core in as well.

She seemed to be picking her words with care. As she spoke, one hand lazily caressed my arm in a familiar, loving way. "Perhaps there is more to you than you have thought."

"What do you mean?" I thought, distantly, that her touch was extremely disarming, and I shouldn't be so ready to listen to what would likely be a crazy theory. And yet, I reflected, she had not said one word that I could say was untrue, or required me to ignore common sense to believe. I knew better than anyone that the "twin sense" Kylie and I shared would be viewed by many as magic. Science explained it as heightened perception and duplicative synapse relays. In earlier times, twins had been granted status as mystics or hunted as evil ones.

"Before, when you were . . . when I was making love to you."

I flushed. "Yes?"

Her voice broke nervously. "Did you see anything?"

"What do you mean?" How could she know?

"Like, me. But different."

Suddenly intense, I said, "Tell me what you saw."

"You," she said quickly, as if holding it in had finally become too much for her. "You, over me. Your hair was thick and massed on your shoulders." Her fingers touched my hair, then my face. "A little thinner. And when I looked around, I saw a kitchen. Not this one. A large open hearth fire, a cat, what I think must have been our clothes on the floor—"

"That's enough." I trembled, then felt a finger of ice flow down my spine. "I don't know how you did that, and maybe someday some scientist will explain it, but I don't understand what you want from me."

She was flushed now, somewhere between annoyance and arousal. "I want your body. That seems pretty plain. I think we have a lot to explore between us and maybe it's older than we are. We might find we like each other, can talk to each other and make each other laugh. Given how rotten my love life has been, that seems like a little bit of bliss to me."

"What are you suggesting? Wait, I know." I laughed dismissively. "Reincarnation. We knew each other in some other life and need to reconnect in this one."

"You don't believe that we go to heaven or hell forever, do you?" My expression must have been plain as she rushed on, "I didn't think so. So we go somewhere. Why not to a new body and to new experiences?" She stepped back a half-pace and tightened Kylie's robe around her.

"There isn't a shred of believable scientific evidence to support it."

"You're wrong about that, and besides, as a theory, reincarnation has very few weak spots."

Openly scoffing, I said, "For example, in the beginning there were only a handful of bodies, but now there's six billion. Where did all those unique souls come from?"

The green in her eyes sparkled. "The most basic act of nature—division. Energy builds to a point and then it divides, just as cells in our bodies do every minute of our life. Souls divide, why not? Nature reuses *everything*. Entropy *always* leads to something new."

I didn't like the way this argument was going, mostly because she was making more sense than I could handle. I was depleted and stressed out, or else I would be able to think of how to debunk her logic. I glanced at the clock, realizing I needed to start getting ready if I wanted to be in the hospital at a reasonable hour. Kylie would be missing me. "Is that where karma comes in?"

"Reincarnation and karmic consequences are not the same thing. The concept of karma is a construct, trying to make sense of how we are born into different situations in life. If karma was a guarantee, then bad things would not happen to good people. Your sister is a good person—nothing she has done deserves this repayment from a vengeful or supposedly beneficent god."

"You got that right," I said before I could stop myself. "Leave Kylie out of this. I need to go, anyway."

"Hayley." She reached for my arm but I shied away. "Oh please, don't be afraid of me."

"I'm not." But part of me was. I braced myself not to flinch when her warm hand rested gently on my forearm.

"I'm not demanding anything of you, only trying to explain who I am. You do not have to believe a word of what I've said. That doesn't upset me at all. I believe, that is what matters to me. You are in charge of your own beliefs."

I wasn't falling for it. I wasn't falling for any of her nonsense. I couldn't. It was all a pose, the understanding, the goodness. How could she be a witch, and tell me about *magic* and *reincarnation* like they made sense, and me listen to her and realize I still did not disagree with a single word she'd uttered, right down to the freedom to believe as I wanted. A freedom I thought every human being deserved and so few were ever allowed to pursue. "Damn right. I choose. I choose to think this is all crazy. And I do have to leave soon for the hospital."

She caught my hand with tears in her eyes. "Today, earlier, that was wonderful." Her eyes, so deeply green, glowed with worry. *Did she not see what I saw? Did I see untrue?*

At her touch, the room had dappled with light, though the winter sun had already set. Herbs tickled my nose and there were birds singing nearby. Summer filled my lungs and I felt as if another set of eyes in me had opened. I saw her, a strong coil of beauty and whimsy, laughing eyes, curving mouth and arms that seemed made in pure magic to hold me this way.

"Perhaps we should retire to the other room where we can lie more comfortably." She drew me past the hearth, the book, the windows spilling over with soft, clear light. "I have more planned for thee."

A voice called from not too far off, "Mistress Lowell? I've come for the syrup thou spoke of."

She darted for her gown whilst I dashed to the bedroom, stifling my giggles at her frantic scramble. I waited, just inside the bedroom door, watching her lace and tie her clothes and pull her cap into place. She looked guilty as sin, some would say, though her voice and manner were calm as she greeted one of our neighbors.

I loved her, had loved her a long while. She was the root of my life, the wellspring of the very blood that pounded in my flesh when her hand stirred me. I began and ended in the welcome of her eyes.

She came to our bed when the neighbor had gone, and her first touch plunged me into fire. No time to remove the laces and gown, and her skirts fell around my shoulders as I pulled that most delicious, red, ripe part of her to my mouth.

Minutes, years passed as I loved her. Seasons fell around me like leaves and when she, too, fell to the bed, her hair was streaked with gray, her face lined with years of laughter. The passion and joy in her eyes were mirrors to mine and our bodies were suffused with the beauty of time. I held her in my arms, feeling her melt like a honeycomb, then grow lighter than feathers. Her eyes met mine with happiness, unflinching, even as I wiped a trace of blood from her cracked lips.

"I am letting go," she whispered. "'Tis my time."

My tears spilled over her face and I lost my words, lost my heart root. The ache of breaking would not let me speak.

"Thee and me are not done. These forty years were not

enough. Let me go, sweetheart, and see me for the next dance. All will be renewed, all is a gift, all is true . . ."

She slipped through my fingers like water and the bed crusted over with bitter leaves. My heart cracked, time split and Aurora said, shaking me softly, "It's true. Come back. It's all true."

I shuddered out of my stupor and could only gaze at her. She would look stunning in another forty years, laughter creasing her face.

She was trying to smile, though her eyes swam with emerald tears. "I liked you with gray hair."

I felt lost. I had believed fervently in not believing, and I knew something was gliding out of my life, no longer needed. "Hold me, Rory, please."

Her arms slid around me and I felt wrapped in her quietness. "You can call me Rory," she said softly. "I like it the way you say it."

The hospital was quiet and chilly and I wanted to go home again, back to my warm bed where Aurora was likely still asleep. We'd returned there and a new kind of passion had overcome us as we explored each other in increasing familiarity. If I wanted to believe, I could say it was a kind of recognition. Our earlier fire was abated and this time was sweet, slow and unbelievably tender. I had showered and dressed quietly, then looked in on her one last time.

Magic.

She asked nothing of me and gave me magic. Were some things in life really free?

Caught on the very edge of wonder, I pushed open the door to Kylie's room and was confronted by my father.

I took two quick steps back as he rose from the chair by her bedside. "What are you doing here?"

"I am being her father, though you'd have kept me out of it until it was too late to save her, if you'd had your way." His deep rumble seemed to rock the floor under my feet.

"How did you know?"

"Next of kin, or had you forgotten?"

I glanced at the bed, and Kylie waved weakly. I took care not to get too close to him as I moved to her bedside. "How are you feeling?"

"Woozy, but better." Her color had improved and she tried to smile. "Did you call him?"

"No." I'd been afraid that Kylie had called him, but now I was angry because someone at the hospital obviously had done so. "He wants to take me to Montpelier, to the church."

"There is no way that is going to happen."

"Life is sacred." He was standing next to me now, looking down at Kylie. "You would let her die, and we will fight for her to live."

"I am out of life, Dad." Kylie was trying hard to speak firmly, but her voice was thready. "Out of life and in a lot of pain. I'm tired."

"Those are the words of a sinner, and you are not that. Unless you have been corrupted." His glance at me was meant to sting, but my armor was fully up. I would not be baited.

"Dad, this is my choice."

"We'll see about that." He smiled and I felt chilled. "You can undo all those papers with a word."

"No," I said. How could he not see how wasted she was, how she'd begun the slide toward death? "You're upsetting her."

"I am bringing her the light of the Lord."

Bow to my will, that's what you really mean, I thought. Bow to my beliefs, my will, my decisions. I abruptly recalled Aurora's simple statements, none of which had required my belief or consent. She asked nothing of me and gave me magic. He wanted to own the most precious parts of Kylie and me, of everyone he met, and give nothing back for it but words.

"You are upsetting her and I won't allow it."

He went around the bed and took Kylie's other hand. And there we were, with her in between us. "I've called a local friend of the church, a legal advocate."

"Dad, don't." Kylie closed her eyes.

He would use her like a wishbone, but I was not playing the game. "All of her papers have been signed, notarized and cleared with hospital legal. I was worried about your interference and so was she. There is nothing you can do."

"I can pray for her to return to the fold—and you to lose your pigheadedness."

Kylie said sharply, "Is that the same way you prayed for it to be Hayley who was sick and not me?"

"She's filled you with lies." He squeezed Kylie's hand and I felt her wince.

"I heard you say it." She tugged weakly on her hand. "That hurts."

He let go, but not immediately. "My friend will be here soon."

"He won't step foot in this room." I patted Kylie's shoulder. "I'll be right back."

I spoke quickly to the first nurse I saw. "We have a situation in my sister's room. My father is upsetting her and he's called some sort of lawyer. I have her power of attorney."

"I'll phone administration," she said, with a tired edge to her voice.

"The other matter is that I didn't call him and neither did my sister, which means someone here did. His number is in her file, but there was no reason to call him."

Her lips pressed together and I got the feeling she suspected who had made the call, but wasn't saying. I didn't care. I just wanted him gone.

When I got back to her room he was praying over her. I rudely interrupted with "She's not dead yet."

"And shall not die if she repents her sins and enters the arms of the Lord."

I wanted to point out that by his reasoning everyone who died was a sinner. Everyone dies. It wasn't fair that it was Kylie's time. I said nothing because arguing with him was pointless since he made no sense.

Kylie's eyes were closed and her face was lined with distress. He'd yet to express any feeling of love or concern for her pain. He didn't see her as a human being, she was a principle, or, at the most, a daughter, which I knew too well was not the same thing as a person.

I bent down to speak into her ear. "I can have him taken out of here."

She nodded. It was all I needed.

I got the security guard. Our father prayed. He told her to repent her sins, her unnatural desires, her lack of faith, to repent her wasted life spent pursuing graven medals. His voice rose and I didn't want to be thirteen again. It wasn't going to happen.

"The Kingdom of Earth reveals only to the pure. You were never cleansed of your sins, but in the Lord you shall be. The crooked are made straight in his glory. Walk tall to the Lord. You cannot crawl with evil. Repent. Leave the influence of disease and perversion."

I shut my ears. By the time the security guard got two more of his ilk, our father was in full foam. I needed to assert no rights—his behavior got him muscled out of the room.

"You will burn for all eternity. Burn forever in the fire of evil and sin! Satan reaches for you with the slimy hands of a woman!"

His voice faded and Kylie's eyes stayed closed. The hospital administrator arrived to apologize for the "clerical error" and did all but produce a waiver for me to sign that promised I wouldn't sue over it. They were lucky there was no one in the other bed to contend with as well.

"I just want to take my sister home."

They got the neurologist in short order. He had no idea what had transpired but wasn't happy with Kylie's vitals. Tomorrow he would decide.

I made them all leave. I turned off the overhead lights and examined Kylie's long-forgotten dinner tray. The soup was cold. There was something that might have been oatmeal in some past decade. I broke open the packet of crackers. "Have something to eat and some water."

"Not hungry."

"I can't take you home if you're not eating."

She frowned but didn't protest when I adjusted the bed so she was upright enough to swallow. She waved the hand with the IV. "I thought this was food."

"Not enough. There's an olive on the salad."

I was crying, on the inside, crying that I was coaxing her to eat a simple little olive and that it was obviously a struggle for her to swallow it. Crying that our father had upset her and worried, deep down, that he'd find some politician who'd run to a judge and force Kylie to do things she did not want. Things I did not want for her.

She did drink nearly a full glass of water, and sipped dutifully at the milk. Encouraged, I told her about the hospital bed that would be delivered tomorrow morning. "It's just like this one, so you'll be more comfortable than in your old bed. I tried to move it and made a mess of it. Aurora helped me get it back."

Kylie tried to grin. "Did she now."

"Yes, she did." I fought down a blush.

"There's something about her." She swallowed a little milk. "Something special I can't figure. I've had weird dreams."

"Bad ones?"

"No. Odd." She pushed the milk carton away and made a strange choking sound. "Hayley."

"What is it?" I reached for the nurse's call button.

"What if . . . what if he's right?"

"About what?"

Her face crumpled as tears escaped. "That I'm going to hell."

"There is no hell, Kylie. It's a bogeyman to make you afraid and agree to whatever their rule is."

"What if there is?" I wiped tears from her cheeks. "I've tried to be good, but I've wanted . . . bad things."

"Who says they're bad? The same people that say there's a hell." I took her hand and if I believed in curses, I'd have cursed our father to suffer every pain Kylie was feeling.

"When I started going to church, with dad . . . there was a preacher who told stories. Of bad people, what happened to them. I had nightmares."

"Sounds like he should have been writing for the *Friday the Thirteenth* movies. And never allowed around young people."

"How can there be nothing? There has to be something."

"If there is, it's not hell." I wanted to tell her about the vision I'd had of some past with Aurora, but how could I? A couple of pictures in my head was nothing to base anything on. Damn my father and his certainty. I had no such certainty to balance against that.

"Then what?" Her tears had stopped and her eyelids drooped. "Then what?"

"I don't know, Ky. I don't know. But when I look at the way nature works, hell makes no sense."

Her hand slipped from mine and I sat with her a few more minutes.

I felt bludgeoned. I was still shaking, a little from the intensity of being with Aurora, and other parts of me—less pleasant—were shivering in anger that my father was anywhere near Kylie. Did he think that dying was easy? That it made it any better for Kylie to be afraid of it? I knew how much morphine she was being given and her face still showed more lines of pain than I liked. I knew how much the loss of her body, her energy, her passion for sports, her zest for living—I knew how much she grieved. It cut me deeply that she was afraid, too.

I wanted my sister back. I wanted my beautiful, brave, bold sister healthy again. I would miss her every hour of the rest of my life. There were places in me that only Kylie ever touched, that only she understood, and they'd be empty and cold. I loved her, and I would not hasten the day she left me.

But I loved her, so I would not hold on to her just for my own comfort.

CHAPTER 7

A delectable, savory aroma assailed my nose the moment I opened the front door. Aurora appeared from the kitchen, wiping her hands on a tea towel.

"Wow," I tried to joke as my stomach growled. "You're even cooking for me?"

"Onion soup, just reheating some I froze a few weeks ago." She hesitated a moment, then grinned as I opened my arms to hug and kiss her. It was a soothing, healing kiss and I sagged slightly against her.

Leaning back, she gazed into my face. "What happened? You're all dark."

"Our father showed up. He tried to get Kylie to go home with him."

"Where's that?" She was still studying me.

"Raving Bible Central in Montpelier. I've never made sense of the sect. Security took him out of her room, but I think he'll be back."

Her thumb caressed the side of my mouth and the next kiss wasn't the least bit rushed. For the first time in my life I felt that I was Home. Home for good. Home because of her.

The steam from the bowl of soup eased the ache of unshed tears. "Okay, you have my permission to cook for me any time you like."

"I'll warn you, I'm vegan, so you might have to get your steak on the sly."

"Oh, you looked in the freezer, didn't you?"

"I was looking for clues about what you like."

I swallowed another spoonful of the savory, warming soup. "This is delicious."

"Thanks." She blushed and it was very becoming. "I'm not moving in, just so you know."

"I didn't think you were." Still, her words gave me a pang. She was home, I felt it in my bones in ways I'd never felt before. I hadn't even known I was searching for this feeling, not until it washed over me in that loving kiss at the door.

"Your life is full," she said slowly. "And it's not a time for decisions like that. Your . . . frame of reference right now is not your own."

"It's Kylie's. She needs me."

"Yes, and you should give her all the energy you can."

I thoughtfully swallowed some sweet onion while recalling our conversation about frames of reference—it seemed so long ago. "You looked a bit smug the day we met, like you had the right answer about the real frame of reference."

"Smug? Well, yes, that sounds like me. It's a fault. I was thinking to myself that there have been people who share my beliefs for thousands and thousands of years. Since the moment nature developed the energy for thought, there has been magic and belief in it."

"You said that our souls set the only timers that matter."

"That matter to us. The planet may predate our souls, but what matters to me, in my existence, is that my soul spans more than this life. Each dance we're given is a gift, an adding on, another layer of magic."

"You make it sound so simple."

"The hardest thing about our world is accepting that you can understand it, every bit of it, if you keep it simple." She grinned and I knew she was both teasing and telling me another piece of her truth.

She gave me magic and asked nothing of me. I very slowly and deliberately said, "I don't know what to think right now, but I promise you that I *will* think about all you have said."

She smiled shyly. "You don't have to believe in anything I've said, but that you take it seriously, consider it respectfully does matter. I realize that now. So thank you."

I brushed my fingertips against hers. "Stay the night with me?"

"I was going to invite you to my place. Because . . . if Kylie comes home you won't be able to."

I nodded agreement. "You're right. And I haven't seen very much of your house."

"I'll give you a tour in the morning. I don't feel like playing tour guide tonight."

Her look was so intent that I flushed. "Oh, you'd look cute in a little uniform. I could be the confused tourist who needs personal attention."

She winked, a bewitching, flirtatious wink. "It's too early to play dress up. Maybe when I know you better."

"Well, I've seen your magic-making room and your, um, magic wand. Perhaps you could at least show me that."

Color ran up her neck and I loved it. We were turned on and blushing like teenagers and part of me was still weeping for Kylie and yet I knew I had to go on living.

I packed a little bag of essentials, made sure I had my cell phone and charger in case the hospital called, and took Aurora's hand at the kitchen door. "Shall we?"

Bast twined around Aurora's legs with a yowl.

"You've got food," I scolded. "You won't perish if you sleep alone for once."

Aurora stooped to scratch Bast's head. "She doesn't under-stand," she cooed at the cat. "Of course you can visit too."

So it was the three of us that crossed the yard. Damn cat always got her way and I could tell there would be times when the two of them would side against me. But that was thinking too far ahead, I reminded myself. Tonight was what mattered. Day by day, that was what mattered.

Bed was what mattered, and Aurora did not give me a tour of

any place but her bedroom. Her rising need caught fire in me and I abruptly could not wait another moment to feel her naked and hot against me.

We rolled over her bed, arms and legs tangling in abandonment. Sharp, like electricity, our passion jolted through both of us.

"Is this a spell?"

"Could be," she whispered in my ear. "Or could be just us. Does it matter?"

"No," I answered, almost in a growl. "But if it's a spell I want to learn it."

"It will be my pleasure." She nibbled her way across my lower lip.

"That," I murmured into her kiss, "is my entire goal in learning it."

Our voices harmonized in the night, then eased to laughter. Kisses ended the day, kisses that were promises of another tomorrow.

I fell asleep to the aroma of her body, her love and the spice of mint and chamomile in the air. My last conscious thought was that one of her dresser drawers was seeping light. The book, I thought, then sleep claimed me.

I stirred in the night, pleased to feel her there. The light changed, from black to green to white and it was Kylie I heard calling out, "Get up, you lagabeds!"

Aurora giggled and pushed me softly. "Thy sister. I'll not get up."

I'd not don a gown just for my sister's modesty, no matter the hour, so I greeted her wrapped in a blanket. "Twas thee I caught abed last week, the sun at full noon, so I'll hear no insults on that account."

"I have come for the eggs and shall leave thee to thy doxy." She skipped lightly to the cellar door and disappeared into the depths. "Thee and she seem partial to Mondays."

"We are partial to all days," I boasted, for it was true. My beloved and I kindled our flame easily. "Thee could say the same any day the week long."

Her light step sounded on the stairs and in moments she was back, egg basket in hand. She never slowed, my sister. She was as fast as I was deliberate. "Thee are not the only one returning to bed. Once these are delivered, I am heading there myself. 'Tis a fine, fine day for love."

"Your doxy is as eager as mine. We are so lucky we ought to be kings."

She grinned at me then cocked her head to the sound of an approaching wagon. "I ran ahead to make this a quick stop. She is in a hurry to get home."

I watched her dance to the open door like a will-o'-the-wisp at midsummer. Leaning out she called, "Don't stop, I shall catch thee up."

"Close that door behind thee, dear sister," I said in parting. I gathered my blanket skirts and headed back to the bedroom. "Blessed be."

"Blessed be," she answered, then the door slammed with a resounding thud.

I startled in bed, my heart pounding. Aurora stirred, then moved close with a sigh. The dark was soft with the scent of her hair. I fell asleep again, and dreamed again and knew in all the time since those years with her I had never been so happy as I was tonight, with her in my arms.

The sheriff examined the restraining order in my hand, then turned wearily to my father. His encampment on my doorstep was not going to last more than ten minutes today. I'd tried letting him in. Kylie had agreed he could visit for thirty minutes a day, initially. But after his second visit had left her in tears and depressed, I felt enough was enough. He wasn't here to comfort her or spend some last few hours dwelling on good times they might have had. He was here to exert his control over her. Never once did he express interest in Kylie as she was. His interest was in her soul.

He couldn't have it. Still filled with wonder on the inside at what I'd glimpsed with Aurora, I could only resist him with steady intensity. He could not have Kylie's soul. It was my house and Kylie agreed, and two days ago a local judge had issued a restraining order.

The number of days left to Kylie was growing short. The two

weeks she'd been home had passed in a blur. I'd finally admitted I could not keep up my classes, and substitutes had been found, much to the department head's annoyance. I had no time for her annoyance, and no time to spend making statements to judges. I closed the door on the vision of the sheriff insisting my father get off my porch, and added it to the list of items I would discuss with the hospital administration at some future date.

Not today. Not tomorrow, either. These days were Kylie's.

I heated water for tea and knew Aurora was at the kitchen door before she knocked. I seemed always to know when she was near these days.

"Good morning," she whispered against my lips. "I saw that it was safe to venture out."

I gathered her into my arms. "Good morning. Yes, battle has been done. Tea?"

"No time. How is she this morning?"

"Groggy, but awake. Go on in, if you want."

I finished making my tea and delighted in the faint, shaky sound of Kylie laughing. She liked Aurora, a lot.

"I've got to get to campus," I heard Aurora say, and she came back to the kitchen to give me one of her whole body hugs.

"I felt today, watching him, that all he wants is Kylie's soul. I believe . . . that she has one." It was a big admission for me. I was trying hard to see the world as Aurora did. "He can't have it."

She studied me seriously, no hint of humor in her eyes. "What would happen if he did somehow get her soul?"

"He can't have it," I repeated stubbornly.

"No, he never can. All that can happen is you think he did. And if you think he did, what happens that's so terrible?"

"Well—" I regarded her open mouthed, not sure I knew the answer.

"Does his hell exist because he believes in it?"

"No." I blinked. How did she make such weighty philosophical issues so simple?

"If he thinks or you think he's got Kylie's soul, what has happened to Kylie's soul?"

"Only what nature determines. I guess . . . I used the word *soul* but that's not what I meant." I sipped my tea and thought it over. "I don't want him to frighten her. I don't want *Kylie* to believe that he has her soul. I don't want her to die, to have the fear of her last breath filled with visions of fire and damnation. That's what I meant."

Aurora nodded. "And I understand, very much, your wanting to fight against that on her behalf. He cannot have her fear and inflict pain. It's how she dies that you are fighting for, not what happens after."

"He's such an extremist. I know perfectly nice, rational Christians who'd agree with me that he is a nutcase. He doesn't represent anything but a bunch of ideas strung together to give him power over others. He's a bully, plain and simple, just using religion for authority. Like so many have over recorded history."

"I think I'd like to sit in on your class next time you teach it." She hugged me again. "Off I go. Call my cell if you need anything."

I watched her hurry down the walk with grace and aplomb, stomping snow and skirting ice as if she'd live here all her life. She'd not even complained of the cold, and today was one I'd consider downright chilly. I loved watching her move.

I joined Kylie in her temporary bedroom, carefully checking the level of solution left in the hanging saline bag, and the level of the collection bag that was hung more discreetly from the lower bed. Her output was healthy—I knew what to look for now. Noting her color, whether she appeared to be in more pain than usual, and her response time to conversation were all things the visiting nurses had taught me to evaluate and take comfort in, when I could. Kylie was a little bit rosy in her cheeks, but she always was after Aurora visited.

"So," Kylie said, her voice thin and raspy. "I like her, you know. Lots."

"Me too."

"I'm glad. You shouldn't be lonely."

Tears filled my eyes, and I didn't try to hide them. Kylie said she understood that I was giving into poignancy and grief. It took too much effort to hold it back. "I don't think I will be."

"You're different." She turned her head to gaze directly at me. "She's made you softer and happier."

"You think? Softer?" I prodded my stomach.

"I mean in a good way. You've a suspicious mind. But lately you seem . . . calm."

"I feel it."

"Even the way you deal with Dad. You're not . . . anything to him. No attitude."

"He doesn't matter to my life, nor to yours. He was in the room when we were conceived but that contribution doesn't buy him anything. He hasn't earned anything."

"He's scared." Kylie licked her perpetually dry lips and I hurriedly gave her water to sip from a straw.

"What makes you say that?"

"Desperate to avoid his own predictions. Ever thought of that?"

"Tell me that a different way," I prompted. "I don't quite understand."

"Sinners die. Everybody dies. Therefore—"

"Everyone is a sinner."

She nodded. "What happens to sinners?"

"Fiery pits of hell, getting stuck with pitchforks, eternal torment, all those fun things."

"Yeah. He must be terrified of dying."

I hadn't thought of it that way, and I couldn't say that doing so increased my sympathy toward him. "And you? Are you afraid?"

"Yes. Pitchforks scare me."

She wasn't joking though she tried to grin as if she was. Her face flinched and I recognized a rise in her pain level. I moved the button within her reach. "Don't tough it out. There's no point."

"If I get a miracle cure," she said grumpily, "I'll make you eat those words." She pressed the morphine button once and the mechanism locked for the next three hours. It had been barely over three since the last one. The neurologist had said when she couldn't make it three hours they'd switch her to one of the heavy-duty designer compounds. "Look at the addiction I'd have to kick."

"You would kick it." We'd joked before about the "miracle cure" and all the trouble it would be in our lives, should it happen. "Driving you to all those support group meetings would really be a drag, though."

"Much better for me to die." Kylie closed her eyes and the lines of pain relaxed. "I get a miracle cure and I'm taking Aurora."

"Hah. Besides, there would be someone else for you."

"What makes you think that?" She frowned slightly, and swallowed and moments later was asleep.

Why indeed, I asked myself. What did I believe? Every time Aurora held me I felt that wonderful feeling of Home. I didn't want to lose who I was in her, but the rest of the world did seem to recede when I gazed into her eyes. She didn't ask me to change but in accepting the magic she had brought into my life, I found myself wanting to change. I wanted to believe in *her*. In the feelings I had when I was around her. I wanted to believe in forevers.

Mystics throughout the ages wrote of their conversions. Epiphanies and raptures, passions and ascents, they took belief outside their known worlds of thought, and merged body and soul into new beliefs. Whether hammered to church doors or found in the path of a rising star, they changed.

I changed.

Fitzgerald's dark night of the soul was about loss and being lost. In my dark night of the soul, I found light and what mattered.

I'd been restless all night. Kylie's meds had been changed a week earlier and she dozed most of the time. But tonight had seemed different. She was awake, and groggy with drugs and pain. She spoke in half-finished sentences and some distress.

I hadn't wanted to leave her to go to bed, and decided I'd ask the morning nurse if she thought Kylie ought to be moved back to the hospital.

"Hayley . . . the pitchforks, you know?"

"I know."

"If they're the last thing I think of . . ."

"They're not real."

"*Twilight Zone* I'd make them real. Gotta stop."

I took her cool, dry hand and squeezed hard enough for her feel it through the layers of numbing meds. "Let's think about something else, then."

"Can't. I don't know what . . . happens."

"When?"

"When I die. I don't want to. I'm so scared, Hay. I don't want to. Pitchforks. Burning." Her breathing was rapidly increasing. "I can hear screaming."

Alarmed, I leaned over her. She'd tightly closed her eyes and the pain was obviously on the rise. The magic button wouldn't respond to her push for another fifteen minutes. "There's no screaming, Ky. None at all."

"What happens? I'm going to hell."

"No, you're not."

She waved a hand as if she wanted to push me away. "You don't believe in anything."

"I do, Ky. I do."

"At least Dad could give me . . . something."

I squeezed her hand again and she didn't respond. "Open your eyes, Kylie. Look at me, please."

"I can smell the fires."

"Look at me, please."

It was an effort for her to respond, but she did. I was looking into her eyes, but they were my own. I was reflected there and saw her, too. "I have *never* lied to you, have I?"

"Tried when we were kids."

"You always knew. I could never fool you. We're twins. We

know." Her eyelids drooped and I shook her slightly. "Stay with me."

"Wanna sleep."

I knew, somehow, she would never regain consciousness. I'd waited too long and not thought about what I would say, but I couldn't let screams of the damned and smells of hellfire be what she carried with her. "You shall, Kylie. But first, listen."

I stroked her forehead and was rewarded by her eyes opening again. "What?"

"I believe in something. Took me a while, but I believe that there are no endings. No place where you will go forever. There is this world, and here is where we dwell. Every turn of our time, we have gifts of life. And we turn again, and live again." My voice broke.

"Why do you believe that? Sounds too easy."

"I'm in love with Aurora, and when I'm with her I feel the turning of my life. Loving her will go with me, always. I found her in this life and it is a new beginning."

She had tears in her eyes but they were also increasingly vacant.

Clutching her hand, my face close to hers, I said, "That is your miracle cure, Kylie. There is no ending. But there are new beginnings."

"Don't lie. Not now."

"I can't lie to you, you know that. Am I lying? Look at me, Kylie," I pleaded, tears trickling down my cheeks. "I believe this. I believe it, finally. Everything is magic. All you have to do now is let go. It's okay to be afraid."

She breathed out and didn't breathe in again as I expected. Just as I was about to panic, she gasped, a great heaving sigh. "I want to believe."

"This will sound crazy, but I knew Aurora before. A long, long life ago. That book, the one with the crazy lettering, it started everything."

Her eyelids fluttered rapidly. "I dreamed . . . about eggs. And a wagon and a woman driving . . . and she kissed me when I jumped in. And I ran in my dream. Like I used to."

"Yes, sweetie, that's it. Yes. It's all true." I was choked and blinded by tears as I pressed the back of her hand to my cheek. There was no time for a past that long ago. She had nothing left in her to recall such distant memories.

"Do you remember the World Cup game, where you ran like the wind? You weren't afraid to try. The sky was so blue that day and you were a blaze of speed across the grass. Think of that, Kylie."

She nodded, weakly, so weakly, and her lips curved in a near smile.

I rested my head on her shoulder, thinking that the last time I had done this she had lived my memory with me even though she'd been in her room and I in mine. I believed now.

Whispering the word I'd learned from Aurora's book, I let us both sink deep into that magical day. I remembered every victorious moment, showing Kylie what I'd always loved about her, including every line of the lithe, powerful body that now, tonight, was at its ending.

"Think of that, how wonderful it was. You stretched so far for that kick . . . a blur going for that pass. How perfect those moments were." My tears splashed on her face and she didn't react.

"You will be that again, *I promise you*. No endings, but new beginnings, always. I believe this, I truly do."

She breathed out and her lips curved slightly. "Beginnings . . ."

Epilogue

G lad you wore boots?" I tried not to laugh as Aurora yanked her foot out of a puddle.

"Spring is more trying than winter. Everything is so muddy! Bast left paw prints on my pillow."

"You let her sleep at your house. Now it's her house."

"There is no *let* when it comes to cats. She'd find her way in, one way or another."

I took a long step to avoid another paving stone sunk below the water level. As nonchalantly as possible, I said, "She'd likely be less confused if she had only one house to live in."

"Are you asking me to move in with you, Hayley Carnegie?"

"Do you want to?"

She caught my hand. "No, no, you have to do better than that. I will not move in with you because it's easier on the cat."

I pulled her to me, heedless of the squishy ground we were navigating. "I want us to live together, Aurora Lowell, I want to because I am in love with you and I want another forty years with you."

"That's better." She kissed me.

As always, a simple kiss made time irrelevant. I'd learned the magic of dismissing time for these moments, to stand with her in the place where we were together. The world could wait.

"You still didn't answer," I said when her lips released mine.

"I think Bast would prefer it, so yes."

"Vixen!" I tickled her furiously, threatening to topple her to the ground.

"Hayley, don't, I'll get soaked through and there's no change of clothes in the car."

"That could make driving home really fun."

"I don't disagree." She laughed into my eyes and I wanted that wonderful green glow around me forever. "But in the meantime, this is not the time nor place, missy."

I let her go and turned my attention to the path again. "One more set, I think, then we go left."

I couldn't yet look at the rows of old and cracking gravestones without thinking of Kylie. Though these plots were hundreds of years old now, some were tended with flowers much like the bouquets that had overflowed at her memorial service. I'd spread her ashes in the cold winter chill from a hill overlooking a river. A beautiful place to join with the wind she had been in her life.

Glancing at the notes I'd made in the cemetery's office, I tugged Aurora's arm. "The Lowells are over here."

"Maybe we should have waited a few more weeks, like you suggested. My toes are soaked."

"C'mon, we're here. We'll go look at the House of the Seven Gables, next, and then, as long promised, we're going to have nice, warm apple cobbler at the Salem Hotel. You can put your boots in front of the fire like everyone else does."

"Sarah Lowell," Aurora read. "Oh look, so many children died, three, this one was two, oh, little Daniel was only two weeks. How sad."

We walked the row of markers slowly. Many couldn't be read at all. Most were for children, she was right. The oldest Lowell at the time of her death was a Deborah Lowell, aged thirty eight.

"No, wait," I corrected. "This one was in her sixties. This is the last marker, too."

"Apple Lowell. Friend to All," Aurora read. "That's sweet." She bent closer, tracing a faded symbol above the name. "Is that a pentagram?"

"In this cemetery? I seriously doubt it. Salem folk in that era were mightily afraid of witches."

"I know. But it's not a cross."

"So." I regarded her bent head. Sunlight on her hair made me think of ripe strawberries. "Worth getting your feet wet?"

"Yes. My ancestors walked here and their bones are here."

"I could have let you come here with Lexi."

"Oh please." She regarded me with a teasing smile. "Never in a million—"

"A million what?" I prodded, when she didn't go on.

Finger trembling, she pointed at the grave marker next to Apple Lowell's.

The name jumped out at me like lightning in a clear sky. I read, "Holly Carnegey, Friend to All."

"It's the same symbol, whatever it is."

"She died one year later, to the day. Also in her sixties."

Aurora gave a funny gasp and pulled me close. A slightly shaking hand wrapped around my arm. She softly said, "These forty years were not enough."

I shivered and we stood there for a few more minutes. Finally, I was able to say, "They weren't enough, sweetheart. All is a gift, so we get another dance."

Her eyes shone in the light, glazed in pure green and shimmering with joyful tears. Looking deep I saw myself there in the depths of her grace and laughter. No endings, only beginnings. And in this new dance that I shared with her, I believed in magic.

SKYCLAD

JULIA WATTS

Part I:

Earth

CHAPTER 1

Chameleon and her coven were working skyclad. Naked except for the ritual jewelry that decorated their fingers, wrists, and necks, the six women stood in a circle in the meadow, moonlight shining silver on their skin.

The high priestess, Chameleon, stood in front of the altar, her wavy honey-blonde hair topped with a silver crown, her arms spread before the members of the coven as if preparing to envelop them all in an embrace. Chameleon let her lips turn up in a slight smile as Iris stepped forward to face her.

As always, Chameleon was struck by how beautiful Iris looked, her short, dark hair crowned with a vine wreath, her eyes aglow with the energy of the ritual, her hands shaking a little as they always did. This slight trembling was one reason Iris was such a great working partner. It was her job to play the human role in the coven's rituals, while Chameleon played the role of the goddess. Iris's trembling was perfect because what human in her right mind wouldn't tremble standing before the goddess?

Yes, Iris was the perfect partner for ritual, Chameleon thought as Iris knelt before her. The two of them hadn't worked out as partners in life, but that was hardly surprising. Life wasn't as beautifully orchestrated and predictable as ritual. If it were, people wouldn't feel the need to invent rituals to bring them comfort.

Chameleon pushed her personal thoughts away, concentrating on embodying the spirit of the goddess as Iris began the Five-Fold Kiss. Bending low, Iris pressed her lips to Chameleon's right foot, then her left, then raised her head to kiss Chameleon's right knee, then her left. For Chameleon, each kiss lit a fire—a sacred fire that burned not just within her but within all the coven members who were circled around them. Iris rose higher on her knees and kissed the spot on Chameleon that symbolized the goddess's womb—that slight swell of her belly below her navel but above her pubic hair. Iris rose higher, brushing her lips against Chameleon's right breast, then her left breast. Finally, standing face to face with the high priestess, Iris leaned in and pressed her lips to Chameleon's as Chameleon's arms opened in a gesture of blessing which included the whole coven. The Five-Fold Kiss was complete.

As always when she enacted sacred rituals, Chameleon thought how much more meaningful these pagan rites were for her than the dreary Protestant rituals she was force-fed as a child and teenager. She remembered sitting in the church sanctuary, wearing a scratchy, freshly ironed pink dress and stiff, shiny Mary Janes, her little brother beside her, his unruly hair tamed with Dippety-Do, his little neck half-choked by the bow tie their mom had forced him to wear.

But church wasn't about being comfortable or natural. It was about fighting off your natural desires—stifling every urge for comfort and pleasure, stripping away the layers of physicality and selfhood until there was nothing left but a clean white soul, pure enough to float up to heaven. And heaven was the whole point of that brand of religion, wasn't it? To reject the ugly ways of the earth so that after death you could stroll through heaven on streets of gold.

Even as a little girl, Chameleon had thought that streets paved with gold sounded tacky. And she didn't think the earth was some ugly thing to be cast aside. Sure, the earth had its problems, but wasn't it people's responsibility to try to fix them? And so much of the earth was so beautiful. She'd take a field of wildflowers over streets paved with gold any day.

And so it was no wonder she'd become a witch—had found a religion which embraced the natural instead of rejecting it. And now her little brother, who had never asked the same questions she had, was the youth minister at the same church they'd gone to as kids. Well, at least they'd both turned out religious, although in her parents' eyes, the religion they and her brother practiced was the only one that counted.

As the coven looked on, Chameleon held up the wine-filled chalice. Iris held the ritual blade high, then dipped it in the wine. The wine consecrated, Chameleon and Iris shared a kiss and a drink. Then Chameleon turned to Graymalkin, the coven's oldest member and self-proclaimed "resident crone." Chameleon kissed Graymalkin's lips and passed her the chalice. Graymalkin drank, and then turned to kiss Belladonna, the coven's youngest and most heavily tattooed and pierced member. And so the cup was passed, with a kiss, to each member of the coven: Belladonna to spiky-haired, wiry Coyote; Coyote, to large, curvy Anansi, who enjoyed saying that unlike the coven's white members, she practiced black magic. Chameleon smiled, pleased, just as she was sure the Goddess was pleased, to see these women with the night sky above them and the soft ground below them, kissing and sharing, at peace with themselves, with nature, and with each other.

It was always awkward the first few minutes after the magic circle was banished. The road from ritual to normal life was a bumpy one, and usually everybody stood around cluelessly for a while until somebody—tonight, it was Coyote—finally said something about the chilly night air that made everybody start walking from the pasture to Graymalkin's farmhouse, where they could put on their clothes—the costumes which returned them to the mundane world.

After a ritual, Graymalkin's bedroom always reminded Chameleon of the girls' locker room in high school: females in various states of undress, talking and laughing. But it was different from high school, too, in that none of the women were judging each other or feeling ashamed of their bodies. The women who, unlike Iris and Belladonna, did not possess what weight and youth-obsessed society defines as a "good" body, still seemed confident of their beauty. Anansi gloried in the sensuality of her soft, rounded fertility goddess's body; Graymalkin took pride in the experience symbolized by every wrinkle and stretch mark; and Coyote was confident in the lithe, ropy frame she shared with her animal namesake.

Chameleon slipped on a long, dark blue dress batiked with dark clouds, moons, and stars.

"Look at you," Graymalkin said, tying back her long, silver hair. "You've put on clothes, but you're still skyclad."

Chameleon smiled. "Well, as a high priestess, I feel I should be a woman of contrasts. Naked but clothed, wise but ignorant . . ."

"Hot but single," Coyote interrupted, grinning as she adjusted her sports bra.

Chameleon grinned back. For Coyote, flirtation and conversation were one and the same. Chameleon didn't mind the "hot but single" comment at all, until she looked away from Coyote and briefly made eye contact with Iris, the reason she was single.

Anansi, seeming to sense the awkward moment, said, "Of course, 'hot but single' isn't really a contrast. It should be hot AND single. Some of us have got a little too much going on to be sharing it all with just one person."

"Fuckin' A," Belladonna said, stomping into her Doc Martens. "Why does everything always have to be about being part of a couple? You know, when I first took up the craft, I was blown away by how much of it is about working in pairs. It looks like we could get beyond that limited pair-bonding idea. I mean, as much as Wicca emphasizes couples, we might as well all get husbands and be Baptists."

Iris, who was standing behind Belladonna, rolled her eyes, but Chameleon could see the younger witch's point. Sure, Belladonna's view was a little extreme, but she was a twenty-year-old theatre arts major at the university and so was prone to making dramatic proclamations. Chameleon knew that Belladonna got on Iris's nerves—Iris had said that Belladonna wasn't mature enough to take the craft seriously—but Chameleon also thought it was important to have at least one very young woman in the coven. Except for Graymalkin, all the other witches were in their thirties, and while everybody agreed it was great to have Graymalkin as an older member, not all of them were as sure about Belladonna's value. To Chameleon, though, the young woman—the maiden— was as important an incarnation of the goddess as the crone. She was happy for Belladonna to be their resident maiden, even if the hickeys that frequently marked Belladonna's neck and breasts made it clear that she did not possess the virginal qualities which the term "maiden" implied.

"I know what you mean," Chameleon said to Belladonna, moving behind the young witch to help her with the zipper of her dress which, like all of Belladonna's dresses, was very short and very black. "Sometimes I get kind of fed up reading about all the pairing off that happens in Wicca. And when you read the older texts it's even more heinous because the assumption is that the pairings will always be male-female."

"Yeah, I hate all that old-school bullshit," Belladonna said.

"But," Chameleon added, as Belladonna turned to face her, "all gender issues aside, there's still something powerful about two people merging . . ."

"No doubt about that," Coyote snickered, wiggling her eyebrows at Anansi, who play-slapped her on the arm.

"Well, sex is one way to merge, but symbolic ritual can do it, too," Chameleon said. "However it happens, though, a lot of magic is created when two people come together as one—like the yin and yang symbols that form a full circle when joined together, and yet even as they merge, each symbol maintains its own identity."

Graymalkin, dressed in a flowing purple caftan, draped her arm around Chameleon's shoulders. "No offense to the High Priestess, but this conversation is getting a little heavy to process on an empty stomach. Who wants to throw the tofu kebabs on the grill while I get the plates and drinks?"

"All hail the grill goddess," Coyote called, raising her arms high.

Everyone filed out of the bedroom to help Graymalkin. Iris, then Chameleon, were the last in the procession. Before Iris walked out the door, she turned around, kissed Chameleon's cheek, and whispered "beautiful" into her ear.

Iris left Chameleon standing in the doorway, her heart and mind racing. Iris had dumped Chameleon two months before, and Chameleon had promised Iris that their ended romantic relationship would have no impact on Iris's status in the coven. But what in the name of Gaia was she supposed to make of that word—"beautiful"—and that kiss?

After the coven got through the few awkward minutes after the ritual, the gathering always turned into a party. The food was spread out on a folding table in Graymalkin's front yard. Seeing the dishes lined up and the women lined up to fill their plates always reminded Chameleon of the Wednesday night potlucks she'd grown up with at the Cartersville Baptist Church. The food was different, of course. The Baptists' Campbell's Soup-based casseroles, Jell-O salads, Bundt cakes, and iced tea had been replaced by the witches' tofu kebabs; hummus; gluten-free, dairy-free-chocolate-free brownies; and a box of cheap red wine. Still, whether the potluck was Baptist or pagan, in some ways they were both the same. Both were opportunities for relaxation and fellowship after a religious service, and at both, the quality of the food was decidedly hit-or-miss.

Chameleon sat down on the ground and nibbled her tofu and sipped her wine. It was the same brand of wine that she and Iris had consecrated in the ritual, but somehow it had tasted better in the chalice than it did in a waxy paper cup. Chameleon thought of Iris penetrating the chalice with her dagger and of the other kind of penetration which that ritual symbolized. Iris had been good at that kind of penetration, too. Think about something else,

Chameleon ordered herself. She focused on her plate, trying not to look at Iris and trying not to look like she was trying not to look at Iris.

"Hey, are you okay?" Graymalkin had sat down on the ground next to her. "You seem a little distracted tonight."

"Oh," Chameleon said. "I hope that doesn't mean that the ritual didn't go well."

"No, it was beautiful." Graymalkin patted Chameleon's hand. "You always make it beautiful. I wasn't talking about you the high priestess. I was talking about you the person."

Chameleon smiled. Graymalkin's greatest gift as a witch and a woman was her ability to see right into a person's feelings. "Yeah, well," Chameleon said, "I guess I'm just tired. It was crazy at the café today." Chameleon felt the intensity of Graymalkin's gaze and knew she wasn't buying that tiredness was the whole story. "Plus, there's a little E.L.W. going on here tonight."

"E.L.W?" Graymalkin knit her brow. "I don't think I'm familiar with that term. Is it from some special pagan tradition?"

"Yes," Chameleon said. "It's from the lesbian tradition. It stands for Ex-Lover Weirdness." She leaned closer to Graymalkin and lowered her voice. "Iris kissed me tonight—not just as part of the ritual, but back in your bedroom after we got dressed. She kissed me and said 'beautiful' and then just left me standing there with my mouth hanging open."

"Well," Graymalkin said as she picked a piece of bell pepper off her skewer, "maybe she's having regrets. I mean, seeing you standing in front of the altar, looking all beautiful, embodying the goddess, how could she not have regrets?"

"Well . . ." Chameleon began. She had been going to say, "Keeping the me who embodies the goddess separate from the me you wake up beside in the morning was never a speciality of Iris's." But she didn't say it because Iris was standing right in front of them.

"Is it okay if I butt in?" Iris said, smiling. Chameleon had always been a sucker for Iris's smile. She smiled all over, the corners of her eyes crinkling, the dark centers of her eyes twinkling. It was an endearing, mischievous grin—part of the reason, along with the keen features and small frame—that Iris had an elfin quality.

"Sure," Chameleon said, smiling back against her better judgment.

"Well, actually, I should probably butt out," Graymalkin said, rising. "I need to run to the freezer and get some Tofutti to go with the brownies."

Still sitting on the ground, Chameleon was sorely tempted to grab Graymalkin's ankles to stop her from leaving.

Iris sat down next to Chameleon and gulped back half a cup of wine. "Uh, Cham . . ." she said, "there was something I wanted to ask you."

Chameleon managed to choke out, "Okay."

"Um . . . the thing is, I had kind of a rough day today, and I'm hitting the wine harder than I probably ought to be. Do you think you can drive me home tonight?"

"Sure. No problem. Um . . . Iris, if you'll excuse me for a minute, I've got an announcement I need to make."

Chameleon got up and walked away, not sure why she felt like she'd just been kicked in the stomach. She didn't know what she'd expected Iris to ask her, but she did know that "Will you be my designated driver?" wasn't it.

Okay, enough of this, Chameleon told herself. It's time to act like a high priestess, not a girl at her first middle school dance. She picked up a serving spoon and clanged it against a metal bowl to get everyone's attention. "Before everybody drinks so much that they become irresponsible for their actions," she said, "I'd like to remind you that we will be meeting to do our Adopt-a-Highway project on Saturday morning. We'll meet at the Quick-E Mart near the site at nine a.m. As I've said before, this is a great opportunity to do some good for our earth and our community. So even though I know there aren't many natural early risers among us, I urge you to overcome your nocturnal instincts and drag your butts out of bed to help us on Saturday morning."

Once the box of wine and the coven members were exhausted and good night hugs were exchanged, Iris sidled up to Chameleon. "Can I still get that ride?" Her East Tennessee accent was exacerbated by wine.

"Hey, it's part of my job as a member of Witches Against Drunk Driving." Chameleon was trying to be casual and funny, but as she well knew, when people *tried* to be casual and funny, they were usually neither, and she was no exception. The truth was she was a wreck. As she and Iris walked to her ancient, battered Toyota with its "My other car is a broom" and "My Goddess gave birth to your God" bumper stickers, she realized the alcohol she smelled wasn't just on Iris's breath. It was also a full paper cup of something harder than wine that Iris had grabbed for the road. "You'd better get rid of that open container," Chameleon said. "If we get pulled over, we don't want to be violating any other taboos besides being dykes and witches."

"Good point," Iris said, chugging the contents of the cup. "The open container is now an empty container."

Chameleon was a bit taken aback by Iris's drinking. Iris had been known to tie one on occasionally, but she didn't usually knock it back this hard. "Are you okay?" Chameleon asked, turning the key in the ignition.

"Sure," Iris said. "Just a bad day, that's all. But I feel great now. It was a bad day, but it's a beautiful night. Look at the stars."

They were driving down the narrow gravel road away from Graymalkin's farmhouse. The starry sky spread over them like a black velvet cape dusted with silver sequins.

"They're amazing," Chameleon said, though she could only glance up at the sky since she needed to keep her eyes on the road.

"Pull over," Iris said. "Stop the car for a minute so you can enjoy the sky."

Chameleon couldn't help smiling. Spontaneous moments like this had been her best times with Iris the year and a half they'd been together. "Well, you know me," Chameleon said, pulling the car to the side of the road. "I'm a sucker for stargazing."

They stood in a green field staring up at the glittering sky. Without Chameleon even noticing it at first, Iris had taken Chameleon's hand. Chameleon felt the power of their connection. She looked away from the stars and at Iris.

Iris smiled. "Come here," she said. She tugged on Chameleon's hand and led her across the starlit field to a dark grove of trees. "Here," Iris said, pulling Chameleon into the darkness of the woods.

"Why are you dragging me here?" Chameleon laughed. "You can't see the stars in here."

"Sure you can," Iris said, grinning. "If you're lying down." She leaned forward and pressed her mouth to Chameleon's, her arms encircling Chameleon, pressing them together breast to breast and thigh to thigh. They had always been a perfect fit. "Tonight," Iris whispered in Chameleon's ear, "when we were enacting the Great Rite, it made me remember what is was like when you and I would come together after a Sabbat, when you would be filled with the goddess, and I . . . I would make love to you and feel that power . . ." She found Chameleon's mouth again and gently pushed Chameleon down to a soft patch of moss that cushioned the ground like Gaia's carpet.

Chameleon lay back on the moss, smelling its sweet earthiness and feeling the sweet pressure of Iris's weight on top of her. She knew she should tell Iris to stop, to wait just a minute so they could talk about what this act was going to mean. They were lesbians, for goddess's sake. They weren't supposed to make a move without hours of processing their feelings. But Chameleon knew what she was feeling at this moment. Desire. Desire that flowed like warm water, drowning her questions, drowning the voice in the back of her head saying, "Don't do this," desire washing over her arms and legs and breasts and belly as Iris peeled off Chameleon's dress, and Chameleon lay naked on the good, clean earth, her breasts and hips and bent knees rising up like hills. And if she was the earth, then Iris was the sky, hovering over her, enveloping her, embracing her like the night sky embraced the earth in darkness.

Iris ran her small, skillful hands over Chameleon's shoulders, over her breasts, belly, and thighs. The words Chameleon knew she should say disappeared from her mind until there was nothing but Iris's hands on her skin, nothing but mouth touching mouth, skin touching skin, earth touching sky. And when Iris's hand entered the source of Chameleon's pleasure, there was nothing else in the whole world except that hand in that dark place, the athame penetrating the wine-filled chalice, the butterfly dipping into the flower's nectar, the yin merging with the yang—the source of all the power in the universe.

Chameleon felt the pleasure and the power fill her until she was full to bursting, overflowing, her bliss pouring out over the mossy earth and her cries piercing the night sky.

When Chameleon opened her eyes, she saw a sky full of sparkling stars. And when she closed her eyes, she could still see them.

Once Chameleon had returned to normal consciousness enough to realize that lying naked on moss made for a very chilly backside, she sat up to see that Iris had already gotten dressed. "Are you sure you want those clothes on?" Chameleon asked. "If you'd like to join me here on the moss, I'd be happy to . . . you know, return the favor."

"I couldn't let you do that," Iris said. "The goddess can be worshiped by her human subjects, but she doesn't worship them back."

Chameleon rolled her eyes. "Iris, I'm not a goddess. I'm just a regular witch like you."

"No," Iris said, offering Chameleon a hand to help her off the ground. "You're not like me. You're a high priestess—the goddess's vessel. And I am only worthy to worship at your altar."

More than once, Chameleon had thought that Iris might be a little nuts when it came to Wicca. Iris was a literalist, and so when Chameleon enacted the part of the goddess, Iris seemed to really think of her as a goddess, which had made their romantic relationship difficult. After all, Chameleon wasn't very goddess-like first thing in the morning, her hair a big mess and her mood a bigger one, her pillow wet with drool. Iris seemed to love going to bed with a goddess, but she was less fond of waking up with a regular woman.

Chameleon could've chosen to argue with Iris, but she decided to chalk Iris's oddness up to excessive alcohol consumption. "I'm assuming you're pretty drunk, or you wouldn't be talking that way."

Iris smiled. "Yeah, I'm still pretty drunk. Are you ready to go?"

"Well, I guess I'd better put my dress on first."

"In case we get pulled over?"

"Yeah."

They held hands walking back through the field. Chameleon's limbs were still heavy and languid with pleasure, but her brain was starting to work overtime. Had this encounter in the woods meant anything other than a few minutes of fun? And if it had, could she and Iris patch their relationship back together?

They rode in silence until they neared the turn-off for Iris's house. "So . . ." Chameleon said, "I could take you to your house. Or you could spend the night at my place. In the morning, I could make you those banana-oatmeal pancakes you like."

"You'd better just drop me at my place," Iris said. "Tempting as those pancakes are, I think I need to be by myself for a while and try to think through what happened today."

Chameleon felt shallow for the irritation she felt when Iris turned down her bed-and-breakfast offer. Clearly, something was really bothering Iris, and as both her high priestess and her friend, she needed to offer help and support. "Are you sure you don't need to talk about what's bothering you? Maybe I can help." She pulled the car over in front of the ramshackle Victorian house Iris shared with two roommates.

Iris smiled and touched Chameleon's cheek. "You already helped. Out in the woods, I needed that so much after . . ." Iris laughed. "You know, you're probably the last person I should be talking to about this."

"What do you mean?"

"The reason I had a bad day was because Jackie broke up with me."

Chameleon racked her brain, trying to remember if Jackie was a name she had heard Iris say before. "And Jackie would be . . . ?"

"My girlfriend."

"Your girlfriend?" Chameleon and Iris hadn't been broken up two full months yet. How had Iris had time to get a girlfriend?

"See, I told you I shouldn't be talking to you about this. For you, it's like, 'Okay, Iris dumped me, so now Iris is the one who gets dumped.' It's only fair, isn't it? Like the Rule of Three."

The Rule of Three was the Wiccan idea that whatever you do, good or bad, will come back to you threefold. Like witch's karma. "Don't tell me what I'm thinking, Iris," Chameleon snapped. "Figuring out my thoughts and feelings was never a strength of yours."

"So now you're mad?"

"Apparently your ability to figure out my feelings has improved. And now if you'll excuse me, I think I need to be by myself for a while."

Iris grinned and shook her head. "Well, you wouldn't be much of a high priestess if you didn't have a flair for drama."

Chameleon didn't grin back. "Good night, Iris." When Iris leaned in to kiss Chameleon's cheek, she turned her face away.

Driving home, Chameleon marveled at Iris's slash-and-burn relationship style. She remembered watching a TV nature program that showed a rose going from a tightly closed bud into full bloom in less than five seconds. That was what dating Iris was like . . . there was no taking it slow, no letting things develop gradually. She moved from first date to full-blown relationship with the speed of time-lapse photography. Of course, the rose in the nature program had also been shown dying alarmingly quickly, its petals falling one by one. This was where the metaphor in Chameleon's mind fell apart. Iris would never stick around to watch the petals dropping off pathetically; once the fullness of a relationship's bloom started to fade, she was out of there.

Chameleon's apartment was a converted garage in Fort Sanders, a funky neighborhood near downtown which was mostly inhabited by UT students and hippie throwbacks. Chameleon had first moved to the Fort when she was a UT student, but with each passing birthday she was moving more fully into the hippie throwback category.

Her garage apartment, which had once housed two cars, provided ample space to house Chameleon, her cat, and her belongings, thanks to a clever combination bookcase/desk/loft bed she and Coyote had built to occupy the center of the large, high-ceilinged room. Underneath the loft bed, a couch and a steamer trunk doubling as a coffee table served as her living room area. A little kitchen was tucked into the back corner of the apartment, and she kept her altar, with its candles, chalice, athame, and goddess statues in a little alcove between the bathroom and the closet door. Many people—Chameleon's family members, especially—had expressed shock that she could make a home out of what was really just one room. But to Chameleon, the space felt safe, womb-like.

She needed to feel safe tonight. Often, after leading a ritual, she felt the need to retreat from people, to go away into herself. Tonight, of course, it was more than that. She had let herself feel for Iris again, even though she knew the problems she and Iris had weren't easily fixable. This was how it had always been with Iris. When Iris made love to her, she treated her with such reverence, but afterward, Iris had always pulled away, making Chameleon feel weak, vulnerable, and decidedly un-goddess-like.

Chameleon changed into her pink poodle pajama bottoms and her Glinda of Oz T-shirt that read, "Are you a good witch or a bad witch?" Taking the question on her T-shirt personally, she thought of the choice she had made to go into the woods with Iris: "Tonight I was a bad witch. But I'll try to do better."

CHAPTER 2

C amille! Hold the tomato on the tempeh sandwich!"
Sally called through the kitchen window.

"Got it!" Chameleon yelled back. Here at the
Moonshadow Café, the vegetarian restaurant where she worked
the lunch shift five days a week, Chameleon was called by the name
her parents gave her. She much preferred her pagan name to her
Christian one, but she chose to use Chameleon only in the coven
and among those in the know. Sally, the Moonshadow's owner, was
a big-hearted, open-minded earth mother type, and Chameleon
knew Sally would be happy to call her by her pagan name or any
other outrageous nomenclature she could think up, but something
stopped Chameleon from using her chosen name in the work-
place—maybe the feeling that using her witch name while slinging
sandwiches might rob it of some of its magic.

Not that she minded slinging sandwiches. Despite her mother's
frequent admonitions that she was wasting her college degree,
Chameleon liked cooking at the Moonshadow. She had been an art
major in college, and working with food and all its different colors
and textures had become a surprisingly satisfying creative outlet
for her. And since Sally gave her free reign with the food as long as
there was no meat on the menu, Chameleon could be as creative as
she wished.

Her favorite idea for the menu, and the favorite of many customers as well, had been the Mashed Potatoes of the Day. Almost any non-dessert item, Chameleon felt, could be delicious when mixed with mashed potatoes. She had known her roasted garlic and shallot mashed potatoes would be good before she even made them, but her favorites were the more adventurous experiments that turned out well, like the avocado and Monterrey Jack mashed potatoes topped with sour cream and homemade salsa, or the root vegetable mashed potatoes that came out a festive hot pink because of the beet juice.

After assembling what seemed like hundreds of tempeh, tofu, roasted eggplant, and portobello mushroom sandwiches, the lunch rush was finally over. Pantomiming wiping sweat from her brow, Sally hung the "closed" sign on the front door. "You know," she said, "the greedy side of me loves that all these yuppies from the downtown offices eat here because healthy food is trendy. But the old hippie dyke side of me liked it better when we were just a cult restaurant for cool people in the know."

"I know what you mean," Chameleon laughed. "Say, I'm experimenting with a new sandwich—a black bean and avocado wrap. You want to be my guinea pig?"

"You know me. I'm always a happy, hungry guinea pig."

They sat down with their sandwiches and chewed thoughtfully. "What do you think?" Chameleon asked.

"Good," Sally said. "Real good. Maybe we should try it for the Monday special."

"Okay." Chameleon pushed her plate away, most of her sandwich uneaten.

"Camille, are you okay?"

"Yeah, just feeling a little funky. Have you ever been dumped by a girlfriend, and then when you see her again, the old spark's there, and—"

"And before you know it, you're in the sack, and then afterward she makes you feel like shit?"

"Yeah," Chameleon said, amazed as always by Sally's perceptiveness.

"Nope, never had it happen," Sally said, then burst out laughing. "Of course I've had it happen. More than once. However, when you've been an out dyke for over thirty years, there's not much that hasn't happened to you more than once."

"Well, it happened last night with Iris and me," Chameleon said. "And I guess I'm worried that the weirdness between us is going to rub off on the coven. It was probably stupid of me to think I could work with her in the coven and not be bothered by it. There's such a strong connection between the emotional and the spiritual."

"If you ask me, the emotional and the spiritual are the same thing," Sally said. "I've never needed religion because I've always had a girlfriend. Sometimes several girlfriends."

"When you're feeling polytheistic?" Chameleon laughed.

"Yeah, I guess you could say that. Listen, the best thing for you to do is talk to Iris the next time you run into her at one of your little witch fests and make it clear that what happened between y'all isn't going to happen again."

"Well, I guess I'll run into her tomorrow," Chameleon said. "We're meeting to do our Adopt-a-Highway project . . ."

"Wait," Sally said. "Your little witch club is doing that Adopt-a-Highway thing?"

"It's a coven, not a witch club. And yes. Caring for the earth is one of our biggest concerns, and I've been wanting us to do more community service."

Sally's mouth was drawn into a straight line. "Well, expect trouble, that's all I'm saying."

Chameleon knew good and well that wasn't all Sally was going to be saying on the subject. "What do you mean?"

"I mean that when the Department of Transportation puts up those nice little signs that say, 'This stretch of highway was adopted by . . . ,' nobody minds when the organization listed is the Lions Club or the Future Farmers of America, but when certain people hear about a stretch of road adopted by witches, they're going to *freak out*."

"Do you really think so? I mean, we're adopting a road, not a Christian child."

"Yeah, well, some people will think if you're allowed to adopt roads, then you're going to be after the Christian children next. Come on, Camille. Your brother's a fundamentalist minister. You know how these people think . . . if you can call it thinking."

Chameleon winced as she recalled the last time she had gone home for Thanksgiving, when her brother had held forth about how the Harry Potter books should be banned because they enticed children into witchcraft. She had nearly come out to them as a witch right there over the Thanksgiving turkey, but given that they still hadn't gotten over her coming out to them as a lesbian four years earlier, she wasn't quite ready to make the leap. So instead she had merely come out as a Harry Potter fan and had given a passionate defense on the value of fantasy in children's literature. Her brother's response was that she had been "brainwashed" and that he would pray for her. Her parents, as always, had smiled at him benevolently, as if they were amazed by his patience with his heathen sister.

"You've got a point, Sally," Chameleon said. "But it isn't like this project is going to attract a lot of media attention. The fundies will probably be so busy picketing over at the abortion clinic that they won't even notice us flying around on our broomsticks picking up trash."

"Maybe so," Sally sighed. "But if I were you, I'd still expect trouble."

Saturday morning dawned clear and sunny. Chameleon loaded boxes of garbage bags into her car, along with the ugly fluorescent vests the Department of Transportation had provided for them, two gallon jugs of herbal tea, some paper cups, and two batches of apple-walnut muffins she had stayed up to make last night. When she pulled into the parking lot of the Quick-E-Mart, Belladonna and Coyote were already there, splitting a package of lurid pink Sno-Ball cakes. Chameleon looked at their chocolate crumb-lined mouths and said, "I stay up half the night baking organic whole-grain muffins for you, and look what you're eating."

"I know we're bad," Belladonna laughed. "It's the lure of the convenience store. They've got some evil stuff in there."

"Actually," Coyote said, "I'm eating this garbage for a very good reason. I figure some refined sugar will make me pick up all that litter extra fast."

"No," Graymalkin said, joining them. "It'll just make you burn out faster. We'll be picking you up with the litter."

"Hey, y'all." Anansi walked up to them. "Sorry if I'm late."

"If you're late, then I am, too," Chameleon said. She looked over to see Raven, Anansi's coltish thirteen-year-old daughter, standing next to her mom. "Hey, Raven, are you here to help?"

Raven, who used to be very talkative but had recently been struck shy by the ravages of adolescence, nodded silently.

"Well, it's great to have some extra woman power," Chameleon said.

"Speaking of woman power, aren't we one woman short?" Coyote said. "Where's Iris, Chameleon?"

"How am I supposed to know?" Chameleon snapped, sounding more defensive than she meant to.

"I don't know," Coyote said, backpedaling. "I just thought she might have called you or something."

"Nope." Chameleon was trying to sound casual. This no-show was typical of Iris—one second pulling you toward her, the next second running as hard as she could away from you. "Okay." Chameleon assumed her getting-down-to-business voice. "There are two kinds of bags. The white ones are for garbage, and the green ones are for recycling. Garbage goes in the dumpster behind the store, and recycling goes in the bed of Coyote's truck. Now why don't we join hands for a moment and give praise to Gaia, our Earth Mother, because she's who we're doing this for."

As the bikers and housewives and NASCAR fans in the parking lot stared, the coven joined hands and praised the earth goddess.

⚜

The cleanup was a success. True, Chameleon found some disgusting things that made her glad she was wearing gloves—dirty diapers, half-eaten, decaying hamburgers, an inexplicably discarded pair of men's briefs—but within two hours, the stretch of road was free of all the detritus of human carelessness. Even though Iris's absence nagged at her a bit, Chameleon felt good.

Tired but happy, the coven members gathered where the Adopt-a-Highway sign with their name on it would soon be planted and toasted each other with herb tea. Any minute, Chameleon thought, a representative from the Adopt-a-Highway program would be here to inspect their work. Once it was approved, the sign bearing the coven's name would be ordered.

The representative arrived twenty minutes late, driving an SUV—not a very environmentally friendly car for someone in her line of work, Chameleon thought. She was a middle-aged, helped-along blonde dressed in a designer track suit and dripping diamond jewelry. "Sorry I'm late, ladies!" Her fuschia-painted lips parted in what Chameleon thought looked like a nervous smile. "I'm Tina Thomas with the Adopt-a-Highway program. It looks like you girls did a terrific job with the cleanup!"

Chameleon tried not to wince at the word "girls" being used to address a group of women who ranged in age from twenty to sixty-four. "Thank you, Tina. So does this mean we have approval to officially adopt this stretch of road and have a sign and everything?"

Tina looked away from Chameleon, only to rest her eyes on Coyote and Belladonna—two members of the coven who were probably even more disturbing to her given their respective butch and goth appearances. Finally, Tina focused on the huge rocks that glittered on her manicured hands. "Well, actually, there's just a teensy problem with the sign—"

"What kind of problem?" Anansi took a step forward, but Chameleon gently touched her shoulder to signal her to stay back.

"Well," Tina said, staring at her nails, "some members of the community have let it be known that they find it inappropriate for a group of w—w—?"

"Witches?" Graymalkin offered helpfully.

"Yes. To sponsor a stretch of road and have their organization's name on the sign. Certain community members feel that a sign reading 'Witches of East Tennessee' might be seen as a way for you to recruit new members."

"Huh," Anansi said. "Funny that when my sisters over at the African Methodist Episcopal church sponsored a stretch of road, nobody worried about them recruiting new members."

"Yes, well," Tina said with a quaver in her voice. "Your organization is different."

"How?" Chameleon said. "I mean, our theology might be different, but we're just another religious group trying to do some good in the community. And it seems to me I recall something about there being religious freedom in this country."

"Well, there's no need to get defensive," Tina said, folding her arms across her chest. "You of course have the right to practice your religion and to do community service. There's actually a very simple solution to this problem. I've already suggested it to my boss, and he's very receptive to the idea. We can put up the sign, but instead of it saying, 'Witches of East Tennessee,' we'll just use the acronym for your organization—W.E.T."

"No," Chameleon said. "That makes it sound like we're being evasive about who we are."

"If it just says W.E.T. people'll think we're a scuba diving group or something," Belladonna said.

"Or that we're selling pussy lube," Coyote said, nudging Belladonna.

Tina's face turned the same shade as her lipstick and fingernails. "Well, clearly I'm not going to get anywhere with you people." She rattled her car keys. "Maybe if you have some time to think, you'll see the reason in my suggestion." She glanced at Chameleon, but didn't make eye contact. "Why don't you call the office next week when you feel calmer?"

"Our attorney will call the office next week," Chameleon said.

"Suit yourself." Tina climbed into her SUV and left them in a cloud of carbon monoxide.

"I didn't know our coven had an attorney," Graymalkin said.

Chameleon shrugged. "It doesn't. But I guess that's about to change."

PART II:

AIR

Chapter 1

Tia Thomas was eating lunch at her desk again. Every day she told herself, I will take a lunch break today. I'll have a nice walk, maybe finally try that little vegetarian place down the street. But then it would get to be twelve and the piles of papers on her desk would show no sign of diminishing, and then it would be 1:15 and she'd have a 1:45 meeting with a client, and so here she'd be once again in her stale office breathing stale air and eating stale peanut butter crackers from the vending machine.

Tia didn't mean to be a workaholic. She always had plans for meals out and movies, for relaxation and yoga classes, but in a firm like this that specialized in helping the underdog, it was hard not to get buried in work. There were a lot of underdogs out there and far too few people who were willing to help them. When she graduated from law school, her mentor had called her "one of the last of the true believers," and she guessed he had been right.

Tia chuckled, thinking how her mama would react to hearing

her agnostic daughter being called a true believer. Belief, in the religious sense of the word, had never been a strong suit of Tia's. Her mama had dragged her to church every time the door was open—to the long services held by the sweaty preacher who jumped up and down like her granny's hyperactive Chihuahua, to children's choir and youth choir practice, to Sunday school. Regardless of what church activity she attended, the message had always been the same: Believe. Have faith.

And her answer had always been the same: Why?

To the teenaged Tia, whip-smart and full of the arrogance of youth, it was always clear that the world was governed by scientific principles, not supernatural ones, and relying on reason made a lot more sense than relying on faith. But when she said things like this, it only made her mama cry about how her baby girl was going to hell.

At least the religion thing took with her two sisters. Selena and LaShea still went to the same church every Sunday where Mama had dragged them their entire childhood. And both Selena and LaShea were former runners-up in the Miss Black Tennessee pageant and were now, in addition to being devout Christians, wives and mothers. At least Mama had managed to raise two out of three of her girls to be who she wanted them to be. And then there was Tia, the agnostic lesbian feminist radical crusading lawyer.

The phone rang, bringing Tia back to the present. "Tia, your one forty-five is here," the receptionist said when she picked up.

How did it get to be 1:45? "Send her in."

When Tia had talked to this woman who was the high priestess or the grand pooh-bah or whatever it was she called herself of the Witches of East Tennessee on the phone this morning, she found herself growing increasingly curious about what such a person would look like. She knew not to expect a pointy hat and warty chin—and knew it was terribly un-p.c. that such an image even crossed her mind—but when it came to what to expect, she was clueless. One of those multiply pierced types with a hair color not found in nature? A hippie chick, maybe? The only thing that would surprise her would be if the high priestess turned out to be a suburban matron with precisely applied makeup and a UT track suit.

"Ms. Thomas?" All of Tia's questions were answered. The witch came closer to the hippie chick category than to any of Tia's other imaginings, but a lank-haired, Manson family type she was not. Her waist-length, honey blonde hair was brushed and luminous, and her light blue eyes, along with the floaty seafoam green dress she wore, gave her an ethereal look. She reminded Tia of the pictures of fairies in old-fashioned children's books.

"Please, call me Tia," she said, rising from her chair and extending her hand.

For such a delicate, airy-fairy creature, the little witch had a firm handshake. "And you can call me Chameleon," she said. "Since you're dealing with me as a witch, you might as well call me by my witch name."

"Oh-kay," Tia said. She always had a problem when people changed their names for religious reasons. She respected people's right to call themselves whatever the hell they wanted to, of course, but she personally always had a hard time wrapping her mouth around fancy religious nomenclature. When she was in college at Fisk, her friend Mikey had converted to Islam and changed his name to Kareem. She always called him Kareem, but she still secretly thought of him as Mikey. But hell, at least he hadn't named himself after a damn lizard.

"Unless you're uncomfortable with it, of course," the witch said, smiling.

"No, I'm not uncomfortable at all," Tia said, hoping it didn't sound like a lie. "Won't you sit down—" Iguana, she thought. Gecko. Gila Monster. But she made herself say "Chameleon."

"Thanks." Chameleon sat down in the leather chair across from Tia's desk, slipped off her clogs, and folded up her legs like a yogi.

"Make yourself comfortable," Tia said, sitting behind her desk. "Would you like some coffee?"

"No, thanks. I don't do the caffeine thing."

"Really? That's amazing. You mean it's actually possible to live without it?"

"Yep. I'm living proof."

"Wow, and you seem so alert and everything." Tia shuffled through her papers. "Well, from what you told me on the phone this morning, you definitely have a case. If the Department of Transportation has allowed other religious organizations to sponsor stretches of highway and put their organizations' names on the sign, then it's a clear case of religious intolerance. What we'll do is file suit against the Department of Transportation in federal court. This is a pretty clear-cut violation of your civil liberties, and we ought to win. But as I'm sure you know, we're right here on the Bible Belt's buckle, and that buckle is decorated with crosses and Confederate flags. If prejudice wins out over justice in this case, it wouldn't be the first time or the last."

"I know we might not win," Chameleon said. "East Tennessee is about as friendly an environment for witches as Salem in the Puritan era."

Tia smiled. For all her strangeness, Chameleon had the kind of smile you had to smile back at. "So why do you stay here? If you don't mind my asking?"

"I don't mind. It's a question I've asked myself more than once, believe me. I guess I stay because if I left it would feel like I was letting the bigots win. If enough of us stay and make our presence known, eventually people are going to have to get used to us."

Chameleon's statement brought an image to Tia's mind. She saw her great-grandmother in her tiny but spotless kitchen, frosting a yellow cake with caramel icing while talking to her teenaged great-granddaughter. "You know," Tia said, "what you just said reminded me of something my great-grandmother said to me one time. She lived in Mississippi all her life, and as you can imagine, she lived through some real ugliness. One time I asked her why she and Pop-Pop had never moved up north to one of the big cities like so many black people of their generation did. She said, 'Because that's what the crackers wanted, baby. To scare us off so they wouldn't have to look at us no more. We wasn't gonna give them the satisfaction.'"

Chameleon laughed. "That's the same spirit all right. Of course, I'm sure your great-grandmother had to put up with a lot more ugliness than I've ever had to."

"Probably ten thousand times more. Your difference is invisible to most people who see you. They just look at you and see a pretty young white woman." Tia just realized she had called Chameleon pretty and wondered if that was unprofessional.

"Yeah, people have to get to know me a little before they decide to hate me. Then they can say, 'Oh, she's a lesbian witch. We knew there was something wrong with her!'"

Tia felt a little jolt of electricity when she heard the word "lesbian." Her gaydar hadn't picked up that vibe from Chameleon, but she'd always had a hard time reading very feminine white women. "I'm one, too, you know. A lesbian, not a witch."

"I thought you might be. I looked up your firm in the *Gay Yellow Pages* to make sure you were gay-friendly."

"Actually, I'm both gay and friendly," Tia said. "So, Chameleon"—she noticed she was getting more comfortable saying Chameleon's name—maybe it was like that game where you repeat a word so many times that eventually it loses its meaning. "I'd like to take this case, but there's something you should know about me first."

"Okay."

"Would you agree," Tia asked, "that everybody is prejudiced?"

"Sure," Chameleon said. "I could rattle off a list of people I'm prejudiced against without even having to work at it. Republicans, people who wear fur coats, right-wing talk radio hosts, televangelists . . ."

Tia laughed. "I share many of your prejudices. But here's one prejudice we don't share. I have this thing about religion. All religion."

Chameleon looked puzzled. "This thing?"

"I don't get religion," Tia said. "I don't see the need for it. The earth is governed by a combination of scientific principles and chaos, and I'm fine with that. I believe in reason, not religion, which is probably why law appeals to me. That being said, though, I would take to the streets and defend anybody's right to practice their religion, as long as I have the right not to practice any religion myself."

"So you're not religious but you believe in religious freedom?"

"Exactly."

"Well, that doesn't strike me as prejudiced at all."

Tia smiled. "Well, that's because I just told you what I think, not what I feel. To be honest, I've always felt that religion . . . whether it's Christianity or paganism or whatever . . . is a little silly. It always strikes me as primitive and irrational."

"But there's a lot of value in the primitive and irrational," Chameleon said, fingering the silver fertility goddess pendant that hung on a chain between her breasts. "Sex, for instance, is primitive and irrational, yet human beings need it."

"Yes, well," Tia said, becoming strangely flustered and removing her gaze from the provocative pendant in its even more provocative location. "But the sex drive—that's biological. There's no biological need for religion." Chameleon looked as if she were about to say something, but before she could, Tia said, "Look. I don't want to get into a debate or anything. I just want to let you know that I am dedicated to defending your religious freedom even if I personally find your religion to be a little . . . well . . ."

"Wacky?" Chameleon offered.

"Yes, okay," Tia said. "But be that as it may, I have to admit I'm almost completely ignorant of Wicca. I mean, I know you aren't devil worshipers or anything like that, but that's about the extent of my knowledge. And after I've filed this suit, the media's going to be all over this story, so I'd better do some quick studying so I can talk about what you believe without sounding like a damn fool."

"Well, why don't you stop by the Moonshadow Café for lunch tomorrow? I'll bring you a bunch of books."

"The Moonshadow Café? Oh, that's the little place up the street I've been meaning to try for a year now."

"Well, you ought to try it," Chameleon said. "I'm the cook, and I'm damn good."

"Really? A witch chef?"

"Yep, but there's no eye of newt on the menu, I promise. It's all vegetarian."

Tia grinned. "Well, okay, I guess I could stop by."

"Lunch will be on the house, and I'll bring you a whole stack of books on Wicca." Chameleon smiled. "If you're prejudiced and ignorant, I figure it's my duty to educate you."

By the time Tia showed up at the Moonshadow Café, a heavy-set middle-aged woman was flipping over the sign on the door to read "Closed." Tia was about to turn tail and go back to the office when Chameleon, wearing an apron over a peasant blouse and long paisley skirt, appeared and opened the door. "Hey! I had given up on you. Come on in."

"I'm sorry I'm late. I seem to fall into some kind of wormhole in the office. I lose all track of time."

"Actually, it's great that you're here now that all the customers have gone. We can have lunch together."

Chameleon escorted Tia to a table and brought her a glass of iced herbal tea, which was better than Tia expected it to be.

"The special today is a risotto with sun-dried tomatoes, bleu cheese, and walnuts. Would you like to try it?"

"It sounds a hell of a lot better than old peanut butter crackers from the office vending machine, which is my usual lunch," Tia said.

"Now you've got to take better care of yourself than that," Chameleon said. "You should come here and let me feed you."

Tia smiled as Chameleon set the plate of warm risotto in front of her. "You're a very nurturing person, aren't you?"

"Yeah, I guess so. That's probably how I ended up being a high priestess."

Tia forked up a mouthful of risotto. Delicious. "Well, your cooking certainly is magical."

"Thank you."

The middle-aged woman who had been putting up the Closed sign emerged from the back room and called, "Camille, I'm gonna take off now and let you two enjoy your lunch. I'm starting to feel like a third wheel around here."

"No, grab a plate and sit with us, Sally," Chameleon said. "There's no reason to feel like a third wheel. Tia's my lawyer."

"Oh," Sally laughed, heading out the door, "is that what you crazy kids are calling it these days?"

What could only be described as an awkward silence followed, but then Tia caught Chameleon's eye, and they both started laughing. "I think Sally's trying to matchmake for me since I just endured the worst break-up ever," Chameleon said.

"Of course, every break-up is the worst break-up ever, isn't it?" Tia laughed.

"It's true. I bet you haven't gone through any of that drama in a long time, though. You seem so stable . . . like you're probably all settled down with somebody."

Tia rolled her eyes. "Girl, I haven't had a steady girlfriend since there was a Democrat in the White House."

"Really? I'd think you'd have to carry a softball bat to keep all the dykes away." Chameleon's face flushed pink. "I'm sorry. That was probably an unprofessional thing to say to your lawyer."

Tia could feel her face heating up, too. Fortunately, her blush wouldn't be as visible as Chameleon's. "Actually, I'm kind of the ugly duckling in my family. Both of my sisters are beauty queens."

"Well, you probably could've been, too, if you'd had the personality for it," Chameleon said. "Which, fortunately, you don't."

"Oh, but my sisters do," Tia laughed. "When we were teenagers I could always be ready to go out in fifteen minutes—I'd brush my teeth, shower, throw on clothes, and that was that. But they'd take hours, ironing their hair, putting on lotions and perfumes, fixing their faces, trying on a dozen outfits. I used to tell them that if the house caught on fire in the middle of the night, I'd be the only one who'd survive because they'd have to put their makeup on and fix their hair before they'd step out the door. LaShea, my oldest sister would always say, 'Well, I'd rather die than walk around with nappy old hair like yours.'"

Chameleon laughed. "It's weird, isn't it, how people can share the same genetic material and have nothing in common at all. My brother is a Baptist minister. We're total opposites."

"Not that opposite. You're both religious leaders."

Chameleon rolled her eyes. "Well, he wouldn't see it that way. If he knew I was a Wiccan high priestess . . . Which, thankfully, he doesn't. When I came out as a dyke to him and my parents, they totally despaired for my soul. If I told them I'm a witch, too, they'd think that was my next step down the road to hell."

Tia found herself laughing in Chameleon's presence a lot more than she thought she would. Tia had thought that a person with Chameleon's religious convictions would be painfully earnest and serious, but she actually had a wicked little sense of humor. A wicked witch, Tia thought, smiling. "Yeah, my family's pretty much decided I'm on the short list for hell, too," Tia said. "Of course, even though I came out to them ten years ago, they still like to pretend I'm just an old maid—like great-aunt Frances, who was a schoolteacher who could never find a man to marry her."

"Probably because she never looked," Chameleon said. "Great-aunt Frances probably had a girlfriend nobody knew about."

"I hope she did." Tia glanced down at her watch and was surprised to see that an hour had passed. "Shit, I'd better get back to the office."

"Oh, I hope I'm not getting you in trouble by keeping you for so long."

"Well, given that this is the first real lunch break I've taken in a year, they probably won't hold it against me if I come back a few minutes late. Plus, you're a client. This is a working lunch."

"I guess it is, isn't it? Well, let me grab those books for you." Chameleon went to the counter behind the cash register and pulled out three books. "I could've brought you a whole library's worth, but I didn't want to overwhelm you. These three are a good start."

Tia looked at the covers of the books: *Dreaming the Dark* by Starhawk, *Drawing Down the Moon* by Margot Adler, and *The Witches' Bible Compleat* by Stewart and Janet Farrar. The first two books wouldn't attract undue attention at first glance, but the sight of the third one, which was jet black with a pentacle and broomsticks on the cover, would be enough to send many a Christian running for crucifixes and holy water. Tia grinned. "I wonder what my mama would do if I left this book lying on the coffee table the next time she comes for a visit."

Chameleon smiled. "It would probably shorten her visit considerably. One time I invited some Jehovah's Witnesses in, and I had that book and my ritual dagger lying out in plain sight. They threw *The Watchtower* on the floor and ran."

"I bet they did." Tia swung the door open. "Well, I should head back."

"Okay, well, just read through those and let me know if you have any questions."

"Now you sound like a Jehovah's Witness."

Chameleon laughed. "I do, don't I? Oh, I was thinking, maybe next Thursday night, if you wanted, you could come to our Sabbat—that's a ritual meeting. That way, you could meet some of the other witches in the coven and get a feel for the group and how it works."

"Sure, that sounds good."

"We always meet out in the country at the farm of one of our coven members. It's kind of hard to find, but if you can call and give me directions to your house, I could pick you up and give you a ride there."

"Okay. I'll call you next week."

Tia was halfway out the door when Chameleon said, "Oh, and just so you know, we work skyclad."

"Okay," Tia said, having no idea what Chameleon meant. "Well, I'll see you."

"Bye."

That evening at home, flipping through *A Witches' Bible Compleat* and seeing photos of a beautiful witch wearing nothing but ritual jewelry, Tia discovered that "skyclad" meant naked.

CHAPTER 2

Tia wondered if she might be coming down with something. She'd only toyed with the salad she'd picked up for dinner. Her stomach felt queasy and shaky, and she couldn't concentrate on anything. She couldn't read. She couldn't watch the news. She couldn't even sit still long enough to pet the damn cat. She hadn't felt this way since . . . since the morning of the bar exam four years ago.

So that's what it was. She wasn't sick. She was nervous.

But why? Sure, Chameleon was going to pick her up in half an hour to take her to the witches' hoedown or whatever they called it. But there was no reason for her to be nervous. She had read enough of the books Chameleon had loaned her to know that Wicca was a harmless, peaceful religion. These witches weren't going to cook her and eat her.

And yes, the witches were going to be naked, but it wasn't like she hadn't seen naked women before. *But it's been a while, hasn't it?* her sex drive whispered. She promptly told her sex drive to shut the hell up. She was going to be mature about this, and it was going to be fine. And besides, she wasn't going to participate. Nobody was going to make her take her clothes off.

But what clothes was she going to wear? If everybody else was going to be cavorting around butt naked, then she'd look pretty stupid wearing the dress slacks and silk blouse and blazer she'd had on all day. She'd look like a cop who'd come to arrest them all for public indecency. She rummaged through her drawers and closets and finally settled on what she usually wore when she wanted to look casual but not sloppy: a pair of broken-in but not too faded Levi's and a white button-down shirt. Because she thought it might be muddy where the witches were frolicking, she put on the big clompy pair of dyke boots she always wore around her mother and sisters just to annoy them.

She brushed her teeth and quickly surveyed herself in the bathroom mirror. She kept her hair cropped so close that it required little care, and her caramel-colored skin was clear enough not to require any makeup. "Good enough," she said, looking at herself. She had often thought that women spent way too much energy trying to achieve perfection in their looks. If they could just look in the mirror and say "good enough," then maybe they could focus their energy on more important things.

When the doorbell rang, she jumped even though it wasn't a surprise. Her tiger-striped cat, as always, raced her to the door, getting tangled around Tia's legs and making her trip. When Tia opened the door, Chameleon was centered in the doorframe like a picture. Her long hair was free and wild around her shoulders, and she was wearing a purple dress printed with orchids. A pentacle with an amethyst in its center hung just below her collarbone.

"Hi," Chameleon said. The cat rubbed against her ankles. "And oh, hi, kitty." She squatted down to give the cat a thorough petting.

"That's Zora," Tia said. "She's the official greeter around these parts."

"Well, she's a beautiful girl," Chameleon said. "My kitty died almost six months ago. I had had her since I was a teenager. I keep telling myself I need to go to the shelter and adopt another cat, but I guess I'm still in mourning."

"I'm sure that's hard," Tia said. "Zora's my first real pet, and I'm surprised how attached I am to her."

"Animals are more reliable companions than a lot of humans,"

Chameleon said, standing back up. "Especially given my recent track record with human companions. Are you ready to go?"

"Yep." Now that Chameleon was here, Tia felt calmer, but there was still a nervous twinge in her stomach.

"I like your house," Chameleon said as they walked down the sidewalk to the car.

"My house isn't as old as a lot of the houses in this neighborhood," Tia said. "It's just from the nineteen twenties. I think a big part of the reason why I wanted it is because it's a bungalow, and when I was little I read this book about a family of bears that lived in a bungalow, and I just loved that word. Bung-a-low," she said, stretching it out.

Chameleon laughed. "So you bought the house so you'd have an excuse to say the word a lot?"

"Basically, yes."

In the car on the way out of town, Chameleon said, "You know, I've never seen you out of your lawyer costume before. It seems kind of strange to see you in jeans."

"I live in them when I'm not at the office. That being said, I'm in the office more often than not. Come to think of it, I've never seen you in jeans either."

Chameleon turned onto a tree-lined road. "I don't own a pair, actually. I just find these loose, flowing dresses to be more comfortable."

"Well, they suit you," Tia said, feeling that twinge in her stomach again. It was strange. Chameleon looked beautiful in flimsy, flowing, flowery garments that Tia—or nearly any other black woman she could think of—wouldn't be caught dead in. She guessed a black woman trying to pull off the Celtic earth mother look would be as ridiculous as those white women who insisted on parading around in dreadlocks and cowrie shells and kente cloth.

Graymalkin's farmhouse was farther out in the middle of nowhere than Tia had been since she used to visit her great-grandmother in Mississippi. There was something about being out in the country that made her nervous. Back in college, her friend Mikey had said one time, "I don't ever leave the city, man. I get out in the country and see all them trees, and I can't help thinking they used to hang people who looked like me from 'em." Tia had never thought of this until Mikey said it, but there had always been something about being in the country that made her uneasy and filled her with a longing for lights and noise and people.

"Isn't it peaceful out here?" Chameleon said as she parked in front of the ramshackle old farmhouse.

"It's quiet, all right," Tia said. "And dark."

"And it's not even full dark yet," Chameleon said. "Wait until you see the stars. No need for streetlights when you've got a sky full of stars. Come on in the house. I want you to meet everybody."

Tia knew there was no way she'd remember all their names. The older one was Graymalkin which was easy enough—gray hair, Graymalkin. And the fine-but-not-femme-enough-for-her-taste sister was named Anansi, which she could remember because she was familiar with the African myth. She was, however, rather shocked to see a sister in the coven, as she had always thought of moonlit goddess worship as a white girl thing.

She was hopeless with the other women's names. The butch one called herself Coyote, and Tia knew she'd be calling her Wolf or Dingo or Poodle by the end of the night. And Iris—the cute, spiky-haired one who seemed to have some weird vibe going on with Chameleon—Tia would never remember which flower she was named after. And as for Belladonna, the little girl with all the metal in her face, Tia couldn't help wondering what name her parents had given her . . . probably one of those cutesy names like Brittany or Tiffany.

Despite her amusement at their creative nomenclature, Tia had to admit that all the women were nice and welcoming and seemed to appreciate what she was doing for them.

"Tia," Graymalkin said, "it's going to take us a few minutes to get ready for the Sabbat. Why don't you make yourself comfortable in the living room and then come out to the back field in about half an hour? You'll be able to find us because we'll have candles burning."

"Okay," Tia said, her nervousness bubbling up a bit.

"Oh," Graymalkin added, "there are some pagan magazines on the coffee table if you'd like to flip through them as part of your education."

Sitting on Graymalkin's living room futon, flipping through a magazine which bore the inexplicably Dr. Seuss-like title *Green Egg*, Tia felt like she did when she was waiting at the gynecologist's office. Except, she thought, I'm not the one who's going to be taking my clothes off.

After amusing herself with the magazine's personals section, which had ads with headings like "Green Man Seeks Goddess" and "Gay Gardnerian Seeks Same," Tia checked her watch and took a deep breath. Time to go outside.

In the far field she saw the flicker of candlelight and shadowy female figures. She could do this, she told herself. It was research, just the same as going over to the law library and poring over the books. Except that the women at the law library weren't naked and engaging in pagan rituals. Stop it, she told herself. You can do this. Glad that she had worn boots, she started across the muddy field.

Graymalkin met her a few yards away from the others, and it occurred to Tia that she had never seen a woman Graymalkin's age naked before. Movies certainly didn't show the bodies of any woman much over 35, as though age made the female body somehow repellent. But Graymalkin's soft curves were beautiful. Stop it, Tia told herself. Look only at her eyes. She was sure Graymalkin had noticed her staring, but when she looked at Graymalkin's face, she seemed as oblivious and comfortable as if she were standing there fully dressed. "You can sit anywhere outside the circle," Graymalkin said. "And I brought a tarp so you don't have to get all muddy. Not everybody likes to wallow around in the earth as much as witches do."

"Thank you," Tia said, suddenly imagining the Sabbat as a kind of mud-wrestling tournament. She sat down on the ground and let herself look up at the coven. There they were, nipples erect in the brisk night air, the moonlight giving their bare flesh an ethereal glow. Skyclad, Tia thought.

All the women were beautiful, and Tia felt a little drunk at the sight of them. Anansi's strong thighs and high, proud rear; Belladonna's sensuous curves padded with baby fat; Iris's tan, athletic frame; Coyote's muscle and sinew; and Graymalkin's pillowy lushness. They were also different yet all so perfect in their own ways that Tia wondered why every woman in the world was not a lesbian.

But then the coven members parted, and Tia saw Chameleon in front of the altar. The amethyst and silver pentacle Tia had noticed earlier now hung between Chameleon's bare breasts, which were full and lovely and tinged with blue in the moonlight. She stood before the other women, her bare feet planted slightly apart, her arms outstretched, offering herself as if to a lover. Tia knew from her reading that the high priestess's job was to play the role of the goddess during rituals. Looking at Chameleon, who managed to be naked and regal at the same time, Tia had to say that the goddess role was one that Chameleon played well.

Tia tried to follow the ritual as best she could, but she found the nudity, especially Chameleon's nudity, extremely distracting. When the witch with the flower name came up to Chameleon and started kissing various parts of her body, including a spot that was so low on her belly it almost wasn't her belly anymore, Tia felt a strange pang—was it jealousy? Why should she feel any possessiveness toward Chameleon? She was just her client, for god's sake. Their relationship was strictly professional, and her only purpose in being here was research. When Chameleon turned around to face the altar, Tia found herself thinking, not a bad ass for a white girl.

Stop it, she told herself, and she managed to control herself fairly well until the witches started taking turns kissing and feeding each other red wine which ran down their chins. Tia followed a streak of red wine as it ran down Chameleon's chin, down her long neck, and disappeared into her cleavage.

What's wrong with you, Tia Thomas? she asked herself. These

women are practicing their religion, and you're watching it like it's a porno movie.

When the ritual was over, Chameleon made a beeline for Tia. "So, what did you think?" she asked, standing in front of her as though she were fully dressed.

Tia wondered if she should stand since sitting down put her on eye level with Chameleon's crotch. But what if she stood up clumsily and fell into Chameleon? That would be even more embarrassing. "Um . . . it was very . . . educational," she finally managed to say.

"Good," Chameleon said. "Well, we're going back to the house to get dressed, then we'll have a potluck."

What was it about lesbians and potlucks? Tia had always despised the randomness of potluck meals. She used to say that her understanding of being a lesbian was that there was only one thing that started with *P* that you had to eat, and "potluck" wasn't it. "I'm sorry I didn't bring anything," she said, managing to stand up without falling onto Chameleon's naked body.

"Oh, we wouldn't want you to bring anything," Chameleon said. "You're already doing so much for our coven as it is, and we're just glad you're here." She draped her arm around Tia in what would have been a casual half-hug, had Chameleon been clothed. As it was, Tia froze, knowing that returning the hug meant touching Chameleon's bare flesh.

"Oh, I'm sorry if that made you uncomfortable," Chameleon said. "I'm so used to being naked that I tend to forget everybody isn't so casual about nudity."

"No problem," Tia said, feeling idiotic because her self-consciousness had showed.

"Poor Tia. I don't guess you're used to seeing your clients in the altogether." Chameleon laughed. "I'll go put my dress back on so you don't have to spend so much time deciding where you should look when I'm talking to you."

Chameleon laughed and took off across the field like a doe. Even though Tia was fully clothed, she felt like she was the one who had been exposed.

❧❧❧

The food at the potluck could have been worse. There were roasted ears of corn and a nice pasta salad and a box of cheap red wine which Tia helped herself to in an effort to overcome the awkwardness of dining with strangers whom she had just seen naked.

After two paper cups of wine, she found it much easier to be sociable. Anansi, it turned out, was from Nashville, too, and so they spent a pleasant half hour talking about places and people they knew in common. Graymalkin was a gracious hostess, circulating and making sure everybody was comfortable and offering around egg-free, gluten-free, dairy-free cupcakes (Tia declined). And all the women wanted to know about the lawsuit—what she thought their chances of success were (pretty good, but would be better outside the Bible Belt) and how long the legal process would take (longer than anybody would want it to).

Overall, Tia had to admit that she found the coven to be made up of kind, sincere women who were surprisingly intelligent given their propensity for dancing around stark naked. And they all seemed so comfortable together . . . well, all of them except Chameleon and Iris. There was definitely something going on there. Except for during the ritual, the two women had largely avoided each other, and when contact was unavoidable, their interchanges had been awkward. Tia remembered Chameleon alluding to a bad breakup and wondered if Iris could be the source of it.

When Tia looked at her watch, she was surprised to see how late it was. She leaned over to Chameleon. "I don't want to spoil the party, but I have to get up pretty early for work in the morning."

"Oh, of course," Chameleon said, smiling. "I tend to forget that everyone isn't as nocturnal as we are. Just let me do my good night hugs and then we'll get you home."

Tia noticed that Chameleon's hug with Iris was less close and lingering than her hugs with the other coven members. Once they were in the car, Tia said, "So that breakup you were telling me about . . . it was with Iris, right?"

Chameleon laughed. "Wow, you lawyer types really are observant, aren't you?"

"Yep. It must be hard, her still being in the coven."

"And still being my working partner. But I figured it would be awfully petty for me to kick her out just because she dumped me. I figure the more time that passes, the easier it will get."

"You're a nicer person than I am," Tia said. "I would've kicked her butt out."

"Well, I might have, too, if deep down I hadn't felt like we needed to break up. Iris and I had problems. She always liked the high priestess version of me better than the everyday me."

"Kind of like having a crush on a movie star and thinking the real person will be just like that big image on the screen."

"Exactly." They were getting near town now, and Tia felt comforted by the sight of the city lights. "So," Chameleon said, "what did you think of the Sabbat?"

Tia searched for words. "I thought it was . . . without a doubt . . . the most beautiful religious service I've ever attended."

They were at a stop light, and Chameleon turned toward her, grinning. "Would that be because you happened to be surrounded by naked women?"

"Well, that helped, yeah." Tia laughed.

"But I'm curious . . . what is your impression of our religion?"

Tia didn't want to be put on the spot after midnight after a long day, but here she was. "Well . . . that you're kind, nurturing people who care about each other and the earth."

"That didn't answer my question. You just said what you thought of us, not what you think of Wicca."

Tia grinned. "Hell, maybe you should be the lawyer. Okay, here's what I think: there's nothing offensive about your religion at all. In fact, it's very nice. But maybe it's a little too nice for the world we live in."

"What do you mean?"

"I mean that in a world this fucked up, where people are oppressed or killed or penniless while corporate giants are growing fatter and fatter . . . how can you say some benevolent goddess is in charge of this world? Surely if a goddess was in charge, the world would be a kinder place."

Chameleon parked the car in front of Tia's house. "But you see, the world is in such a sorry state because people have turned away from what the goddess represents . . . from peace and nurturing and living in harmony with nature. If people would embrace these principles, the world would start to heal." Chameleon's eyes were wide and very blue, even in the darkness.

"I told you you're a better person than I am," Tia said.

"Why?"

"Because you believe that kind of change is possible."

Chameleon reached out and placed her hand on Tia's. "But you believe in change, too. If you didn't, you'd be making money hand over fist working for some evil corporation instead of being over-worked and underpaid at a little firm that helps the downtrodden." She smiled. "Like me."

"Okay, so we're both nice people." Chameleon hadn't taken her hand away from Tia's, and her soft touch radiated a strange energy Tia couldn't explain. Tia heard herself saying, "You know, I finished reading *The Witches' Bible*. If you want to come in for a minute, I'll give it back to you."

"Okay." Chameleon smiled. "Wow, you finished it, huh? You're a fast reader."

"That's what got me through law school."

Inside the house, the cat rubbed against Chameleon's ankles while Tia retrieved the book.

"So what did you think of it?" Chameleon asked when Tia handed the book back to her.

"It was interesting . . . I was kind of surprised, though, how much of witchcraft is based on heterosexuality . . . the female energy versus the male energy and all that. It all seemed surpris-ingly . . . straight."

"Well, as I always tell my youngest coven member, who's forevermore complaining about the heterosexism of 'old school'

Wicca, the energy from ritual is all about polarity, and male-female polarity is just one kind of many. People can be of the same sex and still be polar opposites in terms of their personalities. And that polarity can generate tremendous energy . . . and tremendous attraction."

Tia could usually explain all of her actions. She didn't normally do anything without thinking it through first and weighing the pros and cons. But now she just acted. She did something that had she been in control of her reason, she never would have done. It was almost as if she had been bewitched.

Tia took a step toward Chameleon, placed her hands on Chameleon's shoulders, leaned forward, and kissed her on the mouth. Tia felt Chameleon's soft lips part in response, then heard *The Witches' Bible* fall to the floor with a thud and felt Chameleon's arms snaking around her waist.

They kissed without stopping to breathe. Chameleon's back was pressed to the door as Tia leaned into her, finally moving from Chameleon's lips to kiss down her long white neck to her collarbone, her hands sliding down Chameleon's silky dress, down the swell of her breasts and the curves of her hips.

The weight of their passion dragged them to the floor, and somehow Tia was on her back with Chameleon straddling her. Tia watched as Chameleon pulled her dress over her head. She wasn't wearing any underclothes, and Tia gasped to see the beauty she had admired from a distance now so close. Chameleon lay down over the length of Tia's body and leaned in for a long, slow kiss. Tia flipped her over, and soon she was kissing Chameleon's throat and down to her lovely breasts. No wonder she plays the role of a goddess, Tia thought. She certainly has the body for it. But then Tia's head was empty of all thoughts as she moved her hands and mouth over Chameleon's skin, touching and tasting, her senses blissfully alive.

When she parted Chameleon's thighs, she felt for a moment that she could understand the pagan fertility cults and the worship of such a dark and magical place, the source of both life and pleasure. When she slipped one finger, then another, into that place, the holiest of holies, it felt like warm, wet silk. Soon there was nothing but their rhythm, the rocking back and forth and Chameleon's cries and panting combining into a song of pleasure. When Tia felt Chameleon tremble beneath her and felt Chameleon's muscles tighten around her hand, she knew their song of pleasure had reached its crescendo.

After Tia caught her breath, she laughed to see the havoc they had wreaked on her living room floor. They had rolled on the Oriental rug until it was a crumpled mess. They had knocked over the cat's scratching post (the cat was in the corner, staring at them judgmentally), and Chameleon had somehow ended up with her head under the glass-topped coffee table. "Are you okay under there?" Tia asked.

"Sure. Just enjoying the view." Chameleon scooted out from under the table. "You wouldn't happen to have one of those things called a bed, would you?"

Tia grinned. "As a matter of fact, I do. I just kind of forgot about it in the heat of the moment. However, my experience has been that lying on my bed is somewhat more comfortable than lying under my coffee table."

Chameleon laughed. "Maybe we should try it, then."

Tia helped Chameleon up and led her down the hall to the bedroom. When she had bought the house, she had fixed up the bedroom to be deliberately sexy, with pen-and-ink nudes hanging on the wall and an inviting queen-sized bed. Until tonight, though, the only creature that had taken Tia and her bed up on its invitation had been Zora the cat.

"So tell me," Chameleon said, stopping her at the edge of the bed. "Why is it that you still have all your clothes on, and I've been naked for an hour?"

"It must be your pagan tendencies."

"Maybe so." Chameleon ran a finger across Tia's lips. "But from what you just did to me, I think you might have some pagan tendencies yourself." She undid the top button of Tia's shirt.

"After all, nobody's a rationalist in the bedroom . . . not if they want to have a good time anyway. Are you having a good time, Tia?"

"Um . . . yes." Tia was suddenly shy, yet at the same time she didn't want Chameleon to stop undressing her.

Chameleon was unbuttoning Tia's shirt with maddening slowness, undoing a button, then kissing the bare skin down to the next button. When she reached Tia's cleavage, she purred, "ooh . . . look . . . a bra!" as if Tia were wearing some kind of exotic fetish garment. Once Tia's shirt was off, Chameleon went to work unbuttoning her jeans. She yanked them down and sighed, "And white panties!"

"Are you making fun of my undies?"

"No . . . not at all. It's just that it's been so long since I've been with a woman who wore them. But I love the challenge." She put her arms around Tia's back, unhooked her bra, and pushed her back on the bed.

"Better get rid of those panties, too," Chameleon said, sliding them down Tia's hips.

Tia lay on her back with Chameleon leaning over her, Chameleon's hands flat-palmed against Tia's skin, tracing circles over Tia's shoulders, breasts, and belly. A pleasurable heat radiated from Chameleon's touch—heat which seemed like more than could be generated by human hands. How does she do that? Tia wondered, but then her mind stopped, and all she did was feel the warmth and the strokes that relaxed and aroused her at the same time. Soon Chameleon's hands were replaced by her mouth, and Tia gasped to feel the wet warmth of Chameleon's lips and tongue on her breasts, belly, and—her gasp was almost a scream—her inner thighs. When Chameleon's tongue touched down on that most sensitive spot, Tia dug her nails into the sheets. It was good good good good good, and it had been so long since anyone had found that spot, and this was the best she could ever remember it being, now, this moment when her thoughts were silent and there was nothing but pure pleasure washing over her.

"Damn," Tia said, when Chameleon cuddled up next to her. "Damn, you're good at that."

"Well, you know, I chose the name Chameleon because the chameleon symbolizes change and adaptation to change." Chameleon paused to kiss Tia's shoulder. "But the Chameleon is also known for having a very agile tongue."

"Mmm," Tia purred. "You know, I feel like I could sleep for three days. Which, I guess, means I'd better set the damn alarm clock."

Chameleon snuggled up against Tia's back. "Is it okay if I stay here tonight?"

Tia rolled over and took Chameleon in her arms. She knew that if she listened to her thoughts, she would start backing away. But it had been so, so long since she had held a woman like this. "Please," she whispered. "Stay."

PART III:

FIRE

CHAPTER 1

Chameleon wondered if she should be worried. When Tia had woken up early that morning to go to the office, Chameleon had invited her to the café for lunch, and Tia had said she'd come. But now lunch hours were over. Sally had put up the closed sign, emptied the cash register, and headed for the bank. Chameleon had packed up the day's unsold food to deliver to the nearby homeless shelter. It was ten minutes past the time she usually locked up, but she kept finding little excuses not to leave—a knife that needed to be cleaned better, some tofu she could put in to marinate overnight. She felt ridiculous for waiting around—after all, Tia had probably just gotten hung up at the office like the workaholic she was—but she couldn't help herself. Last night . . . she still felt aftershocks of pleasure when she thought about it.

As she was cubing the tofu, there was a soft knock at the door, and she rushed out of the kitchen to see Tia, holding an umbrella that wasn't doing much to protect her from the torrential rain. Chameleon smiled to see her, but felt a surge of panic when her smile was not returned. She took a deep breath and opened the door. "Hey. Come in. I saved some of today's special for you if you want some."

"No, thanks," Tia said. "I just came to talk. Do you have a minute?"

"Sure. Why don't you sit down at least?"

They sat at a table for two. Chameleon noticed that Tia wasn't making any eye contact with her at all, which could only mean bad news. As if Tia's announcement that she came "to talk" wasn't a bad omen anyway.

"Listen, Chameleon," Tia said, looking down at her hands—hands that Chameleon remembered quite fondly from the night before. "Last night was . . . was . . ."

"Great?" Chameleon offered.

Tia produced a weak smile. "Yeah, it was. But I've been thinking it was probably the kind of thing that only needs to happen once."

I will not cry, Chameleon told herself. I will not cry. "Why's that?"

"Well," Tia said, "there are lots of reasons, the first being that I'm your lawyer. For me to have an intimate relationship with you while you're my client . . . well, it's highly unprofessional. I could be disbarred for it."

"Well, I can understand that," Chameleon said. "I certainly wouldn't want to put your career in danger. And after all, I won't be your client forever."

"No," Tia said, still not looking at her, "but you'll be my client for quite a while. This case could go on for a year or longer. It wouldn't be fair for me to ask you to wait just in case we have . . . something."

"I'm a very patient girl," Chameleon said, making a futile attempt at humor.

"It's more than just that," Tia said, studying the tabletop. "You and I are such completely different people. With me, life is all about reason and evidence and facts. And you . . . you're out there naked in the moonlight talking about magic and goddesses and things . . . things you can't *prove*."

"So you deal with the rational aspects of the universe, and I deal with the irrational ones. Between the two of us, we've got the whole universe covered."

Tia shook her head, looking exasperated. "But shouldn't everything be rational? Chameleon, like I'd said, I'd fight to the death to defend your right to practice your religion, but to be lovers with somebody who spends so much time on ethereal things? I'd end up trying to convert you to my way of thinking. And I'd hate myself for trying to change you . . . like I was some kind of missionary for agnosticism."

"Well . . ." Chameleon said, her voice cracking despite her attempt not to cry. "I'm sorry you regret what happened last night."

"Oh, I don't regret it," Tia said, looking at Chameleon for the first time. "It was beautiful . . . a beautiful memory." She reached out and touched the tear that was slipping down Chameleon's cheek. "I need to go. I'll be in touch about the case."

Like an automaton, Chameleon walked back to the kitchen to finish cubing the tofu. Precisely and efficiently, she cubed three full packages of the stuff. It was only as she was dropping the cubes into the marinade that she realized she was crying. She wondered if tears in the tofu compromised its essential vegetarianism.

Chameleon returned to her apartment, planning to strip off her work clothes, burrow under the covers in her loft bed, and stay there indefinitely. Passing by her answering machine, she noticed it was flashing that she had four messages. Maybe, she thought, one of them's from Tia. Maybe she was just scared. Maybe she realizes now that you can't dump a woman before you've even officially gotten together with her. She took a deep breath and pushed "play."

"This message is for Camille Masters," a perky female voice which was definitely not Tia's chirped. "This is Tracy London from Channel Eight News. Your attorney told me I could reach you at this number. I'd like to get together and talk with you about the case you and your . . . group have filed in federal court . . ."

Chameleon pushed the "next" button: "Camille Masters, Brad

Turner from WJAX-TV. I was hoping you could answer a few questions about this whole witches adopting a highway business—that is, if you're not going to turn me into a toad or anything, har, har, har . . ."

Chameleon winced and hit the "next" button again. "This is Shelley Sheldon, Channel Six News . . ." Next. "Camille Masters, this is Stuart Williams from the *Herald* . . ."

Chameleon pressed "stop." Well, her personal life was a wreck, but at least she was a media darling. She washed her face, made a cup of camomile tea to calm her nerves, and decided to call everyone back except that Brad guy. He obviously didn't need her to turn him into a toad; he already was one.

For some reason, both of the TV reporters wanted to interview her in front of the federal courthouse downtown. She arranged to be there at four for a sort of informal press conference with the two TV reporters and the guy from the *Herald*. Chameleon put on a long sage-green dress and pulled out her pentacle necklace so it was prominently displayed. When she looked in the mirror, her face was a mess of puffy eyes and splotchy skin. This was not the look she would have chosen for her TV debut.

When Chameleon arrived in front of the federal courthouse, it was clear why the reporters had wanted to interview her there. The courthouse steps were packed with people: men in three-piece polyester suits straight out of a 1978 Sears catalog; other men in jeans and flannel shirts, their hair cut military short; women with scrubbed, makeup-free faces and never-cut hair, wearing loose, long-sleeved dresses and sensible shoes; other women with beauty shop hairdos and ladylike suits looking like the honorary daughters of Phyllis Schlafly—all of them carrying hand-lettered signs with slogans like NO SUCH THING AS A GOOD WITCH, DON'T TURN ROUTE 25 INTO A HIGHWAY TO HELL, and THOU SHALT NOT SUFFER A WITCH TO LIVE.

Chameleon couldn't breathe. Was this the twenty-first century, or had she just time traveled to the days of the witch hunts? Had she been lured here by the media so that these crazed villagers could burn her at the stake?

But then she saw something that made being burned at the stake seem like an attractive option. There, at the stop of the stairs in front of the white-columned courthouse, was Tia, looking gorgeous and professional with half a dozen microphones and tape recorders in her face.

I can do this, Chameleon told herself. I can speak to Tia in front of all these reporters and all these hate-filled protesters without crying. She took a deep breath, whispered "Goddess preserve me," and headed up the steps, past the demonstrators who were so busy chanting, "Witches, turn or burn!" that they didn't even notice that she, the enemy, was among them.

Tia met her at the top of the steps. "Hi," she said, the same way you'd say hi to your two o'clock appointment, not to the woman whose naked body you had licked the night before.

"Hey." Chameleon was surprised that her voice didn't come out choked and squeaky. "So, what's with all these protesters? Was it a slow day at the abortion clinic or something?"

Tia looked like she might smile but thought better of it. "I'm sure they're enjoying having something novel to protest. I told you when the news of this suit hit, it was going to be big. These reporters are practically drooling over the sensationalism. Don't be surprised if they slap a pointy black hat on your head. Oh and listen . . ." She touched Chameleon's forearm, but like a lawyer, not a lover. "I talked to them quite a bit about the legal basis for our case, so you might want to focus on what a peaceful, harmless religion Wicca is . . . you know, do a little pagan PR."

"Sure," Chameleon said, wondering if there were any emotions hiding beneath Tia's professional exterior. "No problem."

"Okay, take care," Tia said. "I'll be talking with you soon."

Trying to shake off her emotions like a drenched dog shaking off water, Chameleon joined the throng of reporters. It was amazing how alike the two women reporters looked in their just-so suits and their over-coiffed hair which screamed, "don't touch me." Their faces were carefully shellacked with makeup, and they held their microphones in manicured hands. Newsbots, Chameleon thought.

The balding, shlumpy newspaper guy stood back from the newsbots wearing a sweat-stained, dingy sport shirt and jeans he probably bought back when the Watergate scandal was on the front page. For all his sloppiness, Chameleon liked him way better than the newsbots. At least he seemed like a real person.

"So, Ms. Masters," the blonde newsbot said, her candy apple red lips spreading into a beauty pageant smile, "you're the chairperson of Witches of East Tennessee?"

"We don't really have terms like 'chairperson' in Wicca," Chameleon said. "We're not a corporation or anything. I'm the high priestess of the coven, and my witch name is Chameleon." Chameleon watched the newsbots smile encouragingly, the same way they might smile at an insane, but basically harmless street person who was holding forth on some conspiracy theory.

"Miss Ch-Chameleon," the brunette newsbot said, "what would you say to people such as these protesting today who say that witchcraft is devil worship and that by publicly sponsoring a roadway, you're exposing the community—especially young people—to dangerous influences?"

"Well, I would disagree, obviously." Chameleon tried for an ingratiating smile, but given the day she was having, smiling was not an easy task. "It's a common misunderstanding to confuse Wicca with devil worship, but the Christian ideas of God and Satan just aren't a part of our beliefs. We practice an earth-centered religion, based on the cycles of nature and using the goddess as a metaphor for the bounty and seasons of the earth. And since we do value the earth so much, it only makes sense that we would want to participate in a program like Adopt-a-Highway in which we can care for and nurture a little patch of our earth."

"Chameleon," the shlumpy newspaper guy said, not choking on her name at all, "do you think this controversy is just another example of the increasing religious intolerance in our country?"

Chameleon could have kissed the top of his shiny head. Finally, an intelligent question. "Yes, I do. This is the same kind of intolerance you read about every day: Muslim and Sikh children sent home from public schools on dress code violations simply because their clothing or hair length is proscribed by their religion. Christian prayers said at public sporting events. For a country which supposedly guarantees religious freedom, the U.S. certainly seems to favor the Christian religion over all others."

By the time Chameleon finished the press conference she was utterly exhausted, but she did feel like she'd made some pretty good points. It would be interesting to see if any of those points actually showed up in the coverage.

Chameleon didn't own a TV, so she headed over to Coyote's house to watch the 11 o'clock news. By 10:30, Coyote's apartment had turned into the setting of an informal coven meeting, with Belladonna and Anansi showing up to watch too.

"Well," Coyote said, passing beers all around. "I had no idea that being the only coven member to own a flat-screen TV would make me so popular."

"I think you're the only coven member who owns a TV, period," Anansi said, twisting open a bottle of Rolling Rock.

"Well, I've got to have it to watch the Lady Vols games," Coyote said.

"But you always *go* to the Lady Vols games," Belladonna laughed. "You've got season tickets."

"I still tape 'em at home, though, so I can watch 'em on TV later," Coyote said.

"So," Belladonna said, "how does it feel to be a regional lesbian stereotype?"

"I refuse to be called a stereotype by a girl wearing all black and smoking a clove cigarette."

"Shh, it's coming on," Anansi said over the news' canned theme song.

When the blonde newsbot's face appeared on the screen, Belladonna yelled, "Eeew! It's Newscaster Barbie!"

"Trust me, she's even scarier in person," Chameleon said, sipping her beer. She still felt wretched from Tia's brush-off, but being in a roomful of friends was smoothing away some of the sharper edges of her pain.

They sat through ten minutes of stories on robberies, murders, and maimings before the newsbot chirped, "In other news, some local citizens are up in arms about the fact that a group calling themselves Witches of East Tennessee has asked to participate in the Adopt-a-Highway program. Based on those citizens' concerns, the county has denied permission for Witches of East Tennessee to post the name of their organization on an Adopt-a-Highway sign. W.E.T., as the group calls itself, has countered with a lawsuit claiming discrimination. Today I talked to people on both sides of this controversy at the federal courthouse."

A thick-necked, middle-aged man with a buzz cut appeared on screen. "Some things," he proclaimed, "just ain't right. You let witches adopt a road, the next thing you know they'll be trying to adopt our children and turn them into witches, too."

One of the daughters of Phyllis Schlafly appeared next, a Nutrasweet smile on her face. "We're just here to protect the children," she said.

"What children?" Belladonna yelled at the TV. "What fucking children?"

"Shh," Coyote hissed.

Tia was onscreen next, staring into the camera confidently. "I tell you what," Anansi said, "our lawyer is *fine*."

Chameleon winced even as she agreed with her.

"By letting the Greater Bethel A.M.E. Church adopt a stretch of highway," Tia was saying, "the county set a precedent that it is acceptable for a religious organization to not only adopt a stretch of highway but to have the name of their organization appear on the highway adoption sign. Witches of East Tennessee is a legitimate religious organization which should have its name displayed like any other organization. We are confident that the federal court will agree in the spirit of upholding religious freedom for all Americans."

Next, Chameleon saw her own face appear with the name

Chameleon in quotation marks under it, along with the word "witch." She listened to her Wicca-is-not-devil-worship speech, but the whole time she could only think of how strange and nasal her voice sounded and how beaky her nose looked. She was stark naked in front of the coven on a regular basis, but being on TV fully clothed made her feel much more exposed and vulnerable.

"Hey, you kicked ass!" Belladonna said.

"Our high priestess is media-savvy," Anansi added.

Coyote chucked Chameleon on the shoulder—it hurt a little—and passed her another beer.

"Thanks." So . . . Chameleon thought, she was completely in control as a high priestess and completely helpless in her personal life. So what else was new? "Anybody want to order a pizza?" she asked.

It was Sabbat night again. As always, Chameleon set up the altar in the pasture, then went back to the house to get ready for the ritual. It was almost time to start, and Anansi, Coyote, Belladonna, and Graymalkin were gathered in the bedroom, undressing as Celtic music played softly on the stereo. "Has anybody seen Iris?" Chameleon asked. Without a working partner, there could be no ritual.

"Well, actually, I ran into her at the Food Co-Op this afternoon," Coyote said. "And I don't know how you're going to take this, but . . ." Coyote took a deep breath and put her hand on Chameleon's shoulder. "She told me she had been seeing the high priestess of this coven in Maryville. She said she might start going to their Sabbats instead . . . that she hadn't made up her mind."

"Well, I don't see her here, so apparently she did make up her mind," Anansi said.

Chameleon was near tears. Despite how Tia had hurt her, despite being publicly under fire as a witch, she had comforted herself that at least things were going well within the coven. And now she couldn't even say that anymore. "It would've been nice of her to tell me. I mean, who she sleeps with is her business, but standing me up for a Sabbat . . . that's the coven's business."

"She's not thinking about the coven," Belladonna said. "She's thinking about her new high priestess's pussy. The girl is a total groupie."

"I could do her part tonight," Graymalkin said. "I know I'm not ideal, but Goddess knows I've been a witch long enough to be able to do the ritual."

"Would you?" Chameleon said. That was so like Graymalkin—always willing to step in and help in the face of disaster. "That would be great."

Graymalkin did know the choreography of the ritual, but even as she went through each motion, Chameleon knew the Sabbat was going badly. Through no fault of her own, Graymalkin, the comforting crone of the coven, just didn't generate the right chemistry to be Chameleon's working partner.

Usually by the end of a ritual Chameleon felt exhilarated, more alive than she felt at any other time. But tonight's ritual left her drained and depressed. As soon as it was polite to do so, she said her goodnights and left. Why stick around when there was no magic in the air?

Chameleon unlocked her door, wondering if a private ritual might help her feel better. Perhaps the Tarot could give her some guidance. On her way to fetch her deck from the rosewood box where she kept it, she noticed the flashing light of the answering machine. She remembered a line Dorothy Parker supposedly said whenever the phone rang: "What fresh hell is this?" Could it be more newsbots? Or one of those devastatingly attractive yet intimacy-fearing women who were prone to screwing and abandoning her? She pushed "play" only to discover that it was worse, much worse: "Camille, it's your mom. Your daddy and brother and I are coming into Knoxville tomorrow to pick up a few things at that big Christian bookstore out west. Anyway, we thought it'd be fun if you went out to dinner with us. We'll be at your . . . well, it's not really a *house*, is it? We'll be at your little . . . *place* around six o'clock. See you then."

Chameleon had to sit down. When that didn't help, she put her head between her knees, which didn't help much either. This was weird. Too weird. Her parents never thought "it would be fun" if she went to dinner with them. Indeed, they were embarrassed to be seen in public with her. Even though they only lived about an hour away from Knoxville, Chameleon rarely saw them more than twice a year, when she made her much-dreaded obligatory winter and summer visits. Chameleon's mother had only been in her house—or her "little place"—once, and the whole time she'd kept talking about what a bad neighborhood it was, her eyes darting frantically as if she were in danger for her life.

Her father regarded Knoxville as a hotbed of vice and had never visited her at all, and her brother—what the hell was he doing tagging along? Didn't he have some loaves and fishes to multiply or some water to turn into non-alcoholic grape juice or something?

And then it hit her. Her parents, who lived only three counties away, were in the Channel 8 News viewing area. And while they didn't watch the news every night, she'd be willing to bet, given the way her luck had been running, that they watched it last night. In her mind she saw her face as it had appeared on the TV screen with the caption "'Chameleon'—Witch."

This was bad. All kinds of bad. Well, she thought, she could always hide out at Coyote's or Graymalkin's tomorrow night, and when her family showed up, she just wouldn't be there. But then she thought of Iris running out on the coven without a word of explanation. Would standing up her parents really be any different? No, she should stay and talk to them. She had already come out to them as a lesbian; she might as well come out to them as a witch . . . or at least come out to them personally instead of just doing it on TV. After all, she was proud of who she was, and if her family cut her off entirely, didn't she already have a loving and supportive family in the form of the coven? She could do this, she told herself. She could. But right now, she needed to cry a little.

CHAPTER 2

Five-fifty p.m. and Chameleon was a total wreck. She had debated calling another member of the coven to go along with her for moral support, but then decided this was too much to ask, even of a close friend. Chameleon knew her family, and she knew they would regard each of her friends with suspicion: Graymalkin because they wouldn't understand why Chameleon would have a friend who was so much older than she was; Coyote because she was so butch; Belladonna because she was so goth; and Anansi because she was a member of an ethnic group Chameleon's parents most frequently referred to as "those people." She wouldn't make her friends suffer just because she had to.

When there was a knock at the door, Chameleon jumped as if it were a gunshot. She closed her eyes, said a quick prayer to the goddess, and went to open the door. Her mother, father, and brother stood framed in the doorway with fixed smiles on their faces that made them look like particularly overenthusiastic door-to-door salespeople.

Chameleon's father and brother were wearing nearly identical dark suits and actually looked pretty nearly identical otherwise, except that Camille's father's sandy brown hair was now only a clown-like fringe over his ears, whereas her brother's hairline had only begun to creep backward. Chameleon's mom was wearing one of her standard "cute" outfits—a fuschia sweater decorated with kittens playing with balls of lime green yarn. Her slacks were the same shade of green as the yarn, and her shoes were the same shade of fuschia as the sweater. Chameleon's mom was the queen of "cute" outfits in what she called "festive" colors. Opening the woman's closet door was like opening a giant box of Crayolas.

"Hi, honey!" Chameleon's mother crowed. She gave Chameleon an arm's length hug and a feather-light, guaranteed-not-to-smudge-the-lipstick kiss on the cheek.

"Hey, Mom. Hey, Dad." Chameleon's dad did not offer a hug or a greeting, and she didn't make a move to force him. "Hey, Cameron."

"Hey, sis." Cameron gave Chameleon a half-hug of the back-patting variety.

"So," Chameleon's mother chirped. "Are you hungry?"

Nauseated was more like it. But Chameleon still climbed into her parents' gigantic, environmentally toxic SUV with its "God Bless America" and "Abortion Stops a Beating Heart" bumper stickers and settled in for the ride to West Knoxville. Chameleon's parents refused to eat at any of the restaurants in the downtown or university area because they were "not nice." Chameleon assumed that this label also applied to the restaurant where she cooked.

In the strip mall land that was West Knoxville, Chameleon's dad pulled into the parking lot of the Parmesan Piazza, a pseudo-Italian chain restaurant which served a variety of overcooked pastas drowned in red sauce. At the table, a cute waitress with a small tattoo of a Congee character on her hand said, "Welcome to the Parmesan Piazza. Can I start you folks off with some wine?"

Yes, a bottle of Merlot and a straw for me, Chameleon thought, but her father said, "We don't drink alcohol, and neither should you. I'll have a sweet tea, please."

"Sweet tea, sweet tea," Chameleon's mother and brother echoed, while Chameleon, still wishing for wine, settled for a Pellegrino.

"What's that you ordered?" her mom asked suspiciously.

"Just water, Mom. It's an Italian bottled water."

When the waitress set the bottle of Pellegrino down in front of Chameleon, her mom let out a nervous titter. "Well, it doesn't really *look* like bottled water, does it? It looks like a bottle of wine or beer or something." She looked around at the other tables as if she expected people to be pointing accusatory fingers. "I sure hope everybody *knows* it's water."

When the salads arrived, Cameron said, "Shall we pray?" Chameleon's parents bowed their heads and closed their eyes along with Cameron, who intoned, "Bless this food to the nourishment of our bodies . . ."

Chameleon sat, eyes open and head unbowed. The cute waitress, passing by, gave her a supportive pat on the shoulder, as if to say, *I know you're in hell, and I pity you.*

Over plates of pasta that were so splattered with red that they resembled something in a horror movie, Chameleon, in an attempt to make chit-chat, asked her mom, "So how are things at dear old Carter County High?" Her mother was a home economics teacher who had been quite upset when Chameleon, as a high school student, had refused to take even one of her classes.

"Well, things are all right, I suppose," Chameleon's mother sighed. "But I tell you, sometimes I just get so discouraged with these girls today. You should see what they wear to school—skin-tight T-shirts cut off above their belly buttons, skin-tight jeans that come below their belly buttons. Some girls even have a ring in their belly buttons. I swear, I don't know what it is with girls today and their belly buttons . . ."

"I wish it was just about belly buttons," Cameron said. "But it's about more than that—these girls showing off their bodies, making themselves available to boys. With morality on the decline like it is, I'm so proud of our youth group members who take the chastity pledge."

Chameleon choked on her Pellegrino. "A chastity pledge? Is that anything like a chastity belt?"

Cameron smiled a fake-patient smile. "No, it's simply when teenagers—or if they're preteens, it's even better—sign a pledge saying they won't engage in sexual activity until they're married."

Chameleon laughed for the first time all evening. "But that's ridiculous! Most teenagers are so mixed up they can't even promise what they'll be doing tomorrow—let alone promise that they won't do what every raging hormone in their horny little bodies is telling them to do every second!"

"But human beings are not animals, Camille," Cameron said. "They can fight those hormones. I always tell the kids in youth group, whenever you're on a date, sitting in a car in the dark, just think, what would Jesus do?"

"And how are contemporary teenagers supposed to know what a rabbi who's been dead for thousands of years would have done in that situation?" Chameleon shot back, her voice a little louder than she intended it to be.

"Dessert, anyone?" The waitress had appeared at the table.

"I think," Chameleon's father said, "we're ready for the check."

As the gas-swilling SUV pulled up in front of Chameleon's house, she said, "Well, it was good to see you all. Thank you for dinner."

"We were wondering if we could come in for a few minutes," Chameleon's mother said. "We need to talk to you about something, in private."

Here it comes, Chameleon thought. "Sure, okay."

In her little living room area, Chameleon's mother, father, and brother sat bunched together on the little sofa that was the only place to sit except for pillows or beanbag chairs. "Can I make anyone a cup of tea?" Chameleon asked.

"Camille," her mother said, "your father and I saw you on the news last night. He was so upset I thought he was going to have a heart attack. We called Cameron, and he came over and we prayed about it until the Lord told us we had to come talk to you."

"Well, I'm sorry you saw me like that without any warning," Chameleon said. "If it had crossed my mind that you might be watching the news, I would have called you first so it wouldn't have been such a shock. But I've had a lot on my mind lately, and . . ."

"Camille, your father and I are just so upset we don't know what to do. First, you told us you were a . . ."

"Lesbian?" Chameleon thought she'd save her mother the trouble of saying the word.

"And now there's this, and I guess this is just the next logical step from the other, but . . ."

"Mother, you really need to get out more. I didn't become a witch because I'm a lesbian. The world is full of lesbians who aren't witches and witches who aren't lesbians."

"You tell your mother she should get out more," her father spat, his face turning magenta. "Well, I say *you* should stay in more and read your Bible."

"Dad, I don't even own a Bible anymore."

Cameron reached inside his blazer, took out a small Testament, and held it out to her.

"Cameron," Chameleon said. "I went to church and Sunday school with you all those years, remember? I know what the Bible says, and there's a lot of good stuff in it. But overall, it's just not the path for me."

"It's the only path, sis," Cameron said, his voice calm and even.

"It is not the only path. Haven't you ever heard of Buddhists and Hindus and Muslims? They have paths, too. Shoot, there are even different paths to take within Christianity . . . new church franchises are popping up every day." Chameleon was interrupted by the ringing phone. At first, she thought she'd let the machine get it, but then she thought of her parents sitting there listening with horror to the kind of lesbian and Wicca-related messages that she tended to get and ran to pick up the receiver. "Hello?"

"Chameleon? This is Tia."

Talking with the woman who ditched her yesterday in front of her proselytizing family . . . suddenly, spontaneous combustion seemed like an attractive option. "Um . . . yeah?"

"You sound kind of rattled. I think I might have handled things pretty badly yesterday. I apologize."

"My parents and brother are here right now."

"They are? Shit, that's terrible, isn't it?"

"It sure is," Chameleon said in a sweet, cheerful tone.

"Say, do they live close enough to Knoxville that they saw you on the news?"

"That's right."

"Oh, girl, I am so sorry for you right now. Listen, the main reason I was calling is that all this media attention might help us get a court date sooner than we thought. I've got some papers for you to sign, and if I can get them to you to sign tonight, I can file them in the morning, and things should really swing into motion."

"Why don't you bring them on over?" Something about the way her family was coming after her made her want to have her lawyer present, even if her relationship with her lawyer was a little complicated.

"Are you sure? With your folks there?"

"I'm sure. I live in the Fort . . . in the garage apartment behind the big house on thirteen ten Clinch Avenue."

"Thirteen ten Clinch? I'm just down at the law library right now. I can be there in two minutes."

Chameleon hung up the phone, feeling strangely relieved. "Sorry . . . that was my lawyer. I guess you saw her on TV last night, too."

"That was the other thing we wanted to talk to you about," Chameleon's mother said.

"My lawyer?"

"Well, your lawsuit, really." Chameleon's mother's eyes were misty. "You have to understand, honey, that this story is all over the TV and newspapers, and even if you just use some made-up name, everybody back home still sees your face and knows who you are. And how does it look when people see you calling yourself a witch and starting trouble and they say, 'Isn't that Brother Cameron's sister? Isn't that Bill and Bonnie's daughter?' Think about how that affects us, Camille. You're thirty years old. It's high time you grew up and started thinking of other people."

"I am thinking of other people, Mother. And I think that protecting people from religious intolerance is a little more important than protecting you from small-town gossip."

The knock on the door reassured Chameleon that she was no longer to be alone with her family. She opened the door to Tia, who was stunning in a jade green silk blouse and black pants. Chameleon made a gagging expression to indicate how the evening was going, then said, "Hi, Tia. Why don't you come in and meet my family?"

"Thank you, Chameleon." Tia strode into the room, all lawyerly confidence.

"Tia, these are my parents, Bonnie and Bill Masters. And this is my brother, Cameron."

"A pleasure." Tia shook hands all around.

Chameleon's parents and brother shook Tia's hand but did not make eye contact with her. Chameleon burned with shame to think that this was probably the first time her parents had touched skin so much darker than their own.

"My mom was just telling me how she thinks we should drop the lawsuit," Chameleon said.

Tia raised her eyebrows but smiled at Chameleon's mother. "With all due respect, Mrs. Masters, dropping the lawsuit would be a terrible idea. It's very important that this issue is made public. It's a matter of protecting people's civil liberties."

"Civil liberties is just a word liberals use when they want to send this country farther down the road to moral decay," Cameron said.

"Civil liberties is two words, actually," Tia said, and Chameleon stifled a giggle. "Now, Chameleon, if you'll just read through these documents and sign them, we should have a court date in no time."

"Just a minute, Miss," Chameleon's father said, standing up to face Tia. "Listen, I know good and well why you don't want to drop the lawsuit, and it doesn't have a thing to do with civil liberties or any of that hogwash. You don't want to drop the suit because it's money out of your pocket, and being a business man myself, I can understand that." He reached into his pocket and pulled out a checkbook and a pen. "Listen, I don't know how much my daughter is paying you for your services, but I'm willing to double it if you'll drop the case."

Chameleon was in shock. Her father was notoriously tight with money. When she was a kid, her mom always bought their clothes off-season to save money and drove to the grocery store two towns over when it was selling hamburger cheaper than the store down the street, all so she didn't have to listen to Chameleon's father carp about wasted money. And here he was, ready to write a check for an undisclosed sum to protect his family from the shame brought by his prodigal daughter.

"Mr. Masters, are you asking me to betray your daughter for thirty pieces of silver?" Tia laughed. "Well, it's not going to happen. I won't be bribed because I'm not in this for the money. My commitment to this case goes a lot deeper than that. As a matter of fact, Chameleon might not have told you this, but I'm a witch, too." Tia shot Chameleon a glance that said *don't blow this*, and Chameleon tried to keep a calm expression.

"You're one, too?" Cameron said, his mouth hanging open.

"That's right," Tia said. "As a matter of fact, Chameleon, did you notice that the moon is waning?"

"Uh—yes," Chameleon said, wondering if Tia had lost her mind.

"Well, shouldn't we do our ritual then? You all can join us." And then, to Chameleon's amazement, Tia started taking off her clothes. She unbuttoned her silk blouse and slid down her pants. "We always perform our rituals naked," she said. "There's even a special term for it, isn't there, Chameleon?"

"Skyclad," Chameleon said, unzipping her dress and letting it fall around her feet.

Cameron jumped up. "This is an abomination before God!"

"What is?" Chameleon said. "Our bodies? Our natural selves? We're not an abomination." She looked at Tia who was standing straight-backed and majestic. "We're beautiful."

Chameleon's family was standing up as if to leave, but they were frozen. In order to get to the door, they'd have to pass uncomfortably close to Chameleon and Tia. "Shall we draw the circle?" Tia said. "Chameleon, where's your ritual dagger?"

"It's a terrible thing," Chameleon's mother sobbed, "to know that your own child is going to hell."

"Well, we tried," Chameleon's father said.

Cameron pussyfooted past them with Chameleon's parents following, all of them averting their eyes. "I'll be praying for you, sister," he said. "It's never to late to get saved."

"And I'll be praying to the Goddess for you," Chameleon yelled as they walked out the door. "It's never too late to open your mind."

After the door slammed, Chameleon looked at Tia, and Tia looked back at her. They both broke up laughing at the exact same second. When Chameleon could finally speak, she said, "What got into you?"

"I don't know," Tia said, still laughing. "I mean, there I was, feeling like the liberal scapegoat on one of those pundit shows on Fox News, and then I thought, people like this are always trying to force their religion down other people's throats. What if we tried the same thing on them?"

"Well, it sure got them out of here in a hurry. I don't know what I would've done if you hadn't shown up."

"I don't know, Chameleon," Tia said, looking her in the eyes. "There's something about being in your presence that makes me do things I wouldn't normally do."

"It's our polarity," Chameleon said, looking back at her. "It generates all kinds of energy."

"Maybe so, and it's exciting. But it's also scary. I mean, the reason I went and made that speech to you in the restaurant was I got scared. Scared that I had lost control and gone to bed with a client, but also scared because you really got to me. And I'm so rational that intense emotions tend to terrify me."

This confession was more than Chameleon had even hoped for. "Well, do you think that after you're not my lawyer anymore, maybe I could help you explore your emotions and you could . . . I don't know . . . maybe help me learn to balance my checkbook or something?"

Tia smiled. "Maybe so." She leaned over and reached for her clothes.

"Aw, you're not going to put your clothes on, are you?"

"Hey now, I'm still your lawyer."

"Does that mean I can't look?" Chameleon stepped a little closer to Tia. "Come here. I promise I won't touch you."

Tia stepped toward her. "You really are a witch, aren't you?"

They stood naked, face to face, close enough to touch, but not touching. "I just want to look at you," Chameleon said. "You can look at me, too."

Chameleon traced her eyes over the lines of Tia's cheekbones, over the fullness of her parted lips, over her neck which begged to be kissed but which she would not kiss, not yet. She gazed at the muscles of Tia's upper arms and how they tapered down to the soft crook that divided upper arm from forearm—a crook that, like the crook at the back of the knee, was good for licking, but which she wouldn't lick, not yet. With her eyes, she loved the planes of Tia's collarbones and her full, round breasts with nipples like chocolate kisses. She loved the slight swell of Tia's belly and the way it led down to the soft nest of curls in which, Chameleon knew, a lovely night orchid bloomed. She remembered the orchid's scent and taste but knew she would have to content herself with the memory for now.

But there was something moving between them that was more powerful than memory—more present and alive. As Chameleon gazed at Tia and felt Chameleon gaze back at her, their gazes became a kind of touch, and the air between them fizzed and popped with the energy of it. "Do you feel it, Tia?" Chameleon whispered.

"Yes," Tia breathed. "I can't explain it, but I can feel it."

Chameleon smiled, staring into Tia's gold-flecked eyes. "That's because it's magic."

Epilogue:

Water

Chameleon and her coven were working skyclad. Athena, Chameleon's working partner, stepped forward and knelt before her, preparing for the Five-Fold Kiss. As always, Athena was stunned by Chameleon's beauty as she enacted the role of the goddess.

While Athena only believed in the goddess as a metaphor, she did think that if a real goddess actually walked among humans, she would look like Chameleon on the night of a Sabbat. Athena leaned forward and kissed Chameleon's delicate, white foot, then her other foot. She kissed one knee, then the other, then rose to kiss Chameleon's belly—the goddess's womb, the source of life. As the other coven members watched, Athena kissed Chameleon's beautiful breasts and then rose to meet her lips in a kiss which sent energy surging through the entire coven.

A year and a half ago, before she met Chameleon, if somebody had told Tia that she'd be joining a coven, taking the "witch name" Athena, and becoming the high priestess's working partner, she would have handed a psychiatrist's card to the person who had made the suggestion. But life was unpredictable, and so was love.

After the court ruled that Witches of East Tennessee could both adopt a stretch of highway and mark it with a sign bearing their name (a sign which would be defaced and replaced numerous times after the court's decision), Athena and Chameleon began to take full advantage of the fact that their relationship was no longer a professional one.

The first time they had made love as a real couple, Chameleon had insisted that they do it not in either of their houses, but in the open space of nature, where they could be free of all encumbrances. Driving in the country, they found a stretch of river about waist-deep with a waterfall splashing nearby. Water, Chameleon had explained, was the element of love.

At first Tia had been shy—what if some hikers or hunters stumbled upon them? But as they splashed and laughed, she started to feel freer, so that when Chameleon's lips pressed against hers, she kissed back with equal passion. The gentle movement of the water provided the rhythm for their lovemaking, and as Chameleon moved with her, Tia felt as if she were opening up, opening herself up to possibilities she had never imagined. And each day since then with Chameleon, she had opened up a little more.

Tia still believed in reason—that was why she had chosen Athena, goddess of wisdom and justice, as her namesake. And she still spent her days constructing arguments, providing evidence, and using reason to help those in need. But her nights were spent with Chameleon, and in the darkness as she embraced Chameleon, Tia also embraced another side of life that was mysterious, full of wonder, beyond the limits of reason.

CONTRIBUTOR BIOS

Julia Watts was once banned from a book fair in North Carolina when the organizers discovered the non-heterosexual nature of her books. The organizers explained that they refused to host authors whose books dealt with either lesbianism or witchcraft. At that point, Watts swore she would eventually write something that dealt with both lesbianism and witchcraft. "Skyclad" is the happy result of this ambition. Watts is the author of the Lambda Literary Award-winning novel, *Finding H.F.*, as well as the novels *Wildwood Flowers*, *Phases of the Moon*, *Piece of My Heart*, and *Wedding Bell Blues*. She lives with her family in Knoxville, Tennessee.

Therese Szymanski wanted to be a stuntperson when she grew up; thus, she started playing with the big dogs at an early age. Reese has continued to live her life in a way that allows for urban surfing, playing with swords, running with scissors, doing beer runs on fire trucks, driving 125 through Arizona, and occasionally jumping off buildings. She's written seven books in the Lammy Finalist Brett Higgins Motor City Thrillers series, edited *Back to Basics* (which made the Publishing Triangle's list of notable lesbian books for 2004), *Call of the Dark*, and *The Perfect Valentine* (with Barbara Johnson). She's been short-listed for a Spectrum Award, contributed to a few dozen anthologies, is an award-winning playwright, and works as a copywriter and designer.

From ages four to forty, **Karin Kallmaker** wanted to be Mary Poppins. Or Samantha Stevens. Though she can't twitch her nose or slide up a banister, plenty of magic has happened in her life. She fell in love with her best friend at the age of 16, and still shares her life with that same woman, and their two children, nearly 30 years later. The author of more than twenty romances and fantasy-science fiction novels (including the Lambda Literary Award winner *Maybe Next Time* and numerous finalists), she recently began expanding her repertoire to include explicit erotica. As Karin says, "Nice Girls Do."

Born in Dieburg, Germany, Lambda Literary Award finalist and über-femme **Barbara Johnson** is the author of the bestselling lesbian novels *Stonehurst*, *The Beach Affair*, *Bad Moon Rising*, and *Strangers in the Night*. Her short stories have appeared in almost a dozen anthologies. Her novella "Charlotte of Hessen" appeared in *Once Upon a Dyke: New Exploits of Fairy Tale Lesbians* (a 2005 Lambda Literary Award finalist) from Bella Books. An animal rights activist, Barbara has a weakness for rescuing strays and shares her life with four adorably dysfunctional cats, a big old bulldog, and a frisky Jack Russell.

Barbara's resources for "Sea Witch" included *Spells for the Solitary Witch* by Eileen Holland; *The Complete Idiot's Guide to Wicca and Witchcraft* (Second Edition) by Denise Zimmerman and Katherine A. Gleason, from which she took the spells used in "Sea Witch;" and http://www.wicca.com/celtic/cc002.htm.

The picture on the title page of Sea Witch is of Barbara's beloved late cat, Isis.

Publications from
BELLA BOOKS, INC.
The best in contemporary lesbian fiction

P.O. Box 10543, Tallahassee, FL 32302
Phone: 800-729-4992
www.bellabooks.com

BELL, BOOK & DYKE: NEW EXPLOITS OF MAGICAL LESBIANS by Kallmaker, Watts, Johnson and Szymanski. 320 pp. Reluctant witches, tempting spells, and skyclad beauties—delve into the mysteries of love, lust and power in this quartet of novellas.
1-59493-023-6 $14.95

ARTIST'S DREAM by Gerri Hill. 320 pp.When Cassie meets Luke Winston, she can no longer deny her attraction to women . . .   1-59493-042-2 $12.95

NO EVIDENCE by Nancy Sanra. 240 pp. Private Investigator Tally McGinnis once again returns to the horror filled world of a serial killer.   1-59493-043-04 $12.95

WHEN LOVE FINDS A HOME by Megan Carter. 280 pp. What will it take for Anna and Rona to find their way back to each other again?   1-59493-041-4 $12.95

MEMORIES TO DIE FOR by Adrian Gold. 240 pp. Rachel attempts to avoid her attraction to the charms of Anna Sigurdson . . .   1-59493-038-4 $12.95

SILENT HEART by Claire McNab. 280 pp. Exotic lesbian romance.
1-59493-044-9 $12.95

MIDNIGHT RAIN by Peggy J. Herring. 240 pp. Bridget McBee is determined to find the woman who saved her life.   1-59493-021-X $12.95

THE MISSING PAGE A Brenda Strange Mystery by Patty G. Henderson. 240 pp. Brenda investigates her client's murder . . .   1-59493-004-X $12.95

WHISPERS ON THE WIND by Frankie J. Jones. 240 pp. Dixon thinks she and her best friend, Elizabeth Colter, would make the perfect couple . . . 1-59493-037-6 $12.95

CALL OF THE DARK: EROTIC LESBIAN TALES OF THE SUPERNATURAL edited by Therese Szymanski—from Bella After Dark. 320 pp.   1-59493-040-6 $14.95

A TIME TO CAST AWAY A Helen Black Mystery by Pat Welch. 240 pp. Helen stops by Alice's apartment—only to find the woman dead . . .   1-59493-036-8 $12.95

DESERT OF THE HEART by Jane Rule. 224 pp. The book that launched the most popular lesbian movie of all time is back.   1-1-59493-035-X $12.95

THE NEXT WORLD by Ursula Steck. 240 pp. Anna's friend Mido is threatened and eventually disappears . . .   1-59493-024-4 $12.95

CALL SHOTGUN by Jaime Clevenger. 240 pp. Kelly gets pulled back into the world of private investigation . . .   1-59493-016-3 $12.95